BENEATH WEST SENECA

BENEATH WEST SENECA

P HARTWELL

This is a work of fiction. Similarities to real people, places, or events are entirely coincidental.
BENEATH WEST SENECA

Second Edition. April 26, 2026.

ISBN: 978-1-969929-20-5
Written by P. Hartwell.

Dedication

To the unyielding curiosity that resides in the heart of every child, To the brave explorers who venture beyond the familiar paths, And to the quiet courage found in the rustling leaves and the shadowed woods of West Seneca.

This story is dedicated to all those who believe that even in the most ordinary of places, extra-ordinary secrets lie waiting to be unearthed. It is for the young minds that question, the hearts that seek truth, and the spirits that refuse to be deterred by the unknown. May you always find wonder in the world around you, and may your own adventures be filled with as much discovery and resilience. For the parents who warn with love, and for the children who, with bravery and wit, learn to navigate the complexities of the world, transforming fear into understanding and whispers into truth. May the spirit of Joseph live on in every child who dares to look a little closer, listen a little harder, and believe in the power of their own discoveries, illuminating the hidden corners of history and the human heart, proving that even the smallest among us can bring the greatest light to the darkest of secrets. The scent of pine, the creak of wood, the mysteries hidden in plain sight – these are the threads that weave the tapes-try of our shared human story, a story best understood when bravely pursued.

1

The Whispers of West Seneca

West Seneca, 1852. The name itself conjured images of vast, untamed lands stretching out to an unseen horizon, a place where civilization was a fragile seedling pushing its roots into rugged soil. Nestled at the edge of an immense, whispering forest, the village was a testament to human resilience and a beacon of nascent hope against the encroaching wild. Its structures were a patchwork of necessity and determination: rough-hewn cabins, their logs still bearing the scent of the forest they were carved from, huddled together as if for warmth and protection. Chimneys, often crooked and puffing plumes of gray smoke, were a constant reminder of hearths and homes, the heartbeats of this fledgling community.

At the center of this sparse collection of dwellings stood the general store, a hub of activity and a vital artery of supply. Its wooden facade, weathered by sun and wind, bore the marks of countless transactions, the silent witness to the bartering and trading that sustained them. Inside, the air was a heady mix of dried goods, canvas, and the ever-present aroma of lamp oil. Shelves laden with bolts of fabric, sacks of flour, and metal tools spoke of the hard-won comforts and necessities of frontier life. Beyond the store, a small, unadorned church, its steeple reaching tentatively towards the heavens, offered a place for spiritual solace and communal gathering. Its modest size reflected the village's youth, a quiet promise of faith in a land often challenging its very foundations.

The very air of West Seneca was a character in itself, thick with the pervasive scent of pine needles, damp earth, and the occasional, musky hint of animal life stirring in the dense woods. This olfactory tapestry was a constant reminder of the vast, unexplored territories that pressed in on all sides, a wild and formidable presence that both inspired and intimidated. The rustling of leaves was not just the sound of wind; it was the murmur of a thousand secrets, the breath of an ancient, indifferent wilderness. The dappled sunlight that filtered through the dense canopy cast shifting patterns on the dirt paths, illuminating the determination etched on the faces of the villagers and the quiet anticipation of a future yet unwritten.

Life in West Seneca was a symphony of simplicity and arduous labor. The days were dictated by the sun's arc and the demands of survival. Every resident played a part, their lives intertwined by a shared reliance on one another. A broken tool, a harsh winter, a failing crop – these were not individual calamities but communal challenges to be met with shared effort and mutual support. The men, with their calloused hands and weathered skin, ventured into the woods to hunt, to trap, or to clear land, their strength and knowledge of the wilderness their most valuable assets. The women, equally strong and resourceful, managed the homesteads, tended to the gardens, preserved food, mended clothes, and cared for the children, their resilience a cornerstone of the community's stability.

Evenings brought a temporary respite, a chance to gather around crackling fires, share stories, and reaffirm the bonds that held them together. Yet, even in the warmth of their homes, the wilderness remained a tangible presence, its sounds amplified in the darkness – the hoot of an owl, the distant howl of a wolf, the creak of trees swaying in the wind. These were the lullabies of the frontier, a constant reminder that beyond the comforting glow of their lanterns lay a world that was both beautiful and unforgiving. The hum of progress, though present in the clearing of new land and the construction of new cabins, was always underscored by the lingering presence of the unknown, a sense of mystery that clung to the very air they breathed. The frontier was not just a place; it was a state of being, a continuous negotiation between the will to build and the power of the wild.

This inherent tension, this constant dance between the known and the unknown, was perhaps most keenly felt by young Joseph. At ten years old, he possessed a spirit as untamed as the woods that bordered his home. His was a restlessness that found no solace in the predictable rhythms of village life. While other children might be content with games of chase around the general store or helping their mothers with chores, Joseph's eyes were perpetually drawn to the line where the cleared land met the dense, shadowed forest. He was a boy driven by an insatiable curiosity, a perpetual "why-asker" who found the answers provided by adults often insufficient, leaving him with more questions than before.

His mind was a sharp, inquisitive tool, constantly probing, dissecting, and questioning the world around him. This trait, while admirable in its own right, often led him into minor scrapes and landed him in the stern, yet loving, gaze of his parents. A fallen branch that looked out of place, a bird's unusual call, a strange pattern of stones – these were not mere observations for Joseph; they were puzzles waiting to be solved. He possessed an innate ability to see the extraordinary in the ordinary, to find the threads of mystery woven into the fabric of everyday existence. His bright, alert eyes seemed to absorb every detail of his surroundings, always scanning the horizon, always seeking what lay beyond the familiar paths and the watchful eyes of the adults who cautioned him against straying too far.

His parents, a man of the woods and a woman of steadfast practicality, often found themselves holding their breath when Joseph was out of sight for too long. His father, a man whose hands were as familiar with the heft of an ax as they were with the gentle touch needed to carve a bird from wood, understood the wilderness in a way Joseph was only beginning to grasp. His mother, whose days were a meticulous dance of cooking, cleaning, and tending to their small plot of land, saw the world through a lens of pragmatic caution, her heart perpetually braced for the potential dangers that lurked just beyond the village's protective embrace.

They would often sit with him in the evenings, their voices carrying the weight of earnest concern. "Joseph," his father might begin, his voice a low rumble like distant thunder, "the forest is a beautiful place, but it is also a wild one. It does not suffer fools gladly." His mother would add, her brow furrowed with worry, "We've heard tales, son, stories of hunters who ventured too deep and were never seen again, of travelers who lost their way in the fog and never found their path back." These were not intended as idle threats to frighten him, but rather as earnest attempts to instill a healthy respect for the inherent dangers of their environment, a respect that was vital for survival on the frontier. They spoke of respecting boundaries, of listening to warnings, not to stifle his spirit, but to ensure he carried his spirit safely, to preserve the peace of mind of those who loved him and the fragile harmony of their small community.

But for Joseph, the wilderness was not merely a landscape of potential peril; it was a siren's call, an irresistible lure. The unexplored territories surrounding West Seneca were more than just trees and earth; they represented a realm of infinite possibility, a vast, uncharted territory where secrets lay waiting to be unearthed, where adventures untold whispered on the wind. He felt an almost magnetic pull towards these places, a primal urge to venture where others, even the most seasoned villagers, feared to tread. This innate curiosity, this burning desire to know what lay hidden, far outweighed any learned caution or fear of retribution. The very things that warned him away seemed to beckon him closer. The rustling leaves were not merely the sound of nature; they were an invitation, a promise of discoveries waiting to be made, of truths that might lie concealed beneath the verdant canopy. The distant, melodic calls of unseen birds were not just background noise; they were cryptic messages, urging him onward, fueling his imagination with the promise of the unknown.

And so, it was inevitable that one bright, crisp morning, driven by a dare he'd made to himself or simply by the sheer, uncontainable force of his curiosity, Joseph found himself standing at the very edge of the familiar. He had stepped off the well-worn paths, the ones his father had trod countless times, the ones that led to reliable hunting grounds or foraging spots. He was venturing into the periphery, the transition zone where the cultivated edges of the village gave way to the untamed heart of the forest. The trees here grew taller, their branches thicker, their dense foliage weaving a tighter, more intricate tapestry overhead, plunging the forest floor into a perpetual twilight. The silence here was different; it was not the peaceful quiet of an empty clearing but a profound, expectant hush, a silence that seemed to hold its breath. The very air felt charged with a subtle tension, a palpable awareness that he had crossed an invisible threshold. As he moved deeper, his eyes, ever watchful, began to notice things. Markings etched into the bark of ancient trees, too deliberate to be the work of animals, too unusual to be natural. Patches of earth that seemed strangely disturbed, as if something had been buried or unearthed with a haste that belied the quiet of the woods. These were not grand pronouncements, but subtle hints, almost imperceptible whispers in the language of the wild, the first delicate threads of a mystery that would soon begin to unravel.

He followed the faint impression of a trail, a barely discernible path through the undergrowth, its passage marked by a scattering of displaced leaves and the occasional snapped twig that seemed too clean, too precise to be accidental. It was a route that spoke of infrequent use, of a secrecy that discouraged discovery, and its very elusiveness intensified Joseph's thrill. This was no trodden way; it was a hidden artery, a secret vein coursing through the heart of the wilderness, and the mere act of following it felt like a transgression, a forbidden exploration. The trees loomed overhead, their ancient trunks like silent sentinels, casting a dappled, eerie light that painted shifting mosaics on the mossy ground. Shafts of sunlight pierced the canopy here and there, creating isolated pools of brightness that only served to accentuate the surrounding gloom.

As he ventured further, the path winding and twisting like a serpent's trail, his foot nudged against something solid, partially obscured by the rich, dark loam. With a surge of adrenaline, he knelt down, his fingers digging into the yielding earth. It was a wooden box, its surface weathered and softened by time and the elements, its edges softened by countless seasons of rain and sun. Yet, there was something about it, a peculiar craftsmanship, a subtle elegance in its construction that set it apart from the crude utilitarianism of most things made in West Seneca. It felt ancient, as if it had slumbered in this spot for decades, perhaps even centuries, waiting for a curious hand to disturb its long repose. The object felt out of place, a foreign artifact dropped into the natural tapestry of the forest, not belonging to the wild itself, nor resembling anything familiar from the simple lives of the villagers. Its very strangeness immediately captivated Joseph, sparking his keen interest and hinting at a story untold, a past deliberately hidden away, waiting for the right moment to be revealed.

Joseph carefully lifted the box from its earthy bed, brushing away the clinging soil. He examined it closely, his brow furrowed in concentration. It was not locked, but the lid seemed to fit snugly, a testament to its sturdy construction. He ran his fingers over its surface, tracing the faint lines and subtle indentations that marked its form. There were no visible carvings, no overt symbols that he could recognize, yet there was a feeling about it, a palpable aura of mystery that clung to the wood like the scent of aged pine. He tried to discern its purpose, to imagine what it might have held, but it remained an enigma, a silent testament to a forgotten existence. It was made of a wood he didn't recognize, darker and more resilient than the familiar pines and oaks of the surrounding woods. The object felt old, carrying with it a tangible sense of history, a weight of time that deepened his resolve to understand its significance. It became his personal puzzle, a solitary key that he felt certain would unlock a door to a world he had never known existed, a world hidden just beyond the veil of his everyday reality.

As he carefully placed the wooden box into the confines of his satchel, ensuring it was hidden from casual view, a sound reached his ears, faint at first, then growing more distinct. It was the sound of hushed voices, speaking in low, urgent tones, followed by the sharp snap of a twig from further along the barely-there trail. Then, a distant, metallic clang, sharp and resonant, cutting through the forest quiet. He froze, his heart leaping into his throat. He was not alone. Whatever he had found, whatever secret this secluded place held, it was clearly connected to others who were actively using this hidden area. This realization sent a jolt of apprehension through him, a sudden awareness that his solitary exploration had inadvertently stumbled into a hidden world, a clandestine operation. The thrill of discovery was now tinged with a growing sense of unease, a primal instinct that whispered of caution and the potential for unseen danger.

With the mysterious box now safely stowed, Joseph turned his steps back towards West Seneca. The familiar trees seemed to press closer now, their shadows deeper, their silence more profound. His mind, however, was a whirlwind of images and sounds: the faint trail, the unearthed box, the hushed voices, the metallic clang. He clutched the satchel, its weight a constant, tangible reminder of the secret he now carried. The playful, unfettered curiosity that had driven him into the woods earlier that morning had transformed, shifting into a more serious, almost urgent pursuit of understanding. He could not shake the pervasive feeling that this object was more than just a quaint relic or a forgotten trinket; it was a clue, a key, a tangible piece of a much larger, more complex puzzle. And it had ignited a fire within him, a burning resolve to uncover the truth, no matter the obstacles, no matter the cost. The wild whispers of West Seneca had begun to speak directly to him, and he was determined to listen.

Joseph was a whirlwind of a child, a ten-year-old boy perpetually caught between the earthbound realities of West Seneca and the boundless expanse of his own imagination. His spirit, untamed as the wind that swept across the open plains, found the predictable routines of village life a suffocating constraint. While other children his age were content with games of tag that circled the dusty perimeter of the general store, or found satisfaction in helping their mothers with the endless chores of homesteading, Joseph's gaze was invariably drawn to the enigmatic boundary where the last vestiges of cultivated land surrendered to the deep, shadowed embrace of the forest. He was a boy possessed by an insatiable hunger for knowledge, a constant interrogator of the world, whose nimble mind was forever probing, dissecting, and questioning. The adults' pronouncements, often delivered with the finality of established fact, rarely satisfied him, leaving him not with answers, but with a cascade of further inquiries.

His intellect was a keen, bright blade, honed by an innate curiosity that refused to be dulled by routine or complacency. This sharp inquisitiveness, while a testament to his burgeoning intelligence, frequently landed him in predicaments that tested the patience of his parents. A fallen branch that seemed out of place, a bird's call that struck a discordant note in the usual symphony of the woods, a peculiar arrangement of stones in the dirt – these were not mere observations to Joseph; they were puzzles, each one a tantalizing enigma demanding his immediate attention. He possessed an uncanny knack for discerning the extraordinary hidden within the mundane, for tracing the subtle threads of mystery woven into the very fabric of everyday existence. His bright, alert eyes, like those of a watchful hawk, seemed to absorb every detail of his surroundings, constantly scanning the horizon, perpetually seeking what lay beyond the well-worn paths and the ever-present, cautious gazes of the adults who implored him not to stray too far.

His parents, a man whose life was intrinsically linked to the rhythms of the forest and a woman whose very essence was defined by practicality and unwavering resilience, often found themselves holding their collective breath whenever Joseph ventured beyond their immediate sight. His father, a man whose hands were as adept at wielding an ax with precision as they were at coaxing delicate forms from blocks of wood, possessed an intimate understanding of the wilderness, a knowledge that Joseph was only beginning to acquire. His mother, whose days were a meticulously choreographed ballet of domestic duties – cooking, cleaning, tending their small plot of land, and weaving practical garments – viewed the world through a lens of pragmatic caution. Her heart was in a perpetual state of quiet preparedness, braced against the myriad potential dangers that lay coiled just beyond the village's fragile, protective embrace.

In the quietude of the evenings, when the day's labor had ceased and the stars began to prick the darkening sky, they would often sit with him, their voices imbued with a genuine, palpable concern. "Joseph," his father might begin, his voice a low, resonant rumble that echoed the distant threat of thunder, "the forest is a place of great beauty, but it is also a wild and unforgiving one. It does not suffer the careless or the foolish lightly." His mother, her brow often creased with a familiar line of worry, would add her own gentle admonition, "We have heard tales, son, stories passed down from those who ventured too deep into its heart and were never seen again. Tales of hunters who became lost in the swirling mists, of travelers who, losing their way, never found their path back to the warmth of home." These words were not intended as idle threats designed to frighten him, but rather as earnest attempts to instill within him a healthy and necessary respect for the inherent perils of their frontier existence, a respect that was absolutely vital for survival in such an environment. They spoke of respecting boundaries, of heeding warnings, not to stifle the vibrant spark of his spirit, but to ensure that he carried that spirit safely, to preserve the peace of mind of those who loved him dearly, and to maintain the delicate harmony of their small, striving community.

But for Joseph, the wilderness was far more than merely a landscape fraught with potential peril; it was a siren's call, an irresistible, magnetic allure. The unexplored territories that sprawled outwards from the edges of West Seneca held for him a significance that transcended mere geography. They represented a realm of infinite possibility, a vast, uncharted territory where secrets lay dormant, waiting to be unearthed, where adventures untold whispered on the wind, beckoning him forward. He felt an almost primal, magnetic pull towards these untamed places, an innate urge to venture where even the most seasoned villagers, those who navigated the woods with practiced ease, hesitated to tread. This inherent curiosity, this burning, unquenchable desire to discover what lay hidden, far outweighed any instilled caution or any fear of admonishment or punishment. The very warnings that were meant to keep him away seemed, paradoxically, to draw him closer. The rustling of the leaves was not simply the sound of nature's breath; it was an intimate invitation, a whispered promise of discoveries waiting just beyond the next bend, of truths that might be concealed beneath the dense, verdant canopy. The distant, melodious calls of unseen birds were not mere background noise; they were cryptic messages, urging him onward, fueling his fertile imagination with the exhilarating promise of the unknown.

And so, it was on one particularly bright, crisp morning, propelled by a dare he had silently issued to himself or simply by the sheer, uncontainable force of his burgeoning curiosity, that Joseph found himself standing at the very threshold of the familiar. He had deliberately stepped off the well-trodden paths, the ones his father had traversed countless times, the routes that led to reliable hunting grounds or familiar foraging spots. He was venturing into the periphery, the subtle transition zone where the carefully cultivated edges of the village abruptly surrendered to the deep, untamed heart of the forest. Here, the trees grew taller, their branches thicker, their dense foliage weaving a more intricate, more impenetrable tapestry overhead, plunging the forest floor into a perpetual, hushed twilight. The silence here was qualitatively different; it was not the peaceful quiet of an empty clearing, but a profound, expectant hush, a silence that seemed to hold its breath, waiting. The very air itself felt charged with a subtle, yet palpable tension, an undeniable awareness that he had crossed an invisible, yet significant threshold. As he moved deeper into this hushed realm, his eyes, ever watchful and observant, began to perceive details that spoke of a hidden narrative. He noticed markings etched into the rough bark of ancient trees, markings that were too deliberate to be the work of wild animals, too unusual to be attributed to natural phenomena. He observed patches of earth that appeared strangely disturbed, as if something had been hastily buried or recently unearthed with a furtive urgency that belied the profound stillness of the woods. These were not grand proclamations, but subtle hints, almost imperceptible whispers in the ancient language of the wild, the first delicate threads of a profound mystery that was beginning, slowly but surely, to unravel before his very eyes.

He followed the faint impression of a trail, a barely discernible path that wound its way through the dense undergrowth, its passage marked by a scattering of displaced leaves and the occasional, unnervingly clean snap of a twig, too precise to be accidental. It was a route that spoke of infrequent use, of a deliberate secrecy that discouraged casual discovery, and its very elusiveness only served to intensify Joseph's growing excitement. This was no casually trodden way; it was a hidden artery, a secret vein coursing through the very heart of the wilderness, and the mere act of following it felt like a transgression, a forbidden exploration into a world not meant for him. The ancient trees loomed overhead like silent, stoic sentinels, their massive trunks casting a dappled, eerie light that painted shifting, abstract mosaics on the mossy ground below. Shafts of sunlight, piercing the thick canopy at irregular intervals, created isolated pools of startling brightness that served only to accentuate the enveloping gloom that surrounded them.

As he ventured further along this clandestine path, the route winding and twisting with the sinuous grace of a serpent's trail, his foot nudged against something solid, something partially obscured by the rich, dark loam of the forest floor. With a sudden surge of adrenaline coursing through his veins, he knelt down, his fingers eagerly digging into the yielding earth. What he uncovered was a wooden box, its surface weathered and softened by the relentless passage of time and the persistent elements, its edges smoothed by countless seasons of rain and sun. Yet, there was something undeniably distinctive about it, a peculiar, almost elegant craftsmanship, a subtle sophistication in its construction that immediately set it apart from the rough, utilitarian objects that were the standard of everyday life in West Seneca. It felt ancient, imbued with the weight of ages, as if it had slumbered undisturbed in this secluded spot for decades, perhaps even centuries, patiently awaiting a curious hand to disturb its long and silent repose. The object felt profoundly out of place, a foreign artifact deliberately dropped into the natural, organic tapestry of the forest, neither belonging to the wild itself nor resembling anything familiar from the simple, unadorned lives of the villagers. Its very strangeness, its incongruity, immediately captivated Joseph, sparking his keenest interest and hinting at a story long untold, a past deliberately hidden away, waiting for the opportune moment to be revealed.

Joseph carefully lifted the wooden box from its earthy bed, his movements deliberate as he brushed away the clinging soil. He examined it closely, his brow furrowed in a posture of intense concentration. The lid was not secured by any visible lock, yet it fit snugly, a testament to its sturdy and precise construction. He ran his fingers over its surface, tracing the faint lines and subtle indentations that marked its form, searching for any clue to its origin or purpose. There were no visible carvings, no overt symbols that he could readily recognize, yet there was a palpable aura about it, a distinct feeling of mystery that clung to the wood like the lingering scent of aged pine. He tried to discern its purpose, to imagine what forgotten treasures or secrets it might have once held, but it remained an enigma, a silent testament to a forgotten existence, a relic from a time and place entirely unknown to him. It was crafted from a wood he did not recognize, a darker, more resilient timber than the familiar pines and oaks that dominated the surrounding woods. The object felt profoundly old, carrying with it a tangible sense of history, a heavy weight of time that only deepened his resolve to understand its significance. It quickly became his personal puzzle, a solitary key that he felt certain would unlock a hidden door to a world he had never even suspected existed, a world concealed just beyond the translucent veil of his everyday reality.

As he carefully placed the mysterious wooden box into the confines of his satchel, ensuring it was well hidden from any casual view, a faint sound reached his ears, at first almost imperceptible, then gradually growing more distinct. It was the murmur of hushed voices, speaking in low, urgent tones, followed by the sharp, definitive snap of a twig from somewhere further along the barely-there trail. Then, a distant, metallic clang, sharp and resonant, cut through the profound quiet of the forest with an almost violent suddenness. He froze, his heart leaping into his throat, the sudden realization striking him with the force of a physical blow. He was not alone. Whatever secret this secluded place held, whatever he had inadvertently stumbled upon, it was clearly connected to others who were actively, and perhaps clandestinely, using this hidden area. This stark realization sent a jolt of apprehension coursing through him, a sudden, visceral awareness that his solitary exploration had unexpectedly led him into a hidden world, a clandestine operation unfolding in the heart of the wilderness. The exhilarating thrill of discovery was now irrevocably tinged with a growing sense of unease, a primal instinct that whispered a clear and urgent message of caution and the distinct potential for unseen danger.

With the mysteriously acquired box now safely stowed, its presence a comforting yet unsettling weight against his side, Joseph turned his steps back towards the familiar, albeit now subtly altered, paths leading to West Seneca. The trees that had seemed like friendly giants earlier that morning now appeared to press closer, their shadows deepening, their silence becoming more profound, more watchful. His mind, however, was a tempestuous whirlwind of images and sounds: the faint, almost invisible trail, the unearthed wooden box, the hushed, urgent voices, the sharp, metallic clang. He clutched the satchel tightly, its weight a constant, tangible reminder of the secret he now carried, a secret that felt both exhilarating and terrifying. The playful, unfettered curiosity that had so readily driven him into the woods earlier that morning had transformed, shifting into a more serious, almost urgent pursuit of understanding. He could not shake the pervasive, insistent feeling that this object was far more than just a quaint relic or a forgotten trinket; it was a clue, a key, a tangible piece of a much larger, infinitely more complex puzzle. And in unearthing it, he had ignited a fire within him, a burning, unyielding resolve to uncover the truth, no matter the obstacles that lay ahead, no matter the ultimate cost. The wild whispers of West Seneca had begun to speak directly to him, and he was utterly determined to listen.

The evening had settled over West Seneca like a soft, gray quilt, punctuated by the flickering glow of lamps spilling from the few scattered cabins. The scent of woodsmoke and baking bread, usually a comforting balm, did little to soothe the gnawing unease that had taken root in Joseph's chest. He sat at the rough-hewn table in their cabin, the mysterious wooden box tucked away in his satchel, its silent presence a constant, buzzing reminder of his clandestine adventure. Across from him, his father, Elias, meticulously sharpened his hunting knife, the rhythmic rasp of steel against stone a familiar sound that normally spoke of preparedness and self-sufficiency. Tonight, however, it seemed to carry a more somber tone, an unspoken acknowledgment of the fragility of their existence on this frontier. His mother, Martha, her hands usually busy with mending or preparing the evening meal, sat by the hearth, her gaze fixed on the dancing flames, her usual quiet efficiency replaced by a contemplative stillness.

Elias finally set his knife down with a soft thud, his broad hands resting on the table. He turned his steady gaze towards Joseph, his blue eyes, usually warm and crinkled at the corners from years spent squinting against the sun, now held a depth of concern that Joseph had seen before, but never felt quite so acutely. "Joseph," he began, his voice a low rumble, like distant thunder on a summer evening, "your mother and I... we've noticed you've been spending more time at the edge of the woods lately." He paused, choosing his words with the careful deliberation of a man navigating treacherous terrain. "More time than is perhaps wise."

Martha turned from the hearth, her face illuminated by the firelight, casting a gentle glow on her features, which were etched with the quiet strength of a woman who had faced hardship and emerged unbroken. "The forest is a beautiful place, Joseph," she said softly, her voice a melodic counterpoint to Elias's deeper tones. "It provides for us, it shelters us. But it is also a place that demands respect. A place that holds its own counsel, and does not readily give up its secrets." She moved to sit beside Elias, her hand finding his, a silent gesture of solidarity and shared worry. "We don't want to stifle your spirit, son. We know you have a mind that races ahead, that sees things others miss. That is a gift. But gifts can sometimes lead us down paths we are not yet ready to walk."

Elias nodded, his gaze never leaving Joseph's face. "Your mother is right. I've spent a lifetime in those woods, Joseph. I know their moods, their tricks. I've seen men, strong men, good men, wander in with a song on their lips and the scent of adventure in their nostrils, only to have the trees swallow them whole. The paths you think you know can shift with the wind. A familiar stream can suddenly become a raging torrent after a storm. And the creatures within... they are magnificent, yes, but they are also wild. Their instincts are far sharper, far more primal than anything we understand in the safety of our homes." He picked up a small, smooth stone from the table, turning it over and over in his fingers. "There was a trapper, a man named Silas, who came through here a few years back. Thought he knew these woods like the back of his hand. He was following a particularly fine pelt, he said, just a little further in than usual. His wife waited for him. And waited. They found his traps, his rifle, but Silas himself... the forest kept him."

Martha's voice was barely a whisper, yet it carried the weight of profound sorrow. "And then there was the year of the deep snow. A young couple, new to the settlement, their wagon broke an axle just beyond the creek. They decided to make for the nearest cabin, thinking it was only a short walk. They underestimated the distance, and the sudden whiteout. The search party found them huddled together, frozen. They had been so close, so agonizingly close, to safety. But the snow, it can erase everything. It can make a familiar landmark disappear in an instant."

Joseph listened, his heart a heavy weight in his chest. He knew his parents weren't trying to scare him with fanciful tales; they were recounting genuine dangers, the harsh realities of their world. He thought of Silas, the trapper, a man he'd only seen once or twice, a quiet figure with a weathered face and knowing eyes. The idea of that man, so capable, simply vanishing, was a chilling thought. He glanced down at his satchel, feeling the distinct outline of the wooden box through the canvas. It was far from the usual places he explored, and the voices he'd heard... they hadn't sounded like friendly villagers.

"I understand," Joseph said, his voice perhaps a touch too quick, too eager to reassure them. "I know the woods can be dangerous. But I'm careful. I always pay attention."

Elias leaned forward, his gaze intense. "Paying attention is one thing, Joseph. Having the experience, the ingrained knowledge of what to *look* for, that's another. It's the subtle signs. The way a deer holds its ears, the sudden silence of the birds, the scent on the wind that tells you a predator is near. It's a language you learn over years, through trial and error, through mistakes that can cost you dearly.

We're not asking you to be afraid, Joseph. We're asking you to be wise. To be patient. The forest will still be there when you are older, when you have learned more, when you are better equipped to understand its whispers."

Martha reached out and gently cupped his cheek, her touch soft but firm. "There are boundaries, Joseph. And sometimes, those boundaries are there to protect us, not to limit us. When you step beyond them without the proper understanding, you're not just risking yourself. You're risking our peace of mind. Every moment you are out of sight, our minds conjure every terrible possibility. And on the frontier, Joseph, those possibilities are not always imagined." Her voice cracked slightly, and she squeezed Elias's hand tighter. "We love you, son. More than anything. And that love makes us... vigilant."

Joseph looked from his father to his mother, seeing the genuine fear etched beneath their stern pronouncements. He knew they weren't trying to crush his adventurous spirit, but rather to safeguard it, to ensure it didn't lead him to a premature end. He thought of the markings on the trees, the disturbed earth, the peculiar wooden box that felt like it held a secret far older and more complex than any simple woodland tale. He knew, with a certainty that both thrilled and terrified him, that he couldn't simply turn his back on what he had stumbled upon. The warnings were necessary, he understood that. But they also served as a stark reminder that whatever he had found, it was significant enough for others to be moving in secrecy, and for his parents to fear what might lie beyond the familiar safety of West Seneca. The whispers of the woods were growing louder, and Joseph, despite his parents' earnest pleas, felt an irresistible pull to decipher their meaning.

The earnest pleas of his parents, though rooted in love and a deep understanding of the frontier's unforgiving nature, did little to dampen the burgeoning excitement within Joseph. He understood their fear, he truly did. He saw the worry lines etched around their eyes, the way his mother's hand instinctively sought his father's when recounting tales of loss. He knew they weren't trying to chain him, but to guide him, to protect him from the sharp edges of a world that offered both sustenance and peril in equal measure. Yet, their very warnings, their vivid descriptions of unseen dangers and swallowed men, served not as deterrents, but as fuel to a fire that had already been ignited within him. The unknown wasn't merely a place of potential danger; it was a siren's call, a vast, uncharted canvas upon which his imagination could paint its most daring adventures.

West Seneca, while his home, felt increasingly like a gilded cage. The familiar routines, the predictable rhythm of daily life, the well-worn paths through the woods that his father had taught him – they all spoke of safety, of certainty. But Joseph's spirit yearned for the unpredictable, for the thrill of stepping into a narrative where the ending was not preordained. His parents spoke of the woods as a place that demanded respect, that held its counsel. Joseph heard it differently. He heard it as a place that guarded treasures, that whispered forgotten histories to those brave enough to listen. Every rustle of leaves, every distant bird call, every shadow that danced between the trees – they were not just sounds and sights of the natural world; they were invitations, coded messages from a realm that beckoned him to explore its hidden depths.

His father's stories of Silas, the trapper who vanished, painted a picture of a man whose competence was no match for the forest's caprice. Joseph, however, couldn't shake the image of Silas not as a victim, but as a seeker, someone who pushed boundaries, who ventured just a little further because the promise of a finer pelt, a richer discovery, was too compelling to resist. And the young couple, frozen so close to safety, their journey tragically cut short by a sudden whiteout – Joseph imagined their final moments not as despair, but as a desperate, albeit ill-fated, attempt to uncover something new, to forge a path where none existed. His parents emphasized the caution needed, the ingrained knowledge of subtle signs. Joseph, however, felt an intuitive understanding stirring within him, a nascent ability to interpret these signs, not as warnings of impending doom, but as clues to a larger, unfolding mystery.

The wooden box, now safely stowed in his satchel, was the physical manifestation of this pull. It was an anomaly, an object that did not belong to the familiar tapestry of frontier life. Its presence spoke of secrets far older than West Seneca, of a history that predated the settlers and their struggles. His parents' fear was for his physical well-being, a natural and commendable concern. But Joseph's burgeoning curiosity was about something far more profound: the uncovering of truth, the understanding of forces that lay beyond the immediate and the tangible. He felt a kinship with those who dared to venture into the wilderness, not out of recklessness, but out of an insatiable hunger for knowledge, for experience, for the sheer, unadulterated thrill of the unknown.

The vast expanse of the wilderness wasn't just trees and undergrowth to Joseph; it was a repository of untold stories, a living testament to the enduring mysteries of existence. He saw the winding rivers not as potential floodwaters, but as pathways to forgotten lands. He saw the towering mountains not as impassable barriers, but as silent sentinels guarding ancient secrets. The very act of venturing into these unexplored territories was, for him, a form of communion, a way to connect with a primal, untamed aspect of the world that resonated deep within his soul. His parents' cautionary tales, while heeded, were also subtly reinterpreted through the lens of his own burgeoning adventurous spirit. The danger they highlighted was simply another facet of the allure; it was the very edge of the known world, the frontier of discovery, that called to him most powerfully.

He imagined himself not as a lost soul, but as a pioneer of a different sort, charting not just geographical territory, but the uncharted realms of knowledge and understanding. The whispers his parents spoke of – the subtle signs in the woods – Joseph felt them not as pronouncements of danger, but as an ancient language, a dialect of the wild that he was beginning to decipher. The rustling leaves were not a warning of unseen predators, but the murmur of ancient trees sharing their long-held wisdom. The distant calls of unseen birds were not merely animalistic cries, but the melodic strains of a symphony played for those with ears to hear. The wild expanse was a living, breathing entity, and Joseph felt an overwhelming urge to become a part of its grand narrative, to trace its hidden contours, to unravel the enigmas it held within its verdant embrace. His innate curiosity was a compass, pointing him resolutely towards the horizon, towards the places where the maps ended and the true adventure began. He knew, with a certainty that vibrated through his very bones, that the most profound discoveries lay just beyond the familiar, in the territories where others feared to tread.

The familiar worn track that led from the edge of West Seneca's cultivated fields into the embrace of the woods was a boundary Joseph had crossed a thousand times. It was the path to berry patches, to the stream where he fished with his father, to the quiet groves where he'd sought solace and whispered secrets to the wind. But today, it felt different. Today, it was a gateway. The sun, a benevolent eye peering through the canopy, cast dappled patterns on the leaf-strewn earth, a comforting familiarity that belied the growing sense of unease prickling at Joseph's skin. He'd told his parents he was going to check the snares his father had set, a plausible enough excuse to venture beyond the immediate safety of their homestead. But his heart hammered with a different purpose, a silent pact he'd made with himself. He was going further.

The moment he stepped off the well-trodden trail, the world subtly shifted. The air grew cooler, infused with the scent of damp earth and pine needles, a fragrance that was both invigorating and vaguely foreboding. The trees, once friendly sentinels of his known world, now pressed closer, their bark rougher, their branches more tangled, creating an almost impenetrable wall of green. The vibrant greens of summer seemed to deepen, taking on richer, more somber hues, as if acknowledging the intrusion of something new. Sunlight, which had been a generous presence just moments before, now fought its way through the dense foliage in scattered, hesitant beams, creating long, wavering shadows that danced with an unsettling life of their own. The usual chorus of birdsong seemed muted, replaced by a profound, almost watchful silence that pressed in on Joseph's ears, amplifying the sound of his own breathing, the thudding of his heart against his ribs. This was not the familiar woods; this was the periphery, the hushed antechamber to a wilder, more untamed realm.

He moved with a deliberate, almost cautious grace, his eyes scanning every detail. His father had taught him to read the woods like a book – the snap of a twig could mean a deer, the disturbed moss could indicate a badger's den, the scattering of leaves might signal a fox on the prowl. But here, the usual signs were overlaid with something else, something that whispered of human presence, yet was disturbingly alien to the patterns of their own settlement. He noticed a tree, a sturdy oak, its bark bearing a series of deliberate, shallow gouges. They weren't the haphazard scrapes of a bear, nor the territorial marks of a buck. These were precise, almost geometric, arranged in a pattern that seemed too ordered to be natural, too deliberate to be accidental. His fingers traced the rough edges of the incisions, the wood still slightly soft, suggesting they were not ancient. Yet, their purpose eluded him, an enigma etched into the living wood.

Further on, the ground beneath his worn leather boots felt strangely disturbed. Not the soft yielding of leaf litter, but a subtle unevenness, as if something had been dragged, or perhaps, buried. He knelt, brushing away the surface detritus. Beneath, the soil was darker, richer, and strangely compacted. There were no clear footprints, no distinct impressions, but the very texture of the earth felt *wrong*, like a wound in the otherwise natural landscape. He dug his fingers into the soil, feeling a faint, almost imperceptible coolness that seemed to emanate from within. It was a sensation that sent a shiver down his spine, a primal instinct recoiling from something it couldn't quite define.

He continued to press onward, drawn by an invisible thread. The silence was no longer just an absence of sound; it was an active presence, a palpable weight in the air that seemed to absorb the rustle of his movements. It felt like holding one's breath, a moment of suspended animation before a storm. He found himself listening for sounds that weren't there – the imagined snap of a twig behind him, the phantom whisper of movement in the undergrowth. His imagination, so often his companion in solitary exploration, now felt like a mischievous sprite, conjuring specters from the deepening shadows.

The trees grew denser still, their branches interlocking overhead, forming a verdant ceiling that allowed only slivers of light to penetrate. The air became heavy, carrying a faint, almost metallic tang that he couldn't place. He paused, straining his senses. It wasn't the smell of blood, not the earthy decay of fallen leaves. It was something sharper, something that pricked at the back of his throat. He remembered his mother's hushed tales of the old times, of strange occurrences in these woods, of things that defied explanation. He had always dismissed them as the fanciful ramblings of a frontier populace seeking to imbue their surroundings with an aura of mystery. But standing here, on the cusp of the unknown, those tales began to feel less like folklore and more like fragmented memories of a forgotten truth.

He noticed another anomaly, this time more jarring. A cluster of stones, arranged in a rough circle, half-hidden by a curtain of ivy. They were not native to this particular soil; their colors were too varied, their shapes too regular. They seemed out of place, like misplaced pieces of a puzzle. He cautiously approached, his heart pounding a frantic rhythm against his ribs. As he brushed away the clinging ivy, he saw that the stones weren't simply placed; they were deliberately positioned. One of them, larger and darker than the others, bore markings. Not gouges this time, but etched symbols, intricate and angular, unlike any script he had ever seen. They seemed to absorb the scant light, their depths hinting at secrets held for millennia. He traced a symbol with a tentative finger, feeling a strange resonance, a faint hum that seemed to vibrate through his very bones. It felt ancient, powerful, and utterly alien.

Joseph felt a strange mixture of fear and exhilaration. His parents' warnings echoed in his mind – the dangers of straying too far, of venturing into places where the familiar comforts of home could not reach. But the deeper he ventured, the more he felt a profound sense of purpose, a conviction that he was on the precipice of something significant. These signs, these subtle disturbances in the natural order, were not random. They were deliberate, intentional, and they spoke of a presence that was far more complex and ancient than he could have ever imagined. The woods, which he had always perceived as a place of natural beauty and simple dangers, were revealing themselves to be something far more profound, a repository of secrets waiting to be unearthed.

The deeper he went, the more the woods seemed to whisper to him. Not in words, but in the subtle language of the wild: the way the branches bent as if to guide him, the pattern of shadows that seemed to coalesce into fleeting shapes, the unnerving stillness that felt more like a deliberate pause than a natural quiet. He found himself instinctively drawn towards a particular direction, a pull that felt as undeniable as gravity. It was as if the very air was charged with an unseen energy, leading him deeper into its enigmatic heart. The known world of West Seneca receded, its comforting familiarity replaced by the growing allure of the unknown, the tantalizing promise of discovery that lay just beyond the veil of ordinary perception. His initial steps had been tentative, driven by a burgeoning curiosity, but now, he felt an undeniable compulsion, an instinctual drive to unravel the mysteries that lay hidden within the shadowed depths of the perilous outskirts.

2

The Unearthing of a Secret

The well-trodden path, once a beacon of familiarity, now felt like a forgotten memory as Joseph pushed further into the dense undergrowth. He'd left the last vestiges of the worn track far behind him, a conscious severance from the known. It was here, in the hushed embrace of the ancient trees, that he stumbled upon it – a whisper of a trail, a mere suggestion of a passage through the untamed wilderness. It wasn't carved by the steady tread of boots or the passage of carts; it was something far subtler, a delicate scar etched into the very fabric of the forest.

The path, if it could truly be called that, was a barely discernible parting of the ferns and mosses. It weaved and meandered, not with the purposeful straightness of a hunter's route, but with an almost organic sinuosity, as if following the unseen contours of the land or the subtle currents of the air. Overhead, the canopy closed in, a verdant, interwoven ceiling that allowed only fragmented slivers of sunlight to pierce through. These celestial shards, when they landed, illuminated patches of the forest floor in an ethereal glow, casting long, dancing shadows that shifted and writhed with every passing breeze. The air was thick with the scent of damp earth, decaying leaves, and something else – a faint, elusive fragrance that Joseph couldn't quite place, a hint of exotic bloom or ancient, undisturbed soil.

His initial steps onto this unmarked route were tentative, each footfall measured, his senses hyper-alert. The silence here was profound, a palpable entity that seemed to swallow the usual forest sounds. The chirping of birds, the rustling of small creatures, even the sigh of the wind through the leaves seemed to recede, leaving a stillness that pressed in on his ears. It was a silence that felt observant, as if the woods themselves were holding their breath, waiting to see what this intruder would do. He felt a thrill, a potent cocktail of exhilaration and trepidation, coursing through him. This was no longer a casual exploration; this was a journey into the heart of the unknown, a venture beyond the established boundaries of his world.

The trees flanking this phantom trail were older, larger, their bark gnarled and furrowed like the faces of ancient storytellers. Some bore strange, twisted limbs that seemed to reach out, beckoning him onward, while others stood sentinel, their branches laced together to form natural archways. The undergrowth here was thicker, a riot of ferns, brambles, and flowering plants that Joseph didn't recognize. They brushed against his legs as he passed, their damp leaves leaving cool trails on his skin. He noticed that the usual signs of animal passage – the scuff marks of deer hooves, the disturbed earth of a badger's burrow – were absent. This trail, it seemed, was not frequented by the common inhabitants of the woods.

As he followed its winding course, the sense of being watched intensified. It wasn't the watchful gaze of a predator, but a deeper, more pervasive awareness. He imagined ancient eyes peering from behind the moss-covered trunks, unseen presences that had long dwelled in these secluded depths. His father had often spoken of the old legends, of the spirits that inhabited the deep woods, of places where the veil between worlds was thin. Joseph had always dismissed them as fanciful tales, meant to keep children close to home. But now, on this secret path, those stories began to stir, taking on a new, unsettling reality.

The trail itself was an enigma. At times, it would widen slightly, revealing a scattering of unusually smooth, gray stones, arranged in a way that hinted at deliberate placement rather than natural occurrence. At other times, it would narrow almost to invisibility, forcing him to push through dense thickets, his clothes snagging on unseen thorns. It was as if the path itself was alive, shifting and concealing itself, revealing its secrets only to those who were truly seeking them. He found himself constantly looking for clues, for any sign that might explain its existence. Were these the tracks of some long-forgotten people? Had a hermit once carved this way? Or was it something far older, something intrinsically tied to the very soul of the forest?

He stopped for a moment, taking in his surroundings. The dappled sunlight, filtering through the dense foliage, created an almost kaleidoscopic effect on the forest floor. It illuminated patches of vibrant green moss, punctuated by the dark, rich hues of damp earth. A fallen log, covered in a thick carpet of fungi, lay across the path, forcing him to clamber over it. As he did, he dislodged a cluster of ancient, brittle leaves, and a faint, almost metallic scent rose into the air. It was a smell that spoke of time, of decay, and of something else... something that resonated with a strange familiarity, a forgotten echo in his memory.

His heart hammered against his ribs, a drumbeat against the pervasive silence. Every sense was on high alert, absorbing the details of this alien landscape. He noted a particular tree, an ancient oak, whose bark was deeply furrowed, almost like a map. Within one of the deeper crevices, he saw something glinting. He reached out, his fingers brushing against something cool and smooth. It was a shard of what looked like polished stone, embedded deep within the bark. It was a deep, lustrous blue, unlike any stone he had ever encountered in the region. As he touched it, a faint warmth seemed to emanate from it, a subtle vibration that ran up his arm. He tried to dislodge it, but it was firmly lodged, as if fused with the tree itself. The feeling of being on the cusp of a profound discovery intensified, a heady mix of awe and a creeping unease. This was no ordinary forest.

He continued his trek, the unseen trail his unwavering guide. He found himself noticing details he would have overlooked before: the peculiar arrangement of pebbles at the base of a towering pine, the unnatural smoothness of a particular rock face, the way certain vines seemed to grow in deliberate, spiraling patterns. These were not the random quirks of nature; they were subtle signatures, hints of an intelligence that had shaped this landscape long before human eyes had ever set foot here. The sheer antiquity of the place began to weigh on him, a sense of immense time compressed into the towering trees and the shadowed earth.

The further he ventured, the more the world seemed to recede. The familiar landmarks of West Seneca – the distant call of a hawk, the faint outline of the hills that framed their valley – were completely obscured by the dense growth. He was utterly alone, enveloped by the silence and the shadows. Yet, he didn't feel entirely isolated. There was a presence here, a subtle hum of life that was both comforting and deeply unsettling. It was the life of the ancient forest, a pulse that beat in time with something far older than himself.

He came to a small clearing, a sudden, unexpected break in the trees. The sunlight here was more direct, illuminating a patch of ground where the vegetation seemed strangely sparse. In the center of the clearing stood a single, weathered stone monument, roughly shaped like a pillar, about as tall as Joseph himself. Its surface was covered in intricate carvings, symbols that were both alien and strangely familiar, swirling patterns that seemed to twist and writhe in his peripheral vision. He approached it with a mixture of reverence and apprehension, his hand reaching out to touch the cool, rough surface. The stone felt alive beneath his fingertips, vibrating with a subtle energy. He traced one of the symbols, a spiral with radiating lines, and a sudden, fleeting image flashed through his mind – a glimpse of stars, of distant nebulae, of a sky utterly alien to his own.

He gasped, stumbling back, his heart pounding. What was this place? Who had created this monument, and for what purpose? The sheer strangeness of it all was overwhelming, yet it also fueled his resolve. He knew, with a certainty that chilled him to the bone, that he had stumbled upon something extraordinary, something that had been deliberately hidden, waiting to be unearthed. The unmarked trail had led him here, to the heart of a secret that lay buried beneath the verdant skin of the forest, a secret that was now beginning to stir within him. He felt a profound sense of responsibility, a dawning understanding that his journey was just beginning, that the path ahead, however daunting, was one he had to follow. The woods had called to him, and he had answered, stepping off the edge of the known world and into the embrace of an ancient mystery. The faint trail, barely visible, beckoned him further, promising answers to questions he hadn't even known to ask, drawing him deeper into its enigmatic embrace.

The path, a mere suggestion etched into the forest floor, continued its winding dance, drawing Joseph deeper into the hushed embrace of the ancient woods. Each step felt deliberate, a measured intrusion into a realm that time seemed to have forgotten. The dappled sunlight, filtering through the impossibly dense canopy, painted shifting mosaics of light and shadow on the ferns and mosses underfoot. The air, thick with the scent of damp earth and decaying leaves, carried an underlying perfume, something elusive and faintly sweet that Joseph couldn't quite identify. It was a fragrance that hinted at secrets, at forgotten blooms and soils undisturbed for centuries. He felt a profound sense of solitude, yet paradoxically, a feeling of being observed, as if the very trees held ancient eyes, their gnarled branches like silent, watchful sentinels.

He was so engrossed in the subtle shifts of the path, the almost imperceptible changes in the undergrowth, that he nearly missed it. A patch of earth, disturbed in a way that felt unnatural, snagged his attention. It was a slight depression in the loam, as if something had been pressed into the ground, or perhaps, something had emerged. His gaze, already sharpened by the pervasive mystery of his surroundings, zeroed in on the anomaly. Beneath a scattering of decaying leaves and a fine layer of dark, rich soil, a hint of unnatural color peeked through. Curiosity, a potent force that had propelled him this far, now surged with renewed vigor.

He knelt, his fingers brushing away the debris with a careful, almost reverent touch. The soil was loose here, as if it had been recently, though subtly, disturbed. As he cleared away the fallen foliage, a shape began to emerge, a form that seemed utterly alien to the organic chaos of the forest. It was neither wood nor stone, at least not in any way he recognized. The material was smooth to the touch, cool and unyielding, with a dull, metallic sheen that caught the limited light. It was a deep, almost bruised violet, a hue that seemed to absorb rather than reflect the surrounding greens and browns.

Joseph's breath hitched. He had seen many things in his short life – the weathered wood of the village homes, the rough-hewn stone of the church, the polished surfaces of his mother's few precious trinkets. But this... this was unlike anything he had ever encountered. It was a fragment, a shard of something larger, embedded in the earth as if it had fallen from the sky or been thrust from some unfathomable depth. The edges were worn, smoothed by time or perhaps by the very earth that cradled it, yet they retained a subtle angularity, a suggestion of a deliberate form. It was curved in places, with faint, almost imperceptible lines etched into its surface, patterns that seemed to hint at a language he couldn't comprehend.

He dug around it, carefully loosening the soil. The object was roughly the size of his palm, and as he worked it free, he felt a faint, almost imperceptible vibration emanating from it. It wasn't a mechanical hum, but something more organic, like the resonant thrum of a plucked string that lingered long after the initial sound. The vibration sent a shiver down his spine, a primal instinct that whispered of the unknown. It felt ancient, imbued with a power that was both fascinating and vaguely unsettling.

Once free, he turned the object over in his hands. It was heavier than it looked, its weight substantial and grounding. The violet color deepened in certain lights, almost black in the shadows, then revealing hints of sapphire and amethyst when the light struck it just right. He ran his thumb over the etched lines. They were incredibly fine, precise, and seemed to follow a repeating, geometric sequence that was both intricate and strangely hypnotic. It wasn't a pattern he could easily decipher; it felt more like a fragment of a vast, complex design, a single note in an unseen symphony.

His mind raced, trying to categorize this peculiar find. Was it a fragment of a tool? But what tool would be made of such material, and be carved with such meticulous detail? Could it be a jewel, a precious stone unlike any known to the civilized world? Yet, it lacked the inherent sparkle, the crystalline clarity of a diamond or emerald. It was subdued, possessing a deep, internal luminescence that seemed to draw the light in rather than refract it. It felt more like a piece of a celestial body, a fragment of something that had traveled across unimaginable distances.

He looked around the clearing, his eyes scanning the ground, searching for any other clues, any indication of what this object might be or where it came from. There was nothing. The forest floor here was as undisturbed as it had been in the surrounding woods, save for the small patch where he'd made his discovery. It was as if this singular item had been placed here, or had fallen here, in complete isolation.

The strangeness of it all was intoxicating. It was a tangible piece of the mystery that had drawn him off the beaten path. His father, a man of practicalities and hard work, would likely dismiss it as a curious rock or a piece of discarded metal. But Joseph felt a deeper connection, a resonance with the object that transcended mere curiosity. It spoke of a hidden history, a forgotten past that lay buried beneath the familiar landscape of his home.

He carefully wrapped the violet shard in a clean handkerchief, the cool material a stark contrast to the warmth of his hand. He tucked it into the inner pocket of his waistcoat, the slight weight a constant reminder of his peculiar discovery. As he stood, brushing the loam from his knees, his gaze swept across the clearing once more. The path, the very one that had led him here, seemed to vanish into the dense undergrowth on the other side of the clearing, beckoning him onward. The object in his pocket felt like a key, a silent testament to the secrets that lay waiting to be unearthed in these ancient woods. The quiet hum of the forest seemed to grow louder, charged with a new significance, a sense of anticipation for what lay further along the unseen trail. The discovery had amplified the allure of the unknown, transforming his exploration from a simple walk into a profound quest. He knew, with a certainty that settled deep in his bones, that this was no ordinary forest, and his journey was only just beginning. The violet shard was a tangible promise, a whisper from a forgotten age, urging him to delve deeper into the heart of the enigma. The sun, a distant observer through the leaves, cast longer shadows, and the air seemed to thicken with unspoken tales. He adjusted the object in his pocket, its cool presence a steady anchor against the rising tide of his excitement and trepidation. The next step along the path felt like stepping further into a dream, a dream woven from the very fabric of the ancient forest and its hidden, extraordinary secrets.

The object, cradled in Joseph's hands, felt like a fragment of a fallen star, a secret whispered from the void. Its violet hue was not merely a color, but a depth, a velvety darkness that seemed to drink in the muted light of the forest. Holding it closer, he could discern subtle variations within this dark luminescence, glints of almost indigo and streaks of a deep, bruised plum. It was as if the object contained its own miniature cosmos, a universe compressed into a tangible form. The surface, cool and impossibly smooth, offered no purchase for his fingertips to find any discernible grain or texture, unlike any natural stone or worked metal he had ever encountered. It possessed a density that belied its size, a satisfying heft that spoke of materials far removed from the everyday.

As he turned it this way and that, seeking any clue to its manufacture or purpose, his gaze fell upon the etched lines he had noticed earlier. They were not random scratches; they were impossibly fine, precise, and arranged in patterns that spoke of deliberate intent. These were not glyphs or runes he recognized from the faded scrolls in the village library or the inscriptions on ancient tombstones. Instead, they were abstract, almost fractal in their complexity, curving and intertwining in a way that suggested an internal logic, a language utterly alien to his understanding. Some sections appeared as tightly coiled spirals, others as sharp, angular zigzags that seemed to represent a form of mathematical precision. He traced them with the tip of his forefinger, feeling a faint, almost electric tremor pass from the object into his skin. It wasn't a sensation of heat or cold, but a subtle vibration, a silent resonance that seemed to hum just below the threshold of his hearing.

What purpose could such an object serve? It was too small to be a tool for any practical craft he knew. It was too smooth and devoid of sharp edges to be a weapon, or at least, any weapon fashioned by human hands. Its material was unknown, its markings incomprehensible. He held it up against a patch of sunlight, hoping for some reaction, some display of its inner nature. Instead, the light seemed to be absorbed, the violet deepening, the etched lines remaining stubbornly inert. There was no reflection, no glimmer, no indication that it was meant to interact with the visible spectrum in any conventional way.

He closed his eyes, trying to attune himself to the object's subtle thrum. It felt... old. Immeasurably old, older than the trees that surrounded him, older than the very hills on which his village stood. It carried the weight of epochs, a silent witness to eras long past. This wasn't the worn patina of age on a familiar artifact; this was the profound stillness of something that had existed outside the conventional march of time. The vibration, so faint yet persistent, was like the echo of a colossal event, a forgotten song sung in a language of energy and matter.

Joseph's mind, usually so adept at logical deduction and the sorting of observations, found itself adrift in a sea of unanswered questions. He tried to conjure comparisons, to anchor this strange artifact to something known. Perhaps it was a fragment of a celestial map, its patterns depicting constellations unknown to him. Or maybe it was a key, not to a physical lock, but to a deeper understanding, a forgotten piece of knowledge. The idea of it being a 'key' resonated with a peculiar intensity, a feeling that this enigmatic shard was the first step in a much larger revelation.

He imagined the countless possibilities, each more fantastical than the last. Could it have been part of a device of immense power, crafted by beings who understood the very fabric of reality in ways he could only dimly perceive? Or was it a relic from a civilization predating his own, a civilization whose understanding of science and art was so advanced as to appear magical? The more he pondered, the more the object seemed to shrink from definition, its very resistance to categorization becoming its most defining characteristic. It was not a 'what,' but a profound 'why.'

He carefully placed the violet shard back into the handkerchief, the soft fabric a stark contrast to its unyielding nature. The weight in his pocket was a constant, tangible reminder of the mystery he had unearthed. He looked back at the small depression in the earth where it had lain, a subtle scar on the forest floor. It was as if the earth itself had grudgingly relinquished its secret, presenting it to him with a silent plea for comprehension.

The forest, which had seemed merely mysterious before, now felt imbued with an even deeper, more profound sense of hidden purpose. Every rustle of leaves, every creak of a branch, seemed to carry a hidden meaning, an echo of the object's silent song. His initial curiosity had been a spark; this discovery had fanned it into a consuming flame. He felt a pull, an irresistible urge to understand, to unravel the enigma that had presented itself so unexpectedly. This object was not just a find; it was a summons, a challenge to his perception of the world. It was the first thread of a tapestry he had not known existed, and he was compelled to follow it, wherever it might lead. The faint vibration he still felt, even through the handkerchief and his clothing, was a constant reminder that the world was far stranger and more wondrous than he had ever dared to imagine. It was a silent testament to the fact that beneath the veneer of the familiar, lay realms of the unknown, waiting to be explored.

He stood for a long moment, the silence of the woods broken only by the symphony of nature's subtle sounds. The object in his pocket was more than just a curiosity; it was a puzzle piece that hinted at a picture he couldn't yet see. Its enigmatic nature was not a barrier, but an invitation. It beckoned him to look beyond the obvious, to question the accepted truths, and to seek the hidden narratives woven into the very fabric of his world. He could feel a shift within himself, a subtle re-calibration of his purpose. The simple exploration had transformed into a quest, a personal journey into the heart of an ancient secret. The violet shard was his solitary companion, a silent confidant in this burgeoning pursuit of understanding. The sun, now beginning its slow descent, cast elongated shadows, making the trees seem to lean in, as if sharing their ancient wisdom with the young man who had dared to disturb their slumber. He adjusted the object once more, its cool weight a grounding force against the exhilarating swirl of apprehension and anticipation that now coursed through him. The path ahead, already beckoning, now seemed an illuminated corridor into a realm of profound, undiscovered truths. He was no longer just a boy wandering in the woods; he was an explorer at the precipice of a forgotten history, and the violet shard was his cryptic guide. The subtle vibration seemed to intensify, a silent promise of the revelations that awaited him, a tantalizing whisper of the extraordinary concealed within the ordinary.

He examined the surface of the object again, running his finger over the impossibly fine etchings. They formed a series of interconnected geometric shapes, each seemingly derived from the one before it, a fractal progression that spiraled outward. There were no straight lines in the conventional sense, but rather curves that bent at precise, unnatural angles, creating intricate patterns that resembled both celestial charts and microscopic biological structures. He found himself trying to mentally "unfold" the patterns, to see if they could be flattened into a coherent map or diagram. But the curvature of the object's surface, combined with the complexity of the etchings, made it impossible to discern a starting point or a definitive end. It was a fragment, he was certain, a mere sliver of a much grander design.

He tilted the object, letting the faint light play across its violet depths. The material itself seemed to possess a subtle iridescence, a pearlescent quality that shimmered just beneath the surface when viewed at certain angles. It was not the metallic sheen of polished silver or the glassy reflection of obsidian, but something far more organic, akin to the inner surface of a seashell or the wing of a particularly rare butterfly. Yet, it was cool to the touch, unyielding, suggesting a composition far more robust than any biological material he knew. This duality, the organic appearance coupled with the mineral coolness, was another layer to its profound enigma.

What was it made of? He pressed his thumbnail against it, expecting some give, some resistance that would indicate hardness. There was none. His nail slid across the surface as if it were made of polished ice. He tried to scratch it with a small, sharp pebble he found near his feet. The pebble, hard enough to score wood, left no mark whatsoever on the violet shard. It was as if the object existed on a different material plane, impervious to the abrasive forces that shaped the world around him. This realization sent a shiver of awe and a prickle of fear down his spine. Its resilience was a testament to its unknown origin, a silent declaration of its alien nature.

Joseph's mind raced, trying to fit this inexplicable find into any existing framework. He had read of ancient legends, of artifacts imbued with magical properties, of celestial objects that had fallen to earth. But those were stories, bedtime tales designed to frighten or entertain. This was real. It was solid, tangible, and it rested in his hand, vibrating with an unseen energy. He felt a growing conviction that this object was not a mere curiosity, but a key—a key to unlocking a deeper truth about his world, a truth that had been hidden away for untold ages. The forest had yielded its secret, but it was a secret that opened more questions than it answered. It was a riddle etched in a language of light and matter, and Joseph felt an unshakable resolve to find its solution. The profound mystery of the object had not diminished his desire to understand; it had magnified it, transforming a simple walk in the woods into a momentous quest. He was now a custodian of a secret, a fragment of a story that begged to be told, and he felt an immense responsibility to listen, to learn, and to discover. The violet shard, nestled in his palm, felt like the first domino in a chain reaction of revelation, and he was ready to push it.

The forest, which moments before had seemed an arena of pristine solitude, now felt alive with a different kind of energy. Joseph's keen ears, honed by years of navigating the woods, picked up a subtle shift in the ambient sounds. It wasn't the familiar symphony of rustling leaves and chattering squirrels; this was something... other. A faint murmur, too low to decipher words, drifted on the breeze from the direction he had intended to continue. It was the sound of voices, hushed and urgent, that spoke of secrets shared, of clandestine meetings. Then, a sharp, distinct snap of a twig, too heavy to be an animal's careless step, echoed through the trees, closer than he liked. He froze, the violet shard, still warm from his touch, a comforting weight against his thigh, now a tangible link to this sudden intrusion.

His initial exhilaration, the pure wonder of his discovery, began to curdle into a potent mixture of apprehension and a heightened awareness. The woods had always been a sanctuary, a place of predictable rhythms. Now, they felt like a stage for an unseen drama, and he, the accidental audience member, had stumbled upon a scene far more complex than he could have imagined. He held his breath, straining to identify the source of the disturbance. Was it other children, playing some elaborate game? The sound of the twig snap, however, had a deliberate weight to it, a calculated pressure that suggested something heavier, more purposeful than youthful exuberance.

He instinctively reached for the object in his pocket, his fingers closing around its smooth, cool surface. The faint vibration, still perceptible through the thick wool of his trousers, felt like a heartbeat against his own. It was a grounding sensation, a reminder of the tangible reality of his find, even as the intangible threat loomed. He pressed himself closer to the rough bark of an ancient oak, its gnarled trunk offering a semblance of concealment. His eyes scanned the dappled shadows, seeking any flicker of movement, any anomaly in the familiar tapestry of green and brown.

The hushed voices continued, a low murmur that seemed to weave through the rustling leaves. He couldn't make out individual words, but the tone was unmistakable: secretive, intent, perhaps even conspiratorial. It was the sound of people who did not wish to be overheard, who had sought out this secluded corner of the forest for a reason. And he, Joseph, had inadvertently intruded upon their privacy. The thought sent a fresh wave of unease through him. What if they were the ones who had lost the object? Or worse, what if they were actively searching for it, and he had just become an obstacle?

A metallic clang, faint but sharp, cut through the murmuring voices. It was the sound of metal striking metal, a percussive, resonant noise that was utterly out of place in the natural soundscape. It was too deliberate, too distinct, to be a coincidence. It spoke of tools, of something being worked, or perhaps of some kind of signaling. Joseph's mind raced, trying to piece together the fragments of information. Hushed voices, a deliberate twig snap, the clang of metal – it all pointed to a hidden activity, a presence in this normally deserted part of the woods.

His senses, already heightened by the discovery of the violet shard, now went into overdrive. Every distant bird call seemed amplified, every shadow seemed to deepen and conceal a watchful presence. He felt a primal urge to retreat, to flee back to the familiar safety of his village, to forget this unsettling encounter. Yet, the object in his pocket, with its silent hum and inscrutable etchings, held him tethered. It was a mystery he had unearthed, and now it seemed that this mystery was not confined to him alone. Others were involved, and their presence, their activities, were undoubtedly connected to the very thing he now held.

He edged his way further along the oak's broad trunk, trying to gain a better vantage point without revealing his own presence. The undergrowth was thick here, a dense tangle of ferns and brambles that provided excellent cover. He moved with a stealth born of instinct, his small frame adept at navigating the forest floor without a sound. He had always been a quiet observer, more comfortable watching from the periphery than being at the center of attention. This situation, however, demanded a new level of vigilance, a silent, almost predatory awareness.

The voices shifted, seeming to move slightly further into the woods, but still audible. He could now discern a rhythm to their speech, a cadence that suggested a conversation, albeit a hushed one. He imagined them – who were they? Men, women, children? Their age, their purpose, all remained shrouded in the same mystery as the object itself. He pictured rough, calloused hands working with unseen implements, faces illuminated by the dim forest light, their whispers carrying the weight of shared knowledge.

He noticed the subtle signs of their passage that he had previously overlooked. A faint disturbance in the moss on a fallen log, a few leaves that seemed to have been pushed aside with more force than an animal would exert, a barely perceptible indentation in the soft earth that was too regular to be natural. These were the traces of human, or at least intelligent, activity, indicators of a presence that had been here, and likely still was. The secluded clearing where he had found the shard was not as untouched as he had initially believed. It was a place that had been visited, perhaps even frequented, by others.

The thought of others seeking the same artifact, or something related to it, was both thrilling and terrifying. It validated the object's significance, suggesting it was not merely a random anomaly but something of value, something sought after. But it also placed him in a precarious position. He was an interloper, an accidental witness to their clandestine affairs. If they discovered him, if they realized he possessed the object, what would happen? His mind conjured images from the adventure stories he devoured – hidden treasures guarded by fierce protectors, ancient secrets sought by shadowy figures.

He carefully extracted the violet shard from his pocket, cradling it in his palm. Even in the muted light filtering through the canopy, its deep luminescence was captivating. The faint vibration seemed to pulse in time with his own quickening heartbeat. He felt an almost magnetic pull towards the source of the sounds, a desperate need to understand the context of his discovery. The object was a question, and these unseen individuals might hold the answer.

He moved with agonizing slowness, inching his way around the dense thicket that separated him from the direction of the voices. The air grew heavy with anticipation, the silence between the sounds more profound. He reached the edge of the clearing where he had found the object, his eyes sweeping across the small, circular depression in the earth. It was exactly as he had left it, a stark reminder of the moment of revelation. But now, the surrounding woods seemed to hold a new significance, a potential for danger.

He crouched low, peering through a gap in the ferns. In the distance, perhaps fifty yards away, he could see a slight disturbance in the undergrowth. It wasn't a clear view, but he could discern movement, shadows that shifted with a purpose. The hushed voices were clearer now, though still indistinct. He thought he could make out the murmur of what sounded like instructions, of quiet directions being given.

Then, he saw it. A brief, almost imperceptible flicker of light, emanating from behind a large clump of ferns and thicket. It was a soft, diffused glow, not the harsh glare of a lantern or a torch, but something gentler, more controlled. It pulsed for a moment, then vanished. What could be producing such a light in the depths of the forest, at this hour? It was another piece of the puzzle, another element that defied simple explanation.

He pressed himself further into the concealment, his heart hammering against his ribs. The thrill of discovery had been replaced by a gnawing anxiety. He was no longer a curious boy exploring nature; he was a trespasser, an unwilling participant in a clandestine operation. The object in his hand, once a source of wonder, now felt like a dangerous burden, a beacon that might inadvertently draw attention to him.

He tried to recall the exact path he had taken to reach the clearing. The violet shard had been unearthed from a small, almost insignificant mound of earth, nestled beneath the roots of an ancient oak. He had been drawn to that spot by an inexplicable intuition, a feeling that something lay hidden there. Had they intended for him to find it? Or had he stumbled upon something they were trying to conceal? The questions swirled in his mind, each one adding another layer of complexity to his predicament.

He continued to observe, his gaze fixed on the area where he had seen the movement and the faint light. He heard another sound, a soft scraping, as if something were being dragged across the forest floor. It was a dry, rustling noise, interspersed with the occasional muffled thud. Whatever these individuals were doing, it involved some sort of laborious activity, something that required more than just a brief conversation.

The sheer secrecy of their actions was what unnerved him the most. If they were engaged in a legitimate activity, why the hushed voices, the deliberate concealment? The forest was vast and largely unpopulated; there was no need for such extreme caution unless their purpose was something they wished to keep hidden from the world. And if it was something hidden, was it something good or something ill?

He remembered the strange, almost ethereal vibration of the object in his hand. It felt ancient, imbued with a power he couldn't comprehend. If this object was indeed significant, then it was plausible that others would seek it, perhaps even fight for it. He was a solitary boy, armed with nothing but his wits and a mysterious artifact. Against an unknown group engaged in covert activities, he felt alarmingly vulnerable.

He decided to make his move. Staying here, frozen in the undergrowth, was becoming increasingly risky. If they discovered him, his situation would be far worse. He needed to extricate himself from this predicament, to get back to the safety of the village and consider his next steps. But as he prepared to disengage, a new sound reached his ears, one that sent a cold dread creeping down his spine. It was a low, guttural growl, a sound that was far too primal, too menacing, to be human. It was followed by the unmistakable heavy tread of large paws on the forest floor.

Joseph's breath hitched. He had not heard that sound before, not in this part of the woods. It was the sound of a predator, a creature of considerable size and power. And it seemed to be approaching the very area where the hushed voices and the metallic clang had originated. Whatever was happening here, it had just become infinitely more complicated. The hidden activity he had stumbled upon was now apparently accompanied by a much more ancient, and potentially more dangerous, presence. The thrill of discovery had definitively vanished, replaced by a stark, chilling realization: he was caught in the middle of something far larger, and far more perilous, than he could have ever imagined. His immediate concern was no longer just being discovered by the people; it was about surviving whatever was now making its presence known. He felt a sudden, overwhelming urge to retreat, not just out of fear of being seen, but out of a deep, instinctual terror of the unknown forces that seemed to converge in this hidden pocket of the forest. The violet shard, clutched tightly in his hand, now felt less like a key and more like a target, drawing him into a nexus of danger he was ill-equipped to navigate.

The familiar scent of damp earth and pine needles clung to Joseph's clothes, a comforting, albeit now slightly unnerving, reminder of his afternoon's excursion. The forest, usually a boundless playground of imagination, had revealed a hidden facet, a layer of intrigue that had irrevocably altered his perception. With each step away from the hushed voices and the unsettling sounds, Joseph felt the weight of the violet shard in his pocket grow heavier, not in a physical sense, but in the burgeoning significance it represented. The initial exhilaration of discovery had matured, morphing into a potent, almost unshakeable, curiosity. He wasn't just a boy who had found a pretty stone; he was a boy who had stumbled upon a secret, a secret that whispered of hidden agendas and unseen presences. The question that burned brightest in his mind was not *what* he had found, but *why*.

The path back to West Seneca seemed longer than usual, each twist and turn of the familiar trail now viewed through a lens of heightened awareness. The rustling of leaves, once a soothing lullaby, now sounded like the furtive steps of unseen observers. The chirping of birds, a cheerful chorus, could have been coded signals. Joseph found himself glancing over his shoulder more often than not, his young mind conjuring scenarios that played out the unsettling sounds and whispers he had overheard. He imagined shadowy figures, cloaked in the deepening twilight, their faces hidden, their intentions masked. The image of the faint, pulsing light he had glimpsed flickered in his memory, an anomaly that defied any natural explanation he could conceive. It wasn't the friendly glow of a farmer's lantern or the warm hearth of a village home. It was something alien, something that belonged to the hushed conversations and the metallic clang.

He clutched the shard tighter, his fingers tracing the intricate etchings that seemed to swirl and converge under his touch. They were unlike anything he had ever seen, patterns that spoke of an ancient language, a forgotten craft. The object hummed with a faint, almost imperceptible energy, a constant thrum that resonated deep within him. It was a tangible connection to the mystery, a physical anchor to the questions that swirled relentlessly in his thoughts. Was this object lost, or deliberately placed? Was it a treasure, a tool, or something else entirely? The answers, he suspected, were far more complex than a simple game of hide-and-seek.

As he emerged from the treeline, the familiar silhouette of West Seneca came into view, its chimneys exhaling wisps of smoke into the evening sky. The sight usually brought a sense of comfort and belonging, but tonight, it felt like a temporary reprieve. The secret he carried felt too large for the quiet familiarity of his village. It was a secret that had unfolded in the wild, untamed heart of the forest, and he suspected its origins, and perhaps its destiny, lay far beyond the cobblestone streets and thatched roofs of home. His mind, usually occupied with the simple joys of childhood – the next game of marbles, the prospect of supper, the anticipation of a good book – was now consumed by a singular, burning question: what was this object, and who else was looking for it?

He quickened his pace, the setting sun casting long, distorted shadows that danced like spectral figures at the edge of his vision. He bypassed the usual route home, opting for a less-trafficked path that led him past the old blacksmith's forge, its doors now shut for the night. Even here, a midst the familiar structures of human endeavor, the unease persisted. The metallic clang he had heard in the woods echoed in his memory, a sharp counterpoint to the gentle rhythm of his own footsteps. What was being forged in that secluded clearing? And why the need for such profound secrecy?

He reached his own small cottage, the scent of baking bread – his mother's familiar aroma – a welcome anchor to reality. He pushed open the creaking door, the warmth of the hearth washing over him. "Joseph, is that you, dear? You're later than usual," his mother called from the kitchen, her voice a comforting melody. He mumbled a reply, his mind still a thousand miles away, lost in the depths of the whispering woods. He needed to process what he had experienced, to sort through the jumbled fragments of sound, sight, and sensation.

He retreated to his room, the small space that usually felt so expansive now seeming confining. He sat on the edge of his bed, pulling the violet shard from his pocket. Under the soft lamplight, its luminescence seemed to intensify, the internal glow pulsating with a steady, rhythmic beat. He held it up to his eye, tracing the impossibly fine lines with his gaze. They seemed to shift and rearrange themselves as he looked, hinting at a depth and complexity that defied his understanding. This was no ordinary stone, no mere geological anomaly. This was a key, a cipher, a fragment of something far grander and more enigmatic.

The playful curiosity that had led him into the woods that morning had been replaced by a more serious, almost urgent, quest. He felt a pull, an innate desire to understand the meaning behind this discovery. It was as if the shard itself was an extension of his own burgeoning awareness, a catalyst that had awakened a dormant part of his mind. He remembered the hushed voices, the deliberate sounds, the sense of clandestine activity. These were not the actions of children playing a game, nor the innocent ramblings of forest dwellers. These were people with a purpose, a purpose that seemed intrinsically linked to the object he now held.

He lay back on his bed, the shard resting on his chest, its faint warmth seeping through his shirt. His mind raced, piecing together the puzzle. The forest, usually so predictable, had revealed its secrets grudgingly, and only to him. He had been drawn to that specific spot, as if guided by an unseen hand. And now, he was left with a profound sense of responsibility, a feeling that this secret was now his to safeguard, and his to unravel. The question was no longer confined to a simple curiosity; it had become a burning imperative. He needed to know the truth, to understand the significance of the violet shard and the shadowy figures who operated in the hidden corners of his familiar world. The path ahead was uncertain, fraught with the shadows he had glimpsed, but the fire ignited within him was too bright to be extinguished. He would seek answers, no matter the cost. The unearthing of a secret had just begun, and Joseph knew, with a certainty that settled deep in his bones, that his life would never be the same. The simple act of finding a peculiar stone had unlocked a hidden world, and he was compelled to explore it. The weight of this new knowledge pressed upon him, a silent promise of adventures and dangers yet to come, all stemming from that single, luminous object.

3

Unraveling the Cryptic Thread

The violet shard lay on his worn wooden desk, catching the afternoon sun that streamed through his window. Joseph, usually an impatient boy when it came to waiting for meals or the end of lessons, found himself utterly absorbed, his sense of time dissolving into the intricate details of the object. He had already spent the better part of an hour just turning it over and over in his hands, feeling the cool, smooth texture of its surface, the unexpected heft it possessed despite its size. Now, illuminated by the light, its true nature began to reveal itself, or rather, its refusal to reveal itself.

He brought it closer to his eye, his breath misting the crystalline surface momentarily before it cleared. The faint, internal luminescence seemed to pulse with a slow, steady rhythm, a silent heartbeat within the stone. It was this internal light that had first drawn him in, a soft, ethereal glow that seemed to beckon from the forest floor. Now, he could see that this light wasn't uniform. It flickered and shifted, concentrated in certain points within the shard, creating a mesmerizing, almost hypnotic effect. He wondered if this was some form of phosphorescence, but even to his young mind, it felt different, more... alive.

His fingers, nimble and accustomed to the fine work of mending fishing nets and whittling small figures, now traced the almost imperceptible lines etched into the shard's exterior. They weren't the rough cuts of a tool or the random striations of a natural break. These were deliberate, impossibly fine lines, arranged in a complex, geometric pattern. At first glance, they appeared to be mere decorative swirls, but as Joseph tilted the shard, angling it this way and that to catch the light, a new dimension emerged. It was as if the lines themselves held a hidden depth.

He held it at a precise angle, his eye squinting in concentration. For a fleeting moment, the swirling lines seemed to coalesce, forming faint, stylized symbols. They were unlike anything he had ever encountered. They bore no resemblance to the familiar script of the village schoolmaster, nor the ornate lettering on the pages of his mother's worn prayer book. He racked his brain, sifting through his limited visual vocabulary. Could they be ancient runes? He'd heard tales from old Silas, the village elder, about markings left by long-forgotten peoples, but those stories always felt like fanciful myths. Now, holding this shard, the myths felt a little closer to reality.

He tried to sketch them in his notebook, a tattered volume filled with his observations of flora and fauna, interspersed with attempts at drawing the world as he saw it. The pencil felt clumsy in his hand, his lines too thick, too crude to capture the delicate precision of the etchings. He managed to approximate a few of the shapes, a series of interlocking triangles, a spiral that seemed to twist into itself endlessly, a single, sharp angle that reminded him of a bird's wing in flight. But these were mere approximations, ghostly echoes of the original. The true essence of the symbols remained elusive, veiled in their own inherent mystery.

Joseph then turned his attention to the subtle differences in the shard's coloration. It wasn't a uniform violet. Deeper, almost indigo hues swirled within the lighter lavender, interspersed with veins of a startlingly bright amethyst. These color shifts weren't random. They followed the same intricate patterns as the etchings, as if the color itself was a form of inscription, a visual language communicating something he couldn't yet decipher. He pressed the shard against the page of his notebook, hoping to capture the subtle gradients, but the paper only absorbed the light, rendering the complex hues into a dull, flat purple.

He began to compare the symbols to anything that might hold a parallel in his world. He remembered the carved wooden gargoyles that adorned the eaves of the old chapel, their faces contorted in expressions of ancient warnings. Their lines were bold, stylized, but they lacked the fine, almost impossibly delicate nature of the shard's markings. He thought of the patterns in the frost that formed on his windowpane on cold mornings, intricate and fleeting, but governed by the predictable laws of crystallization. These symbols on the shard seemed to defy such natural order.

He even considered the recurring motifs in his mother's embroidered linens, the wildflowers and vines that adorned their humble table cloths. These were familiar and comforting, but they spoke of the earth, of growth and seasons. The symbols on the shard felt otherworldly, hinting at a design that was not born of nature, but of a mind that conceived of patterns far beyond human comprehension. He traced one particular symbol, a series of concentric circles with a single, sharp line bisecting them, and it sparked a faint, distant memory. Where had he seen something like that before?

Was it in one of the old books his father had left behind, filled with leather-bound tales of distant lands and forgotten constellations? His father, a scholar of sorts, had a small collection of books that were now carefully preserved by his mother, too precious to be read by eager young hands. Perhaps one of those volumes held a clue. He made a mental note to search through them later, a flicker of hope igniting within him.

He also recalled the faded murals on the interior walls of the abandoned mill on the edge of town, remnants of a time when the mill had been more than just a crumbling edifice. Those murals depicted scenes of local history, of harvests and festivals, but there were also more abstract patterns painted in the corners, designs that had always seemed out of place, almost alien. Could the shard's symbols bear a resemblance to those forgotten decorations?

The longer he studied the shard, the more he realized that its clues were not readily apparent. They were subtle, layered, designed to be discovered, perhaps, only by someone with the patience and the keenness of observation to truly look. The faint luminescence, the intricate etchings, the subtle shifts in color – each element felt like a piece of a larger puzzle, a coded message waiting to be translated.

He tried to force the symbols into a known language, to see if any part of them aligned with the Greek alphabet his father had tried to teach him, or even the rudimentary pictograms he'd seen in a book about ancient civilizations. Nothing fit. The shapes were too fluid, too organic, yet too mathematically precise at the same time. It was a paradox that only deepened his fascination.

He picked up the shard again, its weight a comforting presence in his palm. He could feel a faint vibration emanating from it, a subtle tremor that seemed to resonate with the very air around it. Was this a power source? A communication device? Or simply a manifestation of its unique material composition? He ran his fingertip over a particularly sharp intersection of lines. It felt as though he was touching the edge of an impossibly small, impossibly intricate mechanism.

He held it up to the light once more, tilting it, rotating it, searching for any hint of a seam, a button, a hidden switch. The surface was utterly seamless, a testament to a craftsmanship that transcended anything he had ever witnessed. There were no external moving parts, no obvious way to activate or interact with it. Its secrets were clearly held within, locked behind the enigmatic language of its design.

Joseph's initial excitement was now tempered by a growing sense of frustration, but it was a productive frustration, the kind that fueled a detective's resolve. The object was not giving up its secrets easily, and that, he felt, was precisely the point. It was a challenge, a silent dare. Someone, or something, had created this, imbued it with these cryptic markings, and left it for someone to find. And he, Joseph, had found it.

He decided to try a different approach. Instead of looking for what the symbols *meant*, he started to consider *how* they were made. The lines were so fine, so perfectly consistent, that no earthly tool he could imagine could have created them. He thought of the finest needle, the sharpest quill, but even those would leave a visible mark, a trace of their passage. The lines on the shard seemed to have been... grown, or etched by light itself. This led him to consider the possibility that the object was not entirely of this world, or at least, not crafted by conventional means.

He spent the next hour meticulously cataloging every detail in his notebook. He drew diagrams of the shard's overall shape, noting its subtle asymmetry, the way its edges were not perfectly flat but curved inward slightly, like a lens. He tried to measure the spacing between the etched lines, using the width of his own fingernail as a rough guide, but found the measurements inconsistent, suggesting that the patterns were not based on simple arithmetic ratios.

The fact that the symbols appeared and disappeared depending on the angle of the light also struck him as significant. It implied a deliberate interaction with external stimuli, a responsiveness that was characteristic of a living organism, or perhaps, a sophisticated piece of machinery. He tried shining his lamplight directly onto the shard, but this seemed to wash out the symbols, flattening them into indistinguishable lines. It was only with the softer, more diffuse light of the sun, filtered through the windowpane, that the hidden meanings began to emerge.

He remembered a story his father had read to him once, about a hidden city said to be built of crystal, where the very light of the sun was used to power the inhabitants' devices. At the time, it had been a captivating fairy tale. Now, holding the violet shard, the fairy tale felt like a premonition.

He carefully placed the shard back into the oilskin pouch he had used to carry it. He couldn't risk damaging it, not now that he understood its potential significance. He felt a profound sense of responsibility, the weight of this discovery pressing down on him. This wasn't just a beautiful object; it was a mystery, a coded message, and he was the only one who had found the key. The silent clues within the violet shard were a testament to a hidden world, and Joseph was determined to unlock its secrets, one cryptic symbol at a time. The forest had yielded its first whisper, and he was ready to listen to the rest of the story, no matter how complex or how dangerous it might prove to be. He closed his notebook, the sketches of the inscrutable symbols a testament to his first tentative steps into a vast, unknown territory. The journey had just begun.

The sun, which had seemed so full of promise just hours ago, now cast long, disquieting shadows across the village as Joseph made his way back. His return from the woods, usually a simple transit from the wild to the familiar, felt different. The violet shard, nestled safely within his oilskin pouch, was a tangible piece of the unknown, a secret he carried not just in his hand, but within his very perception. The world, which had seemed so straightforward and predictable, was now subtly reconfigured, its edges blurred by the unsettling hum of what he had unearthed.

As he passed the communal well, where a few women were drawing water, their chatter, usually a lively cacophony of gossip and domestic concerns, struck him with a new resonance. He slowed his pace, not out of any deliberate attempt to eavesdrop, but because his newly awakened sensitivity seemed to amplify every sound, every inflection. He heard fragments, disconnected words that, to anyone else, would have been mere background noise.

"...best keep it quiet, Elara," a gruff voice, belonging to old Thomas, the blacksmith, rumbled. He was speaking to Elara, the baker's wife, her face usually creased in perpetual good cheer, now unusually drawn.

"Quiet? How can we keep it quiet, Thomas? It's not as if it's a secret we can bury again," Elara replied, her voice a low, worried murmur.

Joseph's heart gave a strange lurch. *Bury it again?* The phrase, innocent enough on its own, felt loaded with implication when paired with the context of secrecy. He continued walking, his ears straining, catching another snippet as he moved past the village tavern, its doors swung open, spilling the scent of ale and pipe smoke onto the dusty street.

"...the old ways... they don't understand," a man's voice, slurred with drink but laced with a peculiar urgency, drifted out. It was likely Silas, whose pronouncements were often cryptic even in his cups. *The old ways.* The phrase echoed the hushed legends old Silas himself sometimes spun, tales of the forest and its hidden power, of a time before the village was established, when the land itself held sway. Joseph had always dismissed them as the ramblings of a lonely old man. But now, with the violet shard pulsing with its silent enigma, these fragments of conversation began to coalesce, forming a disturbing pattern.

He walked down the familiar lane leading to his small cottage, the worn cobblestones a comforting, if now strangely insufficient, anchor to reality. He noticed other groups of villagers, their conversations ceasing abruptly as he approached, only to resume in hushed tones once he had passed. It was a subtle shift, a barely perceptible reticence, but it was there, a tangible curtain drawn across their interactions.

He saw Martha, the weaver, talking animatedly with her neighbor, Anya. As Joseph drew nearer, Martha's animated gestures ceased, and she cast a quick, almost fearful glance in his direction. Anya's response was a sharp, almost imperceptible nod, her eyes meeting Martha's with a shared, unspoken understanding. Then, as Joseph passed, Anya turned back to her neighbor, her voice a low whisper that was entirely lost to him, but the intent, the deliberate lowering of their voices, was unmistakable.

He tried to recall the exact moment the feeling had shifted. Was it when he found the shard? Or had the unease been present, latent, even before that, a subtle undercurrent he had simply failed to perceive? The secluded trail, the one he had always considered just a shortcut, a forgotten path overgrown with brambles, now seemed significant. He had followed it because it was less traveled, a place where he could escape the usual village bustle and commune with the quiet solitude of the woods. But now, he wondered if it was less traveled for a reason.

He remembered the peculiar stillness of that path, the way the birds seemed to fall silent as he ventured deeper. He had attributed it to the dense canopy, the way it filtered the sunlight into a dappled gloom. But what if it was something else? What if the forest itself was holding its breath, guarding its secrets?

His mind raced, trying to connect these disparate threads. The hushed conversations, the averted glances, the phrases about keeping things quiet and the old ways – they all pointed to a shared knowledge, a collective understanding that was being deliberately withheld from him, from everyone else in the village. And somehow, he suspected, the violet shard was the key that had unlocked this veil of secrecy, not just for him, but for the villagers themselves.

He reached his cottage, its familiar facade a welcome sight. His mother was within, her movements usually characterized by a gentle, rhythmic hum of domestic activity. Today, however, he noticed a subtle tension in her shoulders as she stirred a pot over the hearth. She looked up as he entered, her expression softening into a smile, but it was a smile that didn't quite reach her eyes.

"Joseph, dear. You're back. Supper will be ready soon," she said, her voice calm, perhaps a little too calm.

He walked over to the worn wooden table, placing his satchel on it. The oilskin pouch, with its precious contents, felt warm against his leg. He hesitated, then met his mother's gaze. "Mother," he began, his voice lower than usual, "I was in the woods today, near the old Whispering Creek."

His mother paused her stirring, her hand hovering over the pot. Her eyes widened almost imperceptibly, and a shadow crossed her face. "The Whispering Creek? It's a difficult path, Joseph. Full of thorns."

"I know," he said, watching her closely. "But I found something there. Something... unusual." He didn't know how to phrase it, how to bridge the gap between the tangible reality of the shard and the intangible world of secrets it seemed to represent.

His mother turned back to her pot, her movements a little more jerky now. "The woods hold many things, Joseph. Some things are best left undisturbed."

Her words, so similar to the whispers he'd overheard, struck him with a chilling familiarity. It was as if a silent pact of silence was being enforced, a communal agreement to ignore what was clearly evident. He felt a surge of frustration, a desperate need to break through this wall of unspoken understandings.

"But Mother," he pressed, "this was different. It was... a stone, violet in color, and it had strange markings on it. It seemed to glow." He watched her face, searching for any flicker of recognition, any hint that she knew what he was talking about.

His mother's back was to him, but he could feel her stiffen. She remained silent for a long moment, the only sound the gentle bubbling of the stew. Then, she let out a soft sigh, a sound that seemed to carry the weight of years. "Joseph, sometimes... sometimes what we see, what we find, is not meant for us to understand. Not yet, anyway."

She turned then, her eyes meeting his with a look of profound sadness mixed with a weary kind of resignation. "The world is a complicated place, my son. And some stories are best kept in the quiet."

Her evasiveness, her subtle redirection, confirmed his suspicions. The villagers weren't just being casual in their hushed tones; they were actively policing information, reinforcing a silence that seemed to surround the very woods he had explored. The shard wasn't just a discovery; it was a catalyst, a disruption to a carefully maintained equilibrium of ignorance.

Later that evening, as he sat at the table, the stew offering little comfort, he listened to the sounds of the village settling down for the night. The usual creaks and groans of the cottage, the distant barking of a dog, the occasional murmur of voices from a neighboring house – all seemed amplified, imbued with a new significance. He imagined the villagers, behind their closed doors, perhaps engaging in conversations similar to the ones he'd overheard, reinforcing the unspoken rules, reiterating the importance of discretion.

He thought again of the secluded trail, the one leading to Whispering Creek. He had always enjoyed the sense of adventure it offered, the feeling of stepping off the beaten path. Now, the path itself felt like a conspirator, a route leading away from the ordinary and into a realm of hidden truths. The thorny bushes, the gnarled trees, the way the light struggled to penetrate the dense canopy – it all felt like a deliberate attempt to deter casual explorers, to protect something precious, or perhaps, something dangerous.

He remembered his father's books, the ones his mother kept so carefully preserved. He had only been allowed to look at them under strict supervision, and even then, only at the more accessible tales. But he recalled images from some of the older volumes, faded illustrations of symbols and patterns that had seemed alien and intriguing. He resolved to try and find those books, to search for any possible connection, any clue that might shed light on the cryptic markings on the violet shard. His father, with his quiet wisdom and his love for the written word, might have left behind more than just a legacy of knowledge; he might have left behind a key.

As he lay in his bed that night, the violet shard wrapped carefully in a soft cloth beside him, he could still hear the echoes of those hushed conversations. "Keeping it quiet." "No one must know." "The old ways." They were no longer just snippets of overheard chatter; they were pronouncements, edicts from a hidden council of village elders, their authority wielded not through formal decree, but through a pervasive atmosphere of shared, unspoken understanding.

He closed his eyes, but sleep did not come easily. The image of the violet shard, its internal luminescence pulsing like a captured star, was burned into his mind. It was a tangible representation of the mystery that had so suddenly descended upon his quiet village, a mystery that seemed to be woven into the very fabric of their lives, a secret that had been guarded for generations, and that he, Joseph, had inadvertently stumbled upon. The path to Whispering Creek, once just a forgotten trail, now felt like the beginning of a perilous journey into the heart of a profound enigma, a journey that would force him to confront not just the secrets of the woods, but the secrets of his own village, and perhaps, the secrets of the past itself. The hushed conversations were not just whispers of caution; they were echoes of a long-held fear, a fear that he was now beginning to understand.

Joseph found himself tracing the outline of the markings on the violet shard with his fingertip, the smooth, cool surface a stark contrast to the turbulent thoughts churning within him. Each line and curve felt like a deliberate stroke, a piece of a language he couldn't yet comprehend. He remembered his father, a man of few words but profound observation, once remarking on the importance of 'reading between the lines,' not just in books, but in the world around them. At the time, Joseph had thought it a poetic flourish, a fatherly homily. Now, it felt like a directive. The markings *were* lines, and he had to read them, understand their meaning.

His mind, usually occupied with the predictable rhythms of village life – the planting seasons, the harvest, the simple joys of childhood games – was now a buzzing hive of speculation. The hushed conversations he'd overheard were like scattered puzzle pieces, each bearing a fragment of a larger, more complex picture. He recalled his mother's tight-lipped silence when he'd mentioned the Whispering Creek, her hurried change of subject, the almost imperceptible tightening of her jaw. It wasn't just a disinclination to discuss the creek; it was a carefully constructed wall of avoidance. He remembered a time, years ago, when he'd been curious about the old abandoned well at the edge of the woods, the one the villagers steered clear of. His father had simply said, "Some places hold shadows, Joseph. Best not to disturb them." At the time, he'd imagined literal shadows, the kind cast by trees. Now, he wondered if his father had meant something far more profound, something rooted in secrets and perhaps, fear.

He thought of the object itself, the violet shard. It wasn't a natural stone, not like the grey river rocks or the speckled granite of the hills. It had an unnatural luminescence, a faint pulse that seemed to resonate with something deep within him, a feeling he couldn't quite name – anticipation, perhaps, or a prickle of unease. His father's study, a room usually off-limits to him unless accompanied, had been filled with ancient tomes and maps. Joseph remembered poring over faded illustrations of constellations, of strange symbols used by long-forgotten peoples. Could these markings be similar? He pictured his father, hunched over a brittle page, his brow furrowed in concentration, trying to decipher similar enigmas.

He started to construct hypotheses, each more fantastical than the last. Could the shard be a fragment of a fallen star, imbued with celestial power? The legends of meteorites sometimes spoke of strange properties, of metals unknown to earthly smiths. But the markings... they felt too deliberate, too intentional for a cosmic accident. Then his mind drifted to tales of ancient treasures, of buried hoards left by long-lost civilizations, hidden away for safekeeping. The village, nestled in its valley, had a history that stretched back further than anyone could precisely recall. There were whispers of older settlements, of people who had lived on this land before the current inhabitants arrived, their stories swallowed by time. Was the shard a relic of those forgotten times? A piece of jewelry, perhaps, or a tool of some ancient craft?

But another possibility, a darker one, began to creep into his thoughts. The furtiveness of the villagers, the way conversations died when he approached, the warnings about keeping quiet – these didn't feel like the custodians of a lost treasure. They felt more like guardians of a dangerous secret. He remembered the hushed discussions about 'the old ways,' a phrase that always carried a subtle undertone of disapproval or apprehension among the adults. What were these old ways? Were they connected to the land itself, to some power that the modern villagers feared or misunderstood? He recalled old Silas, the village elder, often muttering about the 'balance' of things, about the 'humors' of the earth. Silas's pronouncements were usually dismissed as the ramblings of age, but now, Joseph wondered if they held a kernel of forgotten wisdom.

He sat by the hearth, the flickering firelight casting dancing shadows on the walls. He felt like a detective in one of the adventure stories he devoured, piecing together clues in a world that was suddenly far more mysterious than he had ever imagined. The violet shard was his central exhibit, the unspoken witness to a hidden narrative. He thought about the specific words he'd heard: Elara's worried comment about not being able to "bury it again," old Thomas's gruffness, Silas's cryptic remarks about "the old ways." Each phrase was a thread, and he was trying to weave them into a coherent tapestry.

He remembered another incident, from a few summers ago. A traveling merchant had passed through the village, a man with exotic wares and even more exotic tales. He'd brought with him a small, intricately carved wooden box, which he claimed had belonged to a wise hermit. When he'd opened it, a faint, sweet scent had emanated from within, and the villagers had gathered around, mesmerized. But after a few hours, the merchant had quickly packed it away, his demeanor shifting from jovial to guarded. Joseph had overheard him speaking to his host, the innkeeper, in hushed tones. "Best keep it closed," the merchant had whispered, "some things are meant to sleep." The innkeeper had nodded gravely, his usual hearty demeanor replaced by a rare seriousness. Joseph had felt a similar sense of unease then, a feeling that something potent and perhaps dangerous was being contained. Was the violet shard something like that? Something that needed to be kept contained, its nature deliberately obscured?

He closed his eyes, trying to visualize the exact location where he'd found the shard. The gnarled oak, its branches twisted like arthritic fingers, the thick carpet of moss, the peculiar stillness of the air. He had pushed aside a cluster of ferns, revealing a small hollow in the earth, and there it had been, nestled amongst the roots, its violet light a beacon in the gloom. He hadn't felt fear then, only a profound sense of discovery, an almost magnetic pull towards the object. But now, recalling the palpable shift in the atmosphere, the way the very air seemed to hum with an unseen energy, he understood that his finding wasn't a mere happenstance. It felt like an invitation, or perhaps, a summoning.

He thought about his father's books again. His mother kept them in a locked chest, citing their fragility. But Joseph had a key, a small, tarnished brass key his father had given him years ago, telling him, "For when you are ready to truly learn." He hadn't understood the significance then, but now, the thought of those books, of the knowledge they might contain, was a powerful lure. If the markings on the shard were ancient symbols, there was a chance his father, a scholar in his own right, might have encountered something similar in his research. He pictured himself unlocking the chest, the scent of aged paper and ink filling the air, the promise of answers held within those brittle pages. He could almost feel the weight of the books in his hands, the texture of the vellum, the faint ink of forgotten languages.

He stood up and walked to the small window of his cottage, looking out at the darkening landscape. The familiar contours of the hills were softened by the twilight, the village lights appearing like scattered embers. The sense of isolation, of being on the cusp of a revelation that the rest of his world was deliberately ignoring, settled upon him. He felt a strange mix of excitement and apprehension. This was no longer a simple childhood adventure; it was a descent into a mystery, a quest that had begun with a violet shard and was now leading him into the shadowed corners of his own community, and perhaps, into the depths of its forgotten history. The hushed conversations were not just whispers; they were a symphony of apprehension, a lullaby of secrets sung to keep the truth at bay. And Joseph, the accidental audience, was beginning to learn the melody. He decided then and there that he wouldn't let this mystery remain unsolved. The violet shard was more than just an object; it was a key, and he was determined to find the lock it belonged to, no matter how deeply it was buried. His father's words echoed in his mind once more: "Some things are worth seeking, Joseph, even when the path is obscured." And the path, he knew, was just beginning to reveal its obscurities.

The allure of the violet shard, coupled with the growing unease sparked by hushed village conversations, compelled Joseph to action. A second expedition was necessary, not a reckless plunge into the unknown as his first visit had been, but a deliberate, cautious foray. The forest, which had once seemed a benign playground, now held a distinct edge, a palpable awareness of his presence. He felt its ancient gaze upon him, scrutinizing his intentions. His parents' veiled warnings, once easily dismissed as overcautiousness, now resonated with a chilling gravity. He recognized the subtle shift within himself: the carefree curiosity had been replaced by a keen, almost predatory, focus. This was no longer a game of discovery; it was an investigation.

He chose his timing with meticulous care. Early morning, before the first tendrils of smoke curled from cottage chimneys, before the farmers began their daily rounds. The air was crisp, carrying the damp, earthy scent of the waking woods. He moved with a newfound stealth, his footsteps deliberately light on the dew-kissed moss. Each snap of a twig, each rustle of leaves, was amplified in the pre-dawn quiet, and he instinctively flattened himself against the rough bark of trees at the slightest hint of sound, his heart hammering against his ribs. He was no longer just a boy exploring; he was a shadow, slipping through the emerald labyrinth.

His route was the same as before, yet his perception of it had transformed. He noted the way the sunlight, still hesitant to break through the dense canopy, cast elongated, distorted shadows that seemed to writhe and shift with a life of their own. He paid closer attention to the natural sounds – the chirping of early birds, the distant bleating of sheep – filtering them for anything discordant, anything that spoke of human intrusion or unusual activity. The familiarity of the path was overlaid with a layer of heightened awareness, each familiar landmark now a potential hiding place or a vantage point for observation. He found himself pausing more frequently, not to admire the scenery, but to listen, straining his ears for the faintest murmur of voices, the crunch of boots on the forest floor, the distant clang of metal. The forest felt alive, not just with nature, but with secrets, and he was determined to unearth them.

He reached the clearing where he'd first found the violet shard. The gnarled oak stood as a silent sentinel, its branches reaching out like skeletal fingers. The moss, still clinging to its roots, seemed to absorb the scant light, creating an area of perpetual twilight. Joseph circled the base of the tree, his eyes scanning the ground with a meticulousness that bordered on obsession. He was looking for anything he might have missed, any disturbance in the earth, any displaced stone, any sign that someone else had been here recently, or perhaps, that his initial discovery had not been as solitary as he'd believed. He remembered the specific hollow where the shard had lain, a small indentation that seemed almost too perfect, too deliberately concealed. He knelt, his gloved hands brushing away loose soil and fallen leaves, meticulously examining the area.

The feeling of being watched intensified here, in this very spot. It wasn't a physical sensation, but a psychic pressure, a prickling awareness that made the hairs on the back of his neck stand on end. He imagined eyes peering from behind the dense foliage, unseen observers who might have witnessed his earlier find, or worse, who might be waiting for him to return. He recalled his father's advice about 'reading between the lines,' and now he applied it to the environment itself. Were the twisted branches of the oak a natural formation, or a deliberate marker? Was the peculiar stillness of the air in this clearing a product of the dense trees, or something more?

He began to search the immediate vicinity, moving outward from the oak. He pushed aside thick ferns, peered into the shadowed crevices between moss-covered rocks, and sifted through piles of decaying leaves. He was searching for more shards, for remnants of whatever object the violet fragment belonged to, or perhaps, for something that could explain its presence. He found small, unremarkable stones, fragments of bark, and the occasional fallen acorn, but nothing that resonated with the strange energy of the violet shard. Yet, he persisted, driven by an almost primal need to understand.

He noticed a faint trail, almost entirely obscured by undergrowth, leading away from the oak and deeper into the woods. It wasn't a well-worn path, more like a faint impression in the earth, as if something had been dragged or carried this way at some point. His pulse quickened. This was a new clue, a deviation from his previous exploration, a potential indication of the shard's origin or its intended destination. He hesitated for a moment, a knot of apprehension tightening in his stomach. Was this trail meant to be discovered, or was it a deliberate misdirection? But the drive for answers, for confirmation of his growing suspicions, outweighed his fear.

He followed the faint trail, his movements becoming even more cautious. The forest grew denser here, the canopy so thick that only dappled patches of sunlight managed to penetrate. The air grew cooler, more humid, carrying the scent of damp earth and decaying vegetation. He moved slowly, his senses on high alert, constantly scanning his surroundings. He listened for the telltale sounds of pursuit, for any sign that he had been followed or observed. The silence here was profound, broken only by the drip of water from unseen leaves and the occasional chirp of an insect. It was a silence that felt heavy, pregnant with unspoken meaning.

The trail led him to a small, overgrown dell, a secluded hollow shielded by a dense ring of ancient trees. In the center of the dell, partially hidden by a thick tangle of brambles, he saw it – a shallow, circular depression in the earth, as if something large and heavy had once rested there, or perhaps, been buried. The ground around the depression looked disturbed, the moss and soil dislodged, but time and the elements had worked to conceal the exact nature of the disturbance. He approached it slowly, his heart pounding. This felt significant. This felt like the place where the violet shard had come from.

He knelt by the edge of the depression, his eyes tracing the subtle contours of the earth. He could see faint traces of what looked like a darker, richer soil mixed with the lighter topsoil, suggesting that the earth had been dug and replaced. He reached into his satchel and pulled out a small trowel, a tool he'd brought specifically for this purpose. He began to gently scrape away the surface layer of soil, his movements deliberate and controlled. He was careful not to disturb the area too much, wanting to preserve any potential evidence.

As he dug, he uncovered fragments of something dark and brittle, unlike the surrounding earth. He picked up a piece, turning it over in his fingers. It was hard, almost like petrified wood, but with a strange, almost metallic sheen. He sniffed it; it had a faint, acrid odor, not unpleasant, but unusual. He continued to dig, unearthing more of these fragments, which seemed to be pieces of a larger, broken object. They were irregularly shaped, some curved, some jagged, but all possessed the same dark, brittle quality. He wondered if this was what the violet shard had once been a part of.

He carefully placed the fragments into a separate pouch, labeling it with the location and the date. He then turned his attention back to the depression itself. He scraped away more soil, his trowel occasionally hitting something harder beneath the surface. He continued to dig, meticulously clearing the area. It became apparent that the depression was deeper than he had initially thought, and the fragments he had found were merely scattered remnants.

Then, his trowel struck something smooth and unyielding. He froze, his breath catching in his throat. He carefully brushed away the surrounding soil, revealing a section of what looked like polished stone. It was dark, almost black, and strangely cold to the touch, even through the trowel. He continued to work, uncovering more of the object, which seemed to be a large, circular stone or perhaps, a metal disk, buried just beneath the surface. Its edges were smooth and rounded, and as he cleared more of the area, he began to discern faint etchings on its surface.

The etchings were similar in style to the markings on the violet shard, though more worn and less distinct due to their prolonged contact with the earth. He traced them with his finger, a thrill of recognition coursing through him. These were the same angular lines, the same complex curves, the same alien script. He felt a surge of triumph, a confirmation that he was on the right track, that his instincts had been correct. This was connected. This was significant.

He worked tirelessly, carefully excavating the circular object. It was larger than he had anticipated, perhaps three feet in diameter, and surprisingly heavy. As he cleared more of its surface, he realized it wasn't a stone at all, but a disc made of a dark, metallic material he didn't recognize. It was intricately patterned, the etched symbols forming a complex, spiraling design that seemed to draw the eye inward. The violet shard, he now understood, was likely a fragment broken from this larger disc, its luminescence perhaps a byproduct of the disc's material or its hidden purpose.

He marveled at the craftsmanship, the sheer artistry of the object. Who could have made this? And why was it buried here, in this remote part of the forest? The questions multiplied, each one raising further mysteries. He ran his hands over the etched symbols, trying to decipher their meaning, but they remained stubbornly enigmatic, a language lost to time. He wondered if his father, with his vast collection of ancient texts, had ever encountered anything like it.

As he worked, he noticed something else. Around the perimeter of the disc, almost entirely hidden by the roots of the trees and the overgrown vegetation, were several smaller, irregularly shaped indentations, as if other pieces had once been attached to it or fitted into it. He carefully investigated these indentations, finding more of the dark, brittle fragments, some of which were curved, suggesting they were parts of a larger, more complex structure. It was clear that this disc, whatever its purpose, had once been part of something even grander, something that had been broken apart.

He felt a growing sense of awe, and also, a profound unease. The sheer antiquity of the object, the alien nature of its design and markings, hinted at a history far older and stranger than anything he had ever known. He thought again of the villagers' hushed tones, their evasiveness, their fear of 'the old ways.' Could this disc, and the violet shard, be connected to those forgotten traditions? Was this something the villagers actively sought to conceal, something they feared would resurface and disrupt their lives?

He continued to excavate, but his progress was slow and arduous. The disc was firmly embedded in the earth, and the surrounding roots of the ancient trees made it difficult to get a proper purchase. He realized he couldn't move it by himself. He needed help, but whom could he trust? His parents' reaction to the shard had been so telling, so fearful. To reveal this disc would likely invite even greater alarm, perhaps even confiscation. He was caught in a dilemma, wanting to understand, yet fearing the consequences of his discovery.

He spent the rest of the morning meticulously documenting his findings, sketching the disc, the indentations, and the surrounding dell. He took rubbings of the etched symbols, hoping that perhaps by transcribing them, he might find a pattern, a key to their meaning. He carefully re-covered the disc, leaving it in its resting place, as it was too large and heavy to transport. He then gathered the scattered fragments he had found and placed them in his satchel.

As he prepared to leave, he cast one last look at the dell. The sun had risen higher now, and shafts of light pierced through the canopy, illuminating the clearing in an almost ethereal glow. The disc, partially revealed, seemed to thrum with a hidden energy, a silent testament to its mysterious past. He felt a profound connection to it, a sense of responsibility to unravel its secrets.

He made his way back through the forest, his mind buzzing with a thousand thoughts. The initial trepidation had given way to a determined resolve. He knew now that his suspicions were not unfounded. There was something extraordinary hidden within the familiar landscape of his village, something that the adults were trying to keep buried, literally and figuratively. He clutched the pouch of fragments in his satchel, the weight a tangible reminder of the secrets he carried. The forest no longer felt merely watchful; it felt complicit, a silent guardian of a much larger enigma. He understood that this second expedition had not provided answers, but it had certainly deepened the mystery, opening a door to a world far more complex and perilous than he had ever imagined. The thread he had begun to unravel had just become much, much thicker.

The dell, with its newly unearthed circular artifact, felt like the heart of the mystery. Joseph, however, was not one to linger without further probing. The initial excitement of discovery, while potent, was tempered by a growing realization of the enormity of what he had stumbled upon. The disc, with its intricate etchings, was a tangible link to a past that defied easy explanation, but it was also just one piece of a much larger, fragmented puzzle. He knew instinctively that more fragments, more clues, lay waiting to be found, scattered like forgotten breadcrumbs through the ancient woods. The faint trail he had followed to this secluded spot, barely a whisper on the forest floor, might not have been the only path leading from the initial clearing.

He spent the remainder of the afternoon systematically expanding his search outwards from the dell. The undergrowth here was thick, a chaotic tangle of ferns, brambles, and fallen branches that made progress slow and arduous. He moved with a renewed sense of purpose, his eyes meticulously scanning the ground, his hands pushing aside vegetation with practiced care. He was not just looking for more fragments of the dark, metallic material; he was searching for any anomaly, any sign of human or unnatural intervention that might betray the presence of other hidden objects or caches.

His efforts were rewarded, not with another large artifact, but with something far more subtle, yet equally significant. Tucked beneath the gnarled roots of a particularly ancient-looking beech tree, about twenty yards north of the dell, he found a small, tightly bound bundle of what appeared to be dried animal hide. It was remarkably well-preserved, considering its apparent age, the sinew lashing it together still holding firm, though brittle to the touch. His heart gave a hopeful leap. This felt deliberate, hidden. Carefully, using the tip of his trowel, he worked to loosen the soil around it, and then gently lifted the bundle.

Unwrapping it proved to be a delicate operation. The hide was dry and stiff, and he feared it might crumble. He worked with painstaking slowness, his breath held, his fingers nimble. As the last layers of hide fell away, he revealed not a tool, nor a weapon, but a collection of flat, smooth stones. They were roughly palm-sized, each one meticulously etched with symbols that were undeniably similar to those on the disc and the violet shard. However, these etchings were sharper, clearer, as if these particular stones had been more recently exposed to the elements, or perhaps, protected from them in a unique way.

There were seven stones in total, each bearing a different, yet interconnected, series of markings. He laid them out carefully on a patch of cleared moss, his mind racing to find a pattern. Some symbols seemed to represent celestial bodies – a stylized sun, a crescent moon, and what looked like a cluster of stars. Others were more abstract, angular and geometric, reminiscent of the script he'd seen on the disc, but arranged in distinct sequences. He recognized some of the recurring motifs, the spiraling lines and the sharp, diagonal strokes, but the overall arrangement on each stone seemed to tell a different part of a story, or convey a different piece of information.

One stone, in particular, caught his attention. It depicted what looked like a rudimentary map. A series of interconnected lines formed what could be a crude representation of the local landscape – the winding path of the river, the outline of the distant hills, and a cluster of markings that seemed to indicate the village. But what truly set it apart were several small, circular etchings dotted across the map, each one positioned at a significant point. One of these points coincided precisely with the location of the dell where he'd found the disc. Another was marked near the gnarled oak where he'd first discovered the violet shard.

This was not merely decorative; it was a guide. A guide to what, however, remained a profound mystery. Were these the locations of other artifacts? Or were they sites of some ancient significance, places where rituals were performed, or knowledge was imparted? The presence of the stones, carefully hidden and etched with such specific details, spoke of a deliberate effort to preserve this information, to pass it down through generations, or perhaps, to ensure its rediscovery by someone who could understand its meaning.

He spent another hour meticulously sketching each of the stones, noting the precise arrangement of the symbols, the subtle variations in their carving. He took rubbings of each one, hoping that the graphite impressions might reveal details that his eyes had missed in the dappled forest light. The weight of this new discovery settled upon him, adding another layer of complexity to the already bewildering enigma. The disc was a key, and these stones were perhaps the cipher needed to unlock its secrets.

His thoughts then turned to the possibility of more than just scattered artifacts. What if there were documents, written records from whoever had created these objects? The idea seemed improbable, given the fragile nature of parchment and paper in the damp forest environment, but the careful preservation of the hide bundle suggested that its creators had understood the importance of safeguarding their knowledge.

He decided to backtrack, not along the faint trail to the dell, but towards the original clearing where he had found the violet shard. He reasoned that if this was a significant location, it might have been a focal point for other activities or discoveries. He moved with a heightened awareness, scrutinizing the base of trees, the hollows in fallen logs, and any unusual rock formations. He was searching for anything that seemed out of place, anything that might have been overlooked in his first, less-informed visit.

It was near the base of the gnarled oak, nestled amongst a thick growth of moss and ferns, that he found it. Partially obscured by a heavy, rotting log, was a small, weathered wooden box. It was surprisingly intact, though the wood was dark and soft with age. A thick, almost petrified layer of moss had grown over its lid, making it blend almost seamlessly with its surroundings. He felt a surge of adrenaline. This was it. This had to be what he was looking for.

Prying the box open was a challenge. The wood was brittle, and the moss had acted like a sealant. He used his trowel again, carefully working at the edges. With a soft groan of ancient wood, the lid finally gave way, revealing the contents within. It was not a treasure trove of gold or jewels, but something far more valuable to Joseph.

Inside the box lay a collection of rolled-up parchments, tied with faded, brittle cords. Alongside them were several small, intricately carved wooden figurines, their details worn smooth with time, and a single, unbroken violet shard, identical to the one he possessed. He handled the parchments with the utmost reverence, his fingers trembling slightly. They were incredibly fragile, and he could already see some of the ink beginning to fade.

He unfurled the first parchment carefully. It was covered in a dense script, far more complex and flowing than the angular markings on the disc and stones. It was a language he didn't recognize, a beautiful, alien calligraphy that seemed to dance across the page. He scanned the document, looking for any familiar elements, any recognizable patterns, but found none. It was as if he was looking at a book written in an unknown tongue.

However, scattered within the text, almost like deliberate annotations, were small, detailed drawings. These drawings mirrored the symbols on the stones – the celestial bodies, the geometric patterns, and the stylized representations of the landscape. One drawing depicted the gnarled oak tree, with a small circle drawn at its base, mirroring the map-like stone. Another showed the disc, its circular form clearly illustrated, with lines radiating outwards.

He unrolled the second parchment. This one was different. While still bearing the unfamiliar script, it also contained a series of diagrams, almost like blueprints, showing how various pieces, including the disc and the violet shard, might fit together. There were also crude but effective sketches of what appeared to be celestial events – comets streaking across the sky, phases of the moon, and constellations. It was clear that the creators of these artifacts had a profound understanding of astronomy, or at least, their own unique interpretation of it.

The third parchment seemed to be a more personal account, though its meaning was lost to him. It contained longer passages of the script, interspersed with what looked like emotional notations, small sketches of faces contorted in expressions of joy or sorrow, and symbols that he interpreted as perhaps representing life or death. He felt a strange sense of connection to the anonymous author, a shared human (or perhaps, not-so-human) experience across the vast chasm of time.

The wooden figurines were equally enigmatic. They were small, no more than a few inches high, and vaguely humanoid in shape, but with elongated limbs and large, almond-shaped eyes. They were carved with remarkable detail, suggesting a high level of craftsmanship, but their purpose remained elusive. Were they representations of the people who created these artifacts? Or were they meant to serve some ritualistic or ceremonial function? He carefully placed them back into the box, alongside the intact violet shard, his mind already formulating theories.

As the sun began to dip lower in the sky, casting long shadows through the trees, Joseph knew he had to return. He couldn't carry the box; it was too fragile, and he didn't want to risk damaging its contents. He carefully re-covered it with moss and leaves, marking the location mentally, and with a small, almost imperceptible scratch on the trunk of a nearby tree. He took the seven etched stones and the remaining fragments of the dark, brittle material from his satchel. He also made sure to leave the original violet shard in its place at the base of the oak, a silent testament to his initial discovery.

The walk back to the village was a blur of intense thought. The initial thrill of discovery had been replaced by a sobering awareness of the immense task ahead. He had found more than just a single anomalous object; he had uncovered a trail of interconnected clues, suggesting a hidden history, a forgotten civilization, or perhaps, something far more ancient and alien. The coded messages, the astronomical references, the crude maps – they all pointed to a deliberate, sophisticated attempt to communicate something important across the ages.

He looked at the stones in his hand, their cool surfaces a stark contrast to the warmth of his own skin. He recognized the symbols now, not as random markings, but as a nascent language, a visual lexicon of a people who had once inhabited this land, or perhaps, had visited it with purpose. The question of who they were, where they came from, and why they had left these remnants behind, gnawed at him. He felt a growing sense of responsibility, a conviction that these discoveries were not meant for him alone, but for a purpose yet to be revealed. The thread he had found was indeed thick, and it was leading him down a path that was only just beginning to unfold. The silent woods, which had once seemed merely a backdrop to his life, now felt like a repository of secrets, whispering their ancient tales to anyone willing to listen.

4

The Shadow of Manifest Peril

The unearthed disc and the collection of etched stones were no longer mere curiosities; they had become an obsession. Joseph found himself drawn back to the woods, not with the casual curiosity of a boy exploring his backyard, but with the focused intent of a man on a vital quest. The forest, once a place of simple wonder, now felt charged with a deeper, more resonant meaning. Each rustle of leaves, each snap of a twig, seemed to echo the ancient whispers he was beginning to decipher. He spent hours poring over the stones, tracing the familiar symbols, trying to discern the narrative woven into their patterns. The parchment, too, lay spread out in his room, a tantalizing but frustrating puzzle of an unknown language. He realized with growing certainty that the forest held more secrets, and that the carefully preserved fragments were just the beginning.

It was during one of these reflective afternoons, while sketching the intricate markings from memory in his worn notebook, that Joseph first noticed the subtle shift in the village atmosphere. It wasn't a dramatic change, no sudden clamor of alarm, but a creeping, almost imperceptible alteration in the way people interacted. He overheard snippets of hushed conversations in the market square, words like "unease" and "strangers" and, most disturbingly, "meddling." Old Man Hemlock, usually a garrulous fountain of village gossip, spoke in low tones with Mrs. Gable about unusual lights seen near Blackwood Ridge, and the increasing reluctance of livestock to graze too close to the deeper parts of the forest. Joseph instinctively felt these whispers were connected to his discoveries, a vague premonition settling in his gut.

The casual glances from villagers he passed on the cobbled lanes no longer felt entirely friendly. They lingered a moment too long, carrying a subtle weight of unspoken inquiry. It was as if their eyes were trying to probe beneath his youthful exterior, searching for the secrets he was so desperately trying to unravel. Young Sarah, who usually offered him a bright smile and a shared piece of gossip, now seemed to shy away, her gaze averted as he approached. Even his own parents, though they'd always been supportive of his inquisitive nature, began to ask more pointed questions about his long excursions into the woods. "Are you sure you're not going too far, Joseph?" his mother had asked, her voice tinged with an unfamiliar concern that wasn't solely about his well-being. "The woods can be tricky, especially as the days grow shorter."

He remembered a particular exchange overheard while he was ostensibly examining the produce at the baker's stall. Two older men, their faces etched with the weariness of hard labor, were talking with a gravity that caught his attention. "They say the old tales are stirring again," one of them muttered, his voice barely above a whisper. "Talk of things best left undisturbed. The old ways, they were there for a reason, weren't they?" The other man grunted in agreement. "Aye. And some folks, they forget that. They go digging where they oughtn't, poking at things that have slept for centuries. Bad business, that." Joseph felt a prickle of unease crawl up his spine. Were they referring to him? Was his innocent exploration perceived as "poking at things"? The words "outsiders" and "those who pry too much" echoed in his mind, suddenly imbued with a chilling significance.

The whispers seemed to coalesce into a palpable sense of apprehension that permeated the very air of the village. The once familiar rhythm of daily life felt slightly off-kilter. The boisterous laughter from the tavern seemed muted, the usual jovial greetings exchanged between neighbors were shorter, more guarded. There was a collective holding of breath, a shared awareness of something unknown lurking just beyond the periphery of their everyday lives. Joseph, armed with his strange artifacts and the nascent understanding they offered, felt like a lightning rod for this unspoken tension. He was no longer just a curious boy; he had become a focal point of a burgeoning unease, a catalyst for fears that had long been dormant.

He found himself more watchful during his excursions. The familiar paths seemed to hold new shadows, and the deeper woods, which had always been a place of adventure, now felt like a territory under surveillance. He'd catch himself glancing over his shoulder, convinced he heard footsteps or the rustle of movement that wasn't the wind. The silence of the forest, once comforting, now seemed pregnant with unseen eyes. He began to understand that the warnings, which he had initially dismissed as the superstitious ramblings of villagers prone to exaggeration, were perhaps more grounded in reality than he had ever imagined.

The artifacts themselves seemed to hum with a new urgency. The symbols on the stones, which he had meticulously copied into his notebook, appeared to shift and rearrange themselves in his mind's eye, as if trying to impart their meaning more directly. He spent hours comparing them to the script on the parchment, searching for any Rosetta Stone that would unlock the alien language. He had a growing suspicion that the parchments weren't just records, but possibly instructions, or a narrative that explained the purpose of the disc and the shards. The more he looked, the more he felt the vastness of what he had stumbled upon, and the greater the sense of being observed became.

One evening, as he was carefully examining one of the smaller etched stones under the dim glow of his oil lamp, he heard a distinct cough from outside his window. He froze, his heart leaping into his throat. The sound was too close, too deliberate, to be a stray animal. He quickly extinguished the lamp, plunging the room into darkness, and crept to the window. Peering through a gap in the curtains, he saw nothing but the familiar, moonlit outline of the village street. Yet, the feeling of being watched persisted, a cold knot in his stomach. He stayed there for a long time, listening to the night sounds, the soft chirping of crickets and the distant hoot of an owl, but the subtle unease remained, a constant hum beneath the surface of the ordinary.

He recalled the old woodcutter, Elias, who lived on the edge of the village, a man known for his solitary nature and his intimate knowledge of the forest. Elias rarely spoke to anyone, preferring the company of trees, but he was a respected figure, his word carrying weight. Joseph had seen him in the market earlier that day, his weathered face set in an uncharacteristically grim expression. They had exchanged nods, as they always did, but Elias's eyes had held a deep, troubled look that unnerved Joseph. Later, he'd overheard Elias talking to the innkeeper, his voice a low rumble that carried clearly in the quiet afternoon.

"The signs are there, John," Elias had said, his voice laced with a weariness that spoke of long familiarity. "The earth itself is restless. Those who stir it... they don't always understand what they're waking."

This cryptic remark, coupled with the hushed conversations and the watchful eyes, created a tapestry of mounting anxiety. Joseph felt a growing conviction that his discoveries were not merely archaeological finds, but potent relics that carried a weight of history, perhaps even danger. The warnings, once vague pronouncements about the inherent mystery of the woods, now seemed to point towards an active, perhaps even hostile, presence. The feeling of being an outsider, of prying into secrets that were meant to remain buried, was no longer a theoretical concern; it was a tangible, growing reality. The shadows in the woods had begun to lengthen, not just with the setting sun, but with the deepening sense of peril. He knew, with a certainty that settled deep in his bones, that he was no longer alone in his quest, and that whatever forces had shaped the past were now beginning to take notice of his present. The intricate etchings on the stones, once mere patterns, now felt like dire omens, and the weight of their unspoken message pressed down on him, heavier with each passing day. He had unearthed more than artifacts; he had unearthed a history that was perhaps still very much alive.

The woods, once a sanctuary of boundless curiosity, had begun to feel like a labyrinth of hidden eyes and listening ears. Joseph's excursions, once fueled by the exhilarating rush of discovery, were now punctuated by a gnawing apprehension. The symbols on the disc and stones, which had previously spoken of a captivating past, now seemed to whisper warnings, their intricate patterns a language of caution. He found himself constantly scanning his surroundings, every snapped twig or rustle of leaves sending a jolt of adrenaline through him. The playful thrill of uncovering ancient secrets was slowly being overshadowed by the stark realization that those secrets might be actively guarded.

It was a crisp autumn afternoon, the air alive with the scent of decaying leaves and damp earth, when the shift from unease to outright alarm occurred. Joseph had ventured deeper into the woods than usual, following a deer trail that wound its way towards the rumoured entrance of a series of caves rumored by the older villagers to be haunted. He carried his notebook, a stub of charcoal, and a growing sense of foreboding that clung to him like the damp mist beginning to gather. He was examining a cluster of particularly unusual rock formations, their surfaces etched with faint, geometric patterns that mirrored some of the markings on his retrieved artifacts, when he heard it – the unmistakable sound of heavy boots crunching on dry leaves, far too deliberate to be an animal's passage.

His blood ran cold. He immediately dropped to a crouch behind a thicket of ancient ferns, his heart hammering against his ribs like a trapped bird. He hadn't made a sound, or so he thought, but the approach was too direct, too purposeful. The footsteps grew closer, accompanied by the low murmur of voices. He couldn't make out the words, but the tone was hushed, conspiratorial. He dared to peer through the dense foliage, his breath catching in his throat. Two figures emerged from the trees, clad in dark, nondescript clothing, their faces obscured by the low-hanging branches and the deepening twilight. They weren't villagers; their posture, their measured stride, spoke of a different kind of purpose. They moved with a predatory efficiency, their eyes sweeping across the terrain as if searching for something, or someone.

Joseph held his breath, straining to remain as still and silent as the ancient trees that surrounded him. The figures paused near the rock formations he had been studying, their heads bent together in a low discussion. He caught a glimpse of one of them pointing towards the very spot where he had been standing moments before. A chill, far colder than the autumn air, snaked down his spine. They were looking for him, or at least for evidence of his presence. He realized with a sickening lurch that they might have seen him, or heard him, despite his best efforts at stealth. The playful thrill of discovery was gone, replaced by a primal urge to escape, to vanish.

The figures began to move again, their path taking them in the direction he had come from, towards the main deer trail that led back to the village. This was his chance. As soon as they had moved out of his immediate line of sight, Joseph scrambled to his feet, not daring to make a sound. He moved with a newfound urgency, his senses heightened to an almost unbearable degree. Every rustle of leaves, every creak of a branch, sounded like an alarm. He abandoned the deer trail, opting instead for a more circuitous route, plunging through denser undergrowth, his hands and arms scraped by thorns and rough bark.

He could hear the distant sounds of their movement, their voices carrying faintly on the wind, and it spurred him on.

He stumbled through the fading light, his lungs burning, his legs aching. The familiar woods, usually a comforting embrace, now felt menacing, a labyrinth designed to trap him. He ran until he was sure he had put a significant distance between himself and his pursuers, then he crept through the undergrowth, his ears straining for any indication that he was still being followed. He hid behind massive oaks, flattened himself against moss-covered rocks, his eyes darting nervously from shadow to shadow. The playful curiosity that had driven him into these woods had been replaced by a gnawing fear, a stark understanding that his pursuit of the past had attracted the attention of those who preferred it to remain buried.

He stayed hidden for what felt like an eternity, the silence of the forest now a heavy, suffocating blanket. The sun had dipped below the horizon, casting long, distorted shadows that seemed to writhe with unseen threats. He imagined those figures, their silent, purposeful movements, their intent eyes, and his heart pounded with a renewed urgency to return home. He finally ventured out of his hiding place, moving with a cautious haste, his eyes constantly scanning the periphery. He reached the edge of the woods as true darkness descended, the familiar lights of the village a welcome, albeit distant, beacon.

The encounter had been terrifyingly close. He had heard them, seen them, and they had been searching the very ground he had been exploring. It wasn't just his imagination; there were people out there, actively patrolling these woods, people who were clearly not interested in sharing the secrets he was uncovering. The simple joy of his pursuit had been irrevocably altered. The artifacts, once magical keys to a forgotten world, now felt like dangerous contraband. He understood, with a clarity that chilled him to the bone, that his explorations had moved beyond mere childish fascination and had entered a realm of tangible peril. The playful thrill of discovery was gone, replaced by the cold, hard reality of a game where the stakes were far higher than he had ever anticipated. He had touched something ancient, something powerful, and it had clearly not gone unnoticed. The shadows of the woods no longer held only the mysteries of the past; they now held the very real threat of the present.

The chill that had settled into Joseph's bones after his encounter in the woods lingered long after he'd returned to the relative safety of his home. The primal fear had subsided, replaced by a grim determination. His parents' hushed warnings, once dismissed as the anxieties of overprotective guardians, now echoed with an unsettling prescience. They had spoken of guardians, of those who protected the forgotten places, and the figures he had glimpsed certainly fit that description. But their presence wasn't a mere abstract threat; it was a tangible manifestation of the peril they had alluded to. The woods, he now understood, were not just wild; they were actively managed, their secrets kept under lock and key.

The following days were a delicate dance between his insatiable curiosity and his newfound wariness. He found himself revisiting the edges of the woods, not venturing in as recklessly as before, but observing, looking for anything out of the ordinary. The very trees seemed to hold a new significance, their gnarled branches and thick undergrowth no longer just natural features, but potential hiding places, silent sentinels. He began to notice subtle shifts in the environment, anomalies that, when viewed through the lens of his recent experience, painted a chilling picture.

His first concrete discovery came a week later, on a grey, drizzly afternoon. He had decided to explore a less-trodden path, one that led away from the usual routes and towards a dense, almost impenetrable section of forest bordering the old abandoned quarry. His parents had always warned him away from this particular area, citing unstable ground and unseen hazards. Now, he understood their reticence likely stemmed from more than just natural dangers. As he navigated the slippery, leaf-strewn ground, his foot caught on something buried beneath the detritus. He knelt, brushing away the wet leaves and mud. It was a snare, a crudely fashioned loop of thick wire, cleverly disguised with twigs and moss. It wasn't the kind of trap meant for rabbits or squirrels; the wire was too heavy, the mechanism too robust. It was designed for something larger, something that might wander off the beaten path. The sheer malice of its placement, so close to a frequented trail, sent a fresh wave of unease through him. It felt like a deliberate warning, a clear sign that this area was considered off-limits.

Joseph carefully documented the snare in his notebook, sketching its intricate, deadly design and noting its precise location. He resisted the urge to disarm it, a small voice of caution reminding him that interfering might draw unwanted attention. He continued his cautious exploration, his eyes now scanning the ground with a heightened awareness. A little further on, he encountered another unsettling sight. A small, dilapidated trapper's cabin, long forgotten and presumed to be falling apart from neglect, showed signs of recent activity. The door, which he vaguely remembered being half-rotted and ajar, was now firmly shut, secured with a heavy-duty padlock. More disturbingly, a small, crudely carved wooden effigy, resembling a stylized bird with sharp, angular wings, was nailed to the cabin's doorframe. Its eyes, two dark, unblinking points, seemed to bore into him. It wasn't folk art; it had the unsettling, almost primitive quality of a warding symbol, a potent deterrent. The cabin itself was isolated, miles from any farmstead, and the padlock and effigy spoke of a deliberate attempt to keep people out. Whatever was inside, or whatever happened here, someone wanted it hidden.

These weren't isolated incidents. Over the next few weeks, Joseph meticulously mapped out the subtle disturbances he found. He discovered a section of forest, perhaps fifty yards square, where the undergrowth had been meticulously cleared, leaving the bare earth exposed. There were no signs of logging, no felled trees, just a perfectly circular patch of disturbed soil, as if a giant, invisible hand had swept the area clean. It was unnatural, jarring against the wild chaos of the surrounding woods. He found a series of deep, deliberate scorch marks on the bark of several ancient oak trees, forming a triangular pattern that seemed to emanate from a central point. The marks were too precise, too uniform to be the result of lightning strike or a careless campfire. They felt like a brand, a territorial marker.

One crisp morning, he stumbled upon a seemingly innocuous but deeply disturbing find: a small, woven basket, intricately crafted from reeds, lying partially concealed beneath a pile of moss. Inside, nestled amongst dried leaves, were three smooth, dark stones, each marked with a single, precise symbol. These were not the symbols from the disc or the standing stones he had been studying; these were simpler, almost abstract. One resembled a coiled serpent, another a stylized eye, and the third, a simple cross with a circle at its center. The basket itself was tied shut with a length of what looked like animal gut, and a faint, almost imperceptible scent of something acrid, like burnt herbs, clung to it. It felt like an offering, or perhaps a warning, left specifically for him. He recognized the craftsmanship as being similar to some of the older, more rural traditions he had read about in his local history books, but these had a stark, ominous feel.

Joseph collected the basket, his gloved hands trembling slightly. He felt a growing sense of being watched, of being tracked. The feeling wasn't just paranoia; it was the logical conclusion of these deliberate, targeted disturbances. Someone was actively patrolling these woods, leaving behind not just physical traps, but symbolic deterrents. These were the "perils" his parents had spoken of, no longer abstract warnings but concrete manifestations of a hidden agenda. They were designed to subtly redirect, to subtly frighten, and ultimately, to stop anyone from delving too deep into the woods' secrets.

He started to notice patterns in the placement of these signs. They appeared more frequently on the paths leading towards the ancient standing stones, and near the hidden cave entrance he had discovered. It was as if these markers were forming a perimeter, a series of subtle but firm barriers. The snare was on a secondary trail, guarding a less obvious approach. The cabin, with its locked door and effigy, was nestled deeper in, guarding a more secluded area. The cleared patch of earth was near the very spot where he'd first found the disc, a place of significant power. The scorched trees marked a boundary, a line that was not to be crossed. And the basket, with its unsettling contents, felt like a direct message, a warning delivered to his doorstep, or rather, his hiking trail.

The implications were staggering. This wasn't a natural wilderness he was exploring; it was a managed territory, overseen by individuals who were deeply invested in keeping its secrets. The casual curiosity that had led him here was no longer innocent. He was encroaching on something, disturbing something that had been deliberately concealed for generations. His parents' fear, he realized, was not unfounded. They hadn't just been worried about him getting lost or injured; they had known about these guardians, these protectors. They had understood the forces at play, forces that operated in the shadows, leaving behind these subtle, chilling signs.

He found himself retracing his steps, meticulously re-examining the areas where he'd found these anomalies. He noticed how the snare was placed in such a way that it would be nearly impossible to see if one wasn't looking for it, blending seamlessly into the undergrowth. He saw how the effigy on the cabin door wasn't just nailed there; it was carved with an unsettling precision, its dark wood almost seeming to absorb the light. The cleared patch of earth wasn't just bare; it was meticulously raked, as if to ensure no stray leaf could conceal a hidden object. Every detail spoke of a careful, deliberate effort.

The subtle psychological warfare was as effective as any physical barrier. The snare instilled a primal fear of injury. The effigy evoked a sense of dread and superstition. The cleared earth felt violating, an unnatural scar on the landscape. The scorch marks were a clear sign of ownership, a territorial claim. And the basket with its cryptic stones was a direct message of exclusion. These were not random acts of vandalism; they were calculated deterrents, designed to discourage further exploration and to communicate a clear message: you are not welcome here.

Joseph began to question the nature of his quest. Was he merely a curious boy trespassing on private land, or was he an unwitting intruder into something far more ancient and significant? The artifacts he possessed, the disc and the stones, suddenly felt heavier, imbued with a dangerous allure. They were not just relics; they were keys, and it was clear that whoever had left these signs did not want those keys to be used, or perhaps, to be found. His parents' hushed conversations, their worried glances, their insistence on caution – all of it coalesced into a terrifying realization. They had known. They had understood the invisible boundaries and the unseen watchers that Joseph was only just beginning to perceive.

He started to feel the woods in a new way. The rustling leaves were no longer just the sound of the wind; they were whispers of vigilance. The shadows were no longer just the absence of light; they were pockets of unseen observation. The very air seemed charged with an unspoken warning. The playful thrill of discovery was being systematically eroded, replaced by a gnawing anxiety, a constant awareness of being on the precipice of something dangerous. The signs were clear, the perils were manifesting, and Joseph knew, with a chilling certainty, that his journey into the past had now led him directly into a present that was actively guarded, and deeply hostile to his curiosity. The woods, once a playground for his imagination, had become a battlefield of intentions, and he was an unarmed combatant, armed only with a notebook and a burgeoning, terrifying understanding.

The crudely fashioned snare, the effigy nailed to the decaying cabin door, the unnervingly precise scorch marks etched into the ancient oaks, and the small, reed basket containing its cryptic stone offerings—these were no longer mere historical curiosities or isolated signs of trespassing. Joseph's understanding of them had irrevocably shifted. They were not simply markers of a territory; they were active deterrents, meticulously placed, and imbued with a purpose far beyond simple deterrence. The object he now held – the smooth, dark stone etched with a symbol resembling a coiled serpent, discovered within that moss-laden basket – felt less like a piece of forgotten history and more like a freshly lit fuse.

He turned the stone over in his gloved palm, its coolness a stark contrast to the rising heat of apprehension in his chest. It was surprisingly light, yet possessed a dense, significant weight. The symbol, when held under the dappled sunlight filtering through the dense canopy, seemed to possess a subtle depth, almost as if the stone itself was subtly shifting, the carved lines deepening and then receding. This was no accidental etching; it was deliberate, almost alive. He remembered the acrid scent that had clung to the basket, the phantom smell of burnt herbs and something else, something sharp and metallic. It was a scent that now seemed to linger around the stone itself, an almost imperceptible whisper of power or perhaps, of something far more sinister.

The immediate implication was stark: this wasn't just a wilderness being guarded; it was a secret, and this stone, this object, was intrinsically tied to it. The careful placement of the traps and wards, the deliberate clearing of the earth, the territorial scorch marks—they all pointed to a conscious, organized effort to keep something hidden. And now, with the stone in his possession, Joseph felt the chilling certainty that *he* had become a part of that hidden narrative, a player in a game he hadn't realized he'd joined. The warnings his parents had issued, once veiled in layers of parental concern, now seemed like a chillingly accurate prophecy of the tangible perils that awaited him. They hadn't just been warning him about the woods; they had been warning him about the people who protected its secrets, the unseen custodians who ensured that certain things remained buried, forgotten, and undisturbed.

He recalled the hushed conversations between his parents, the way their eyes would flick towards the window when the woods were mentioned, the anxious undertones in their voices when discussing local folklore. They had spoken of guardians, of those who *watched*. At the time, he'd interpreted it as a metaphorical description of a natural instinct to protect ancestral lands. Now, the realization dawned with icy clarity: they had meant individuals. Real people, with intent, and with the means to enforce their will. This stone, and whatever it represented, was clearly something they deemed vital to keep concealed, and he, by finding it, had inadvertently made himself a person of interest. The mere act of holding this object felt like an admission of guilt, a declaration of intent that he had not even made.

The journey back from the forest that day was a far cry from his usual, almost carefree rambles. Every snapping twig, every rustle of leaves, every bird call seemed to be amplified, carrying with it a new, menacing resonance. He imagined eyes watching him from the dense thickets, unseen sentinels assessing his every move. The feeling was no longer a vague paranoia; it was a concrete awareness of being observed, of being cataloged. The symbols, the traps, the wards – they were not just to keep intruders out; they were also to identify and perhaps, to *manage* those who, like him, stumbled upon something they shouldn't have. The stone in his pocket was not just a clue; it was a beacon, a declaration that he had crossed a threshold, a physical manifestation of his trespass.

He began to piece together the fragmented whispers he'd overheard in the village, the half-forgotten local legends that had always seemed like charming superstitions. The tales of strange lights in the woods, of people disappearing without a trace, of unearthly sounds carried on the wind – they no longer sounded like fanciful ramblings. They sounded like echoes of a hidden reality, a society operating just beneath the surface of the ordinary, safeguarding its secrets with an ancient, unyielding resolve. The careful concealment of the quarry, the abandoned cabin, the very *peril* his parents had spoken of – it all coalesced into a single, terrifying conclusion: the village itself, or a significant portion of it, was complicit in this elaborate deception.

The object was more than a clue; it was evidence. Evidence that someone was actively invested in maintaining a particular narrative, or more accurately, in suppressing another. The symbols weren't just esoteric markings; they were a language, a code, understood by those who belonged to this hidden order, and a stark warning to those who did not. The serpent on the stone... he recalled a similar motif in some of the older carvings he'd seen on the disc, though cruder, less refined. Was this an emblem of a specific faction, a particular lineage, or a representation of the very essence of what was being protected? The acrid scent, the burnt herbs – he remembered reading about their use in ancient purification rituals, or as components in obscure concoctions meant to ward off or attract certain energies. The implications were profound. Whoever had left this basket, whoever had placed these symbols, was not merely a territorial landowner; they were participants in practices that hinted at something far older, far more potent, and infinitely more dangerous than he could have imagined.

Joseph found himself reviewing his notes from the previous weeks, his sketches of the traps and wards suddenly taking on a new significance. He saw the progression, the increasing boldness of the deterrents. The snare was a physical deterrent, a primal threat. The effigy was psychological, playing on superstition. The scorch marks were territorial claims. But the basket, with its carefully chosen stones and potent scent, felt like a direct communication, a deliberate placing of an artifact designed to be found by *him*, or at least by someone who fit his profile – a curious, persistent individual delving into the forgotten history of the area. It was an escalation.

He began to understand that the 'manifest peril' his parents had alluded to was not a vague, atmospheric threat, but a very real, human (or perhaps, *almost* human) agency. The guardians weren't abstract entities; they were people, residents of the surrounding villages, or perhaps a select few from his own, who had taken it upon themselves to become the custodians of the woods' secrets. Their methods were subtle, their presence often unseen, but their intent was unmistakably clear: to keep the past buried, and to actively deter anyone who sought to unearth it. This stone, this object, was a direct challenge to their authority, and by extension, to their very existence. Possessing it meant he was now marked, identified as a threat to their clandestine operations.

The weight of the stone in his pocket was a constant, unsettling reminder. It was no longer just a mysterious artifact; it was a target, a symbol of his unwelcome intrusion. He felt the unspoken question hanging in the air: why him? What was it about his exploration, his questions, his very presence, that had drawn the attention of these hidden protectors? Was it simply his persistence, his refusal to be deterred by minor obstacles, or was there something more? Had his examination of the disc, his research into local history, somehow flagged him as a potential threat to their carefully constructed silence?

He thought about the older inhabitants of the village, the ones who rarely ventured out, who spoke in hushed tones of 'old ways' and 'forgotten pacts'. Had they always known? Were these guardians drawn from their ranks, their silent vigil a continuation of ancient traditions passed down through generations? The thought sent a shiver down his spine. He had always viewed these whispers as quaint folklore, harmless remnants of a bygone era. Now, they seemed like a chillingly accurate description of a present-day reality. The peril was not a phantom conjured by fearful imaginations; it was the calculated, determined effort of individuals who believed they were upholding a sacred trust, a trust that required their active, often aggressive, participation.

The stone felt heavier still. It was a tangible link, a direct piece of evidence of a conspiracy of silence. He realized that the warnings were not just about the physical dangers of the woods, but about the very real, present danger posed by those who sought to preserve its secrets. They were the shadows that his parents had warned him about, the unseen forces that manipulated the periphery of his perception. They were the reason the paths were subtly altered, the reason certain areas felt inherently off-limits, the reason the very air seemed to hum with an unspoken warning. And this object, this serpent-marked stone, was the undeniable proof that his curiosity had not gone unnoticed. He was no longer an observer; he was a participant, and the game was just beginning to reveal its terrifying stakes. The woods were not just wild; they were guarded, and he had just picked up the key to a door someone desperately wanted to remain locked.

The stone, cool and unnervingly potent in his pocket, was no longer just an object of academic curiosity. It was a physical manifestation of the unseen forces that had begun to warp the edges of his reality. The prickling sensation of being watched, which had initially been a subtle undercurrent of paranoia, had solidified into a stark certainty. The woods, once a sanctuary for exploration and discovery, now felt like a labyrinth guarded by silent, unseen sentinels. Every rustle of leaves, every creak of a branch, seemed to carry an implicit threat, a warning whispered by the very wind that stirred the ancient trees. His parents' veiled anxieties, once dismissed as the overprotective concerns of parents who didn't fully grasp his passion, now echoed with chilling prescience. They had spoken of guardians, of those who *watched*, and Joseph now understood with a visceral clarity that they had meant real people, custodians of a secret so fiercely guarded that it had birthed a clandestine society within the very fabric of his familiar world.

The immediate instinct, the natural human response to such escalating peril, would have been to retreat. To abandon the quarry, to forget the symbols, to discard the serpent-etched stone and erase the unsettling knowledge it represented. To pretend he had never found the basket, never noticed the scorch marks, never felt the chilling significance of the effigy. But for Joseph, the very act of being threatened, of being so profoundly and subtly targeted, had ignited a fire within him, a stubborn defiance that eclipsed his fear. The danger, far from being a deterrent, had become a catalyst. It had taken his intellectual curiosity and forged it into an unyielding resolve. If these guardians were so determined to keep their secrets buried, there had to be a reason, a compelling importance that transcended mere territoriality. And understanding that reason, he believed, was the only true path to safety. To flee would be to acknowledge their power, to surrender to their hidden dominion. To press on, however, was to reclaim his agency, to assert his right to know, and perhaps, to expose the truth before it consumed him.

He began to move with a newfound caution, a stealth that belied his years. His expeditions into the woods were no longer spontaneous forays but meticulously planned operations. He studied his maps with an intensity that bordered on obsession, identifying less-traveled paths, noting the subtle shifts in terrain that might indicate hidden trails or concealed entrances. He paid closer attention to the flora, recognizing the specific plants used in the ritualistic basket, noting where they grew most abundantly. He became a ghost in the familiar landscape, his movements fluid and deliberate, his senses heightened, constantly scanning his surroundings for the slightest anomaly – a disturbed patch of earth, an unnatural stillness, the faintest scent that didn't belong. The days of simply documenting were over; now, he was observing, analyzing, and planning, his mind a battlefield where apprehension warred with an unshakeable commitment to uncover the truth.

The weight of the stone in his pocket was a constant, tactile reminder of the stakes. It was no longer just a puzzle piece; it was a key, a tangible link to a conspiracy that extended far beyond the hushed whispers of local folklore. He revisited his sketches, the crude drawings of traps and wards now appearing as sophisticated defense mechanisms, each one a testament to the guardians' commitment and ingenuity. The snare, a simple physical barrier; the effigy, a psychological deterrent rooted in ancient fears; the scorch marks, a territorial claim etched in fire; and the basket, a deliberate offering, a deliberate message. Each element was a step in their escalating efforts to deter intrusion, and he, by collecting the stone, had become the ultimate trespasser, the one who had crossed an invisible but undeniably present line. His parents' warnings, once abstract pronouncements about the dangers of the unknown, had now acquired a concrete and terrifying form. They hadn't been warning him about the wildness of nature; they had been warning him about the fierce, possessive guardianship of its secrets, and the people who embodied it.

He remembered fragments of conversations overheard in the village square, hushed exchanges between elders that he had previously dismissed as the rambling of old age. Tales of strange lights in the deep woods, of hunters who vanished without a trace, of eerie melodies carried on the night air. These were no longer just fanciful stories to fill the quiet hours. They were echoes of a hidden conflict, a society operating in the shadows, their actions punctuated by disappearances and unexplained phenomena. The peril his parents had so cryptically mentioned was not a phantom, but a very real, very human force, a force that wielded the wilderness itself as an extension of its will. He began to suspect that the carefully cultivated ignorance of the villagers was not merely a product of their environment, but an active participation in the ongoing deception, a collective agreement to maintain the silence that protected their hidden world.

This realization shifted his perspective entirely. The guardians were not some distant, mythical protectors of ancient lore; they were likely his neighbors, the people he saw every day, their faces etched with the mundane details of village life. The very ordinariness of their outward existence made their hidden purpose all the more chilling. Were they perpetuating traditions passed down through generations, their vigilance a sacred duty? Or had some more recent event, some unearthed discovery, solidified their resolve to enforce absolute secrecy? The thought that his own community might be complicit in this elaborate charade gnawed at him. He found himself scrutinizing the faces of those he knew, searching for any flicker of recognition, any hint of the hidden knowledge they might possess. The suspicion cast a pall over his familiar world, transforming casual acquaintances into potential adversaries, the innocent into the complicit.

His resolve, however, was not dampened by this unsettling possibility; it was amplified. If the guardians were among them, then the secret they guarded must be of paramount importance, something that impacted the very heart of their society. He felt a growing certainty that understanding this secret was not just a matter of satisfying his own curiosity, but a necessity for his own safety, and perhaps, for the safety of others who might stumble upon the same path. The more he learned, the more he realized the potential danger of remaining ignorant. The guardians' methods, while subtle, were undeniably effective. They had managed to keep their secret hidden for generations, and if he was to navigate this increasingly perilous terrain, he needed to do so with a clarity of purpose and a strategic mind, armed with knowledge rather than driven by blind instinct.

He began to see the woods not as a collection of trees and trails, but as a complex system of defenses and indicators, a language written in the landscape itself. The placement of the traps, the types of symbols used, the subtle alterations of the terrain – they all spoke of a sophisticated understanding of both the natural world and human psychology. He started to draw parallels between the symbols he'd encountered and ancient iconography, seeking patterns that might reveal the origins and nature of the group responsible for this elaborate network of concealment. The serpent on the stone, for instance, was a potent symbol in many ancient cultures, often representing cyclical renewal, primordial power, or hidden knowledge. Was this the nature of the secret they were protecting?

The acrid scent that had accompanied the stone, the phantom smell of burnt herbs, began to appear in other contexts. He recalled instances where a similar, faint aroma had seemed to cling to the air near certain remote areas of the forest, areas he had previously dismissed as having peculiar soil compositions or unusual vegetation. Now, he recognized it as a deliberate marker, a subtle signal of their presence, a ritualistic element woven into the fabric of their territorial claims. These were not the actions of simple poachers or territorial landowners; these were the practices of individuals deeply connected to ancient beliefs and rituals, committed to preserving something they considered sacred, or perhaps, something they deeply feared.

The danger was palpable now, a low hum of awareness that never quite left him. He knew he was treading on dangerous ground, that his continued investigation was an act of defiance against a powerful, organized entity. But the more he understood, the more he was convinced that the greatest peril lay not in confronting the truth, but in succumbing to the enforced ignorance. His parents' fear, he now understood, was not just for his physical safety, but for the potential corruption of his spirit, the erosion of his independence by the insidious power of secrecy and control. He would not let them dictate his understanding of the world, not when the world held such profound and compelling mysteries. His resolve had solidified, hardening into a quiet, unwavering determination to see this through, to understand the shadows, and to emerge from the encroaching darkness with the truth as his shield. The quest had become more than just an investigation; it had become a personal crusade, a test of will against an ancient, silent power.

5

The Web of Deception

The woods had become his silent schoolroom, but the village was fast becoming his most perplexing lecture hall. Joseph understood, with a dawning dread that was nevertheless tinged with a grim exhilaration, that his hunt had expanded beyond the rustling leaves and hidden trails. The guardians were not solely creatures of the forest; they were woven into the very fabric of his community, their secrets cloaked in the mundane routines of daily life. His parents' pronouncements about the "watchers" and the "hidden ones" now resonated with a chilling clarity. They weren't speaking of spectral figures or mythical beasts, but of flesh-and-blood individuals, his neighbors, whose familiar faces concealed an ancient, vigilant purpose.

He began by focusing on the periphery, the individuals whose lives seemed tethered to the shadowed heart of the surrounding woods. Old Man Hemlock, the taciturn woodcutter whose cottage stood at the very edge of the forest, became a primary subject of his clandestine observations. Hemlock was a man of few words, his movements slow and deliberate, his gaze often fixed on some unseen point in the distance. Joseph had always attributed this to the quiet contemplation of a man nearing the end of his days, content with his solitary existence. Now, however, he saw a different kind of watchfulness in the old man's eyes, a keenness that suggested he was not merely observing the changing seasons, but the comings and goings of those who dared to trespass in the deeper woods. Joseph would linger near Hemlock's property, feigning an interest in the variety of fungi clinging to the decaying logs, his ears straining to catch any snippet of conversation that might drift from the open doorway of the cottage. He noticed that Hemlock received infrequent visitors, men who arrived on horseback, their faces often obscured by the brims of their hats, and who departed as silently as they arrived. Their interactions were brief, marked by curt nods and hushed exchanges, and invariably, they carried small, tightly wrapped parcels that seemed to disappear into the depths of Hemlock's well-worn satchel. What were these parcels? Not provisions, Joseph reasoned, as they were too small and too infrequently delivered. Were they messages? Supplies? Or perhaps something more tangible, a physical manifestation of their clandestine network?

Then there was Elara Vance, the village healer. Her knowledge of herbs and poultices was legendary, her hands possessing a gentle efficacy that soothed both physical ailments and troubled spirits. Joseph's mother often spoke of Elara's uncanny ability to find rare medicinal plants, hinting that the healer possessed an intuitive understanding of the forest's bounty that bordered on the supernatural. Now, Joseph viewed her wisdom with a new, calculating eye. Elara's excursions into the woods were more frequent and extensive than those of any other villager, often lasting for days at a time. She always returned with baskets overflowing with an array of flora, some familiar, others utterly alien to Joseph's botanical knowledge. He recalled seeing her once, near the very clearing where he had discovered the serpent-etched stone. She had been kneeling by a cluster of moonpetal blossoms, her movements graceful and precise, her brow furrowed in concentration as she carefully extracted the delicate petals. She hadn't seemed to notice him, hidden as he was behind a thicket of ferns, but he remembered the peculiar, almost ritualistic way she handled the plants, as if she were performing a sacred rite. He wondered if her connection to the woods was more than just a professional one. Did she supply specific herbs for the guardians' rituals? Was her healing a cover for a deeper, more involved role in their operations? He noticed that certain villagers, those who seemed to hold positions of subtle authority – the miller, the blacksmith, even the mayor – would often seek Elara out for private consultations, their visits marked by the same hushed tones and furtive glances he had observed in Hemlock's visitors. There was a shared understanding, a silent language passing between them that excluded all outsiders, including himself.

His attention was also drawn to the weekly market days, events that had always seemed innocuous, a simple occasion for villagers to trade goods and exchange gossip. Now, Joseph saw them as subtle theaters of operations. He began to position himself near the stalls of certain individuals, not to purchase anything, but to observe their interactions. The baker, a jovial man named Thomas, whose loaves were always the first to sell out, would often engage in brief, almost imperceptible exchanges with others. A quick touch of hands as a coin was passed, a low murmur exchanged over a shared barrel of apples, a furtive glance exchanged across the bustling square – these were the minutiae that Joseph meticulously cataloged in his mind. He noted that Thomas had a small, almost invisible scar above his left eyebrow, a detail that seemed insignificant until he saw a similar marking on the jawline of a stranger who had briefly conferred with Old Man Hemlock at the edge of the woods. Were these marks of allegiance? A subtle way for members of this hidden society to recognize each other in plain sight? He started to pay more attention to who bought from whom, and more importantly, who *didn't* buy from whom. There were subtle exclusions, patterns of avoidance that spoke volumes.

The mayor, a man named Thorne, a stern figure whose authority was rarely questioned, seemed to engage in a more overt, yet still discreet, network. Thorne would often convene small, informal meetings in the back room of the general store, ostensibly to discuss village affairs. Joseph, peering through the grimy windowpane, would see

Thorne speaking with Hemlock, Elara, and the blacksmith, Mr. Abernathy, their faces serious, their gestures animated, as if engaged in matters far weightier than crop yields or boundary disputes. Abernathy, a man whose powerful hands were as adept at forging iron as they were at mending a broken wagon wheel, was another enigma. His forge was a place of constant activity, the ringing of hammer on anvil a familiar sound in the village. But Joseph had observed Abernathy on rare occasions, when the forge was cold and the villagers had retired for the night, emerging from a small, almost hidden cellar beneath his workshop, carrying what appeared to be intricately carved wooden objects, wrapped in rough burlap. He never saw where these objects went, only that Abernathy would disappear into the shadows with them, his powerful frame seeming to melt into the darkness.

The realization that these individuals, pillars of his community, might be the very guardians he had come to fear, was a deeply unsettling one. It painted his familiar world with a sinister hue, transforming friendly nods into guarded assessments and casual greetings into potential probes. He began to experiment with subtle approaches, trying to gauge their reactions. He once asked Elara Vance about a particular, unusually shaped leaf he had found near the stream, feigning ignorance of its properties. Her response was polite but guarded, her eyes assessing him with an intensity that made him feel as though she was dissecting his very soul. She provided a general answer, describing it as a common woodland plant, but her hesitation, the almost imperceptible tightening of her lips, told him she knew more. It was a subtle denial, a redirection that confirmed his suspicions. He had touched upon something she was not meant to discuss, and her practiced deflection was a testament to her ingrained loyalty to the hidden order.

His investigations took on a more systematic approach. He started to map the village itself, marking the residences of those he suspected, noting their daily routines, their usual companions. He used his keen powers of observation, honed by his solitary explorations, to detect anomalies. A window shutter closed at an unusual hour, a lamp burning late into the night, a carriage that appeared only after dark, its destination the outskirts of the village – these were all clues, breadcrumbs leading him further into the labyrinth. He began to frequent the tavern, not for the ale, but for the opportunity to overhear conversations. The men gathered there often spoke of the woods, of hunting, of strange occurrences that were dismissed as the ramblings of overly imaginative minds. But Joseph listened for the undertones, the veiled references, the moments of shared silence that followed a particularly cryptic remark. He learned to differentiate between genuine ignorance and willful omission. He saw the way certain men would quickly change the subject when the conversation veered too close to the "old ways" or the "sacred grounds." He noticed the exchanged glances between the mayor and the blacksmith whenever someone mentioned unusual lights seen deep within the forest.

One evening, under the guise of delivering a message for his mother, Joseph found himself near the mayor's estate. The imposing house, usually well-lit, seemed to be holding its breath. Only a single lantern flickered in the study window, casting long, distorted shadows across the manicured lawn. He hid behind a towering oak, his heart pounding a rhythm against his ribs that felt amplified in the suffocating silence. He saw Thorne emerge from the house, not to address the villagers as was his custom, but to meet with a cloaked figure who had appeared seemingly from nowhere. They spoke in hushed, urgent tones, their words swallowed by the rustling leaves. Joseph strained to catch anything, but the distance and the wind were too great. He did see, however, Thorne hand the figure a small, dark object before the figure melted back into the shadows as quickly as they had arrived. The gesture was quick, almost furtive, and it cemented Joseph's belief that the mayor was more than just an observer; he was a central player, a facilitator in whatever operations these guardians conducted.

He began to document his observations meticulously, not in his usual detailed sketches of flora and fauna, but in coded notes and cryptic diagrams. He created a lexicon of symbols for the individuals he suspected, a visual shorthand to represent their roles and their interactions. The serpent for the clandestine society itself, the oak for Thorne, the hearth for Abernathy, the moon petal for Elara, the ax for Hemlock. He started to chart their movements, their meetings, their patterns of communication. He noticed that certain individuals would converge at specific points in the village, often coinciding with the arrival of an unseen presence from the woods. He realized that the seemingly random interactions of village life were, in fact, carefully orchestrated exchanges, a complex web of communication and coordination designed to maintain their secrets and their power. The more he observed, the more he understood that the guardians were not a monolithic entity, but a network, a society with its own internal hierarchies and methods of operation, all bound by a shared commitment to a secret that held immense significance. His passive observation had evolved into active reconnaissance, and the weight of that knowledge settled upon him, a heavy cloak of responsibility and growing peril. He was no longer just an observer; he was a student of their secrets, and the lessons he was learning were whispered in the shadows of his own home.

The pieces, once scattered and seemingly unrelated, began to coalesce, forming a picture far more intricate and disturbing than Joseph could have imagined. His meticulous observations, the coded notes scribbled in the margins of his father's old ledgers, the hushed conversations he'd managed to decipher, were no longer mere fragments of suspicion; they were threads in a tapestry of deception that stretched back generations. The turning point, the moment the true nature of the secret began to reveal itself, arrived not through a grand discovery, but through the quiet persistence of a seemingly insignificant artifact.

It began with the baker, Thomas. Joseph had grown increasingly fascinated by Thomas's seemingly innocuous exchanges at the market. There was a peculiar pattern to how he handed over loaves of bread, a subtle flourish of the wrist that often accompanied the transfer of a coin, or sometimes, nothing at all. Joseph had noticed that Thomas's left hand, the one that often brushed against the recipient's as he made the transaction, bore a faint, almost invisible scar above the left eyebrow. It was a detail he had initially dismissed, but the memory of a similar marking on a stranger conferring with Old Man Hemlock lingered. He decided to focus his attention on Thomas.

One market day, Joseph positioned himself strategically, feigning an interest in the plump, ruddy apples piled high at a neighboring stall. He watched as Thomas served a steady stream of customers, his movements practiced and efficient. Then, he saw it. A regular customer, a farmer named Silas, approached Thomas's stall. Silas, a man known for his quiet nature and his unwavering loyalty to the village council, held out a small, intricately carved wooden bird. It was the kind of object Joseph had seen Abernathy the blacksmith carrying in his cellar. Thomas took the bird, examined it with a practiced eye, and then, with the same peculiar flourish of his left hand, passed Silas a small, unadorned loaf of bread. As their hands brushed, Joseph saw Thomas discreetly slip a tiny, folded piece of parchment into Silas's palm. The entire exchange lasted no more than five seconds. Silas pocketed the parchment and moved on, leaving Joseph with a gnawing curiosity.

That night, Joseph's mind raced. What could a small wooden bird and a folded piece of parchment signify? He remembered his father's occasional cryptic remarks about "carrying the message" and the importance of "discreet couriers." He also recalled Elara Vance's words about certain plants holding "hidden properties," a phrase that now seemed to echo with a new, sinister meaning. He knew he needed to understand the communication method.

The opportunity arose a few days later. Joseph, under the guise of delivering a basket of freshly picked berries to his aunt, who lived near the edge of the village, made his way past Thomas's bakery. The scent of warm bread filled the air, a comforting aroma that now seemed tainted with suspicion. He noticed that Thomas was not at his usual post. Instead, a younger apprentice was tending the counter.

Joseph, feigning a need to ask about a special order, entered the bakery. While the apprentice was distracted by another customer, Joseph's eyes scanned the well-worn wooden counter. He noticed a small, dark stain near the edge, as if something had been spilled and wiped away hastily. Driven by an impulse he couldn't quite explain, he discreetly ran his fingers over the spot. He felt a faint stickiness, and when he brought his fingers to his nose, he detected a faint, sweet scent. It was the scent of honey, but with an unusual, almost floral undertone. He recognized it from a particular type of wild honeysuckle that grew only in the deepest parts of the woods, near the ancient standing stones.

The next morning, armed with this new information, Joseph sought out Silas. He found the farmer tending his fields, his face etched with the familiar lines of hard work. Joseph approached him casually, complimenting him on his robust crops. Silas responded politely but distantly. Joseph then casually mentioned the market day, and the quality of Thomas's bread. Silas nodded, his gaze fixed on the horizon.

"Fine baker, Thomas," Silas said, his voice gruff. "Always has the best loaves."

"I noticed you received one yesterday," Joseph said, trying to keep his tone casual. "A special one, perhaps?"

Silas stopped his work, his eyes narrowing almost imperceptibly. "Just a regular loaf, lad. Nothing special."

Joseph pressed on, his heart pounding. "I saw you pass something to Thomas. A wooden bird, I believe. And he gave you a small piece of paper."

Silas's jaw tightened. He turned to face Joseph fully, his usual mild demeanor replaced by a stern intensity. "You have sharp eyes, Joseph. Too sharp for your own good, perhaps." He paused, then lowered his voice. "Some things are best left unobserved, especially by those who do not understand their purpose."

"But I want to understand," Joseph insisted, his voice barely a whisper. "What is it all for? What is the secret?"

Silas looked at him for a long moment, his gaze piercing. Finally, he sighed, a sound of deep weariness. "It is not a secret I can explain, boy. It is a duty. A burden." He glanced around, as if ensuring they were alone. "The bird... it is a token. A sign of safe passage. The parchment... it carries coded instructions. For those who need to know."

"Instructions for what?" Joseph demanded.

For the protection of West Seneca," Silas replied, his voice flat. "For the continuation of what has always been."

Joseph's mind flashed back to his parents' hushed conversations about the "watchers" and the "hidden ones," and the ancient pact that bound their community. He looked at Silas, a man he had always seen as a simple farmer, and saw now the weight of a hidden responsibility.

"Protection from what?" Joseph asked, his voice trembling with a mixture of fear and anticipation.

Silas hesitated, as if weighing his words carefully. "From those who would exploit what this land holds. From those who would disrupt the balance." He gestured vaguely towards the deep woods. "There are things in this world, Joseph, that are not meant for the common eye. Ancient powers, forgotten pacts. West Seneca is a sentinel, standing guard over something precious."

Joseph's mind struggled to grasp the enormity of what Silas was implying. It wasn't just about smuggling, or some petty crime. This was about something far older, something tied to the very land itself. He thought of the serpent-etched stone, the peculiar rituals his mother had alluded to, and the unsettling energy he sometimes felt emanating from the heart of the forest.

"So, you are all... guardians?" Joseph ventured, the word feeling both alien and fitting on his tongue.

Silas gave a short, humorless laugh. "In a manner of speaking. We ensure that the legacy of our ancestors is maintained. That the sacred trust is honored." He then looked directly at Joseph, his expression softening slightly. "You have a keen mind, Joseph. You see what others do not. But understanding is one thing, entanglement is another. Be cautious."

With that, Silas turned back to his fields, resuming his work as if the conversation had never happened. Joseph stood there, stunned, the pieces clicking into place with terrifying clarity. The secretive meetings, the coded messages, the hushed conversations – they were all part of a meticulously organized network, a clandestine society dedicated to protecting West Seneca and its hidden purpose. The sweet scent of honeysuckle on his fingers suddenly felt heavy with the weight of generations of secrets.

He knew then that his perception of West Seneca, of his neighbors, of his very life, had been irrevocably altered. The idyllic frontier settlement was a facade, a carefully constructed illusion hiding a complex, ancient underbelly. His investigations had moved beyond simple curiosity; they had led him to the heart of a conspiracy, a conspiracy woven into the fabric of his community, dedicated to preserving a secret that was as vital as it was dangerous. His commitment, he realized with a chilling certainty, had just deepened immeasurably. He was no longer just a boy exploring the woods; he was a witness, and perhaps, unknowingly, a potential inheritor of this profound and perilous legacy. The nature of the secret was not one of simple crime, but of ancient duty, a silent war waged by his own people to safeguard something of immense power and consequence, hidden away in the very heart of their quiet village.

The revelation from Silas, coupled with the lingering scent of that peculiar honeysuckle, had not merely confirmed Joseph's suspicions; it had ignited a fervent desire to dissect the intricate mechanisms of this hidden society. The "duty" and "burden" Silas had spoken of were no longer abstract concepts but tangible forces guiding the actions of his neighbors. Joseph understood that the wooden bird and the folded parchment were not isolated incidents, but keystones in a much larger, more complex operation. He began to meticulously review his own notes, the jumbled fragments of overheard conversations, and the seemingly disconnected occurrences that had previously baffled him. He felt a growing certainty that a discernible pattern lay beneath the surface, a hidden rhythm to the village's clandestine activities.

His focus sharpened on the dates. The market day Silas had been observed was not the first time Joseph had noticed something unusual. He remembered a similar, albeit less overt, exchange involving Abernathy the blacksmith a few weeks prior, coinciding with the annual harvest festival. Abernathy had been unusually reticent that day, his usual jovial demeanor replaced by a grim preoccupation. Joseph recalled Abernathy meticulously polishing a set of ornate metal hinges, his movements precise and almost ritualistic. At the time, he'd dismissed it as Abernathy's typical fastidiousness, but now, the memory sparked with new significance. Could the festival have been a cover, a convenient time for these discreet transactions to occur under the guise of communal celebration? He made a note to investigate Abernathy's movements more closely around important village events.

The recurring motif of the serpent also weighed heavily on his mind. He'd seen it etched on the ancient standing stones, a symbol his mother had once alluded to with a strange mixture of reverence and fear. He'd also noticed it subtly incorporated into the design of the carved wooden bird Silas had given Thomas. Was the serpent a mark of membership, a signature of their shared purpose? Or did it represent something more profound, something connected to the "ancient powers" Silas had mentioned? He recalled the peculiar, almost hypnotic way the serpent symbol seemed to writhe in his vision when he'd first encountered it near the standing stones, a sensation that had both thrilled and unnerved him. He began sketching the serpent symbol repeatedly, trying to capture its essence, its inherent power. He wondered if this symbol was a key, a visual cipher that unlocked the meaning behind the coded messages.

He also started to pay closer attention to the geography of these exchanges. The market square, the baker's shop, Abernathy's forge, and the secluded clearing near the standing stones – these were the locations he'd observed significant events. But were these the only places? Silas's mention of the "deepest parts of the woods" and the "ancient powers" suggested a connection to the natural world, to places untrodden by most villagers. Joseph remembered Elara Vance's cryptic words about certain plants holding "hidden properties." Could the specific locations be tied to the flora or fauna of West Seneca, to natural cycles that dictated the timing of their operations? He envisioned a map of the village and its surroundings, marking each point of interest, searching for any geographical correlation, any subtle alignment that might reveal a hidden network.

The sweet, floral scent of honey, faint but persistent, had also become a crucial clue. He had associated it with the wild honeysuckle near the standing stones, a plant known for its potent fragrance and, according to local lore, its subtle medicinal properties. Could the honey be a form of communication, a way to subtly mark messages or exchange information? He recalled that Thomas had a small apiary behind his bakery, a fact he'd always found charmingly rustic. He wondered if the honey Thomas used in his baking, or perhaps a specially prepared concoction, played a role in their clandestine activities. Perhaps a specific type of honey, gathered from a particular patch of wildflowers, was a signal in itself. He decided to procure some of Thomas's honey, not for consumption, but for analysis. He needed to understand if that distinctive floral undertone was indeed the same scent he had detected on the bakery counter.

The nature of the coded messages also became a focal point of his investigation. Silas had described them as "coded instructions." Joseph's father's ledgers, with their seemingly random notations and asterisks, began to appear less like mundane accounting and more like a cypher waiting to be deciphered. He remembered his father's habit of annotating passages in books, often with seemingly irrelevant observations or single, cryptic words. Could these annotations, scattered across various texts, be fragments of a larger code, perhaps intended to be read in conjunction with specific symbols or locations? He started to meticulously cross-reference his father's journals with the symbols he'd observed and the locations he'd identified, searching for any overlap or hidden connections. The idea of a living code, passed down through generations, began to take shape in his mind.

He began to see a rhythm in the seemingly disparate events. The exchange with Silas at the market occurred on a Tuesday. The festival with Abernathy was a Saturday. He started charting these events on a calendar, looking for any recurring temporal patterns. Were there specific days of the week, or phases of the moon, that seemed to be favored for these clandestine activities? He recalled his mother's mention of certain lunar cycles influencing "harvests" and "gatherings," and how some villagers still observed ancient superstitions tied to celestial movements. This was no longer just about isolated incidents; it was about a meticulously orchestrated series of events, a temporal dance of deception.

He considered the possibility that the "hidden properties" Elara Vance had spoken of were not purely medicinal, but perhaps related to the transmission of information. Could certain plants or herbs be used to create inks that faded unless treated, or to produce scents that conveyed specific meanings? He remembered Elara's extensive collection of dried herbs and roots, and her deep knowledge of botany. She was a woman of considerable intuition and foresight, and her words now seemed laden with a significance he had previously overlooked. He needed to understand her role, her potential involvement, and whether her knowledge of natural remedies extended to the realm of secret communication.

The initial thrill of discovery began to be tempered by a growing sense of unease. The scale of the operation, the apparent depth of the deception, suggested a threat far greater than he had initially imagined. This was not a simple matter of smuggling goods; it was about preserving something ancient and powerful, something that had earned the unwavering loyalty and vigilance of generations. The quiet serenity of West Seneca was a carefully crafted illusion, a peaceful facade masking a profound and enduring struggle. He felt the weight of this realization settle upon him, a chilling premonition of the dangers that lay ahead. He was no longer an observer, but a participant, whether he wished to be or not. The web of deception was vast and intricate, and he was already caught within its silken strands, desperately trying to unravel its secrets before it ensnared him completely. His father's legacy, his mother's hushed warnings, and Silas's stoic pronouncements all converged, painting a picture of a community bound by an ancient, formidable purpose, a purpose that was now unfolding before his young eyes.

He decided to revisit the standing stones, not just to sketch the serpent, but to feel the aura of the place, to try and absorb some of its inherent power, the power Silas had alluded to. He felt a strong pull to that ancient site, a place where the veil between the ordinary and the extraordinary seemed thinnest. He would go at dusk, when the shadows lengthened and the world began to blur, to see if the symbols revealed themselves more clearly in the fading light. Perhaps the standing stones themselves were a repository of knowledge, a silent witness to centuries of the village's hidden history. He carried with him a small, smooth stone he'd found near the river, a stone that felt oddly warm to the touch, and he wondered if it might serve as a conduit, a way to connect with the energy of the place.

The baker, Thomas, with his deceptively simple profession, had become a central figure in Joseph's growing understanding. The subtle flourish of his hand, the invisible scar, the intimate knowledge of passing coded messages – it all pointed to a man deeply embedded in the village's secret life. Joseph recalled other instances where Thomas had displayed an uncanny awareness of events, a seemingly prescient knowledge of who needed what, and when. It wasn't just the bread; it was the subtle guidance, the unspoken arrangements that Thomas facilitated. He remembered Thomas's unusually keen interest in Joseph's father's health in the months leading up to his passing, a concern that had seemed almost paternal, yet now felt deeply suspicious. Could Thomas have been privy to his father's knowledge, or perhaps even involved in orchestrating his silence? The thought sent a shiver down Joseph's spine.

He then turned his attention to the blacksmith, Abernathy. Abernathy was a man of iron and muscle, his life seemingly dedicated to shaping metal. Yet, Joseph remembered the peculiar tools he had seen in Abernathy's cellar, tools that seemed too refined for ordinary blacksmithing, bearing intricate etchings that resembled the patterns found on the serpent-marked stone. Abernathy's participation in the festival, his uncharacteristic quietness, and his meticulous polishing of the ornate hinges now suggested a deeper involvement than mere craftsmanship. Were these hinges part of some larger mechanism, some hidden apparatus crucial to the village's secret purpose? And what about the cellar? Joseph had only glimpsed its contents, but the memory of those unusual tools, glinting in the dim light, haunted him. He resolved to find a way to gain access to Abernathy's cellar, to examine those tools more closely, and to understand their function within this clandestine network.

The concept of a "sentinel" village, a guardian of ancient powers, began to solidify. It was a role that demanded constant vigilance, a silent dedication to protecting something invaluable from external threats. The threat, as Silas had alluded, came from those who would "exploit what this land holds." Joseph's mind conjured images of greedy merchants from distant towns, or perhaps even more shadowy figures, seeking to uncover and harness the hidden energies of West Seneca. His father's death, once a personal tragedy, now seemed to him a potential casualty in this ongoing, hidden war. Had his father been too close to uncovering the truth, or perhaps even a casualty of his own role as a guardian?

The timing of these coordinated actions was another piece of the puzzle that gnawed at him. The harvest festival, the market days, and other less obvious gatherings all seemed to serve as convenient cover. He wondered if there were specific celestial alignments or seasonal changes that triggered these activities. His father's journals contained notations about planting and harvesting that went beyond mere agricultural cycles; there were references to specific times for "tending the roots" and "gathering the light." These phrases, once enigmatic, now seemed to describe a ritualistic, perhaps even astrological, calendar guiding the village's secret operations. He painstakingly tried to correlate these notations with the dates of the suspicious events he had witnessed, searching for a temporal synchronicity that would reveal the underlying rhythm of their work.

He remembered a particular passage in his father's journal that spoke of "the turning of the year" and the "awakening of the old." This was written just before the winter solstice, a time of deep darkness and ancient rituals. He recalled that during that period, there had been a series of unusual night gatherings in the woods, hushed meetings that his parents had strictly forbidden him from approaching. The scent of woodsmoke and something else, something wild and earthy, had permeated the air. Now, he suspected those gatherings were not merely social events, but crucial phases in the execution of their duties. He felt a creeping sense of dread as he realized the extent of the deception that had permeated every aspect of village life, even the celebration of the seasons.

The honeysuckle scent, he realized, was not just a marker; it was a signal, a subtle clue embedded within the very environment. The specific wild honeysuckle that grew near the standing stones possessed a unique aroma, and it was likely that the villagers had learned to interpret its presence or its absence as a confirmation or a warning. He envisioned a system where certain plants served as natural signposts, indicating safe passage or warning of impending danger. Elara Vance's botanical knowledge would be invaluable in understanding this aspect of their communication. He needed to approach her, to gauge her awareness and perhaps subtly probe her for information without revealing the full extent of his own discoveries. Her knowledge of herbs, of their hidden properties, might unlock the secrets of the coded messages and the locations.

Joseph's pursuit of this pattern was driven by an instinct for self-preservation. He understood that to navigate this treacherous landscape, he needed to anticipate their movements, to understand the logic behind their actions. If he could predict their next move, he might be able to avoid being caught in their web, or even find a way to expose their secrets to the wider world, though the thought of such a drastic action filled him with trepidation. The villagers were not inherently malicious, but their dedication to their ancient duty could make them dangerous if they perceived him as a threat. He was a boy, after all, and they were seasoned guardians, bound by oaths and traditions far older than himself.

The more he looked, the more he saw. The subtle glances exchanged between villagers, the seemingly innocent conversations that held double meanings, the way certain objects were passed from hand to hand – it was all part of a grand, silent theater. His father's ledgers, once a mundane collection of numbers, now seemed like a cryptic script, a coded narrative of their generations-long vigil. The symbols, the locations, the timing, the scents – they were all pieces of a vast, interconnected system, a testament to the ingenuity and dedication of the people of West Seneca. He knew, with a chilling certainty, that his journey had only just begun, and that the true nature of West Seneca's secret was far more profound and perilous than he could have ever imagined. The pattern was emerging, intricate and terrifying, and he was determined to follow it to its hidden source, no matter the cost. He started to believe that his father had also been following this pattern, and that his death was a consequence of getting too close to understanding it. This made Joseph's mission all the more urgent.

The path forward was not a straight one, Joseph realized with a sinking certainty. The meticulous pattern he had been painstakingly piecing together, the interconnected symbols, locations, and timings, could very well be a carefully constructed illusion, a labyrinth of breadcrumbs designed to lead the unwary astray. The villagers, bound by their ancient duty, were not merely secretive; they were masters of misdirection, artists of the false trail. Every seemingly clear clue, every convenient revelation, now carried the potential for being a carefully planted seed of deception. His father's journals, once his most trusted source, might contain intentional ambiguities, subtle distortions designed to camouflage the true nature of their operations, or worse, to actively mislead anyone who dared to follow.

He recalled the almost theatrical performance Silas had put on at the market, his gruff pronouncements and the conspicuous handing over of the wooden bird. Had it been a genuine exchange, or a deliberate display for his benefit, or perhaps for the benefit of unseen eyes? Silas's words, while revealing, had also hinted at a deeper burden, a commitment that went beyond mere village errands. Joseph had latched onto those hints, eager for any scrap of truth, but now he questioned if Silas himself was a deliberate guide, or a pawn in a larger game, his pronouncements carefully calibrated to steer Joseph in a particular direction. The scent of honeysuckle, so potent and seemingly linked to the standing stones, could be a deliberate olfactory marker, a familiar scent meant to draw him in, while the real secrets lay hidden elsewhere, masked by this pervasive fragrance.

The very nature of the clues he had gathered—the serpent symbol, the ornate hinges, the cryptic notations in his father's ledgers—all seemed too perfectly aligned, too readily interpretable. It was the kind of clarity that often accompanied a well-rehearsed deception. He thought of the story his grandmother used to tell about the trickster raven, a creature that delighted in leading travelers on wild goose chases through the forest, leaving behind a trail of glittering trinkets and enticing sounds, only for the travelers to find themselves lost and bewildered, the trinkets worthless baubles. Was he, Joseph, the unwitting traveler, being led on such a chase by the guardians of West Seneca? The thought was a chilling one, transforming his methodical investigation into a precarious dance on a tightrope of potential lies.

This realization cast a long shadow over his previous assumptions. Elara Vance's hushed pronouncements about the "hidden properties" of plants, her knowledgeable gaze, her seemingly innocent questions about his research – were these genuine expressions of concern, or were they part of a carefully orchestrated attempt to gauge his progress and perhaps plant further misinformation? He remembered her mentioning a specific herb, known for its soporific qualities, a plant she'd said was "useful for peaceful slumber." At the time, he'd dismissed it as a medicinal observation, but now, the word "soporific" echoed with a more sinister resonance. Could she have subtly drugged him, perhaps during one of his visits to her apothecary, to cloud his judgment or subtly influence his findings? The idea, though disturbing, could not be entirely dismissed. The very sweetness of her demeanor, the gentle way she dispensed her herbal remedies, could be a potent form of misdirection, masking a mind far more cunning than he had previously perceived.

Even Abernathy the blacksmith, a man Joseph had always seen as straightforward and dependable, now became a figure of suspicion. His uncharacteristic reticence during the festival, his meticulous work on those peculiar hinges—was it all genuine? Or had Abernathy been directed to behave in a certain way, to draw attention to himself, to serve as a visible, yet ultimately misleading, participant? Joseph recalled Abernathy's strong hands, his weathered face, the air of quiet competence that always surrounded him. It was easy to trust such a man, too easy. Perhaps the misplaced trust was precisely what they were counting on. The intricate etchings on the tools in his cellar, the ones that resembled the serpent markings, could be a deliberate echo, a way to plant the serpent symbol where it served their purpose, making it appear as an organic part of their operations rather than a directed clue.

The entire premise of his investigation, the idea of uncovering a singular, grand secret, began to waver. What if there wasn't one secret, but many, a complex tapestry of deceits woven to protect something far more fundamental? What if the "powers" Silas spoke of were not necessarily benevolent, or even tied to the land in a mystical sense, but represented something entirely different—a valuable resource, an ancient technology, or even a dangerous ideology that the villagers were protecting from the outside world, or perhaps from themselves? The misdirection, in this context, would serve not just to keep outsiders ignorant, but to keep the villagers themselves compartmentalized, each group or individual only privy to the information necessary for their specific role, preventing anyone from grasping the full, potentially terrifying, truth.

He had to begin questioning the very foundation of his assumptions. The standing stones, for instance. He had felt a pull towards them, a sense of ancient power, and he'd seen the serpent etched upon them. But what if the serpent was a common symbol, or even a recent addition, placed there specifically to lend an aura of antiquity and mystery to a mundane location? What if the true meeting points, the actual centers of their clandestine activities, were far more ordinary, disguised by the very mystique they had cultivated? He imagined them deliberately using the standing stones as a decoy, drawing attention to this ancient site while their real operations occurred in the abandoned mill by the river, or the forgotten root cellar beneath the old schoolhouse.

The calendrical patterns, too, were suspect. The correlation between market days and unusual exchanges, the significance of the harvest festival – these seemed too neat. Perhaps the exchanges were deliberately timed to coincide with these events, making them appear as mere coincidences to any observer. He recalled his father's meticulous record-keeping, the way he would mark recurring astronomical events in his astronomical charts. Had his father's notations about celestial cycles also been a form of misdirection, pointing towards a grand, cosmic plan when the reality was far more terrestrial and perhaps more sinister? He imagined the guardians subtly manipulating the perception of time, making their actions appear dictated by natural rhythms when, in fact, they were orchestrating those rhythms themselves.

Joseph's approach had to shift. He could no longer afford to be a hungry seeker, eagerly devouring every scrap of information that came his way. He had to become a discerning analyst, a skilled debunker of his own burgeoning theories. Each piece of evidence needed to be cross-examined, not just for what it revealed, but for what it might be hiding. He had to consider the possibility that Silas's revelations were incomplete, curated to satisfy Joseph's curiosity without revealing the true stakes. Thomas's geniality, his helpful advice, his consistent presence – these were all qualities that made him seem trustworthy, but in a world of deception, trustworthiness could be the most potent weapon of all.

He needed to develop a mental filter, a way to separate the genuine from the fabricated. This meant looking for inconsistencies, for the subtle tells that even the most skilled deceivers might betray. It meant paying attention not just to what was said, but to what was conspicuously omitted. When Silas spoke of the "burden," he had avoided specifics. When Elara Vance discussed herbs, she had been vague about their precise applications in "sensitive matters." When Abernathy polished those hinges, he had offered no explanation for their unusual design. These omissions, these gaps in the narrative, were now more significant than any explicit statement.

The honeysuckle scent, a clue he had clung to with such conviction, now seemed almost too convenient. Its association with the standing stones, a place of perceived power, could be a deliberate strategy to imbue the scent itself with a false sense of significance. What if the scent was used in multiple, unrelated contexts, a ubiquitous aroma designed to create a false sense of connection? He imagined them using it not just near the stones, but also in the vicinity of places they wished to imbue with an air of mystery, or perhaps even in the homes of individuals they wished to associate with their cause. The scent might not be a key at all, but a lock, designed to seal off certain lines of inquiry by presenting a seemingly obvious answer.

His father's legacy, too, was now a subject of doubt. Had his father been a willing participant, a guardian who had left behind a coded testament? Or had his father been a victim, his journals deliberately planted or altered after his death to serve as a tool of misdirection? The idea that his own father's words might be a trap was almost unbearable, yet it was a possibility that had to be entertained. He recalled his father's final days, his increasing frailty, his moments of lucidity interspersed with periods of confused rambling. Had those ramblings contained fragments of truth, or had they been the result of influence, perhaps even intentional poisoning as Elara's soporific herb suggested?

Joseph resolved to approach his future investigations with a healthy dose of skepticism, even paranoia. He would revisit the places he had marked on his mental map, but with a new objective: to look for the deliberate blind spots, the areas that seemed too intentionally obvious. He would scrutinize every overheard conversation, not for the words spoken, but for the subtext, the unspoken implications, and the potential for coded meanings that served a dual purpose. He understood that the web of deception was not just woven with secrets, but also with lies, and that unraveling it would require him to become as adept at recognizing falsehoods as he was at seeking truth. The journey had just become significantly more treacherous, a descent into a hall of mirrors where every reflection might be a distortion, and every path a potential dead end. His survival, and the uncovering of what West Seneca truly guarded, depended on his ability to see through the elaborate charade.

The air in the small study felt heavier than usual, thick with the scent of aging paper and the metallic tang of his own anxiety. Joseph traced the intricate knotwork on the cover of his father's journal, a symbol he'd once found comforting, now imbued with a disquieting ambiguity. His journey had begun with a child's curiosity, a fascination with the whispered legends of West Seneca, and a yearning to understand the shadowed corners of his father's life. But that innocent pursuit had long since evaporated, replaced by a gnawing certainty that he had stumbled into a world far more complex and dangerous than he could have ever imagined. He had been following a trail, but now he understood that the trail was not merely leading him to a destination; it was leading him *through* something, a trial by fire that had already begun to reshape him.

The recent encounter at the old mill, the shadowed figures he'd glimpsed through the dust-choked windows, the palpable sense of being watched – these were not mere anxieties conjured by an overactive imagination. They were tangible proof of a reality that bristled with hidden threats. He had seen the glint of steel, not just the farmer's scythe or the woodsman's ax, but something sharper, something wielded with deliberate intent. And the silence that had fallen upon the millworkers when he'd approached – a silence that felt less like surprise and more like a prearranged signal – had chilled him to the bone. It was the silence of complicity, of a shared, unspoken understanding that excluded him entirely. He had narrowly escaped being noticed, but the experience had irrevocably altered his perception. He was no longer an observer; he was a participant, whether he wished to be or not.

The realization settled over him like a shroud: there was no returning to the life he had known, to the simple days of academic pursuit and youthful exploration. The path back was overgrown, obscured by a growing forest of unanswered questions and tangible dangers. Each clue he had uncovered, each conversation he had pieced together, had served not to illuminate a clear path, but to ensnare him deeper within the intricate web. He thought of the veiled warnings from Silas, the cryptic pronouncements of the elders, the unnerving knowledge displayed by Elara Vance. These were not accidental encounters; they were deliberate interactions, designed, he now suspected, to test his resolve, to gauge his understanding, and perhaps, to draw him into the very heart of the mystery, a moth drawn to a flame that promised both illumination and destruction.

He recalled the fleeting moment when he'd first discovered the hidden compartment in his father's desk, the thrill of uncovering a secret that felt almost sacred. That thrill had been the initial lure, the spark that ignited his investigation. Now, the embers glowed with a dangerous heat. The intricate clockwork mechanism his father had crafted, the one that held the false bottom, wasn't just a clever hiding place; it was a metaphor for the entire operation. Layers upon layers of deception, intricate mechanisms designed to conceal a truth that was far more profound, and perhaps far more perilous, than he had initially imagined. He had already peered through one layer, then another, and with each revelation, the stakes had risen exponentially.

The knowledge he now possessed was a heavy burden, a double-edged sword that promised understanding but threatened exposure. He knew enough to be dangerous, not only to himself but, he now suspected, to the people who were actively working to keep West Seneca's secrets buried. The casual dismissal he had once afforded to the hushed conversations he'd overheard, the coded phrases he'd dismissed as local superstition – these were now potential keys, fragments of a larger narrative that whispered of ancient pacts, of guarded resources, of a power that the villagers were willing to kill to protect. The symbol of the serpent, once a curious mark, now seemed to represent a coiled threat, a predator lying in wait.

He felt it keenly in the quiet hours of the night, a prickling sensation on his skin, the subconscious awareness of eyes upon him even when he was alone. The woods surrounding his ancestral home, once a familiar sanctuary, now seemed to hold an unspoken menace. Every rustle of leaves, every snap of a twig, could be a scout, a sentinel, a silent guardian of the hidden truth. He had started to recognize certain patterns in the comings and goings of unfamiliar faces in the village, the way they lingered too long at the tavern, the furtive exchanges that happened in shadowed alleyways. They were not just villagers; they were custodians of a secret, and he was an intruder who had, perhaps, seen too much.

The moment of realization wasn't a single, dramatic event, but a slow, dawning comprehension, like the gradual emergence of a submerged island. He had been walking a tightrope, and he had finally reached the point where the rope frayed, the drop below too vast to consider retreating. The near miss at the mill, the subtle but undeniable shift in the demeanor of some of the villagers, the increasingly urgent tone in his father's fragmented entries about "unseen eyes" and "necessary precautions" – all these converged into an undeniable truth. He could no longer pretend to be a mere scholar, a curious outsider observing from a safe distance. He was embroiled, entangled, and the very act of seeking the truth had made him a target.

The thought of turning back, of abandoning his quest and trying to erase what he knew, felt like a betrayal. Not just a betrayal of his father's legacy, which was now inextricably linked to the mysteries of West Seneca, but a betrayal of himself. He had tasted the possibility of a truth so profound it could redefine everything he understood about his world. To retreat now would be to condemn himself to a life of perpetual uncertainty, forever haunted by the knowledge that he had stood on the precipice of understanding and flinched. The questions, once a source of intellectual stimulation, had become an insistent, burning need to know.

He stood up from his desk, the worn floorboards creaking beneath his weight. He walked to the window, gazing out at the darkening landscape. The familiar silhouette of the standing stones was barely visible in the twilight, their ancient presence a constant reminder of the enigmatic forces at play. He had been given glimpses, fragments, hints. Now, he knew, he had to pursue the whole. The danger was no longer an abstract concept; it was a tangible presence, a shadow that stretched long and cold across his path. But with that shadow came a strange sense of clarity. The hesitation, the doubt, the cautious probing – these were no longer his primary tools.

He had to commit. He had to embrace the peril, not as a victim, but as a seeker who understood the cost. This was the point of no return. The carefully constructed facade of ignorance had crumbled, and in its place stood a stark, unwavering resolve. He would not be deterred by fear, nor seduced by misdirection. He would press on, not just to uncover the secrets of West Seneca, but to understand the true nature of his father's involvement, and the responsibilities that now, undeniably, rested upon his own shoulders. The web had tightened, but he was no longer simply caught within it; he was now actively, and deliberately, trying to unravel it from the inside, knowing that the slightest misstep could lead to his own undoing. The pursuit of truth had become a dangerous game, and he was ready to play. He picked up the journal again, his grip firm, the weight of its secrets a familiar, and now accepted, burden. His journey had truly begun.

6

The Confrontation Beckons

The weight of his father's journal felt different now, no longer a collection of cryptic scribblings but a blueprint, a guide to a destiny he could no longer outrun. Joseph stood by the window, the last vestiges of daylight painting the ancient woods in hues of bruised purple and deep indigo. The silence outside was no longer peaceful; it was watchful, pregnant with unspoken threats. He had spent days poring over the entries, the coded references, the hurried sketches of unfamiliar symbols and cryptic locations. Each word, each hastily drawn line, was a piece of a puzzle that had ensnared him, drawing him deeper into the shadowy heart of West Seneca. The encounter at the mill had been a brutal awakening, a stark illustration that polite inquiry and scholarly detachment were no longer viable options. He was no longer an observer; he was a target, and his only hope of survival lay in taking the initiative.

He turned from the window, his gaze falling upon the scattered maps and notes spread across his father's desk. The meticulously drawn lines of the local terrain, the annotations marking hidden springs and forgotten paths, the almost obsessive detailing of the standing stones – these were his arsenal. His father, it was becoming increasingly clear, had been preparing for something, something that involved not just the preservation of West Seneca's secrets, but a potential confrontation. Joseph, armed with this newfound, terrifying understanding, realized he had to do the same. He could not wait for the shadows to engulf him completely; he had to step into them, deliberately, strategically.

His limited resources gnawed at him. He had no allies in this place, no one he could truly trust. The villagers, with their wary eyes and guarded smiles, were a closed book, their loyalty to the ancient ways unquestionable. Silas, the old woodsman, had offered cryptic advice, but Joseph suspected Silas himself was bound by unspoken obligations. Elara Vance, with her unsettling knowledge of his father's affairs, was an enigma, her motives as veiled as the secrets of the valley. He was alone, armed only with his intellect, his father's legacy, and a desperate courage born of necessity.

The plan began to coalesce, not as a fully formed strategy, but as a series of calculated risks, each step designed to peel back another layer of deception. He needed a point of leverage, something that would force the hand of whoever was orchestrating this elaborate charade. His father's journal mentioned a "gathering," a clandestine meeting that occurred during specific lunar phases, held in a location known only by a series of encoded symbols. This gathering, Joseph surmised, was where the decisions were made, where the secrets were guarded, where the true power of West Seneca resided. If he could infiltrate this gathering, or at least disrupt it, he might force the perpetrators into the open.

But how to find this location? The symbols in the journal were abstract, seemingly unconnected to any known cartography. He recalled a passage where his father described a particular constellation visible only during the autumn equinox, a celestial marker that corresponded with a terrestrial landmark. The equinox was only a few days away. That would be his window. He spent hours cross-referencing star charts with his father's rough sketches, the flickering lamplight casting long, dancing shadows that seemed to mimic the unseen observers he felt constantly around him.

He remembered a story his father had told him as a child, about a hidden grove deep within the whispering woods, a place said to be a nexus of ancient energy, marked by a peculiar alignment of ancient trees. Could this be the place? The description was vague, steeped in folklore, but his father had always had a knack for weaving truth into his tales. Joseph decided to investigate, to scout the area, to see if any of the symbols from the journal matched the natural markings of the grove.

His limited resources also extended to his physical capabilities. He was an academic, not a woodsman. While his father had taught him some basic survival skills, he was no match for seasoned hunters or trackers. He would need to rely on stealth, on misdirection, on exploiting the element of surprise. He couldn't engage in a direct confrontation; that would be suicide. He had to be a ghost, a whisper in the wind.

He began to gather what he could. A sturdy hunting knife, a flint and steel, a coil of rope – items that felt alien in his hands, yet necessary for the journey ahead. He packed provisions sparingly, knowing he would need to move quickly and lightly. He also retrieved a small, intricately carved wooden bird from his father's desk. It was a seemingly insignificant trinket, but he remembered his father explaining its purpose: it was a sound mimic, capable of replicating various animal calls with astonishing accuracy. This could be his diversion.

The plan began to take shape with a terrifying clarity. He would use the night of the autumn equinox, when the celestial alignment and terrestrial markers would converge. He would travel to the supposed location of the gathering, armed with his father's journal and the wooden bird. His objective wasn't necessarily to join the meeting, but to observe, to identify the key players, and if possible, to gather concrete evidence of their activities. He knew the risk of being discovered was immense, but the alternative – remaining ignorant, waiting for the inevitable – was a far greater terror.

He considered the possibility of a trap, a deliberate lure set by those who wished to silence him. Every clue, every piece of information, might be a carefully crafted piece of bait. He had to be prepared for anything. He thought about the way the villagers had averted their gazes when he'd asked about his father's work, the subtle changes in their tone when the conversation veered too close to the village's hidden history. They were protecting something, and they would protect it fiercely.

His father's journal mentioned a specific ritual performed during the equinox, one that involved the channeling of energy from the standing stones. The location of this ritual, according to the coded passages, was to be revealed through a sequence of movements around the central monolith, a dance of sorts, guided by the moon and stars. Joseph realized that this ritual was likely the "gathering" he sought. If he could be present, unseen, and witness this ritual, he might understand the true nature of what was happening in West Seneca.

He began to practice using the wooden bird, experimenting with different calls. The harsh cry of a hawk, the mournful hoot of an owl, the rustling of unseen creatures in the undergrowth. He needed a sound that would draw attention away from his own approach, a sound that would create confusion and a sense of natural disturbance, masking his clandestine movements.

He also needed to consider his escape route. If he was discovered, he couldn't rely on the open paths. He knew the woods intimately from his childhood explorations, the hidden ravines, the dense thickets that offered concealment. He would use his knowledge of the terrain to his advantage, moving through the less-traveled routes, relying on the darkness and the dense foliage as his allies.

The date of the equinox loomed closer, each day bringing a heightened sense of anticipation and dread. Joseph felt a strange calm settle over him. The fear was still present, a cold knot in his stomach, but it was now tempered by a grim determination. He was no longer the naive boy who had arrived in West Seneca seeking answers. He was a man on the precipice of a profound truth, and he was prepared to face whatever lay beyond it.

He decided to make one final reconnaissance mission to the edge of the woods that bordered the standing stones, a few days before the equinox. He wanted to confirm the celestial alignment his father had described and to observe the area for any signs of unusual activity. He moved with practiced silence, the skills honed by weeks of vigilance. As he approached the clearing, he saw them – two figures, silhouetted against the fading light, near the base of the largest standing stone. They were not villagers he recognized. Their posture was rigid, their movements economical and purposeful, like sentinels on duty. They carried no tools, no hunting implements, but there was an unmistakable air of authority, of vigilance, about them. They were guarding the place.

Joseph melted back into the trees, his heart pounding. His father's journal had warned of "guardians," individuals tasked with protecting the sanctity of the ritual site. These were likely them. Their presence confirmed the importance of the location and the need for extreme caution. He needed a way to bypass them, or to distract them, without revealing his own presence.

He returned to his father's study, his mind racing. He reread the passages detailing the ritual, searching for any mention of defenses, of protective measures, or of any vulnerabilities. His father had alluded to a particular time during the ritual when the guardians' attention was divided, when their focus was entirely on the proceedings. This was his chance. He would have to time his approach perfectly, moving in the brief window of distraction.

The plan was solidified: on the night of the equinox, he would approach the standing stones from the west, using the natural cover of the dense woodland. He would conceal himself within the thick undergrowth overlooking the clearing. He would wait for the ritual to commence, observing the participants and the guardians. When the moment of divided attention arrived, he would use the wooden bird to create a diversion on the opposite side of the clearing, drawing the guardians away. In that brief window, he would attempt to approach the central monolith, perhaps to examine the symbols his father had mentioned, or to leave a subtle marker, a sign that he had been there, that he was watching. He knew it was a high-risk gambit, but the potential reward – undeniable proof, a tangible understanding of West Seneca's clandestine heart – was worth the peril. He would be a phantom, a specter of inquiry, aiming to illuminate the darkness without becoming consumed by it. The confrontation was no longer a possibility; it was an inevitability, and Joseph was finally ready to face it, armed with a plan born of desperation and forged in the crucible of his father's secrets.

The weight of his father's journal, once a mere collection of cryptic scribblings, had transformed into a blueprint, a guide to a destiny he could no longer outrun. Joseph stood by the window, the last vestiges of daylight painting the ancient woods in hues of bruised purple and deep indigo. The silence outside was no longer peaceful; it was watchful, pregnant with unspoken threats. He had spent days poring over the entries, the coded references, the hurried sketches of unfamiliar symbols and cryptic locations. Each word, each hastily drawn line, was a piece of a puzzle that had ensnared him, drawing him deeper into the shadowy heart of West Seneca. The encounter at the mill had been a brutal awakening, a stark illustration that polite inquiry and scholarly detachment were no longer viable options. He was no longer an observer; he was a target, and his only hope of survival lay in taking the initiative.

He turned from the window, his gaze falling upon the scattered maps and notes spread across his father's desk. The meticulously drawn lines of the local terrain, the annotations marking hidden springs and forgotten paths, the almost obsessive detailing of the standing stones – these were his arsenal. His father, it was becoming increasingly clear, had been preparing for something, something that involved not just the preservation of West Seneca's secrets, but a potential confrontation. Joseph, armed with this newfound, terrifying understanding, realized he had to do the same. He could not wait for the shadows to engulf him completely; he had to step into them, deliberately, strategically.

His limited resources gnawed at him. He had no allies in this place, no one he could truly trust. The villagers, with their wary eyes and guarded smiles, were a closed book, their loyalty to the ancient ways unquestionable. Silas, the old woodsman, had offered cryptic advice, but Joseph suspected Silas himself was bound by unspoken obligations. Elara Vance, with her unsettling knowledge of his father's affairs, was an enigma, her motives as veiled as the secrets of the valley. He was alone, armed only with his intellect, his father's legacy, and a desperate courage born of necessity.

The plan began to coalesce, not as a fully formed strategy, but as a series of calculated risks, each step designed to peel back another layer of deception. He needed a point of leverage, something that would force the hand of whoever was orchestrating this elaborate charade. His father's journal mentioned a "gathering," a clandestine meeting that occurred during specific lunar phases, held in a location known only by a series of encoded symbols. This gathering, Joseph surmised, was where the decisions were made, where the secrets were guarded, where the true power of West Seneca resided. If he could infiltrate this gathering, or at least disrupt it, he might force the perpetrators into the open.

But how to find this location? The symbols in the journal were abstract, seemingly unconnected to any known cartography. He recalled a passage where his father described a particular constellation visible only during the autumn equinox, a celestial marker that corresponded with a terrestrial landmark. The equinox was only a few days away. That would be his window. He spent hours cross-referencing star charts with his father's rough sketches, the flickering lamplight casting long, dancing shadows that seemed to mimic the unseen observers he felt constantly around him.

He remembered a story his father had told him as a child, about a hidden grove deep within the whispering woods, a place said to be a nexus of ancient energy, marked by a peculiar alignment of ancient trees. Could this be the place? The description was vague, steeped in folklore, but his father had always had a knack for weaving truth into his tales. Joseph decided to investigate, to scout the area, to see if any of the symbols from the journal matched the natural markings of the grove.

His limited resources also extended to his physical capabilities. He was an academic, not a woodsman. While his father had taught him some basic survival skills, he was no match for seasoned hunters or trackers. He would need to rely on stealth, on misdirection, on exploiting the element of surprise. He couldn't engage in a direct confrontation; that would be suicide. He had to be a ghost, a whisper in the wind.

He began to gather what he could. A sturdy hunting knife, a flint and steel, a coil of rope – items that felt alien in his hands, yet necessary for the journey ahead. He packed provisions sparingly, knowing he would need to move quickly and lightly. He also retrieved a small, intricately carved wooden bird from his father's desk. It was a seemingly insignificant trinket, but he remembered his father explaining its purpose: it was a sound mimic, capable of replicating various animal calls with astonishing accuracy. This could be his diversion.

The plan began to take shape with a terrifying clarity. He would use the night of the autumn equinox, when the celestial alignment and terrestrial markers would converge. He would travel to the supposed location of the gathering, armed with his father's journal and the wooden bird. His objective wasn't necessarily to join the meeting, but to observe, to identify the key players, and if possible, to gather concrete evidence of their activities. He knew the risk of being discovered was immense, but the alternative – remaining ignorant, waiting for the inevitable – was a far greater terror.

He considered the possibility of a trap, a deliberate lure set by those who wished to silence him. Every clue, every piece of information, might be a carefully crafted piece of bait. He had to be prepared for anything. He thought about the way the villagers had averted their gazes when he'd asked about his father's work, the subtle changes in their tone when the conversation veered too close to the village's hidden history. They were protecting something, and they would protect it fiercely.

His father's journal mentioned a specific ritual performed during the equinox, one that involved the channeling of energy from the standing stones. The location of this ritual, according to the coded passages, was to be revealed through a sequence of movements around the central monolith, a dance of sorts, guided by the moon and stars. Joseph realized that this ritual was likely the "gathering" he sought. If he could be present, unseen, and witness this ritual, he might understand the true nature of what was happening in West Seneca.

He began to practice using the wooden bird, experimenting with different calls. The harsh cry of a hawk, the mournful hoot of an owl, the rustling of unseen creatures in the undergrowth. He needed a sound that would draw attention away from his own approach, a sound that would create confusion and a sense of natural disturbance, masking his clandestine movements.

He also needed to consider his escape route. If he was discovered, he couldn't rely on the open paths. He knew the woods intimately from his childhood explorations, the hidden ravines, the dense thickets that offered concealment. He would use his knowledge of the terrain to his advantage, moving through the less-traveled routes, relying on the darkness and the dense foliage as his allies.

The date of the equinox loomed closer, each day bringing a heightened sense of anticipation and dread. Joseph felt a strange calm settle over him. The fear was still present, a cold knot in his stomach, but it was now tempered by a grim determination. He was no longer the naive boy who had arrived in West Seneca seeking answers. He was a man on the precipice of a profound truth, and he was prepared to face whatever lay beyond it.

He decided to make one final reconnaissance mission to the edge of the woods that bordered the standing stones, a few days before the equinox. He wanted to confirm the celestial alignment his father had described and to observe the area for any signs of unusual activity. He moved with practiced silence, the skills honed by weeks of vigilance. As he approached the clearing, he saw them – two figures, silhouetted against the fading light, near the base of the largest standing stone. They were not villagers he recognized. Their posture was rigid, their movements economical and purposeful, like sentinels on duty. They carried no tools, no hunting implements, but there was an unmistakable air of authority, of vigilance, about them. They were guarding the place.

Joseph melted back into the trees, his heart pounding. His father's journal had warned of "guardians," individuals tasked with protecting the sanctity of the ritual site. These were likely them. Their presence confirmed the importance of the location and the need for extreme caution. He needed a way to bypass them, or to distract them, without revealing his own presence.

He returned to his father's study, his mind racing. He reread the passages detailing the ritual, searching for any mention of defenses, of protective measures, or of any vulnerabilities. His father had alluded to a particular time during the ritual when the guardians' attention was divided, when their focus was entirely on the proceedings. This was his chance. He would have to time his approach perfectly, moving in the brief window of distraction.

The plan was solidified: on the night of the equinox, he would approach the standing stones from the west, using the natural cover of the dense woodland. He would conceal himself within the thick undergrowth overlooking the clearing. He would wait for the ritual to commence, observing the participants and the guardians. When the moment of divided attention arrived, he would use the wooden bird to create a diversion on the opposite side of the clearing, drawing the guardians away. In that brief window, he would attempt to approach the central monolith, perhaps to examine the symbols his father had mentioned, or to leave a subtle marker, a sign that he had been there, that he was watching. He knew it was a high-risk gambit, but the potential reward – undeniable proof, a tangible understanding of West Seneca's clandestine heart – was worth the peril. He would be a phantom, a specter of inquiry, aiming to illuminate the darkness without becoming consumed by it. The confrontation was no longer a possibility; it was an inevitability, and Joseph was finally ready to face it, armed with a plan born of desperation and forged in the crucible of his father's secrets.

The stark reality of his situation pressed in on him, heavy and suffocating. He had a plan, a perilous, desperate plan, but even the most meticulously crafted strategies could crumble without the right support. He was acting on instinct and fragmented clues, a lone actor in a play where the script was written in invisible ink. He needed more. He needed confirmation. He needed... an ally. The thought felt like a betrayal of his father's solitary quest, a concession to weakness, but the gnawing fear that he was out of his depth, that his own interpretation of the journal's secrets might be fatally flawed, spurred him forward. He couldn't afford to be proud, not when survival was at stake.

He thought of Old Man Hemlock, the proprietor of the general store, his face a roadmap of weathered kindness and a hint of perpetual suspicion. Hemlock had always treated Joseph with a peculiar blend of deference and caution, as if aware of more than he let on, his eyes often lingering on Joseph's father's name, a flicker of something unreadable passing across his features. Perhaps, Joseph mused, a carefully worded inquiry, a seemingly innocent question about local lore, might yield some unexpected insights. He could frame it as a son's attempt to understand his father's fascination with the region, a longing to connect with the history his father held so dear. It was a delicate dance, a tightrope walk between revealing too much and not enough.

He needed to gauge Hemlock's reaction, to feel the pulse of his unspoken knowledge.

Alternatively, there was Mrs. Gable, the village librarian, a woman of quiet dignity and an almost unnerving intellect. She had been a close confidante of his father, often spoken of in hushed, reverent tones by his late mother. Her vast knowledge of local history and her reputation for discretion made her a potential beacon in the fog of deception. Joseph envisioned approaching her under the guise of researching his family's lineage, seeking access to any old town records or personal papers that might have belonged to his father. He could present his father's journal, carefully omitting the more sensitive and coded passages, framing it as an academic curiosity, a historical document he was trying to contextualize. Her insight into his father's motivations, her understanding of the subtle currents that flowed beneath the surface of West Seneca's placid exterior, could be invaluable. He imagined her eyes, sharp and discerning, poring over his father's notes, piecing together the fragments of a story that even he, the son, was still struggling to comprehend.

But there was also the risk of alarming them, of planting seeds of suspicion that could ultimately backfire, making him an even greater target. If Hemlock or Mrs. Gable were somehow complicit, or if their loyalty lay with the unseen forces that shadowed West Seneca, his overtures could be a death sentence. He needed to be certain, or at least reasonably confident, of their trustworthiness before committing to such a risky course of action. The ambiguity was a constant source of anxiety, each potential interaction fraught with the possibility of miscalculation.

Then there was the alternative: a more direct, evidence-gathering approach. His father's journal had mentioned a small, locked shed behind the old mill, a place his father had referred to as his "repository." The sketches in the journal depicted a peculiar, ornate key, a key that Joseph hadn't yet encountered. If he could find that key, if he could gain access to the shed, he might find more tangible proof of his father's research, perhaps even documents or artifacts that explicitly detailed the nature of the threat or the identities of those involved. The mill itself had been the site of his initial, terrifying encounter, a place steeped in a dark, industrial past that now seemed to whisper of present-day secrets. The shed, he imagined, would be a treasure trove of his father's clandestine work, a physical manifestation of his hidden agenda. He visualized himself picking the lock, his fingers fumbling with the mechanism, the click of the tumblers a small victory in the larger battle.

He also recalled a passage describing a "hidden clearing," a place his father used for observation, equipped with what he vaguely termed "listening devices." The description was maddeningly vague, referencing a particular rock formation and a specific type of moss that grew only in that area. Locating this clearing would require a deep dive into the more obscure geographical details of his father's maps, a meticulous cross-referencing of cryptic symbols and natural landmarks. If he could find this place, he might uncover a more systematic collection of intelligence, perhaps recordings or notes detailing the movements and activities of the unknown parties his father feared. It was a more solitary path, one that relied entirely on his own deductive skills and his father's cryptic guidance, but it also offered the promise of unadulterated truth, free from the potential biases or loyalties of others.

He spent the better part of the afternoon poring over his father's maps again, tracing the faint pencil lines that denoted less-traveled paths and uncharted territories. His father's annotations were dense, a complex tapestry of observations and coded notations. One particular symbol, a stylized depiction of a raven's claw, appeared repeatedly in the vicinity of the old mill. He had initially dismissed it as a navigational marker, but now, with a fresh perspective, he wondered if it signified something more, perhaps a personal insignia or a warning. He decided that a cautious approach to the mill, under the cover of darkness, was necessary. He would search the perimeter, looking for any sign of the shed, any indication of the missing key. The thought of returning to the scene of his previous encounter sent a tremor of apprehension through him, but the potential reward of uncovering concrete evidence outweighed the fear. He had to know.

The memory of his father's hushed conversations, the subtle shifts in his demeanor when certain topics arose, began to solidify in Joseph's mind. His father had clearly been involved in something significant, something dangerous, and he had been preparing for it in secret. The journal was not merely a record of discovery; it was a testament to a vigilant mind at work, a mind that anticipated threats and planned countermeasures. Joseph felt a growing sense of responsibility to continue that work, to bring his father's hidden efforts to fruition.

He walked to the bookshelf, his fingers brushing over the worn spines of his father's collected works on ancient history and local folklore. It was here, amidst the dusty tomes, that his father had spent countless hours, seeking answers to questions that had plagued him for years. Joseph picked up a leather-bound volume on the standing stones of the British Isles, a book his father had often referenced. He flipped through the pages, his eyes scanning the dense text and intricate diagrams. He remembered his father's fascination with the astronomical alignments of these ancient sites, his belief that they were not merely ceremonial, but also acted as conduits for natural energies, energies that could be harnessed or, perhaps, exploited.

His father's journal had mentioned a specific alignment, a convergence of celestial bodies that occurred during the autumn equinox, correlating with a terrestrial phenomenon at the standing stones. This alignment, his father believed, was crucial to understanding the true purpose of the site and the rituals conducted there. Joseph's task, then, was twofold: to decipher the precise astronomical calculations his father had used and to locate the specific terrestrial markers that would confirm the alignment.

He needed a more precise understanding of the celestial mechanics involved. While his father's journal offered coded hints, it lacked the detailed astronomical data required for a definitive calculation. He decided his first step should be to visit the village observatory, a small, often overlooked building on the outskirts of town, which his father had been instrumental in establishing years ago. The observatory housed a wealth of astronomical charts, telescopes, and meteorological records that might shed light on his father's calculations. However, the observatory was often maintained by a single, reclusive astronomer, a Mr. Abernathy, who was known for his eccentricities and his reluctance to share his knowledge with outsiders. Joseph would have to approach him with extreme caution, presenting himself as a curious student eager to learn about his father's passion.

In parallel, he needed to revisit the standing stones themselves. His father's journal contained a sketch of the central monolith, with various points marked and annotated with cryptic symbols. Joseph suspected these markings were not merely decorative but served as a key to unlocking the ritual's mechanics, perhaps indicating specific positions or movements required for the channeling of energy. He recalled his father's habit of making detailed observations of the natural surroundings, noting the types of flora, the subtle changes in the terrain, and the patterns of animal behavior. These seemingly minor details might hold the clue to identifying the specific terrestrial markers his father had alluded to.

He also considered the possibility that his father had left physical clues, hidden in plain sight, perhaps concealed within the very fabric of the village. His father had a fondness for puzzles and games, often incorporating hidden messages and codes into his everyday life. Joseph remembered a specific anecdote his father had shared about a time he'd hidden a valuable letter within the intricate workings of the grandfather clock in their ancestral home, only revealing its location through a series of riddles. Could his father have employed similar tactics in West Seneca? He resolved to examine the village clock tower, the old schoolhouse, even the town's historical society, for any anomalies or hidden compartments that might have escaped his initial notice.

The notion of a hidden meeting place also resurfaced in his mind. His father's journal had alluded to a clandestine gathering, a secret assembly where the true power brokers of West Seneca convened. Identifying this location would be paramount. He decided to focus his efforts on the periphery of the village, exploring the less frequented areas, the abandoned farmhouses, and the overgrown sections of the woods. He would pay close attention to any unusual signs of recent activity, any tracks that seemed out of place, or any discarded items that might suggest a clandestine meeting. His father's journal had mentioned a specific type of wild herb that only bloomed near the supposed meeting site, a detail that Joseph had previously overlooked. He resolved to familiarize himself with this herb, to use it as a natural indicator in his search.

The weight of his father's legacy, once a source of comfort and intellectual curiosity, had now become a burden of responsibility. He was no longer just a son seeking to understand his father's past; he was a custodian of his father's unfinished work, a lone sentinel standing against an unseen enemy. He knew that time was not on his side. The equinox was fast approaching, and with it, the opportunity to uncover the truth, or to be consumed by the shadows that had claimed his father. He would need more than just courage; he would need wisdom, allies, and perhaps, a touch of his father's own uncanny foresight. The path ahead was fraught with peril, but Joseph was no longer content to wait for answers to be revealed. He would seek them out, digging into the very heart of West Seneca's secrets, no matter the cost.

He returned to his father's desk, his gaze sweeping across the meticulously organized papers. His father had been a man of order, and even in his absence, his methodical approach provided a framework for Joseph's own investigation. He picked up a small, leather-bound notebook, separate from the main journal, filled with what appeared to be personal reflections and daily observations. His father's handwriting was neat and precise, a stark contrast to the hurried, coded entries in the larger journal. Joseph began to read, hoping to find a more personal perspective, a glimpse into his father's emotional state and his evolving understanding of the situation.

One entry, dated several months prior, caught his eye: "The whispers grow louder. They sense my attention, my scrutiny. I must be more circumspect. The 'gathering' is not merely a meeting; it is a ratification. A sealing of intentions that extend far beyond the confines of this valley. I fear for young Joseph. If only he knew the true nature of his inheritance." The mention of his own name, coupled with the veiled threat, sent a chill down Joseph's spine. His father had been aware of the danger, and he had been protecting him, keeping him in the dark to shield him from the immediate peril. This realization only intensified Joseph's resolve. He couldn't let his father's sacrifice be in vain.

He then turned his attention to a series of sketches at the back of the notebook. They were rough, abstract drawings, depicting symbols that mirrored those found in the main journal, but with additional, more rudimentary annotations. One sketch, in particular, stood out: a crude representation of a specific constellation, accompanied by a single word: "Orion." His father had mentioned Orion in passing, as a point of reference for celestial navigation, but this seemed to carry a deeper significance. Joseph recalled his father's extensive knowledge of astronomy, his ability to identify stars and constellations with remarkable ease. He decided to cross-reference this sketch with his father's astronomical charts, hoping to pinpoint a specific date or time associated with Orion's prominence in the night sky.

The question of the missing key to the shed at the mill continued to nag at him. He had searched the immediate vicinity of the mill on his previous reconnaissance, but the area was vast and overgrown. He needed a more systematic approach. He remembered his father mentioning a collection of his father's personal effects, stored in a dusty attic trunk at the old family home, long since abandoned and now owned by the village council. His father, the elder Joseph, had been a bit of a collector, and it was possible that the key, or at least a clue to its whereabouts, might be among his grandfather's belongings. This would require a trip to the old homestead, a place filled with ghosts of memories, but a necessary pilgrimage if he was to uncover the truth.

He also considered the possibility of approaching the enigmatic Elara Vance. She had expressed an unusual interest in his father's work and had offered him a cryptic warning about the dangers lurking in West Seneca. While her motives remained unclear, her knowledge of his father's affairs was undeniable. Perhaps a direct, yet cautious, confrontation was in order. He could frame his inquiry as a desperate plea for guidance, a young man lost and seeking to understand his father's complex legacy. He would have to tread carefully, however, gauging her reaction, searching for any sign of deception or ulterior motives. He knew she was tied to the village's secrets in ways he couldn't yet fathom, and her cooperation, or her opposition, could significantly alter the course of his investigation.

The village itself, he realized, was a labyrinth of unspoken rules and hidden allegiances. He had observed the villagers' wary glances, their guarded conversations, their ingrained reluctance to delve into the village's darker history. It was clear that many of them were complicit, either through active participation or through silent consent, in whatever was happening in West Seneca. His father had been an outsider, an academic drawn to the region by its history, and he had clearly unearthed something that had made him a target. Joseph, as his son, was now inheriting that dangerous curiosity.

He decided to focus on one immediate objective: to locate the shed at the mill. He meticulously re-examined his father's journal, searching for any further details about its location or the key. He found a small, almost imperceptible annotation near a sketch of the mill's water wheel: "Beneath the raven's perch." The raven's perch – it was a local landmark, a gnarled oak tree that stood sentinel over the mill pond, its branches twisted and contorted like grasping fingers. His father's cryptic clues were becoming more frequent, more pointed, as if he had anticipated Joseph's need for specific directions. He resolved to return to the mill at dawn, when the light would be softer, less revealing, and conduct a thorough search of the area beneath the ancient oak. The key, he felt, was within reach, a tangible piece of the puzzle that would unlock the next stage of his father's hidden investigation.

The thought of seeking help from a trusted adult, a figure of authority or wisdom within the community, was a recurring one. However, the pervasive sense of secrecy that enveloped West Seneca made such an approach fraught with peril. Who, in this insular village, could be truly trusted? His father had been isolated in his investigations, his trusted confidantes few and far between. Joseph understood the wisdom in that caution. To reveal too much, too soon, could be catastrophic. He needed to gather more concrete evidence, to build a foundation of undeniable facts before approaching anyone, lest his inquiries be dismissed as the ramblings of a grief-stricken son.

His father's journal also mentioned a specific pattern of lights that would appear in the windows of the abandoned rectory on certain nights, a signal that his father had been observing with great interest. He had noted the dates of these occurrences, correlating them with lunar cycles and specific astronomical events. If he could witness this signal himself, if he could observe who or what was responsible for it, it might provide a direct link to the clandestine activities of the village's hidden players. He decided to position himself near the rectory on the next night predicted by his father's notes, hidden amongst the dense foliage, a silent observer in the encroaching darkness. He would need to be patient, to wait for the right moment, and to trust his father's meticulous record-keeping.

The collected information, though fragmented, was beginning to form a coherent, albeit terrifying, picture. His father had been investigating a deeply entrenched secret, a conspiracy that involved a significant portion of the village's population and extended to matters of ancient ritual and possibly, a hidden source of power. The standing stones, the celestial alignments, the clandestine gatherings – all pointed to a deliberate, organized effort to maintain this secret, and to silence anyone who threatened to expose it. Joseph understood that his father's death was not an accident. He had been silenced. And now, the mantle of that dangerous investigation had fallen upon his own shoulders. He could no longer afford to be passive. He had to become an active participant, a hunter of truths in a village that preferred to remain in the dark.

He picked up a small, tarnished silver locket from his father's desk, a family heirloom he hadn't thought about in years. His father had always kept it close, a silent reminder of his mother, who had died when Joseph was very young. He opened it, expecting to find their miniature portraits, but instead, he found a tiny, folded piece of paper, inscribed with a sequence of numbers and a single, cryptic word: "Sundial." He had no idea what it meant. It wasn't a reference to any known sundial in the village, nor did it seem to correspond with any astronomical data. It was another puzzle piece, another breadcrumb left by his father, leading him deeper into the mystery. He carefully refolded the paper and placed it back in the locket, tucking it inside his own pocket. It was a tangible connection to his father, a constant reminder of the quest he was now bound to undertake. The information was slowly, painstakingly, coming together, but the picture it painted was one of profound and ancient danger. He needed to trust his father's instincts, to follow the breadcrumbs, and to prepare for the inevitable confrontation.

The raw, unsentimental logic of his father's coded entries, when pieced together with the faint whispers of local lore and the chillingly precise astronomical data unearthed from the dusty observatory records, finally coalesced into a singular, undeniable focal point. It wasn't a grand, imposing structure, nor a place that screamed of ancient power. Instead, it was a place of quiet neglect, a forgotten corner of the valley that had been deliberately overlooked by generations. Joseph had spent hours poring over his father's geological surveys and the intricate maps he'd painstakingly annotated, cross-referencing the unusual geological formations with the recurring symbols that denoted secrecy and concealment. The constellation Orion, so prominently featured in his father's personal notebook, had been the final, luminous key. His father had meticulously documented its position during the autumn equinox, and with it, a terrestrial marker – a solitary, strangely shaped rock formation, described in the journal as "the sentinel's hand."

Tracing this celestial alignment downwards, onto the crumpled topographical map spread across his father's desk, Joseph's finger landed on a small, almost insignificant area nestled deep within the western ridge of the valley. It was a region marked on most maps as simply "uncharted woods," a no-man's-land that even the most experienced hunters tended to avoid. But in his father's private annotations, this patch of wilderness pulsed with meaning. There were multiple symbols here, clustered together like a cluster of stars on his father's map: a triangle within a circle, repeated multiple times, along with the distinct raven's claw insignia that had appeared so frequently near the mill. His father had also drawn a small, almost childlike sketch of a cabin, its roof half-collapsed, surrounded by a dense thicket of brambles. This, Joseph felt with a certainty that resonated deep within his bones, was it. The target location. The nexus of the secret he had been drawn into.

He pictured the scene vividly, his mind's eye painting the rough contours of the ridge, the dense, ancient trees shrouded in perpetual twilight, the whispering of the wind through their skeletal branches. He imagined the isolation of the place, the sheer remoteness that would lend itself to clandestine meetings and hidden activities. The "sentinel's hand" rock formation, a solitary granite outcropping that vaguely resembled a gnarled, petrified hand reaching towards the sky, would serve as an unmistakable landmark, aligning with the celestial positioning of Orion's belt at the appointed hour. And there, nestled beneath its watchful gaze, would be the decaying cabin, the silent witness to his father's final, desperate investigations.

The cabin itself was a phantom in his father's notes, a place spoken of in hushed tones, a "rendezvous point" for those who operated in the shadows. His father had described it as being remarkably well-hidden, almost camouflaged by the natural growth of the surrounding wilderness. He had mentioned a specific path, barely discernible, that led to its entrance, a path that would only be apparent to those who knew precisely where to look. The ravens, those dark harbingers of ill omen that seemed to flock to West Seneca, were also mentioned in connection with this location, their eerie caws a constant presence that his father had interpreted as territorial markers, or perhaps, even sentinels of their own kind.

He could almost feel the damp earth beneath his feet, the tangled undergrowth snagging at his clothes as he navigated the treacherous terrain. The air would be thick with the scent of pine needles and decaying leaves, a potent, earthy perfume that belied the sinister purpose of the place. He envisioned the silence, broken only by the natural sounds of the forest, but a silence that would carry the weight of unspoken observation, the prickling sensation of unseen eyes watching his every move. His father had written about the unnerving stillness that permeated the area, a unnatural quiet that seemed to absorb all sound, all life. It was a place that held its breath, waiting.

Joseph imagined approaching the cabin under the cloak of darkness, the sliver of moon offering scant illumination. He would need to move with extreme caution, his senses heightened, attuned to the slightest anomaly. The "sentinel's hand" rock would be his guide, its dark silhouette a stark contrast against the bruised indigo sky. The path his father described, the one that was "only apparent to those who knew," would likely be a faint depression in the forest floor, a subtle disturbance in the natural order of things. He would need to tread lightly, to avoid disturbing any tell-tale signs of recent passage.

He imagined the cabin itself: a skeletal structure, its timbers weathered and gray, its windows dark, empty sockets staring out into the night. The collapsed roof would have allowed the elements to reclaim much of the interior, but his father's sketches suggested that the core structure remained intact, a shell that had been deliberately preserved, or perhaps, simply forgotten. He pictured the overgrown brambles, a thorny barricade that would deter any casual wanderer, a natural defense that had served its purpose well for years. Yet, his father had indicated a small, almost imperceptible break in the brambles, a narrow aperture that led to a hidden entrance.

His father had also mentioned a specific type of moss, a vibrant, almost luminous emerald green, that grew exclusively on the north-facing side of the cabin's foundation stones. This moss, he had speculated, was a byproduct of the unique geological composition of the area, a composition that might be tied to the very reason for the cabin's clandestine use. It was another marker, another breadcrumb left by his father, a detail so specific that it could only have been observed through prolonged, dedicated surveillance.

The anticipation, a cold, sharp knot in his stomach, began to tighten. He was no longer just deciphering clues; he was preparing to walk into the heart of the mystery. He visualized himself kneeling by the foundation stones, his fingers brushing against the cool, damp moss, searching for any sign of disturbance, any indication of recent activity. He would be looking for more than just a physical presence; he would be searching for the residual energy of their meetings, the faint echoes of their whispered conversations, the intangible aura of their secrets.

He knew that the location itself might be more than just a meeting place; it could be the source, the origin point from which the influence of West Seneca's hidden society radiated. The standing stones, the astronomical alignments, the secluded cabin – they all seemed to converge in this one, forgotten corner of the valley. His father had believed that this area possessed a unique energetic signature, a confluence of natural forces that made it ideal for their rituals and their machinations. Joseph felt a sense of awe mingled with dread, the dawning realization that he was stepping onto ground that had been trod by those who wielded a power he could only begin to comprehend.

He considered the possibility of encountering others there. His father's journal had alluded to sentinels, individuals tasked with guarding these secret locations, individuals who would not hesitate to eliminate any perceived threat. He imagined them as shadows themselves, blending seamlessly into the darkness, their senses honed to detect the slightest intrusion. He would need to be not just observant, but invisible. His movements would have to be fluid, silent, and utterly deliberate. He would be an intruder in their sanctuary, and his presence would not be tolerated.

He thought about the items he would need to bring. A reliable source of light, though one that would cast the least amount of illumination, perhaps a shielded lantern or a simple candle. His father's journal, the key to understanding his father's journey and the secrets he had uncovered. The small, carved wooden bird, his father's ingenious sound mimic, which he now recognized as a vital tool for diversion and escape. A sturdy knife, for protection and utility, and a coil of rope, for navigating any unexpected obstacles. He packed them with a newfound sense of purpose, each item imbued with the weight of his father's legacy and the gravity of his own mission.

He visualized the moment of arrival. The final approach, the careful scanning of the perimeter, the moment of confirmation as he identified the weathered cabin, partially obscured by the encroaching wilderness. He would pause, take a breath, and then, he would move forward, into the heart of the unknown, ready to confront the legacy his father had left for him. The target location identified, the path laid bare, the confrontation beckoned. He was no longer a mere observer of West Seneca's secrets; he was about to become a participant, whether he wished to or not. The air in his father's study seemed to grow colder, the silence more profound, as he made the final preparations for his journey into the deep woods, towards the place where his father's quest had ultimately led him, and where his own perilous journey was about to truly begin. The cabin was more than just a destination; it was a gateway, and he was about to step through it.

The chill of the pre-dawn air did little to penetrate the resolve hardening within Joseph. He moved through his father's study with a quiet deliberation, each movement measured, each decision weighed. The clues were gathered, the destination fixed, but the journey itself was still an abyss of uncertainty. Now came the practicalities, the grounding of abstract discovery into tangible preparation. His gaze swept over the worn surfaces of the desk, lingering on the tools of his father's trade that had become his own inheritance.

His father's hunting knife, its well-worn leather handle smooth under Joseph's touch, felt like an extension of his own hand. It was more than just a blade; it was a symbol of survival, of resourcefulness. He tested its edge against his thumb, the keenness a familiar reassurance. Beside it lay a sturdy length of oak, a walking stick that his father had crafted himself, its surface etched with a pattern that Joseph now recognized as a stylized representation of the constellation Orion. It was a practical tool, certainly, but also a talisman, a constant reminder of the celestial alignment that had guided him. He hefted it, feeling the reassuring weight, imagining it as a defensive aid, a means to ward off unseen threats in the dense woods.

Next, his attention turned to the lantern. The oil lamp, its glass cloudy with disuse, felt fragile compared to the stark reality of his objective. He carefully cleaned the glass, then found a small, stoppered flask of lamp oil tucked away in a drawer. Filling it was a delicate operation, the dark liquid glinting dully in the faint light. He checked the wick, ensuring it was properly seated, ready to cast its hesitant glow into the encroaching darkness. He understood the need for light, but also the danger of drawing attention. This would be a tool of necessity, used sparingly, its beam carefully controlled.

He also considered the pieces of the puzzle that still lay scattered on the desk. The small, intricately carved wooden raven, a piece of art that now represented something far more sinister. He picked it up, turning it over and over in his fingers. Was there some hidden compartment? Some further message encoded within its delicate form? He had found no such indication, yet a nagging intuition told him it was more than mere decoration. He placed it carefully in his pocket, a tangible link to the very heart of the mystery, a potential key to understanding if not to immediate action. He also unearthed a small, leather-bound diary, separate from his father's main journals. This one was filled with shorter, more cryptic entries, almost like coded observations. One particular passage, dated just a few weeks before his father's disappearance, caught his eye: "The sentinel's eye watches. The silence speaks of preparation. They know the alignment approaches." He tucked this into his satchel as well, a chilling premonition now imbued with a sense of immediate relevance.

His father's satchel, a sturdy canvas bag, was already partially packed with essentials – a waterskin, a small quantity of dried rations, a flint and steel. Joseph added his chosen tools, carefully arranging them so they wouldn't rattle or snag. He felt a strange sense of calm settle over him, a clarity born from the sheer necessity of action. The fear was still there, a cold undercurrent, but it was now overlaid with a steely determination. He was not a warrior, nor a seasoned woodsman, but he was his father's son, and he carried the weight of his father's quest.

He paused before the tarnished hand mirror that lay on his father's vanity. He picked it up, meeting his own reflection. The boy staring back was older than his years, his eyes holding a gravity that belied his youth. The playful spark that had once resided there had been replaced by a somber intensity, a reflection of the darkness he was about to step into. He saw the fear, yes, but he also saw the nascent courage, the flicker of defiance. He had to believe that this was enough. He had to believe that his father's legacy, his father's courage, would somehow guide him.

He remembered his father's quiet strength, his unwavering commitment to truth, even when it led him down dangerous paths. Joseph knew that he was embarking on a journey his father had been forced to abandon, a journey that had ultimately cost him everything. The thought was a heavy burden, but it was also a powerful motivator. He couldn't falter now. He couldn't let his father's efforts be in vain. The fate of whatever secret lay hidden in the woods, and perhaps even the truth of his father's death, rested on his shoulders.

He ran a hand over the smooth wood of the desk, a final farewell to this sanctuary of knowledge. The air in the study felt charged, thick with unspoken anticipation. Outside, the first tentative hints of dawn were beginning to paint the sky in shades of gray and rose, a stark contrast to the encroaching darkness he was about to embrace. He pulled on a thick woolen jacket, the familiar scent of his father's pipe tobacco clinging to it, a comforting anchor in the sea of the unknown.

He took a deep breath, the air filling his lungs, bracing himself for the physical and emotional toll that lay ahead. He was venturing into a world that operated by different rules, a world where shadows held sway and secrets were guarded with lethal intent. His father's meticulous notes had provided the map, but the terrain itself remained untamed, unpredictable. He was stepping out of the familiar into the profoundly alien, armed with little more than his father's legacy and a nascent courage that felt both fragile and impossibly strong.

The thought of the "sentinel's hand" rock formation came to him again. A guide, yes, but also a silent, stoic witness. He imagined it as his father had described it, a gnarled, petrified hand reaching skyward, an ancient sentinel guarding the valley's deepest secrets. This silent guardian, he knew, would be his first true marker, confirming his arrival in the territory his father had identified. The journey to it would be fraught with its own challenges, the rough terrain, the possibility of getting lost, the ever-present threat of encountering those who wished to keep these secrets buried.

He pictured the path his father had hinted at, the one that was "only apparent to those who knew." He imagined it as a subtle break in the undergrowth, a barely perceptible disturbance in the forest floor, a secret whispered by the earth itself. He would need to be hyper-vigilant, his senses on high alert for the slightest anomaly, the faintest sign of passage. His father's journals had stressed the importance of observation, of noticing the details that others overlooked. This would be his primary weapon: a keen eye and an unwavering focus.

He thought about the ravens, the dark birds that seemed to be inextricably linked to West Seneca's hidden society. His father had interpreted their presence as territorial markers, or perhaps even sentinels. He wondered if they would be watching him, their dark eyes following his progress through the trees, their raucous calls a warning to others. He hoped they would mistake him for just another creature of the forest, another transient being passing through their domain.

The weight of his father's mission settled upon Joseph's young shoulders with an almost palpable force. It was a heavy burden, one that few his age would be expected to carry. Yet, he felt a strange sense of peace in this responsibility. It was a connection to his father that transcended death, a tangible continuation of his father's unfinished work. He was not just seeking answers for himself; he was seeking justice for his father, and perhaps, for the truth of West Seneca itself.

He packed a small notebook and pencil, determined to record his own observations, to add his own chapter to his father's legacy. He felt a surge of adrenaline, a tightening in his chest, as he closed the satchel. The time for preparation was over. The time for action had arrived. He cast one last look around the study, a silent promise made to the memory of the man who had inspired this perilous undertaking. Then, with a steady breath, Joseph stepped out of the quiet study and into the uncertain dawn, the unknown awaiting him in the depths of the western ridge. The confrontation beckoned, and he was ready to answer its call.

The moon, a sliver of bone against the inky canvas of the sky, offered little solace. Joseph sat by the window of his father's old room, the rough-hewn wood cool beneath his forearms. The village of West Seneca lay below, a patchwork of muted lights and deep shadows, the silence unnerving. Each creak of the house, each rustle of leaves outside, seemed amplified in the pre-dawn stillness, like whispers of a truth he was about to disturb. The weight of his father's legacy pressed down on him, a heavy cloak woven from love, loss, and an unyielding quest for answers. The meticulous planning, the careful gathering of his father's tools – they were anchors in a swirling sea of uncertainty, yet they did little to quell the tremor in his hands.

He traced the constellations etched onto his father's walking stick, the oak cool and solid beneath his touch. Orion, the hunter, a silent guide through the darkness. His father had always spoken of the stars with a quiet reverence, as if they held the secrets the earth tried to conceal. Now, Joseph felt a kinship with that celestial vigil, a solitary figure waiting for a dawn that promised revelation, or perhaps, further concealment. He replayed the cryptic entries from his father's hidden diary in his mind, the words "The sentinel's eye watches. The silence speaks of preparation. They know the alignment approaches" echoing with a new, chilling resonance. The sentinel. Was it the rock formation, the "sentinel's hand," as his father had called it? Or was it something, or someone, else?

He unclasped the worn leather satchel, its familiar scent of oil and aged canvas a comforting counterpoint to the gnawing anxiety. He checked the waterskin, ensuring it was full, its leather supple. The dried rations, a meager supply, seemed insufficient for the journey he envisioned, yet he knew that speed and stealth were paramount. The flint and steel, a humble yet vital tool, lay nestled amongst the provisions. He ran his thumb over the carved raven, its smooth wood a stark contrast to the jagged edges of the mystery it represented. His father had believed the ravens were more than mere birds; they were watchers, messengers, perhaps even guardians of a hidden order. He wondered if they would be watching him tonight, their keen eyes tracking his movements from the skeletal branches of the ancient oaks.

The lamp, its glass now gleaming after his diligent cleaning, sat on the windowsill. He pictured its hesitant glow illuminating the path ahead, a small beacon against the overwhelming darkness. But the thought of its light also brought a prickle of fear. Light attracted attention, and attention was the last thing he wanted. He would have to be judicious, using it only when absolutely necessary, when the path dissolved into impenetrable shadow. His father's instructions had been clear: observe, remain unseen, and trust the instincts honed by careful study.

He remembered the night his father had disappeared. The quiet unease that had settled over their small cottage, the unanswered questions that hung in the air like dust motes in a sunbeam. He had been so young then, too young to understand the depth of his father's research, too young to grasp the danger he had courted. Now, standing on the precipice of a similar confrontation, Joseph felt a profound sense of both loss and purpose. He was walking in his father's footsteps, not out of obligation, but out of a desperate need to understand, to honor, and perhaps, to avenge.

The village was stirring. A dog barked in the distance, a sharp, insistent sound that cut through the quiet. A light flickered on in one of the cottages, a sign of life that felt both reassuring and a stark reminder of the normalcy he was about to disrupt. He pulled on his thickest woolen jacket, the scent of his father's pipe tobacco a familiar embrace, a ghost of comfort in the encroaching chill. He was not a woodsman, nor a fighter. His father had been a scholar, a seeker of knowledge, and Joseph was his inheritor. But there was a resilience in him, a quiet stubbornness that had been forged in the crucible of grief.

He closed his eyes, picturing the map his father had painstakingly drawn, the intricate details of the terrain, the specific markers that would guide him. The old mill, the whispering creek, the ancient cluster of yew trees. Each landmark was a waypoint, a confirmation that he was on the right path. The "sentinel's hand" rock formation was the ultimate destination, the place where the final truth, or the final danger, awaited. He imagined its weathered, stony fingers reaching skyward, a silent testament to the enduring power of nature and the secrets it guarded.

He stood up, stretching his limbs, a small victory against the stiffness that threatened to betray his apprehension. The air in the room felt heavy, charged with anticipation. He had to move. The night was waning, and the dawn would bring its own set of challenges, its own heightened awareness from those who wished to remain hidden. He picked up the tarnished hand mirror from his father's vanity, its surface clouded with age. His reflection stared back – a boy, yes, but a boy carrying the burden of a man's quest. The fear was a tangible presence, a cold knot in his stomach, but it was tempered by a nascent courage, a fierce determination to see this through. His father's quiet strength, his unwavering pursuit of truth, even when it led him into the shadows, was his inheritance.

He slipped out of the room, the floorboards creaking a soft protest. The house felt eerily empty, a hollow echo of the life it once held. He moved through the darkened halls like a shadow himself, his every sense heightened. He could almost feel his father's presence, a guiding whisper in the silence, urging him forward. He paused at the front door, his hand hovering over the latch. The world outside was a vast unknown, a landscape painted in shades of moonlight and shadow. He was stepping into a realm where the familiar rules of West Seneca no longer applied, a place where secrets were guarded with a vigilance that could prove fatal.

The journey to the sentinel's hand was more than just a physical trek; it was a descent into a labyrinth of his father's making, a deciphering of cryptic clues left behind by a man who had vanished into the very mystery he sought to unravel. Joseph knew that his father had been close, terrifyingly close, to uncovering something of immense significance. The intensity of his father's final journal entries, the hurried, almost desperate tone, spoke of an imminent discovery, and an equally imminent danger. This was not just about finding answers; it was about understanding the forces that had silenced his father, and preventing them from silencing him too.

He recalled the specific phrasing in one of his father's notes: "The subtle disturbance in the natural order, the slight divergence from the expected path – these are the signs. They are not meant to be seen by the casual observer, but by the one who knows where to look." This implied a hidden trail, a path discernible only to those who understood the language of the woods, the silent signals that nature itself offered. Joseph felt a surge of pride, a connection to his father's keen intellect, his ability to perceive the world with an almost supernatural clarity. He had inherited that eye, that ability to see beyond the superficial.

He gripped the oak walking stick, its familiar weight grounding him. It was a tool of navigation, a potential weapon, and a symbol of his lineage. His father had carved it, imbued it with his own spirit, and now it served as a tangible link between father and son, a bridge across the chasm of absence. He thought of the constellation Orion again, its prominent belt a beacon in the night sky. His father had often pointed it out, explaining its significance in ancient lore, its role as a celestial guide. Now, Joseph felt as if Orion itself was watching over him, a silent promise of a clear path through the encroaching darkness.

He remembered the day his father had taken him to the edge of the woods, pointing out the seemingly ordinary rock formations, weaving tales of local legends and hidden wonders. Joseph had been enthralled, imagining secret passages and forgotten treasures. He hadn't understood then that those tales were not just stories, but fragments of a deeper, more dangerous truth. His father had been laying the groundwork, subtly preparing him, perhaps, for the very journey he was now undertaking. The thought sent a shiver down his spine, a mix of awe and trepidation.

The wind picked up, rustling the leaves outside with a sound like hushed whispers. It felt as if the forest itself was acknowledging his presence, a silent observer of his solitary vigil. He looked out at the village one last time, the few remaining lights twinkling like distant stars. It was a world he was about to leave behind, a world of order and familiarity, for a world of ancient secrets and unseen forces. He was ready. He had to be. The memory of his father's hopeful smile, the glint of curiosity in his eyes, spurred him onward. He would not let his father's quest end in unanswered questions. He would not let the shadows win.

The satchel contained not just physical tools, but also the collected wisdom of his father's research. The meticulously drawn maps, the annotated passages from obscure texts, the pressed leaves and carefully cataloged stones – each item was a piece of a complex puzzle, a breadcrumb trail leading him deeper into the unknown. He ran his fingers over the rough paper, feeling the tangible evidence of his father's relentless pursuit. It was a pursuit that had consumed him, ultimately leading him to this precipice, this moment of confrontation.

He took a deep, steadying breath, the cool night air filling his lungs. The faint scent of pine and damp earth drifted through the open window, a primal invitation from the wilderness that lay beyond the village. He was no longer just Joseph, the boy who had lost his father. He was Joseph, the seeker, the inheritor of a dangerous legacy, the one who dared to venture into the heart of West Seneca's hidden truth. The pre-dawn chill was a reminder of the cold reality awaiting him, but it was also a bracing tonic, sharpening his senses, steeling his resolve. He had to trust his father's guidance, his father's instincts, and now, his own. The night was a crucible, and he was about to be tested. He felt the first stirrings of dawn on the horizon, a faint blush of rose painting the eastern sky. It was time. The confrontation beckoned, and he would answer.

7

The Climax Unfolds

The old oak walking stick felt like an extension of Joseph's own arm, its worn smoothness a familiar comfort against the rough wool of his sleeve. Each step he took away from the familiar, shadowed cottages of West Seneca was a deliberate plunge into the deepening night. The village, a cluster of slumbering houses, seemed to hold its breath as he passed, the silence punctuated only by the distant, mournful cry of a barn owl and the frantic thumping of his own heart. He moved with a stealth born of desperation, a silent wraith against the tapestry of shadow. The moon, a mere sliver tonight, offered no illumination, but that was a blessing, not a curse. Darkness was his ally, his cloak, his shield.

He skirted the edge of the common, the dew-laden grass cool beneath the soles of his sturdy boots, a stark contrast to the agitated heat that pulsed through his veins. Every snap of a twig, every sigh of the wind through the skeletal branches of the ancient yews, sent a jolt of adrenaline through him. His father's words echoed in his mind, a constant, low hum of caution: *"They are watchful. They are patient. The stillness is their symphony."* Was that rustle in the undergrowth the passage of a nocturnal creature, or was it the deliberate movement of a pursuer? He couldn't be sure, and the uncertainty gnawed at him, sharpening his senses to a painful degree.

The path he followed was one he had trod countless times before, a winding track through the woods that bordered West Seneca, leading towards the rolling hills that cradled the "sentinel's hand." But tonight, these familiar woods felt alien, imbued with a sinister aura. The trees seemed to lean in, their branches like grasping fingers, the shadows between them deeper, more menacing than he remembered. He imagined eyes watching him from the darkness, unseen sentinels of the secret his father had sought. He kept his gaze fixed on the faint outline of the path ahead, his breathing shallow, controlled. He dared not whistle, dared not hum, dared not betray his presence with any unnecessary sound.

He recalled his father's detailed notes on the local flora and fauna, his observations on the subtle shifts in the wind, the particular calls of birds that indicated a presence not their own. His father had possessed an uncanny ability to read the language of the wilderness, a skill honed through years of quiet observation. Joseph clung to that knowledge, trying to filter his own fear through the lens of his father's teachings. Was that particular stillness in the air a sign of something amiss, or just the natural lull before the dawn?

The weight of the satchel on his shoulder was a constant reminder of the purpose of his journey. It contained not just supplies, but the very essence of his father's last days: the worn maps, the cryptic journal entries, the fragments of strange artifacts. He fingered the smooth, cool obsidian shard tucked securely in a side pocket, a piece of his father's collection that had always held a particular fascination, and a certain unease. His father had written of its unusual properties, its connection to "places of ancient power," and the unsettling feeling it evoked. Now, holding it, Joseph felt a similar prickle of disquiet, as if the very object pulsed with a hidden energy, a silent witness to the events to come.

He reached the old mill, its derelict timbers groaning in the breeze, a silhouette against the faintest hint of pre-dawn light beginning to touch the eastern horizon. The waterwheel, long since seized by rust and disuse, stood still, a skeletal sentinel guarding the entrance to a forgotten era. This was a waypoint, a marker on his father's map, and a place where a particular, unsettling silence usually reigned. Tonight, however, he detected a subtle deviation from that norm. A faint, almost imperceptible humming, a low vibration that seemed to emanate from the very earth beneath his feet. It was too consistent to be the wind, too rhythmic to be natural. He froze, straining his ears, his senses on high alert. Was it the sound of machinery, or something more... organic?

He moved closer, hugging the shadow of the decaying stone wall, his hand instinctively going to the sturdy oak stick. The humming grew marginally louder, a deep resonance that seemed to vibrate through the soles of his boots. He peered through a broken pane of glass, his eyes scanning the interior of the mill. Dust motes danced in the sliver of moonlight that pierced the gloom, illuminating the rusted gears and cobweb-draped machinery. Nothing seemed out of the ordinary at first glance. Then, his gaze fell upon a section of the stone floor, near the massive central grinding stone. It was cleaner than the surrounding area, as if recently disturbed. And the humming, he realized with a chilling certainty, was coming from *beneath* it.

His father's notes had spoken of hidden passages, of subterranean chambers where ancient rituals had once been performed. Could this be one of them? The thought sent a fresh wave of fear through him, but it was mingled with a burgeoning curiosity, a desperate need to understand. He dropped to his knees, ignoring the rough grit of the floor, and began to examine the stones more closely. His fingers, trained by his father's meticulous work, searched for any sign of a seam, a lever, a hidden mechanism. The humming seemed to pulse in time with his own racing heartbeat, an unsettling duet in the oppressive silence.

He found it. A small, almost invisible indentation on one of the larger flagstones, barely discernible to the touch. His father had described such a catch in his journal, a pressure-activated release mechanism. With trembling fingers, Joseph pressed down. There was a soft click, followed by a grinding sound as the stone slowly, reluctantly, began to retract into the floor, revealing a gaping maw of darkness below. The humming intensified, accompanied now by a faint, earthy smell, like damp soil and something else... something metallic, almost acrid.

This was it. The "danger zone" his father had alluded to in his final, frantic scrawlings. This was the threshold he had to cross. He hesitated for a moment, the enormity of what lay before him pressing down on him. The path ahead was shrouded in an impenetrable blackness, and the sounds emanating from it were alien, disquieting. He could still turn back, return to the safety of his father's empty house, and pretend that none of this was happening. But the image of his father's determined face, the memory of his unwavering quest for truth, anchored him. He was not going back.

He pulled out his father's lamp, the tarnished metal cool in his hand. He hesitated, remembering his father's warning about drawing attention, but the darkness below was absolute. He needed light. With a deep breath, he struck the flint and steel. A spark flared, catching the oil-soaked wick, and a hesitant, flickering glow bloomed, pushing back the oppressive blackness. The light revealed a rough-hewn stone staircase, descending steeply into the earth. The air that rose from it was cold, carrying with it the unnerving hum and the acrid scent. It felt like stepping into the mouth of a beast.

He took the first step, his boots crunching on loose gravel. The stone slab slid shut behind him with a final, echoing thud, sealing him in. The darkness of the mill above was replaced by an even more profound, suffocating blackness, broken only by the small circle of light cast by his lamp. The humming seemed to surround him now, a pervasive vibration that filled his ears and seemed to settle in his very bones. He could feel it in the damp stone of the walls, in the stale air he breathed. It was a presence, a tangible force that seemed to emanate from the depths of this hidden place.

He continued his descent, his movements slow and deliberate. Each step was an act of courage, a testament to his resolve. He scanned the walls with his lamp, looking for any clues, any markings his father might have left. The stone was rough and irregular, stained with centuries of damp. There were no carvings, no inscriptions, nothing to indicate what lay at the bottom of this descent. The only constant was the hum, and the growing sense of unease that coiled tighter and tighter in his gut. He thought of the raven carved into his walking stick, its dark eye seeming to watch him from the shadows. He wished for its silent guidance, its own connection to the hidden world his father had so avidly explored.

The staircase finally leveled out, opening into a low, cavernous space. The humming was loudest here, a deep, resonant thrum that seemed to emanate from the very center of the chamber. His lamp cast long, dancing shadows, making the rough-hewn walls seem to shift and writhe. The air was thick, heavy with a cloying, metallic scent that made his eyes water. He held his breath, trying to discern the source of the sound, the origin of the oppressive atmosphere.

And then he saw it. In the center of the chamber, bathed in the faint, ethereal glow of his lamp, was an object that defied explanation. It was large, metallic, and intricately crafted, its surface a dull, burnished bronze that seemed to absorb the light rather than reflect it. Strange, angular symbols were etched into its surface, symbols he didn't recognize, yet which stirred a primal recognition deep within him. The humming emanated from this object, a steady, powerful vibration that resonated with an otherworldly intensity. It was a machine, perhaps, or something far older, far more alien. His father had found it. And whatever it was, it was the heart of the mystery, the source of the danger that had swallowed him whole. He was in the danger zone, and the climax was indeed unfolding.

Joseph crept closer, the rough stone cool against his cheek as he pressed his eye against a narrow gap between two colossal, lichen-covered boulders. The air was thick with the metallic tang he'd noticed before, but now it was underscored by a subtle, almost floral sweetness that was profoundly unsettling. He held his breath, his heart a frantic drummer against his ribs, and willed his eyes to adjust to the dim light filtering from the strange object his father had discovered. The humming, which had seemed to vibrate through his very bones in the subterranean chamber, was muted here, a low, persistent murmur that only served to heighten the tension.

He was in a natural amphitheater, a bowl-shaped depression hidden within the rolling hills, shielded by dense thickets of gorse and ancient hawthorn. The strange, bronze artifact, which Joseph had glimpsed from the mill's depths, pulsed with a soft, internal luminescence, casting an eerie, green-tinged glow across the immediate vicinity. It was unlike anything he had ever seen, a complex interplay of interlocking gears and smooth, obsidian-like panels, all arranged in a pattern that seemed both mathematically precise and disturbingly organic. Runes, the same alien script etched onto the artifact, were also faintly traced onto the exposed rock faces around the clearing, as if the very earth here bore witness to its presence.

Then, he saw them. Figures, cloaked and hooded, moved with a silent, purposeful grace around the artifact. Their movements were not those of ordinary villagers; they were too fluid, too coordinated, too... ritualistic. They seemed to commune with the pulsating machine, their hands hovering over its surfaces, their heads bowed as if in prayer. Joseph's father's frantic scribbles about "devotion" and "the offering" flashed through his mind. This was no clandestine meeting; it was a communion.

One of the figures, taller than the others, with a distinctly different cut to their heavy, dark robes, stepped forward. In their hands, they held a small, intricately carved wooden box. As they approached the artifact, the humming intensified, and the green luminescence of the machine brightened perceptibly. Joseph's breath hitched. He recognized the box. It was the one his father had kept locked away in his study, the one Joseph had always been forbidden to touch. His father had hinted that it contained "the seed of truth," a phrase that had always sounded like a poetic metaphor, but now... now it felt chillingly literal.

The cloaked figure opened the box. Inside, nestled on a bed of dried, dark herbs, was a cluster of glistening, almost crystalline seeds. They seemed to capture and refract the artifact's light, radiating a faint warmth that Joseph could almost feel even from his concealed position. He watched, mesmerized and horrified, as the figure carefully placed the box onto a small, recessed platform on the artifact.

For a long moment, nothing happened. The figures remained motionless, their collective gaze fixed on the machine. Then, with a soft, resonant *thrum*, the artifact began to whir. A fine mist, shimmering with an iridescent quality, began to rise from the seeds. The mist curled around the artifact, clinging to its metallic surfaces, and then, as if drawn by an invisible force, began to disperse into the surrounding air. The floral scent intensified, sweet and cloying, making Joseph's head swim.

He recognized the scent now. It was the same peculiar fragrance that had emanated from the dried herbs found clutched in his father's hand. His father hadn't been hallucinating, nor had he simply been smelling flowers. He had been sensing the residual effects of this... ritual.

The cloaked figures began to stir, their heads lifting. They exchanged silent gestures, and then, one by one, they turned their attention towards the periphery of the clearing. Joseph froze, his blood running cold. Had they seen him? He pressed himself deeper into the shadows, his hands clasped over his mouth to stifle any sound. He was too exposed, too visible. The rocks offered some cover, but the clearing was relatively open, and the pale light from the artifact, though dim, seemed to illuminate everything.

He risked another peek. They weren't looking directly at him, but their gazes swept across the area with an unnerving intensity. Their heads were tilted, as if listening, and Joseph realized with a sickening lurch that they were likely attuned to anything out of the ordinary, any disruption to their carefully orchestrated ceremony. His father had spoken of their "awareness," their ability to sense deviation.

The taller figure, the one who had handled the box of seeds, made a low, guttural sound. It wasn't a word, but a communication, a signal. The other figures began to gather their belongings, their movements still deliberate and silent. They were preparing to leave. Joseph knew he had to do something, but what? He couldn't confront them. He was one boy against a group of individuals who operated with such unnerving precision, who wielded technology or magic – he couldn't tell which – that felt utterly alien.

He watched as they carefully extinguished the artifact's luminescence, plunging the clearing back into near darkness, save for the sliver of moonlight filtering through the trees. Then, with a final, almost imperceptible nod to the inert machine, they melted back into the shadows from whence they came, their cloaks blending seamlessly with the night.

Joseph remained frozen for several long minutes after they had gone, his body rigid with a mixture of fear and disbelief. The clearing was silent once more, save for the rustling of leaves in the gentle night breeze. The sweet, cloying scent still lingered, a phantom whisper of the unsettling event he had just witnessed. He had seen it. The secret was no longer an abstract concept gleaned from his father's cryptic notes; it was a tangible, horrifying reality.

He had witnessed the heart of West Seneca's hidden agenda. The artifact, whatever its true nature, was central to it. And the seeds... what were those seeds? His father had been obsessed with finding them, convinced they held a key to understanding a deeper truth about the village and its enigmatic inhabitants. Now Joseph understood why. These weren't just seeds; they were an ingredient, a catalyst for whatever process the artifact facilitated.

He slowly, cautiously, moved from his hiding place, his legs stiff and trembling. He approached the artifact. It was cool to the touch now, its inner glow extinguished. The runes on its surface seemed fainter, dormant. He ran his fingers over the recessed platform where the box had been placed. It was smooth, unremarkable. He looked around the clearing, searching for any sign of the seeds themselves, but the fine mist seemed to have dissipated completely, leaving no trace.

He thought of his father. Had he known this would happen? Had he intended for Joseph to witness this? The weight of his father's legacy felt heavier than ever. His father had been trying to uncover this secret, to expose it. But what could a single boy do against such a well-organized, clandestine operation?

He knew he couldn't stay here. The risk of discovery was too great. He needed to get back, to process what he had seen, to try and make sense of it all. His father's journal, his maps, the fragments of artifacts – they were all in his satchel. He had to examine them with this new, terrifying context.

As he turned to leave the clearing, his foot scuffed against something small and hard on the ground. He bent down and picked it up. It was a single, dried herb, dark and brittle, retaining a faint, almost imperceptible trace of that peculiar floral sweetness. It was identical to the ones he had seen in the wooden box. A tangible piece of the evidence, dropped in haste, perhaps.

He clutched the herb tightly in his fist, the rough texture a grounding sensation amidst the swirling confusion in his mind. He looked back at the silent, brooding artifact one last time, a monument to a hidden world operating just beneath the surface of his own. The mystery was far from solved; it had only deepened, transforming from an academic puzzle into a dangerous reality. He had seen the secret in action, and now he knew, with a chilling certainty, that he could never unsee it. The path back to West Seneca felt longer, darker, and infinitely more perilous than the journey out. He had stepped through a veil, and he could never truly return to the world he had left behind. The weight of his father's quest, and the truth he had just witnessed, now rested squarely on his young shoulders. He had to be more than just a curious boy; he had to become something more. He had to become the next step in his father's investigation, armed with a truth that could either save them all, or damn him. The silence of the hills seemed to mock him, pregnant with unspoken warnings. He started his journey back, the single dried herb a potent talisman of the dangerous knowledge he now possessed.

The cool night air, which had moments before felt like a suffocating blanket of secrecy, now crackled with a palpable tension that jolted Joseph to his core. The lingering, sickly-sweet scent of the mist seemed to solidify around him, a tangible testament to the alien ritual he had just witnessed. His heart hammered against his ribs, a frantic, trapped bird, as he realized the figures hadn't simply melted away into the darkness; they had been alerted. The soft rustle of leaves behind him, a sound he'd initially dismissed as the wind, now sounded like a deliberate approach. He'd been so focused on the artifact, on the horrifying spectacle of the seeds and the strange mist, that he had forgotten the most basic rule of his father's clandestine investigations: never assume you are unseen.

He didn't dare turn around. The dried herb clutched in his hand, a tiny, brittle fragment of undeniable proof, felt suddenly inadequate, a fragile shield against an encroaching storm. He had to move. Every instinct screamed at him to flee, to scramble back through the gorse and hawthorn and disappear into the welcoming anonymity of the night. But the image of his father, his frantic scribbles, his desperate quest for truth, flashed before his eyes. His father wouldn't have run. He would have stood his ground, demanded answers, even at the cost of his own safety. And Joseph, clutching the remnants of his father's legacy, felt a surge of something akin to defiance bloom in his chest, pushing back the icy grip of fear.

A voice, low and resonant, cut through the silence, not from behind him, but from the edge of the clearing, closer than he expected. "You are not welcome here." It was the taller figure, the one who had handled the box. The voice was devoid of emotion, yet it carried an undeniable weight, an authority that resonated with the same unnerving power as the artifact itself. Joseph slowly turned, his gaze sweeping across the perimeter of the clearing. He saw them now, not coalescing from the shadows, but standing there, patient and watchful, their dark cloaks like extensions of the night itself. They had anticipated his move, or perhaps, they had simply been waiting.

He backed away from the artifact, his eyes never leaving the figures. The clearing, which had seemed so natural and untouched moments before, now felt like a stage, and he, the unwitting intruder. The faint moonlight, previously a comfort, now seemed to illuminate his isolation, casting his solitary figure into stark relief against the darkened landscape. The rhythmic, almost hypnotic murmur of the artifact, though its luminescence was gone, seemed to pulse with a latent energy, a reminder of the profound forces at play here. He was trapped between the silent, hulking machine and the cloaked figures who had so calmly orchestrated their ritual.

"Who are you?" Joseph managed to ask, his voice trembling despite his best efforts. "What is this place? What have you done?" The questions tumbled out, fueled by a desperate need for understanding, a need inherited from his father. He saw a flicker of something in the shadowed faces beneath their hoods – surprise, perhaps, or a grudging acknowledgment of his presence. They hadn't expected him to confront them, only to flee or to remain hidden, a silent witness to their secrets.

The taller figure took a step forward, their movement unnervingly smooth. "You have seen what you were not meant to see," they stated, the words a calm pronouncement of doom. "Your father's curiosity has led you down a dangerous path, boy." The mention of his father sent a fresh wave of cold dread through Joseph. They knew about his father. They had likely been aware of his investigations, perhaps even responsible for his disappearance, or worse.

"My father was trying to understand," Joseph retorted, his voice gaining a fraction of its usual strength. "He wanted to know the truth about West Seneca, about what you people are doing." He gestured vaguely towards the artifact, the seeds, the lingering scent. "This... this is not natural. It's not right."

A low, derisive sound, like dry leaves skittering across stone, came from one of the other figures. "Natural?" another voice echoed, this one higher pitched, almost sibilant. "What is natural, child? The slow decay of all things? The inevitable march of entropy? We offer order. We offer a counter-force to the encroaching void."

Joseph stared at them, his mind struggling to process their words. Counter-force? Encroaching void? This wasn't about some local superstition or a hidden treasure. This was something far grander, far more abstract, and infinitely more terrifying. He remembered his father's journal entries, the increasingly desperate attempts to categorize the village's oddities, the recurring theme of "imbalance" and "restoration." Were *these* the restorers?

"You're poisoning us," Joseph accused, the words spilling out as a sudden, fierce conviction. "That mist... it smelled like... like the herbs in my father's study. The ones he was always trying to analyze. What are you putting into the air? What are you doing to the village?"

The taller figure remained impassive. "We are ensuring continuity. We are safeguarding against... extinction. Your father, in his limited understanding, saw only threat. He failed to grasp the necessity, the profound purpose."

"Purpose?" Joseph's voice rose, the outrage overriding his fear. "My father is gone! And you speak of purpose? What is this artifact? What are those seeds?" He took a step forward, his eyes fixed on the taller figure's hands, which were now clasped loosely in front of them. He saw the faint, almost imperceptible pulse of light beneath the dark fabric of their robes, as if something within their very being resonated with the inert machine.

"The artifact is a nexus," the taller figure replied, their voice still unnervingly calm. "A conduit. And the seeds... they are the means of transference. Of revitalization."

"Revitalization of what?" Joseph pressed, his gaze darting around the clearing. He was acutely aware of his own vulnerability. He had no weapon, no allies, only the desperate courage of a boy who had lost everything and had nothing left to lose. He scanned the faces of the other figures, searching for any sign of humanity, any crack in their unnerving composure. He found none. They were united, resolute, and utterly alien in their purpose.

"Of that which sustains us," the figure stated, a subtle shift in their posture suggesting they were growing impatient. "Your presence here is an anomaly. It disrupts the delicate balance we have so painstakingly maintained."

Joseph understood then. He wasn't just an observer; he was a disruption. A stray variable in their meticulously planned operation. And disruptions, in their world, were likely not tolerated. He could feel their collective attention now, not just focused on him, but *assessing* him, measuring his threat.

"I'm not leaving until you tell me what you did to my father!" Joseph declared, his voice ringing with a raw defiance. He brandished the dried herb he held. "And I have proof! I know what you're using, what you've been doing!"

For the first time, a flicker of something other than cold composure crossed the taller figure's face. It was a subtle tightening of the jaw, a barely perceptible narrowing of their eyes. The others stirred, their silent communication becoming more pronounced, a series of almost imperceptible nods and shifts of weight. They were reacting. His words, his defiance, had struck a nerve.

"You are a foolish child," the taller figure said, their voice losing a sliver of its perfect control. "Playing with forces you cannot comprehend. Your father was a fool. And you are his unfortunate echo."

Suddenly, the ground beneath Joseph's feet vibrated. It wasn't the low hum of the artifact, but a more localized tremor, originating from the direction of the figures. The faint moonlight seemed to warp, as if being pulled towards them. Joseph stumbled back, his eyes wide. The cloaks of the figures seemed to shimmer, to deepen in hue, almost as if they were absorbing the ambient light.

"What are you doing?" Joseph cried out, a genuine note of panic creeping into his voice. The air grew heavy, charged with an unseen energy. He felt a strange pressure in his ears, a disorienting sensation that made him sway.

"Ensuring your silence," the taller figure replied, their voice now a chilling whisper that seemed to emanate from everywhere at once. "For the good of the continuity."

The other figures moved then, not in a coordinated rush, but with an eerie synchronicity, fanning out to encircle him. Joseph's breath hitched. He was truly cornered. The artifact pulsed faintly behind him, a silent, indifferent witness to his plight. He looked from one hooded face to another, a sea of shadows and veiled intent. He had come seeking answers, and he had found only greater questions, and now, a very real and immediate danger. The confrontation had truly begun, and Joseph knew, with a terrifying certainty, that this was no longer just about finding his father. It was about survival. He braced himself, the dried herb still clenched tightly in his fist, a small, desperate symbol of his father's lost quest, and now, his own desperate fight. The silence that descended after the taller figure's final pronouncement was more terrifying than any roar, a silence that spoke of finality, of the inevitable closing of a trap. He could feel their collective focus narrowing, their unseen energies coalescing, directed solely at him. There was no escape. He was about to become another secret buried in the quiet, unassuming hills of West Seneca. He could feel it in the very air, a tangible shift, a tightening of the invisible net that had been cast around him. The game, as his father would have called it, was now entering its most perilous, and perhaps, its final stage. He saw a subtle movement from one of the figures to his left, a raising of a hand, and Joseph instinctively recoiled, his mind racing for any possible action, any counter-move, however futile. His father's voice, a memory now, echoed in his mind:

"The truth, Joseph, is often found in the darkest of places, and protected by the fiercest of guardians." He was certainly in a dark place, and the guardians were proving to be exceptionally fierce. He took a deep, shaky breath, trying to steady himself against the rising tide of panic. He wasn't his father, but he was his son, and he carried the same unyielding spark of curiosity, the same desperate need to understand. That spark, he hoped, would be enough. It had to be.

Joseph's breath hitched, the air thick with unspoken threats and the low, guttural hum of the artifact. He was trapped. The figures, no longer mere shadows, had fanned out, their cloaked forms creating a semi-circle that pressed in on him. The dried herb in his hand felt pathetically small, a brittle sentinel against the encroaching darkness. He could feel their eyes on him, not human eyes, but something else, something assessing and alien. The taller figure, the one who had spoken with such chilling calm, was now the focal point of his attention. Their posture exuded an unnerving patience, as if they had all the time in the world to deal with him. But Joseph knew better. His father's journals had spoken of urgency, of a ticking clock, of a rapidly closing window. These people, or whatever they were, were not here for pleasantries.

"You won't get away with this," Joseph managed, his voice a little steadier now, fueled by a desperate surge of adrenaline. He held up the dried herb, its faint, earthy scent a stark contrast to the metallic tang in the air. "My father found this. He was investigating the strange sicknesses, the disappearances. He knew you were involved." He saw a subtle flicker in the deeper shadows beneath the hood of the figure closest to his left. A ripple of unease? Or perhaps just the play of moonlight on fabric. He couldn't tell, and the ambiguity was a torment.

The taller figure remained unmoved. "Your father was a man of limited perception. He saw a disease where there was a cure. He fought against the very solution that would have saved us all." The words were measured, deliberate, designed to sow doubt, to twist the narrative. But Joseph's father's last frantic entries, his raw fear and mounting desperation, spoke of a different story, one of manipulation and unseen forces at play.

"A cure that poisons the village?" Joseph countered, taking a small step to his right, testing the perimeter. The figures shifted their positions in unison, fluid and unsettling, closing the gap he attempted to create. It was like trying to outmaneuver a living tide. "A cure that makes people forget who they are? That makes them... compliant?" He thought of the vacant stares of some of the villagers, the unnerving placidity that had settled over West Seneca like a suffocating fog. This wasn't healing; it was erasure.

A soft rustling sound, like dry leaves skittering across stone, came from the group. It was a shared communication, a silent agreement that bypassed spoken language. Joseph felt a prickle of fear as the air around him grew colder, the pressure in his ears intensifying. The moonlight seemed to dim, as if being siphoned away. He was in the center of a vortex, and these figures were its architects.

He had to act. Running was an option, but the figures were too close, too well-positioned. They clearly knew this terrain, this clearing, far better than he did. His only hope was to disrupt their carefully orchestrated control. He remembered his father's desperate plea in his final letter:

"Joseph, if you find this, know that the truth is in the whispers. Listen to the silence. There is always a crack, a weakness, if you know where to look."

His gaze swept across the clearing, his mind racing. The artifact. It pulsed with that faint, internal light, seemingly indifferent to the unfolding drama. It was the source of their power, the nexus of their strange ritual. If he could disrupt that...

"You speak of continuity," Joseph said, his voice gaining a desperate, almost theatrical strength. He took a step back, drawing their collective attention towards the artifact behind him. "But what if this 'continuity' is built on lies? What if this 'solution' is just another form of decay?" He feinted a move towards the artifact, as if to touch it, to examine it closer.

The reaction was instantaneous. The taller figure took a swift, decisive step forward, their movement almost too fast to track. "Do not approach the nexus, boy," they warned, their voice losing its measured tone, replaced by a sharp edge of urgency. The other figures also moved, their cloaks billowing, their forms becoming more substantial, more menacing.

This was his chance. While their attention was momentarily focused on his feigned interest in the artifact, Joseph spun around and bolted. He didn't head back the way he came, into the denser woods where they would likely have the advantage. Instead, he veered sharply to his left, towards a jagged outcrop of rocks that loomed at the edge of the clearing. His father had often spoken of the old smuggler's paths in these hills, treacherous routes known only to a few. He hoped, with every fiber of his being, that his father's knowledge extended to this secluded, and now terrifyingly occupied, clearing.

He scrambled over loose scree, his boots slipping on the damp earth. Behind him, he heard the rustle of cloaks and the sound of pursuit, faster than he could have imagined. They were not deterred by the uneven terrain. The pressure in his ears intensified, and a dizzying sensation made his vision blur. It was as if the very air was resisting his movement, trying to hold him back.

He reached the rocks and began to climb, his fingers raw and bleeding as he sought purchase on the cold, unforgiving stone. He risked a glance back. The figures were at the base of the outcrop, their forms silhouetted against the faint moonlight. They weren't climbing, not yet. They were watching him, their stillness more unnerving than any active pursuit. He could feel their silent contemplation, their analysis of his every move.

Then, he saw it. A narrow crevice, barely wider than his shoulders, leading upwards into the darkness between two massive boulders. It was a tight squeeze, a desperate gamble, but it was his only hope. He shoved himself into the opening, the rough stone scraping against his clothes and skin. He pushed upwards, his muscles straining, the confined space amplifying the sense of panic. He could hear them below him, their voices now a low, resonant chant, a series of syllables that seemed to vibrate in his very bones.

The chanting grew louder, more insistent. The rocks around him began to tremble, a deep, resonant vibration that shook him to his core. He thought he saw a faint, phosphorescent glow emanate from the crevice ahead, a trap that was being laid for him, or a pathway to escape. He had to keep moving. His father's warnings echoed in his mind:

"They control more than just the air, Joseph. They manipulate the very fabric of things."

He reached a small ledge, barely enough room to catch his breath. He peered out from the crevice. The figures were no longer at the base of the outcrop. They were dispersed, their cloaks blending with the shadows of the trees, their forms appearing and disappearing with an unnerving fluidity. They were flanking him, anticipating his every move, using the darkness and the terrain to their advantage.

He saw a flicker of movement to his right, and instinctively pulled himself deeper into the crevice. A cloaked figure emerged from the trees, their form impossibly tall, their head tilted as if listening. Joseph held his breath, the dried herb clutched so tightly his knuckles were white. He could feel the warmth of it, a tiny, grounding presence in this overwhelming unreality.

"He went this way," a voice hissed, the sound seeming to slither through the air. It was not one of the figures he had seen before. It was different, sharper, more human, but laced with an unnerving malice.

Joseph's heart hammered against his ribs. They had help. Or perhaps, some of the villagers were complicit, willing participants in whatever grim ritual was unfolding in West Seneca. The thought sent a fresh wave of dread through him. His father had spoken of suspicion, of paranoia within the village, but Joseph had always attributed it to the stress of his investigations. Now, he wasn't so sure.

He pressed himself further into the crevice, seeking any slight advantage. The air here was heavy, stagnant, carrying the faint, cloying scent of the mist he had encountered earlier. He realized, with a sickening lurch, that they were not just pursuing him; they were actively hunting him, herding him.

Then, he remembered something else his father had scribbled in his journal, a seemingly random observation about the peculiar acoustics of the West Seneca hills.

"The echoes here are... amplified," it read. *"A whisper can become a roar, and a spoken word can be turned against you."*

An idea, desperate and dangerous, began to form. He took a deep, steadying breath. He had to make them reveal themselves, to break their cloaked anonymity, even if it meant drawing more attention.

"I'm not afraid of you!" Joseph yelled, his voice echoing unnaturally through the rocky terrain. He let the dried herb fall from his hand, watching it tumble down the rocks, a silent offering to the chaos. "My father was right about you! You're not saving anyone; you're destroying them!"

He waited, his senses on high alert. He heard movement from the trees ahead, the snapping of a twig. He knew they were closing in. He then took another breath and, remembering his father's fascination with ancient communication methods, he let out a long, piercing whistle. It was a signal his father had used when they were out hiking, a call to meet. He hoped, prayed, that it would cause confusion, that it would force a reaction.

The whistle cut through the night air, sharp and clear. For a moment, there was silence. Then, the figures scattered, their movements betraying a flicker of unease. The taller figure's voice boomed, "Cease this foolishness! You cannot escape!"

But Joseph saw it. A flash of movement, a disruption in the pattern of their pursuit. One of the figures, closer to him, had momentarily turned towards the direction of his whistle, a clear indication of their focus being divided. It was the crack his father had spoken of.

With a surge of renewed determination, Joseph scrambled out of the crevice, not back towards the clearing, but along the rock face, heading deeper into the less explored, more treacherous part of the hills. He heard shouts of surprise, of anger, as his sudden change of direction caught them off guard. He was no longer just running; he was actively using his knowledge, however fragmented, to outwit them.

He plunged into a dense thicket of thorny bushes, the branches tearing at his clothes and skin, but providing cover. He could hear them crashing through the undergrowth behind him, their pursuit relentless. But he was gaining a little ground. He pushed on, the adrenaline coursing through him, his mind a whirlwind of fear and a strange, exhilarating sense of purpose. He was no longer the naive boy who had stumbled upon a hidden ritual. He was a hunter now, fighting for answers, fighting for his father, and fighting for his own survival. The fate of West Seneca, he realized, might very well rest on his ability to disappear into these unforgiving hills, and to return with the truth. He stumbled through the darkness, a desperate, fleeting shadow against the ancient, watchful landscape, driven by the memory of his father and the chilling promise of what lay hidden in the heart of West Seneca. He knew that his escape, if he could achieve it, was only a temporary reprieve. They would hunt him, relentlessly. But for now, he was free, a ghost slipping through the fingers of their control, carrying the weight of a secret that could unravel everything. The night was far from over, and the true climax was still unfolding.

The dense undergrowth snagged at Joseph's clothes, each thorn a tiny, sharp accusation. He ran, fueled by a primal instinct for survival, the echo of his own whistle still ringing in his ears, a desperate beacon in the oppressive darkness. The figures were behind him, a persistent rustling of leaves, a murmur of unseen movement that spoke of their tireless, almost inhuman pursuit. His father's words, though, were a constant companion, a mental map guiding him through the fear. *"They control more than just the air, Joseph. They manipulate the very fabric of things."* This wasn't just a chase; it was a battle against unseen forces, against an enemy who bent reality to their will. He risked a fleeting glance over his shoulder, expecting to see the hulking silhouettes of his pursuers. Instead, the moonlight painted eerie, shifting patterns on the forest floor, the trees themselves seeming to twist and warp, playing tricks on his eyes. Were they always this tall? Did that shadow always flicker with such an unnatural luminescence?

He stumbled, catching himself on the rough bark of an ancient oak. The impact sent a jolt of pain through his wrist, but the immediate threat of falling was a welcome distraction from the terror that gnawed at his resolve. He needed a plan, not just to escape, but to understand. His father's final letter had been cryptic, filled with fragmented observations and desperate pleas, but one recurring theme had been the artifact, the humming, pulsating object that sat at the heart of this clearing. It was the source of their power, the anchor of their insidious influence. If he could understand it, perhaps he could understand *them.*

He pushed himself away from the tree and continued his descent, his heart pounding a frantic rhythm against his ribs. The terrain became steeper, the ground slick with dew. He could hear them, closer now, their pursuit gaining a renewed, chilling efficiency. The air grew heavy, imbued with that same cloying scent that had clung to the mist, a scent that was both floral and vaguely metallic, like overripe fruit left to decay. It was the smell of corruption, of something fundamentally wrong.

Then, he heard it. Not the rustle of pursuit, but a different sound, a low, mournful keening that seemed to emanate from the very earth beneath his feet. It was a sound of suffering, of profound loss, and it struck a chord of recognition deep within him. It was the sound he had heard in the hushed conversations of the villagers, in the averted gazes of those who seemed to carry an unspoken grief. It was the sound of West Seneca, a village slowly succumbing to an unseen affliction.

Joseph froze, the sound washing over him. His father's journal entries flashed through his mind: the increased incidence of 'melancholy,' the 'forgotten memories,' the 'docile acceptance' that had fallen over so many. He had dismissed it as the side effects of isolation, of the harsh winters, but this sound... this was not natural. It was a lament.

He cautiously moved towards the source of the keening, the dense foliage providing him with cover. He emerged onto a small, hidden plateau overlooking a deeper ravine. Below, bathed in an ethereal, milky light that seemed to emanate from no discernible source, was a sight that stole his breath. It was the artifact, larger now, or perhaps closer, its pulsing light more pronounced, casting long, distorted shadows that danced like phantoms. But it wasn't the artifact that held his gaze. It was the figures.

They were gathered around the artifact, their cloaks drawn back slightly, revealing not human forms, but something far more alien. Their skin, or what passed for it, was a pale, luminous grey, stretched taut over angular bone structures. Their eyes, set deep within their sockets, glowed with a faint, internal light, devoid of pupils or irises. And around them, seemingly tethered to the artifact by strands of pure energy, were figures. Human figures. Villagers. They stood in a trance-like state, their faces vacant, their bodies swaying gently, as if caught in an invisible current. Joseph recognized some of them – Mrs. Gable from the bakery, old Mr. Henderson who always sat on his porch, even a few of the children he sometimes saw playing by the creek. They were connected to the artifact, their life force, their very consciousness, being siphoned away.

The taller figure, the one who had spoken with such unsettling calm, was now directly before the artifact, their hands outstretched, palms facing the pulsating core. As Joseph watched, a stream of iridescent light flowed from the figure's hands and merged with the artifact's glow. And with each surge of energy, the villagers swayed a little more, their vacant expressions deepening, their forms becoming almost translucent.

His father's words, "*They see a disease where there is a cure,*" echoed in his mind, now twisted into a horrifying new meaning. This wasn't a cure; it was consumption. They weren't healing the villagers; they were draining them, using their life essence to power... what? The artifact? Themselves?

Suddenly, a sharp, metallic clang split the air. Joseph's heart leaped into his throat. He hadn't made that sound. He looked around wildly, his gaze falling upon a discarded metal pipe lying near his feet. Someone else was here. Someone who had also stumbled upon this horrifying tableau.

From the shadows at the edge of the plateau, a figure emerged. It was a man, dressed in the tattered remnants of what looked like a groundskeeper's uniform. His face was gaunt, his eyes wide with a mixture of terror and grim determination. It was Silas, the man who tended to the old cemetery on the edge of town, a man known for his quiet nature and his uncanny knowledge of the local flora and fauna. Joseph had seen him on occasion, a solitary figure always more comfortable with the dead than the living.

Silas's gaze met Joseph's, and in that brief, charged moment, a silent understanding passed between them. Silas gestured frantically towards the figures surrounding the artifact, his lips moving, but no sound reached Joseph's ears over the low hum of the artifact and the unsettling keening. Silas pointed to a cluster of the trance-like villagers, then to a specific spot on the artifact, a node that seemed to throb with a more intense, emerald light.

Then, Silas acted. With a guttural cry, he hurled the metal pipe towards the artifact. It struck the glowing node with a resonant *thwack*, a sound that seemed to momentarily disrupt the artifact's steady pulse. A wave of pure, unadulterated agony erupted from the surrounding figures. The villagers flinched, their eyes momentarily flickering with a spark of recognition, of pain, before their vacant expressions returned.

The cloaked figures whirled around, their luminous eyes focusing on Silas. Their collective, silent judgment was palpable. The taller figure raised a hand, and a blast of pure energy, crackling with ethereal light, shot towards Silas. He dodged, a miracle of agility, the energy beam searing a path through the undergrowth where he had stood moments before.

This was Joseph's chance. The distraction, the disruption – it was everything his father had hinted at.

"There is always a crack, a weakness, if you know where to look." Silas had provided that crack.

Joseph didn't hesitate. He scrambled forward, moving with a speed born of desperation. He lunged towards the artifact, not to touch it, but to observe. He needed to see what Silas had seen, what he had understood. As he got closer, he could feel the artifact's energy, a palpable force that tugged at his very being, attempting to draw him into its hypnotic rhythm. But his father's warnings, and Silas's brave intervention, kept him tethered to reality.

He saw it then. The node Silas had struck. It was a point of connection, a conduit. And the strands of energy connecting the villagers to the artifact weren't uniform; they varied in thickness and intensity. The emerald node seemed to be the primary conduit, the main artery through which the villagers' life force was being systematically drained.

The taller figure was now advancing on Silas, their movements unnervingly graceful, yet imbued with a predatory intent. Silas, armed only with his knowledge of the terrain and his sheer courage, scrambled back, drawing them further away from the artifact and the captive villagers.

Joseph knew what he had to do. His father's journal had a small, faded sketch of a peculiar, almost crystalline plant, accompanied by the note: *"Resonates with unnatural energies. Disrupts ethereal bonds. Handle with extreme caution."* He'd found a small sample of it tucked away in his father's satchel, a dried, brittle sprig that he'd dismissed as another obscure specimen. Now, it felt like a lifeline.

He fumbled in his jacket pocket, his fingers clumsy with adrenaline. He found the small, dried plant. It felt fragile, almost insignificant. But his father had believed in it. He had believed in its potential.

He looked at the artifact, at the pulsing emerald node. He needed something to deliver the plant, something that would amplify its effect. His gaze swept across the plateau. Then he saw it – a collection of smooth, polished stones arranged in a loose circle around the artifact, each one humming with a faint, residual energy. They were resonators, amplifiers.

Ignoring the chilling sounds of Silas's struggle in the distance, Joseph grabbed one of the larger stones. He crushed the dried plant in his hand, its faint, peppery scent filling the air, and pressed the pulverized remains into the stone. He then hurled the stone with all his might towards the emerald node on the artifact.

The impact was far greater than he'd anticipated. The stone didn't just hit the node; it seemed to shatter against it, releasing a wave of iridescent dust that clung to the artifact. For a heart-stopping moment, nothing happened. The artifact continued its rhythmic pulse. The villagers remained in their stupor.

Then, the artifact shuddered. The steady hum faltered, replaced by a discordant screech, a sound like a thousand fingernails dragging across a blackboard. The emerald light flickered violently, then sputtered, as if a flame were being extinguished. The strands of energy connecting the villagers to the artifact snapped, one by one, like taut wires breaking under immense pressure.

A collective gasp rippled through the villagers. Their bodies stiffened, then slumped, as if the invisible tether that had held them upright had been severed. Their eyes, moments before vacant, now widened, filled with a dawning confusion, a flicker of memory returning. They looked around, bewildered, their faces etched with a profound, unsettling sorrow.

The cloaked figures recoiled, their luminous forms seeming to dim, their movements becoming jerky and erratic. The taller figure let out a harsh, alien cry, a sound of pure frustration and rage. The energy that had been flowing into the artifact now seemed to be bleeding back out, creating a chaotic swirl around them.

Silas, battered and bruised, used the moment of disarray to his advantage. He grabbed a fallen branch and, with surprising strength, shoved it into the base of the artifact, attempting to dislodge it from its position. The artifact rocked precariously, its pulsating light now erratic, sputtering like a dying ember.

"You cannot stop this!" the taller figure shrieked, their voice distorted, their form contorting as if in pain. "This is the inevitable cycle! The continuation!"

"Continuation of what?" Joseph yelled back, his voice raw but firm. He had stumbled upon the truth, and it was more terrible than he could have imagined. "Of stealing life? Of erasing souls?"

"We are... caretakers," the figure hissed, their luminous eyes fixed on Joseph. "We preserve. We maintain the balance. Your father sought to disrupt it. He saw only destruction. We see... order. A necessary pruning."

"Pruning?" Joseph spat, the word tasting like ash in his mouth. "You're killing them! You're stealing their memories, their very essence, to power yourselves!" He looked at the confused, suffering faces of the villagers, the dawning horror in their eyes. This was the sickness his father had fought. This was the secret of West Seneca.

Suddenly, the artifact gave a violent lurch, and the ground beneath them trembled. The smaller, polished stones that had surrounded it began to glow with an intense, white light, and the air crackled with an unbearable energy. The cloaked figures screamed, a chorus of alien anguish, as the energy they had been siphoning now seemed to be rebounding, consuming them.

The taller figure, before being enveloped in a blinding flash, turned its luminous gaze directly onto Joseph. "The cost of knowledge," it rasped, its voice fading into the cacophony, "is always paid."

And then, with a final, deafening explosion of light and sound, the artifact vanished. The ground settled, the blinding light receded, and the only remnants of the chaotic scene were the stunned villagers, the scattered polished stones, and the lingering scent of ozone and decay. Silas stood panting, leaning on his branch, his face streaked with dirt and blood, but his eyes held a glint of triumph.

Joseph looked around. The villagers were slowly coming to, their movements sluggish, their minds still reeling. They looked at Joseph, at Silas, at the empty space where the artifact had been, their faces a mask of confusion and dawning comprehension. The truth, raw and brutal, had been revealed amidst the chaos, and the silence that followed was more deafening than any scream. The secret of West Seneca was no longer hidden; it was etched into the very souls of its inhabitants, a scar that would forever mark their lives. Joseph's quest had reached its terrifying, inevitable conclusion, and the world he thought he knew had been irrevocably shattered.

8

The Aftermath of Revelation

The silence that followed the blinding flash was as profound as the noise had been deafening. It wasn't an empty silence, but one filled with the rustling of leaves disturbed by the unseen forces, the ragged breaths of those who had witnessed the impossible, and the slow, dawning comprehension returning to the villagers of West Seneca. Joseph, still reeling from the residual shockwaves of the artifact's destruction, found his gaze drawn to Silas. The grizzled groundskeeper, his face a roadmap of exertion and newfound resolve, was slowly lowering the branch he'd used to ward off the retreating, now dissipated, alien forms. The air, once thick with the cloying scent of corruption and the ozone tang of raw energy, was beginning to clear, carrying only the damp earthiness of the forest floor.

The villagers, blinking and disoriented, were beginning to stir. Their movements were jerky at first, like marionettes whose strings had been suddenly cut. They looked at their hands, at the trees, at each other, their expressions a mixture of bewilderment and a profound, gnawing unease. The vacant stares were gone, replaced by the raw, unvarnished look of shock, of lives violently returned from a stolen dream. Joseph saw the dawning horror in old Mrs. Gable's eyes as she clutched her chest, her breath coming in shallow gasps. Mr. Henderson, who had been swaying placidly by the artifact, now stood rooted to the spot, his jaw slack, his gaze fixed on the empty clearing where the pulsating light had once held him captive. The children, their faces pale and tear-streaked, clung to their parents, their small bodies trembling.

Joseph's father's words, spoken in the hurried scribbles of his final letter, now resonated with chilling clarity: "They see a disease where there is a cure." The 'cure' had been the systematic siphoning of their life force, their memories, their very essence. The 'disease' was the truth, a truth they had fought to suppress, a truth that had been forcibly extracted from the villagers. Now, the truth was laid bare, not just for Joseph, but for every soul present. But the revelation was just the beginning. The aftermath, the securing of this newly unearthed reality, was the paramount concern. The alien entities, or whatever they were, had been repelled, their primary tool of manipulation destroyed, but their influence might still linger. The villagers, though free, were deeply traumatized, their minds undoubtedly fragile and susceptible.

"We need to... we need to make sure this doesn't get buried again," Joseph stammered, his voice hoarse. He looked at Silas, who nodded grimly, his eyes scanning the perimeter of the clearing with the practiced wariness of someone who had spent a lifetime observing the quiet dangers of the natural world. Silas understood the unspoken gravity of their situation. The artifact was gone, but the memory of its power, the knowledge of what had transpired, was a potent, volatile force.

"The letter," Silas rasped, his voice rough with disuse and emotion. "Your father's journal. It's all here. It's the proof." He gestured towards the satchel Joseph had been carrying, a satchel that had served as a repository for his father's clandestine investigations. The contents of that satchel were no longer just the ramblings of a man obsessed, but the irrefutable evidence of a conspiracy that had woven itself into the fabric of their quiet village.

Joseph instinctively reached for the satchel, his fingers closing around the worn leather. Inside, nestled amongst carefully pressed specimens and faded maps, were his father's journals, filled with meticulous observations, sketches, and coded entries. There were also the letters his father had exchanged with other researchers, whispers of similar phenomena in other remote communities, hints of a network far larger and more insidious than Joseph had ever dared to imagine. These documents were the anchors that would tether the fantastical events of the night to tangible reality. Without them, the villagers' fragmented memories might be dismissed as collective hysteria, a shared delusion brought on by fear or some unexplained natural phenomenon.

"We can't just... leave them here," Joseph said, his gaze sweeping over the bewildered villagers. They were beginning to gather in small, hushed groups, their conversations low and uncertain. Some were weeping softly, others stared blankly into the middle distance, their minds still struggling to process the impossible. The alien figures had taken something from them, and the process of reclaiming what had been lost, or at least coming to terms with its absence, would be a long and arduous one.

Silas, with a surprising surge of energy, moved towards the nearest cluster of villagers. "We need to get them back to the village," he said, his voice surprisingly steady. "Safely. They'll need... they'll need comfort. And answers, when they're ready." He offered a hand to an elderly woman who looked particularly distressed, his touch gentle, reassuring.

Joseph understood. The immediate priority was the well-being of the villagers. But the evidence... that needed immediate securing. The forest, while it had concealed the artifact and its horrors, was also the primary witness. If any trace of the artifact's technology, or the alien entities themselves, remained, it could be easily misinterpreted, or worse, discovered by those who would seek to cover up the truth.

He carefully gathered his father's journals and any loose papers that had spilled from the satchel during the chaos. He then began to systematically search the immediate vicinity of where the artifact had stood. His father's notes had spoken of 'resonant stones,' the polished rocks that had surrounded the artifact and amplified its energy. He found several of them, scattered and inert now, their faint glow extinguished, but still possessing a peculiar smoothness, an unnatural symmetry. He collected them, placing them gingerly into the satchel. He also noticed, scattered amongst the debris, what looked like fragments of a crystalline substance – remnants of the artifact itself, perhaps. He scooped these up too, their sharp edges glinting dully in the faint predawn light. The sheer physical evidence was crucial.

"Silas," Joseph called out, his voice carrying a new urgency. "We need to make sure no one else stumbles upon this clearing, not until we've decided how to handle this. And we need to... we need to document what happened here, precisely."

Silas, having helped a few more villagers to their feet, returned to Joseph's side. "The old logging trails," he said, his eyes fixed on the canopy of trees. "They're overgrown now, forgotten for the most part. Anyone coming this way would have to be looking for something specific. But we can't rely on that." He paused, a thoughtful expression on his gaunt face. "There's the old ranger station, further up the ridge. It's abandoned, falling into disrepair, but it's got a solid foundation. And it's out of the way."

"A ranger station?" Joseph considered the suggestion. An abandoned, isolated location would provide security for the gathered evidence, a place where he and Silas could go through the documents without interruption and formulate a plan. It would also serve as a discreet repository, away from the prying eyes of the village.

"It's too exposed," Joseph said, thinking aloud. "If someone is looking for this, they might search abandoned places." He then recalled a passage in his father's journal, a mention of a hidden cellar beneath their own home, a place his father had used for... private experiments.

"My father," Joseph began, his mind racing, "he had a hidden cellar. Beneath our house. It's old, reinforced. It would be safer than an abandoned building."

Silas considered this. "Your house? I know the place. Solid stone. But who knows if it's truly secure from... whatever this was?"

"It's better than anywhere else," Joseph insisted. "At least we know its defenses, its secrets. And the village is too close. We need to move the evidence away from here, before anyone starts asking questions about where the villagers have been all night."

The task was immense, and the weight of it settled heavily upon Joseph's young shoulders. He was no longer just a boy lost in the woods; he was the custodian of a truth that could shake the very foundations of West Seneca. He looked at Silas, a man who had, in the space of a few terrifying hours, become an unlikely ally, a guardian of the secrets his own father had died trying to expose.

"We'll need to move quickly," Silas said, his voice low and determined. "Before the sun is fully up. People will start noticing the villagers are missing. And once they start asking questions..."

"Then we need to have the answers ready," Joseph finished. He looked at the satchel, at the weight of the evidence it contained. It was more than just paper and stones; it was the collected wisdom, the desperate warnings, and the ultimate sacrifice of his father. He had to protect it, not just for his father's memory, but for the future of West Seneca.

As the first tentative rays of dawn began to pierce the dense canopy, Joseph and Silas began the arduous task of guiding the dazed villagers back towards West Seneca. The path was slow, fraught with the silent anxieties of those who had been touched by something profoundly unnatural. Joseph, with Silas close by his side, carried the satchel containing his father's life's work, the physical manifestation of the truth they had fought so hard to uncover. The evidence was secured, at least for the moment, within the confines of that worn leather bag. But the true challenge lay ahead: presenting it, making it understood, and ensuring that the secrets of West Seneca would never again be buried by the shadows. The world had shifted irrevocably, and Joseph knew that the aftermath of revelation would be a long, complex, and perilous journey. He clutched the satchel tighter, the rough texture of the leather a grounding sensation against the swirling chaos in his mind. The proof was here, tangible and undeniable, and it was his responsibility now to ensure that proof could not be erased, its undeniable truth hidden away once more. He would not let his father's efforts be in vain. He would secure the evidence, and with it, the fate of his village.

The first rays of dawn, usually a welcome herald of a new day in West Seneca, painted the sky in hues of bruised purple and hesitant orange, mirroring the unsettled state of the village. The unnatural stillness of the preceding night, punctuated only by the crackle of Elias Thorne's artifact and the subsequent terrified cries, had given way to a different kind of quiet – one pregnant with dawning comprehension and burgeoning dread. Word, carried by the first few villagers who had been roused by the commotion and then by the returning, disoriented souls from the clearing, spread with a ferocity that outpaced even the swiftest gossip. It began as a murmur, a ripple of confused whispers at doorsteps and over garden fences, quickly escalating into a torrent of shock and disbelief that washed over West Seneca.

Old Man Hemlock, whose cottage sat closest to the treeline, was one of the first to venture out, drawn by an instinct older than any man-made clock. He saw Martha Jenkins, her face ashen, stumbling towards her home, her gaze unfocused, her hands fluttering as if trying to brush away an unseen dust. "Martha? What in the blazes...?" he'd croaked, his voice raspy with sleep and a lifetime of unanswered questions. Martha had merely shuddered, clutching her shawl tighter, mumbling about lights, about shadows that moved with an intelligence far too ancient for this quiet valley. Hemlock had then seen others, emerging from their homes with a bewildered air, drawn by the unnatural silence that had fallen after the strange, violent cacophony.

The tale of Elias Thorne's artifact, of the shimmering, alien entities that had been repelled by Silas and young Joseph, of the forced extraction of memories and vitality, was already in motion.

By the time the sun had fully ascended, painting the familiar landscape in its usual golden light, West Seneca was a village transformed. The ordinary routines of the morning were shattered. Milk churns stood forgotten by gateposts. The scent of baking bread hung heavy and unheeded in the air. Instead, knots of villagers gathered in the town square, their faces a mixture of bewilderment and something far more sinister – dawning comprehension. The hushed conversations of the night before, fueled by fear and confusion, had now coalesced into a terrifying consensus. The events in the clearing, the artifact, the entities, Elias Thorne's desperate, final act – it was all true.

Agnes Peterson, the baker's wife, a woman known for her unflinching pragmatism and her booming laugh, stood with her arms crossed, her lips pressed into a thin, angry line. Her husband, Thomas, usually the picture of calm resilience, looked utterly lost, his eyes darting from one bewildered face to another. "It's madness," Agnes declared, her voice cutting through the confused babble. "Pure, unadulterated madness. Elias was always... eccentric, yes, but to invent such a story, to make us all believe... it's cruel!" Her outrage, however, seemed to falter as she met the gaze of Sarah Miller, whose son, little Timmy, had been among those closest to the artifact. Sarah's silence was more eloquent than any outburst. Timmy, usually a vibrant, chattering child, had been withdrawn and listless for weeks, his memories of the previous summer's fishing trip replaced by fragmented, unsettling dreams he couldn't articulate. Now, seeing Timmy's pallor, his vacant stare, Agnes's certainty began to fray.

Others felt a different kind of emotion – a gnawing sense of betrayal. Sheriff Brody, a man who had always prided himself on maintaining order and knowing every soul in his jurisdiction, found himself on the defensive. He had dismissed Elias Thorne's warnings, had chalked up the villagers' recent lethargy to a bad harvest or a touch of the flu. He'd even had a quiet word with Elias's wife, urging her to keep her husband's "flights of fancy" contained. Now, he stood amidst the very people he was sworn to protect, the weight of his own ignorance a crushing burden. "I... I don't understand," he stammered, his voice losing its usual authoritative edge. "How could we not have known? How could Elias have kept such a thing hidden?" His words were met with a barrage of accusatory glances. Old Man Hemlock, his face etched with the dawning horror of a terrible truth, pointed a gnarled finger. "Hidden? Brody, he tried to tell us! He tried to warn us! And you... you shut him down! We all did, in our own way!"

The revelation wasn't a singular event; it was a slow, agonizing unveiling. For some, like Martha Jenkins, it was a terrifying confirmation of the unease that had plagued them for months. They had felt drained, their lives inexplicably muted, their memories hazy. The artifact, they now understood, was not a source of wonder, but of predation. The shimmering figures, not benevolent guardians, but parasitic entities. For others, it was a profound shock, a shattering of their reality. The quiet normalcy of West Seneca, the predictable rhythms of their lives, had been a carefully constructed illusion, a facade maintained by forces they had never suspected.

Joseph, standing beside Silas near the edge of the town square, watched the unfolding chaos with a mixture of apprehension and a grim sense of purpose. He clutched the worn leather satchel, its contents – his father's journals, the meticulously documented proof – feeling heavier than ever. He saw his father's theories, dismissed as paranoia, now validated in the terrified eyes of his neighbors. He saw the relief, too, in the faces of those who had felt inexplicable malaise, their current distress a testament to their freedom. But he also saw the anger, the confusion, the fear that threatened to consume them all.

Silas, his weathered face betraying a weariness that went beyond physical exertion, placed a steadying hand on Joseph's shoulder. "This is only the beginning, lad," he murmured, his gaze sweeping over the increasingly agitated crowd. "The truth, once unearthed, is rarely tidy.

It's messy. And people... people don't always welcome what they've been shielded from."

The disquiet spread beyond the immediate circle of those who had witnessed the events in the clearing. The villagers who had remained in their homes, who had been too unwell, too frail, or simply too occupied with their daily lives to be drawn to the unnatural light, were now catching up. The stories, amplified and distorted with each retelling, painted a picture of a secret war waged on their very souls. The lethargy that had afflicted many, the creeping forgetfulness, the inexplicable sadness that had settled over the village like a persistent fog – it was all attributed to the artifact, to the parasitic entities.

Eleanor Vance, the village librarian, a woman whose life was dedicated to the preservation of knowledge, found herself in a deeply disturbing position. She had always believed in the power of documented fact, in the irrefutable nature of history. But now, the very foundations of her understanding were being questioned. She listened, her brow furrowed, as Mrs. Gable, a regular patron who had been unusually withdrawn lately, recounted her own vague, unsettling experiences – a feeling of being watched, of her thoughts not entirely being her own. Eleanor recalled her own fleeting moments of uncharacteristic forgetfulness, the times she'd found herself staring blankly at a page, unable to recall what she had just read. Were these simply signs of aging, or had the artifact's tendrils reached even into the quiet sanctuary of the library?

The disruption wasn't just emotional; it was social. The established hierarchies, the trusted figures, were suddenly cast in a new light. Sheriff Brody's authority was visibly shaken. Pastor Davies, whose sermons had always offered solace and certainty, found his flock looking to him with a desperate need for answers he couldn't provide. The carefully constructed order of West Seneca was cracking, revealing the raw, unsettling reality beneath.

The gossip, as it always did, coalesced into rumor, and rumor quickly solidified into what many were willing to accept as fact. The story of Elias Thorne, the mad scientist, was being replaced by that of Elias Thorne, the martyr, the man who had sacrificed himself to save them all. Silas, the quiet groundskeeper, a man who had always been on the periphery of village life, was now being hailed as a hero, his stoic presence a comforting anchor in the storm of disbelief. And Joseph, the boy who had always seemed a little too lost in his books, a little too consumed by his father's legacy, was now the keeper of the truth, the inheritor of a perilous legacy.

A young farmer, young Thomas, his face a mask of bewildered anger, accosted Sheriff Brody. "My father," he spat, his voice trembling with rage, "he hasn't been himself for months! He's forgetful, he's... he's not Dad anymore! You said it was just age! Was it that... that thing? Did it take him?"

Sheriff Brody could only offer a helpless shrug, his face pale. He looked at the accusing eyes, the raw pain, and knew he had failed them. He had failed Elias Thorne. He had failed West Seneca. The weight of that failure was almost as crushing as the revelation itself.

The immediate aftermath was a tempest of raw emotions. Outrage mingled with relief, suspicion with gratitude. Some villagers, clinging to the familiar comfort of denial, refused to believe what they were hearing, dismissing it as mass hysteria or the ramblings of a traumatized boy and an old hermit. They sought explanations in natural phenomena, in electrical storms, in the effects of some strange atmospheric condition. But for the majority, the evidence, however unbelievable, was too compelling. The accounts of those who had been closest to the artifact, their fragmented memories and the lingering spectral unease they carried, painted too vivid a picture.

The hushed discussions turned into more open debates, often heated, erupting in the general store, by the well, and in the churchyard. Accusations were hurled, not just at Sheriff Brody and Pastor Davies for their complacency, but at each other. Had someone known more than they let on? Had anyone benefited from the villagers' weakened state? The fragile bonds of community, already strained by the invisible drain on their vitality, now threatened to snap under the immense pressure of this newfound, terrifying truth.

Joseph watched it all unfold, the satchel a constant weight against his side. He understood that the physical evidence was only half the battle. The other half was convincing his neighbors, his friends, the people he had grown up with, that their quiet existence had been a lie, that their reality had been manipulated. He saw the deep-seated need for answers, for explanations, but also the deep-seated fear of what those answers might entail. The truth, as his father had written, was a cure, but it was a bitter one, one that promised to burn away the comfort of ignorance but offered no easy solace.

Silas, ever the pragmatist, surveyed the scene with a weary pragmatism. "They need to hear it all, Joseph," he said, his voice low but firm. "Not just the sensational parts. They need to understand what your father discovered, what he was trying to do. They need to know the risks, and they need to know what we can do now." He gestured towards the satchel. "That needs to be presented. Carefully. But it needs to be presented."

The task ahead was daunting. Joseph felt the immense pressure of his father's legacy, the responsibility of safeguarding the truth. He had the proof, a mountain of meticulously recorded observations, scientific data, and personal reflections. But how to disseminate it? How to make the villagers understand the profound, alien threat that had been lurking in their midst, a threat that had been cleverly disguised as a benign phenomenon? The clearing, once the scene of unspeakable horror, now held the key to their collective understanding. It was there that the unvarnished truth had been laid bare, and it was from there that the path forward, however uncertain, had to begin. The village of West Seneca had awakened to a truth they could no longer deny, and the dawn of this new, unsettling reality was only just breaking. The aftermath of revelation had truly begun, and it promised to be a long, arduous journey for every soul in West Seneca. Joseph felt a tremor of apprehension, but beneath it, a steely resolve. He would not falter. He couldn't. His father's sacrifice demanded nothing less.

The dust had barely settled in West Seneca, but the air was thick with more than just residual particles from Elias Thorne's desperate gamble. A new kind of reckoning was dawning, one born not of spectral invaders, but of human failings. The fragile peace of their frontier existence had been shattered, and the pieces were being reassembled with the harsh cement of accountability. For those who had known, or suspected, Elias Thorne's truth and had chosen silence, or worse, dismissal, the morning brought a chilling clarity. The weight of their complicity, however passive, was beginning to press down.

Sheriff Brody found himself isolated in a sea of accusatory stares. The authority he had wielded with quiet confidence now felt like a brittle mask. He'd always been the bedrock of order, the man who knew every face, every sinew of this community. But his very role had required him to accept the surface reality, to dismiss the whispers of the uncanny as the ramblings of the superstitious or the eccentric. Elias Thorne had been the eccentric. Brody, in his own mind, had been the sensible one, the one who kept the peace by ignoring the cracks in its foundation. Now, those cracks had widened into chasms, and he was exposed, stripped bare of his perceived wisdom. The farmer whose father had suffered the slow erosion of memory, the woman whose child now stared with vacant eyes – their pain was a direct indictment of his oversight, his willful blindness. He had not merely failed to protect them from an external threat; he had failed to believe them when they spoke of it, thereby compounding their suffering. He saw his own name, no longer etched with respect, but with a brand of ignorance and dereliction of duty. The quiet conversations in the general store, the hushed whispers at the well, were no longer about village gossip, but about his dereliction. Old Man Hemlock's accusation, "You shut him down!" echoed in the silence of Brody's own thoughts, a constant, damning refrain. He'd sent Elias away with dismissive words, offered platitudes to his frantic wife, and now, the consequences were not just

Elias's death, but the deep, festering wound of distrust inflicted upon the very people he was sworn to serve.

Pastor Davies, a man accustomed to dispensing divine pronouncements and offering solace, faced a different kind of void. His sermons, typically met with nods of affirmation and bowed heads, were now met with a disquieting silence, a searching gaze that demanded tangible answers, not spiritual comfort. He had heard Elias Thorne's increasingly desperate pleas, had been privy to the unsettling accounts of villagers experiencing inexplicable fatigue and memory lapses. But the teachings he imparted spoke of faith, of enduring earthly trials, not of parasitic entities lurking in the shadows of their own valley, feeding on their very essence. He had counseled patience, had attributed the villagers' malaise to the hardships of frontier life, to the anxieties of the unknown. He had even gently suggested to Elias that perhaps his intense focus on his peculiar research was leading him to see shadows where none existed. Now, confronted with the irrefutable proof and the visceral reality of the artifact's power, Pastor Davies felt the profound inadequacy of his own doctrine. His faith, which had always been a source of strength, now felt like a fragile shield against a truth that defied biblical precedent. He could offer prayers for healing, but he could not undo the damage. He could speak of divine retribution, but he could not bring Elias Thorne back. The villagers looked to him for absolution, for a clear path through this inexplicable darkness, and he could offer only the same bewildered prayers that were now on their own lips. The trust he had cultivated over years, built on the foundation of unwavering faith, was now being tested by the chilling reality of human vulnerability and the incomprehensible nature of their adversary. His silence, his inability to offer a spiritual explanation for the tangible harm inflicted, was a betrayal of the very faith he represented.

Agnes Peterson, the formidable baker's wife, found her pragmatism utterly disarmed. Her initial outrage, her fierce defense of normalcy, had crumbled with the sight of Timmy's listless gaze. Her husband, Thomas, a man who had always looked to her for strength and direction, was now adrift, his usual resilience replaced by a bewildered fear. Agnes had prided herself on her clear-sightedness, her ability to cut through nonsense. She had seen Elias Thorne as a man lost in his own eccentricities, and his warnings as the product of an overactive imagination. Now, she saw the horrifying consequence of her own dismissal. She had encouraged others to view Elias's claims with skepticism, had perhaps inadvertently fueled the very complacency that had allowed the artifact to thrive. Her own moments of forgetfulness, the times she'd found herself staring at a recipe with no recollection of the ingredients, were no longer dismissed as a sign of aging, but as insidious tendrils of the entities' influence. The shame of her own blindness gnawed at her. She had been so certain, so unyielding in her disbelief, and in doing so, had failed to recognize the subtle erosion of her neighbors' well-being. The integrity of their community, of their shared reality, had been compromised, and she, in her own way, had contributed to that compromise by refusing to acknowledge the possibility of a truth that lay beyond her immediate comprehension.

The ripple effect of revelation spread outwards, touching every corner of West Seneca. Those who had been physically unable to attend the clearing, or who had simply been too preoccupied with their daily toil to be drawn by the unnatural light, were now being brought up to speed. The story, passed from neighbor to neighbor, morphed and magnified with each telling, transforming Elias Thorne from a misunderstood recluse into a tragic hero and Silas from a quiet groundskeeper into a steadfast guardian. Joseph, the quiet boy who had always lived in the shadow of his father's scientific pursuits, was now thrust into the unforgiving spotlight, the reluctant custodian of his father's legacy and the keeper of their collective future.

The immediate aftermath, as Silas had predicted, was a tempest of raw emotion. While some clung to denial, finding solace in familiar explanations of unusual weather patterns or mass hysteria, the majority felt the undeniable truth of the events. The palpable exhaustion that had plagued many for months, the creeping forgetfulness, the inexplicable melancholic moods that had settled over the village like a persistent fog – all of it now had a terrifyingly rational explanation. The artifact, the very thing that had promised some form of advanced understanding, had been a voracious predator.

The general store, once a hub of cheerful camaraderie, became a stage for heated debates. Accusations flew, not only directed at the passive figures of authority like Sheriff Brody and Pastor Davies, but also at each other. Had Mrs. Gable, who had recently experienced peculiar memory lapses, known more than she let on about the strange occurrences? Had Elias Thorne's wife, who had pleaded with Brody to take her husband's concerns seriously, been privy to the full extent of his discoveries? The fragile bonds of community, already strained by the invisible drain on their vitality, were now stretched to their breaking point, threatening to snap under the immense pressure of this shared, terrifying revelation.

Joseph, his father's leather satchel clutched tightly against his side, felt the immense weight of responsibility. He possessed the meticulously documented proof, the journals filled with Elias's observations, his calculations, his unwavering dedication to uncovering the truth. But the challenge wasn't merely presenting the evidence; it was convincing his friends, his neighbors, the people he had known his entire life, that their quiet, predictable existence had been a carefully constructed illusion, a facade maintained by forces they had never suspected. He saw the deep-seated need for answers, but also the paralyzing fear of what those answers might truly mean. His father had written that truth was a cure, but a bitter one, one that promised to burn away the comforting layers of ignorance, offering no easy solace.

The communal reckoning began subtly, not with formal pronouncements or courtroom proceedings – such things were luxuries West Seneca could ill afford – but with the quiet erosion of trust and the stark reality of ostracism. The veneer of neighborly goodwill began to chip away, revealing the raw edges of suspicion and accusation. Those who had openly dismissed Elias Thorne's warnings, or who had actively discouraged others from believing him, found themselves on the fringes of conversations, their opinions no longer carrying the same weight. Sheriff Brody's attempts to restore order were met with a weariness that bordered on disdain. His pleas for calm and unity seemed hollow to those who had suffered the consequences of his inaction. He was no longer the steadfast protector, but a symbol of their collective failure to heed the warnings.

Martha Jenkins, who had been among the first to be deeply affected by the artifact's subtle drain, found herself speaking with a newfound authority. Her earlier, frightened mutterings about unseen forces had been dismissed as the ramblings of a woman overwhelmed by stress. Now, her clear, concise recounting of her own experiences, her description of the gradual dimming of her senses and the unsettling blank spaces in her memory, resonated with a terrifying familiarity for many. She became an unlikely voice of truth, her past distress now a testament to her prescience. Her quiet resilience, her unwavering conviction in the reality of what had happened, served as a stark contrast to the wavering pronouncements of the village's leaders.

The loss of trust was a tangible thing, a cold current running through the heart of the community. Doors that had always been open now remained shut. Conversations that had once been casual and open now carried an undercurrent of suspicion. The very fabric of their social interactions had been altered, frayed by the knowledge that some had been privy to a dangerous secret and had chosen to keep it hidden, or had been too fearful to speak out. The concept of community, built on shared experience and mutual reliance, was now tainted by the revelation of deception, however unintentional it might have been for some.

The consequences for those who had actively downplayed Elias's concerns, or who had actively discouraged any investigation into his claims, were particularly severe. While a formal trial was beyond the scope of West Seneca's capabilities, the community's judgment was swift and unforgiving. The respect they had once commanded was replaced by a quiet, but potent, disapproval. Their words were no longer sought; their presence was often met with averted gazes. This ostracism, though lacking the formal structure of legal punishment, was a powerful force in a close-knit frontier village where reputation and social standing were paramount. The baker's wife, Agnes Peterson, bore the brunt of this silent condemnation. Her previous certainty now seemed like arrogance, her dismissiveness a profound disservice to her neighbors. She was no longer simply Agnes Peterson, the baker's wife; she was Agnes Peterson, the woman who had refused to see the truth, even when it stood before her.

Joseph, guided by Silas's steadying presence, understood that justice in West Seneca would not be meted out in a courtroom, but in the rebuilding of trust and the reaffirmation of honesty. The first step was the dissemination of Elias Thorne's findings. The satchel, filled with his father's journals, became the symbol of their truth. Joseph, with a voice that belied his youth, began to read excerpts aloud in the town square, not just the sensational accounts of the entities, but the meticulous scientific observations, the earnest attempts to understand, the desperate struggle to find a solution. He spoke of his father's intention, not to frighten, but to protect.

"My father," Joseph would begin, his voice clear and steady, his gaze meeting the eyes of those who had once dismissed him, "believed in the power of knowledge. He saw a threat, a subtle, insidious danger that was slowly draining the life from our village, and he dedicated his life to understanding it, to finding a way to combat it. He did not want to cause alarm, but to prepare us. And when he realized the danger was immediate, that the artifact itself was a lure, a trap... he did what he believed was necessary. He sacrificed himself to destroy it, to give us a chance to recover."

The initial reactions were a complex tapestry of emotions. Some listened with rapt attention, their faces etched with a dawning comprehension, a painful understanding of what they had unknowingly endured. Others remained skeptical, their ingrained disbelief a stubborn bulwark against the encroaching truth. But as Joseph continued, day after day, sharing the breadth and depth of his father's work, the tide began to turn. The sheer volume of evidence, the logical progression of his father's research, the undeniable correlation between the artifact's presence and the villagers' declining health and vitality – it began to chip away at the walls of denial.

The communal trial, if one could call it that, was a slow, arduous process of collective confession and the gradual rebuilding of faith. Sheriff Brody, humbled and contrite, began to actively seek out those who had suffered, offering not excuses, but genuine apologies and a commitment to being more vigilant, more open to the unusual. He started by personally visiting the homes of those most affected, listening to their stories without interruption, without judgment, and pledging to ensure such a lapse in oversight would never happen again. He understood that his accountability lay not in a verdict, but in a renewed dedication to his duty, a dedication that now included a willingness to believe the unbelievable.

Pastor Davies, too, began to shift his focus. While he still offered spiritual guidance, he also acknowledged the practical realities of their situation. He organized prayer meetings that also served as forums for sharing information and discussing the path forward. He began to speak of resilience, not just in the face of divine tests, but in the face of human error and the need for unwavering honesty within the community. He confessed his own shortcomings, admitting that he had allowed his faith to blind him to the tangible suffering of his flock, and he called for a renewed commitment to truth and transparency among all villagers.

The ostracism, while painful, served its purpose. It was a stark reminder of the consequences of deception and complacency. Those who had been most vocal in their dismissal of Elias's claims found themselves on the receiving end of the community's quiet disapproval. Their words, once influential, were now met with a weary skepticism.

This social consequence, though informal, was a powerful deterrent against future dismissiveness and a potent force in encouraging a more open and receptive attitude within the village.

The concept of justice, in this 19th-century frontier village, was not about retribution in the traditional sense, but about restoring the integrity of the community and ensuring that such a devastating betrayal of trust would never happen again. It was about holding individuals accountable for their actions, or their inactions, and making them understand the profound impact their choices had on the lives of their neighbors. It was about rebuilding the shattered foundations of trust, one honest conversation, one shared confession, one act of renewed commitment at a time.

Joseph's role became central to this process. He was not just the keeper of his father's legacy; he was the living embodiment of his father's dedication to truth. As he continued to share his father's journals, the scientific data, the personal reflections on the nature of the entities and their insidious influence, the villagers began to understand the depth of Elias Thorne's sacrifice and the quiet courage of Silas, who had stood by him. The narrative of Elias Thorne, the eccentric scientist, was being replaced by Elias Thorne, the protector, the man who had given everything to save his community.

The aftermath of revelation was a harsh but necessary cleansing. The raw emotions of anger and betrayal slowly began to give way to a sense of shared purpose. The understanding that they had all, in varying degrees, been victims of a subtle deception, and that some had actively contributed to that deception through their disbelief or silence, forged a new, albeit fragile, sense of unity. The community was irrevocably changed, stripped of its naive innocence, but perhaps, in its place, gaining a deeper appreciation for honesty, vigilance, and the profound courage it takes to face an uncomfortable truth. The justice they sought was not in punishment, but in the collective recognition of their vulnerability, their shared responsibility, and the enduring power of truth, however painful it might be to embrace. The path ahead was still uncertain, but for the first time since the artifact's unnatural glow had faded, the people of West Seneca felt a flicker of hope, a sense of agency, and a quiet determination to rebuild their lives on a foundation of unvarnished reality. They were accountable to each other, and that accountability, in the end, was the beginning of their true healing.

Joseph, clutching his father's worn leather satchel as if it were an anchor in a sea of uncertainty, found himself the reluctant focal point of West Seneca's fractured reality. The boy who had once drifted through the village like a shadow, often lost in the labyrinth of his father's esoteric research, was now undeniably visible. The raw, unsettling revelations of the past few days had done more than expose the insidious influence of the artifact; they had elevated Elias Thorne's son from a mere observer to an active participant in their collective fate. The murmurs that had followed him through the marketplace, once tinged with pity or mild curiosity, now carried a new resonance – a hesitant respect, perhaps even a nascent awe. He was no longer simply Joseph Thorne, the quiet son of the eccentric scholar, but Joseph Thorne, the accidental custodian of a truth that had nearly consumed them all.

Silas, ever the steady presence, stood a few paces behind Joseph, his gaze a silent testament to the boy's quiet fortitude. He saw the shift in the villagers' eyes, the way they now looked at Joseph not as a child lost in his father's theories, but as a young man who had bravely unearthed a devastating secret. Silas had witnessed Joseph's painstaking efforts, the late nights spent deciphering his father's dense, often cryptic, journals, the quiet determination that burned in his young eyes. He had seen the moment of revelation, the almost unbearable weight of knowledge that had settled upon the boy as he pieced together the puzzle. Now, watching Joseph address the gathered townsfolk, Silas felt a swell of pride that transcended his usual gruff demeanor. The boy's voice, though still carrying the lilt of youth, possessed a newfound authority, a clarity born of conviction and the undeniable evidence he carried.

"My father," Joseph began, his voice ringing out in the hushed square, the satchel held a little higher, "did not chase shadows out of madness. He sought understanding. He observed the changes in our fields, the fatigue that settled upon us like a shroud, the way our thoughts seemed to... fray at the edges." He paused, his gaze sweeping across the faces of his neighbors. He saw Sheriff Brody, his usual stern expression softened by a profound weariness and a hint of shame. He saw Agnes Peterson, the formidable baker's wife, her face etched with a sorrow that seemed to have replaced her usual robust confidence. He saw Martha Jenkins, her voice now a source of quiet strength, her past fear transmuted into an unshakeable resolve. "He saw a pattern," Joseph continued, his words gaining momentum, "a subtle predator, feeding on our vitality, on our very essence. And he documented it all."

The journals, bound in Elias Thorne's familiar, sturdy leather, were more than just a record of scientific inquiry; they were a testament to a father's desperate love and a scholar's unwavering commitment to truth. Joseph had spent weeks poring over them, his initial grief for his father gradually giving way to a burning need to understand, and then, to reveal. He had meticulously cataloged the specimens his father had collected – the strange, iridescent dust that clung to the artifact, the samples of soil that showed an unnatural depletion of vital minerals, the recordings of subtle energy fluctuations that had baffled even Elias initially. He had correlated these findings with his father's journal entries, cross-referencing dates, symptoms, and the growing presence of the artifact near the old oak grove.

"This," Joseph declared, carefully extracting a slender, brittle leaf from the satchel, its edges unnaturally desiccated, "was from a tree near the artifact. My father noted how the plants closest to it withered, not from lack of water, but from an unseen depletion. He theorized that the artifact was actively drawing life force, not just from the soil, but from anything it could influence." He held it up, allowing the faint sunlight to catch its pallor. "He was trying to find a way to neutralize it, to shield us, before it was too late."

The sheer meticulousness of Elias Thorne's work was laid bare through Joseph's earnest recitation. He described his father's early hypotheses, the careful exclusion of more mundane explanations – disease, environmental factors, even agricultural pests. He spoke of Elias's growing desperation as his warnings went unheeded, of the lonely nights spent in his study, fueled by coffee and an unshakable conviction that he was racing against an invisible clock. The entries about the subtle shifts in the villagers' moods, the increasing instances of forgetfulness, the inexplicable lethargy – all of it, once dismissed as mere coincidence or the natural hardships of frontier life, now stood in stark, terrifying relief.

"He wrote about the moment he understood," Joseph's voice trembled slightly, but his resolve did not falter. "That the artifact wasn't just a source of energy, as he had initially suspected, but a lure. Something that fed on our very awareness, our consciousness. It was designed to draw us in, to enthrall us, while it drained us." He looked at Sheriff Brody directly. "He tried to tell you, Sheriff. He pleaded for an investigation, for a warning to be issued. But he was dismissed. And that dismissal, I believe, cost him everything."

The accusation hung heavy in the air, not a venomous barb, but a simple, painful truth. Sheriff Brody shifted his weight, his gaze fixed on the ground. He had no words, no defense against the quiet clarity of the boy's statement. He had been wrong, monumentally wrong, and the consequences of his error were laid bare before him, embodied in the son of the man he had failed. The weight of his past decisions pressed down on him, the memory of Elias Thorne's frantic, earnest face before him, a silent reproach.

Joseph continued, detailing his father's final, desperate plan – the meticulous preparation of the containment measures, the intricate diagram of the artifact's resonant frequencies, the chilling understanding that the only way to neutralize its destructive power was to shatter its core, a suicidal act of self-sacrifice. He read passages describing Elias's final moments, not as a madman consumed by his obsessions, but as a man making a profound, agonizing choice to save his community. The raw emotion in his father's words, the love for his family, the regret for the life he would never live, and the fierce hope for West Seneca's future – it all poured out of the satchel, a torrent of truth that washed over the assembled villagers.

The immediate aftermath of Joseph's pronouncements was not a sudden, collective outpouring of relief or remorse. Instead, it was a slow, seismic shift, a recalibration of their understanding of reality. The air, which had been thick with the unspoken anxieties of the recent past, now pulsed with a new, more profound awareness. The villagers looked at each other, truly looked, perhaps for the first time in months, seeing not just familiar faces, but the subtle evidence of the insidious drain their community had suffered. The tired eyes, the absentmindedness, the creeping melancholia – it all made a terrible, undeniable sense.

Agnes Peterson, stepping forward, her voice surprisingly steady, addressed Joseph directly. "Young man," she began, her tone devoid of its usual briskness, replaced by a deep, resonant sincerity, "your father... he was a brave man. And you, his son, you have shown us a courage that belies your years. I... I was wrong to dismiss his concerns. I was proud, perhaps too proud, to believe that I understood the world around me. Your father's work, your presentation of it, has humbled me." She took a deep breath. "My own forgetfulness, the times I'd stand at the oven and not remember what I was baking... I attributed it to age, to stress. But now... I see it was something more."

Her admission, a public confession of her own earlier skepticism, was a powerful catalyst. Others, emboldened by her honesty, began to speak. Thomas Gable, the farmer whose father had suffered from a memory like a sieve, stepped forward, his face etched with a grief that had been amplified by his ignorance. "My father," he said, his voice rough with emotion, "he faded away. We thought it was just old age catching up with him, the hardships of the land. But to think… to think it was this… this *thing*… draining him all along. And I never knew. I never even considered…" His voice trailed off, choked with unshed tears.

Sheriff Brody, his own apology having been met with a stoic, if weary, acceptance, now felt a new wave of responsibility. He saw that the mere acknowledgment of his failure was not enough. The community needed direction, a clear path forward. He approached Joseph, his hand resting on the boy's shoulder, a gesture of both support and shared burden. "Joseph," he said, his voice firm, carrying the weight of his authority, "your father's legacy is now ours to uphold. This satchel, these journals, they are not just your inheritance; they are the foundation upon which we must rebuild. We need to understand this threat, truly understand it, so that we can protect ourselves and ensure that no one else has to suffer as your father did, as we have."

The communal reckoning, as orchestrated by Joseph's painstaking dissemination of his father's research, was not a single event, but a continuous process. The general store transformed from a place of casual gossip into an impromptu classroom, where Joseph, with Silas at his side, patiently explained the complex theories, the scientific observations, the very nature of the entities his father had identified. He didn't shy away from the technical details, the diagrams of energy conduits, the theories of psychic resonance, for he knew that his father's true strength lay in his meticulous, rational approach to the inexplicable.

The villagers, in turn, began to actively participate. They brought forward their own experiences, their own fragmented memories and unsettling sensations, piecing together the collective narrative of their suffering. Martha Jenkins, her voice now confident and clear, recounted how her earlier fears had been dismissed as hysteria, yet how she had continued to observe the subtle changes in her own perception, the way colors seemed muted, the way the laughter of children had lost its sharp, joyful resonance. Her testimony, once overlooked, was now a vital piece of the puzzle, validating Joseph's claims and lending a human face to the abstract scientific data.

Pastor Davies, too, found his role evolving. His sermons, once focused on spiritual solace, now incorporated a new dimension – the importance of vigilance, of questioning, and of an unwavering commitment to truth, even when that truth was unsettling. He spoke of the human capacity for both denial and for profound courage, acknowledging that Elias Thorne had possessed the latter in abundance. He confessed his own limitations, admitting that his faith, while strong, had not prepared him for the tangible manifestations of evil that Elias had confronted. He began to organize community gatherings that were not just prayer meetings, but forums for open discussion, for sharing information, and for collectively strategizing their path forward. He would often ask Joseph to read from his father's journals, allowing the scientific reasoning to complement the spiritual comfort he offered.

The ostracism of those who had been dismissive of Elias Thorne's claims was a natural, albeit uncomfortable, consequence of the revelation. Agnes Peterson, once a pillar of community opinion, now found herself on the periphery. Her past certainty, which had seemed so grounded in practicality, now appeared as a willful ignorance, a blind spot that had endangered them all. While no formal punishment was meted out, the quiet withdrawal of respect, the averted gazes, and the hushed conversations that ceased when she approached served as a potent, if painful, lesson. This social consequence was a powerful reinforcement of the community's newfound commitment to openness and a clear signal that complacency would no longer be tolerated. It was a form of justice that resonated deeply in a society where reputation and social standing were intrinsically linked to trust.

Joseph's role in this process was multifaceted. He was the curator of his father's legacy, the meticulous guardian of his intellectual pursuits. But he was also the bridge between the scientific and the human, translating complex theories into understandable narratives, weaving the objective data with the subjective experiences of the villagers. He organized Elias Thorne's research notes, creating a centralized archive that would serve as a constant reference point for the community. He worked with Sheriff Brody to establish a system of reporting any unusual occurrences, any further signs of the artifact's influence or the entities' presence. He became, in essence, the village's chief investigator, his youth a unique advantage – he was unburdened by the ingrained skepticism that had clouded the judgment of the older generation.

The discovery and subsequent handling of the artifact itself was a critical point. Under Joseph's guidance, and with Silas's practical assistance, they devised a method for its containment, drawing directly from Elias Thorne's detailed schematics. It involved carefully wrapping the artifact in layers of specially prepared lead-lined cloth, a material Elias had theorized would dampen its energetic output. This was not a task undertaken lightly. Joseph, his hands trembling slightly but his resolve firm, carefully followed his father's instructions, the heavy fabric muffling the faint, almost imperceptible hum that had emanated from the object. The process was a tangible manifestation of his father's final act, a continuation of his desperate struggle to protect them. Once contained, the artifact was buried deep within the earth, far from any habitation, a somber testament to the profound danger it represented.

The justice they sought was not a punitive measure, but a restorative one. It was about accountability, about acknowledging the harm done, and about forging a path towards a more honest and vigilant existence. Joseph's role was central to this rebuilding. He had not sought out this position of influence, but it had found him through his father's dedication and his own courage. He had brought the truth to light, a painful, illuminating force that had shattered their illusions but also offered the possibility of genuine healing. The villagers looked to him not just for answers about the past, but for guidance towards a safer future. He was the living embodiment of his father's unyielding pursuit of knowledge and his ultimate sacrifice, a constant reminder of the delicate balance between ignorance and the sometimes-terrifying clarity of truth. The future of West Seneca, no longer shrouded in the subtle, draining influence of the artifact, was now being shaped by the quiet determination of a boy who had inherited not just his father's satchel, but his father's unwavering commitment to the welfare of their community.

The hushed square, moments before filled with the raw vulnerability of confession and the nascent stirrings of community healing, began to disperse. Yet, the palpable silence that followed Joseph's pronouncements was not one of emptiness, but of profound introspection. The routines of West Seneca, so recently disrupted by the unsettling revelations, did not snap back into place as if nothing had occurred. Instead, they fractured, revealing the hairline cracks that had always existed, now widened into chasms by the undeniable truth. The very fabric of daily life had been rent, and the threads, once so familiar, now seemed alien and unpredictable.

The general store, usually a hive of midday activity, where Agnes Peterson, before her humbling admission, would expertly weigh out flour and gossip about the latest harvest, now stood strangely quiet. A few patrons lingered, their faces a mixture of bewilderment and apprehension, their usual cheerful greetings replaced by hesitant nods. Conversations, when they did occur, were hushed, fragmented affairs, revolving around Elias Thorne's discoveries, Joseph's bravery, and the unsettling implications for their own lives. The mundane act of purchasing provisions had become a charged encounter, each interaction weighed down by the unspoken question: *How much have I been affected? How much have I forgotten?*

Agnes herself, her apron dusted not with flour but with the residue of a newly acquired humility, found her once effortless authority wavering. Customers, accustomed to her brisk efficiency, now approached her with a hesitant deference, their eyes flicking towards Joseph and Silas, who had momentarily stepped outside to discuss the logistics of storing the journals securely. Agnes, accustomed to being the unflinching center of her own universe, now felt a strange disconnect from the familiar rhythms of her trade. She caught herself repeating orders, her mind momentarily snagged on a snippet of Elias's research Joseph had shared earlier – something about resonant frequencies affecting short-term memory. Had her own moments of forgetfulness, previously dismissed as the simple fatigue of a long life, been a precursor to this very revelation? The thought was unsettling, a persistent hum beneath the surface of her daily tasks.

Sheriff Brody, his usual authoritative stride now tempered by a visible weariness, found his duties complicated. The petty disputes and minor infractions that typically filled his days seemed trivial in the face of the existential threat they had narrowly averted. He found himself fielding questions not about stolen chickens or bar brawls, but about the nature of the artifact, the potential for its return, and the extent of its influence. His office, once a sanctuary of predictable order, now felt like an information hub for a crisis that had no easy answers. He spent hours poring over Elias Thorne's detailed notes, trying to grasp the scientific underpinnings of the danger they had faced, his frustration mounting with each complex equation he struggled to decipher. He knew he needed to reassure the townsfolk, to project an image of control, but the sheer magnitude of his past misjudgment weighed heavily upon him.

Even the simplest interactions became fraught with a new tension. Neighbors who had shared coffee and confidences for years now eyed each other with a subtle, almost imperceptible suspicion. Had that shared joke that fell flat been due to a lapse in memory? Had that prolonged argument about property lines been fueled by an unnatural irritability, a side effect of the artifact's draining influence? The trust that had underpinned their community, once taken for granted, now felt fragile, like fine porcelain that had been dropped and was being pieced back together with shaky hands.

Martha Jenkins, whose newfound voice had resonated so powerfully in the square, found her own home a site of quiet contemplation. Her husband, a man of few words even on the best of days, now sat by the hearth, his gaze distant, as if trying to recall fragments of conversations they had shared, moments that now seemed to have been dulled by an unseen fog. Martha found herself retracing their shared history, replaying memories with an almost obsessive intensity, trying to distinguish between genuine affection and the subtle, insidious manipulation of an external force. The comfort of their shared past, once a bedrock, now felt like shifting sands.

The children, who had been largely shielded from the direct implications of Elias Thorne's research, were perhaps the most subtly affected. Their games in the village green, once boisterous and uninhibited, now carried a new undertone of caution. A scraped knee was no longer just an accident; it was a potential consequence of reduced awareness, a momentary lapse in the vigilance their parents were now so acutely aware of. The absence of Elias Thorne, the man who had always had a kind word and a fascinating, if often incomprehensible, story for them, now loomed larger than ever. They sensed the shift in their parents' demeanor, the hushed conversations, the worried glances, and it cast a shadow over their innocence.

Silas, ever the pragmatist, attempted to restore a semblance of order by focusing on practical matters. He helped Joseph meticulously catalog and secure Elias's vast collection of notes and specimens, transforming the quiet sanctuary of Elias's study into a makeshift archive. The air in the room, once thick with the scent of old paper and pipe tobacco, now carried the faint, metallic tang of chemicals and the dry rustle of carefully preserved plant samples. Silas worked with a quiet intensity, his gruff exterior a shield against the emotional weight of their task. He knew that if West Seneca were to recover, it would be through diligent, unglamorous work, a process of rebuilding that started with understanding the damage.

Joseph, however, bore the heaviest burden. He was no longer just a grieving son; he was the custodian of a truth that had irrevocably altered his community. The satchel, once a symbol of his father's quiet dedication, now represented a profound responsibility. He found himself constantly revisiting his father's journals, not just to glean information, but to find solace, to hear his father's voice in the carefully penned words, to feel the presence of the man who had sacrificed everything. He felt a deep, unsettling loneliness, the isolation of being the one who knew, the one who had to guide them through the aftermath.

The disruption extended beyond the personal and into the economic sphere. The local craftsman, who had been meticulously repairing wagons, found himself pausing, his tools lying idle as he pondered the implications of his father's research on the very soil that sustained their livelihoods. The farmer, whose fields had shown signs of unnatural depletion, now faced the daunting task of understanding how to restore the land, armed only with fragmented theories and the grim pronouncements of a man who was no longer there to guide him. Every profession, every livelihood, was suddenly cast in a new, uncertain light.

The revelation had, in essence, suspended the natural progression of time in West Seneca. The future, once a predictable continuum of familiar seasons and established traditions, was now an uncharted territory. The past, too, had been recontextualized, its moments of joy and sorrow now tinged with the knowledge of an unseen influence, a subtle predator that had woven itself into the very fabric of their lives. The immediate impact was not a sudden, dramatic upheaval, but a pervasive sense of disorientation, a quiet unraveling of the familiar, leaving the community to grapple with a reality far more complex and unsettling than they had ever imagined. The certainty of the everyday had been replaced by a gnawing uncertainty, and the task of rebuilding their lives, their trust, and their sense of normalcy had only just begun.

The days that followed the revelation were a study in muted disruption. The rhythm of West Seneca, once as reliable as the sunrise, was now syncopated, out of step with itself. The marketplace, usually a cheerful cacophony of vendor calls and animated bartering, had settled into a subdued hum. Vendors found their usual pitches faltering, their minds often drifting to the implications of Elias Thorne's research. Farmer McGregor, known for his booming voice that could carry across the entire square, found himself struggling to engage potential customers, his usual spiel about the crispness of his apples interrupted by a recurring thought: had the artifact's influence made them sweeter, or had it subtly altered their very essence? He'd shake his head, a flicker of bewilderment crossing his weathered face, and offer a hesitant smile, his usual hearty demeanor replaced by a newfound introspection.

Even the simple act of sharing a meal became a more somber affair. Families gathered around their tables, the familiar comfort of shared food now tinged with a subtle unease. Conversations, which had once flowed easily, now often stalled as individuals found themselves searching for words, struggling to recall details of shared experiences. Young Lily Thorne, Joseph's younger sister, who had been blissfully unaware of her father's scientific pursuits until recently, would often ask, "Papa used to tell me stories about the stars. Do you remember, Mama? What did he say about that bright one, the one that looked like a diamond?" Her mother, Sarah, would try to recall, her brow furrowed in concentration, but the clarity was often elusive, the memories blurred at the edges. She'd offer a vague reassurance, a gentle touch, but the unspoken question hung between them: how much of their shared past had been tainted?

The village blacksmith, Elias's closest friend and confidant among the tradesmen, found his forge unusually silent. He'd spend hours staring into the glowing embers, not shaping metal, but piecing together fragmented memories of Elias's increasingly desperate visits. Elias had spoken of "subtle energies" and "vitalistic drain," terms that had seemed like the eccentric ramblings of a brilliant mind pushed to its limits. Now, those words echoed with a terrifying resonance. The blacksmith, a man whose hands were usually steady and sure, found them trembling as he contemplated the possibility that his friend's frantic warnings had been accurate, and that he, too, had been affected, his own focus dulled, his own vigor subtly sapped. He'd sometimes stop mid-swing, the hammer hanging suspended in the air, lost in a sudden, inexplicable forgetfulness.

The local tavern, 'The Weary Traveler,' typically the hub of social life and a place where the day's worries could be momentarily forgotten over a pint, now presented a different scene. Patrons sat in smaller, more isolated groups, their conversations hushed and serious. The usual boisterous laughter was absent, replaced by a low murmur of speculation and concern. Bartender Silas, while outwardly maintaining his usual stoic demeanor, found himself observing the subtle shifts in his patrons. He noticed the increased frequency with which they'd ask for another drink, not out of revelry, but out of a subconscious desire to rekindle a dulled spirit. He saw the way they'd sometimes stare blankly into their mugs, their thoughts seemingly miles away, lost in the labyrinth of their own altered perceptions.

The town council, which normally met weekly to discuss matters of infrastructure and local ordinances, found their agenda completely derailed. The revelation had rendered their usual concerns almost moot. Instead, their meetings became intense, often fractious sessions dedicated to understanding the extent of the damage and devising strategies for mitigation. Sheriff Brody, attempting to exert his authority, found his pronouncements met with a weary skepticism. He'd recall Elias's journals, attempting to explain the scientific principles at play, but the complexity of the information, coupled with the villagers' own lived experiences of subtle cognitive and physical decline, made it difficult to achieve a unified understanding. The very trust that Elias Thorne had sought to build, and that Brody had inadvertently eroded, was now a vital commodity that was desperately difficult to reacquire.

The children's games, too, had changed. The carefree abandon that characterized their play was now tempered by a nascent awareness of their own vulnerabilities. A game of tag might be abandoned mid-chase if a child suddenly felt inexplicably fatigued, their energy reserves seemingly depleted by an unseen force. The simple act of learning, too, was affected. The schoolmaster, a stern but fair man named Mr. Abernathy, noticed a marked decline in his students' ability to retain information. Lessons that had once been readily absorbed now required constant repetition. He found himself struggling to maintain their attention, his own patience tested by a phenomenon he couldn't quite comprehend, a creeping lassitude that seemed to affect not just his students, but his own ability to impart knowledge.

The relationships between villagers were put to a severe test. Husbands and wives, friends and neighbors, found themselves scrutinizing their interactions, searching for signs of manipulation or subtle influence. Had that argument been a genuine disagreement, or a manifestation of the artifact's divisive tendencies? Had that act of kindness been a true gesture of affection, or a calculated response to an alien prompting? The very foundations of trust, built over years of shared experience, began to feel precarious. A sense of isolation began to creep in, as individuals retreated into their own thoughts, uncertain of whom they could truly rely on.

Pastor Davies, while offering spiritual solace, found that his sermons had to adapt. He spoke not just of faith and redemption, but of vigilance and critical thinking. He acknowledged the limitations of human understanding, the ways in which even the most devout could be susceptible to forces beyond their comprehension. He organized prayer vigils not just for comfort, but for clarity, for the restoration of clear thought and purpose. He'd often quote from Elias Thorne's journals, allowing the scholar's meticulous observations to frame the spiritual struggle they faced, emphasizing that understanding the nature of the threat was as vital as faith in overcoming it.

The revelation had created a vacuum, a period where the old certainties had been stripped away, and the new realities were still taking shape. West Seneca found itself in a state of suspended animation, its routines disrupted, its relationships strained, and its future uncertain. The immediate impact was not a singular, cataclysmic event, but a pervasive, unsettling shift in the very atmosphere of the town. The normalcy they had known was gone, replaced by a shared understanding of a profound vulnerability, a secret that had permeated their lives, demanding a complete re-evaluation of everything they thought they knew about themselves and their world. This was the fragile dawn of their new existence, a dawn shrouded in the lingering shadows of revelation.

9

Joseph's Transformation

The hushed square, moments before filled with the raw vulnerability of confession and the nascent stirrings of community healing, began to disperse. Yet, the palpable silence that followed Joseph's pronouncements was not one of emptiness, but of profound introspection. The routines of West Seneca, so recently disrupted by the unsettling revelations, did not snap back into place as if nothing had occurred. Instead, they fractured, revealing the hairline cracks that had always existed, now widened into chasms by the undeniable truth. The very fabric of daily life had been rent, and the threads, once so familiar, now seemed alien and unpredictable.

The general store, usually a hive of midday activity, where Agnes Peterson, before her humbling admission, would expertly weigh out flour and gossip about the latest harvest, now stood strangely quiet. A few patrons lingered, their faces a mixture of bewilderment and apprehension, their usual cheerful greetings replaced by hesitant nods. Conversations, when they did occur, were hushed, fragmented affairs, revolving around Elias Thorne's discoveries, Joseph's bravery, and the unsettling implications for their own lives. The mundane act of purchasing provisions had become a charged encounter, each interaction weighed down by the unspoken question: *How much have I been affected? How much have I forgotten?*

Agnes herself, her apron dusted not with flour but with the residue of a newly acquired humility, found her once effortless authority wavering. Customers, accustomed to her brisk efficiency, now approached her with a hesitant deference, their eyes flicking towards Joseph and Silas, who had momentarily stepped outside to discuss the logistics of storing the journals securely. Agnes, accustomed to being the unflinching center of her own universe, now felt a strange disconnect from the familiar rhythms of her trade. She caught herself repeating orders, her mind momentarily snagged on a snippet of Elias's research Joseph had shared earlier – something about resonant frequencies affecting short-term memory. Had her own moments of forgetfulness, previously dismissed as the simple fatigue of a long life, been a precursor to this very revelation? The thought was unsettling, a persistent hum beneath the surface of her daily tasks.

Sheriff Brody, his usual authoritative stride now tempered by a visible weariness, found his duties complicated. The petty disputes and minor infractions that typically filled his days seemed trivial in the face of the existential threat they had narrowly averted. He found himself fielding questions not about stolen chickens or bar brawls, but about the nature of the artifact, the potential for its return, and the extent of its influence. His office, once a sanctuary of predictable order, now felt like an information hub for a crisis that had no easy answers. He spent hours poring over Elias Thorne's detailed notes, trying to grasp the scientific underpinnings of the danger they had faced, his frustration mounting with each complex equation he struggled to decipher. He knew he needed to reassure the townsfolk, to project an image of control, but the sheer magnitude of his past misjudgment weighed heavily upon him.

Even the simplest interactions became fraught with a new tension. Neighbors who had shared coffee and confidences for years now eyed each other with a subtle, almost imperceptible suspicion. Had that shared joke that fell flat been due to a lapse in memory? Had that prolonged argument about property lines been fueled by an unnatural irritability, a side effect of the artifact's draining influence? The trust that had underpinned their community, once taken for granted, now felt fragile, like fine porcelain that had been dropped and was being pieced back together with shaky hands.

Martha Jenkins, whose newfound voice had resonated so powerfully in the square, found her own home a site of quiet contemplation. Her husband, a man of few words even on the best of days, now sat by the hearth, his gaze distant, as if trying to recall fragments of conversations they had shared, moments that now seemed to have been dulled by an unseen fog. Martha found herself retracing their shared history, replaying memories with an almost obsessive intensity, trying to distinguish between genuine affection and the subtle, insidious manipulation of an external force. The comfort of their shared past, once a bedrock, now felt like shifting sands.

The children, who had been largely shielded from the direct implications of Elias Thorne's research, were perhaps the most subtly affected. Their games in the village green, once boisterous and uninhibited, now carried a new undertone of caution. A scraped knee was no longer just an accident; it was a potential consequence of reduced awareness, a momentary lapse in the vigilance their parents were now so acutely aware of. The absence of Elias Thorne, the man who had always had a kind word and a fascinating, if often incomprehensible, story for them, now loomed larger than ever. They sensed the shift in their parents' demeanor, the hushed conversations, the worried glances, and it cast a shadow over their innocence.

Silas, ever the pragmatist, attempted to restore a semblance of order by focusing on practical matters. He helped Joseph meticulously catalog and secure Elias's vast collection of notes and specimens, transforming the quiet sanctuary of Elias's study into a makeshift archive. The air in the room, once thick with the scent of old paper and pipe tobacco, now carried the faint, metallic tang of chemicals and the dry rustle of carefully preserved plant samples. Silas worked with a quiet intensity, his gruff exterior a shield against the emotional weight of their task. He knew that if West Seneca were to recover, it would be through diligent, unglamorous work, a process of rebuilding that started with understanding the damage.

Joseph, however, bore the heaviest burden. He was no longer just a grieving son; he was the custodian of a truth that had irrevocably altered his community. The satchel, once a symbol of his father's quiet dedication, now represented a profound responsibility. He found himself constantly revisiting his father's journals, not just to glean information, but to find solace, to hear his father's voice in the carefully penned words, to feel the presence of the man who had sacrificed everything. He felt a deep, unsettling loneliness, the isolation of being the one who knew, the one who had to guide them through the aftermath.

The disruption extended beyond the personal and into the economic sphere. The local craftsman, who had been meticulously repairing wagons, found himself pausing, his tools lying idle as he pondered the implications of his father's research on the very soil that sustained their livelihoods. The farmer, whose fields had shown signs of unnatural depletion, now faced the daunting task of understanding how to restore the land, armed only with fragmented theories and the grim pronouncements of a man who was no longer there to guide him. Every profession, every livelihood, was suddenly cast in a new, uncertain light.

The revelation had, in essence, suspended the natural progression of time in West Seneca. The future, once a predictable continuum of familiar seasons and established traditions, was now an uncharted territory. The past, too, had been recontextualized, its moments of joy and sorrow now tinged with the knowledge of an unseen influence, a subtle predator that had woven itself into the very fabric of their lives. The immediate impact was not a sudden, dramatic upheaval, but a pervasive sense of disorientation, a quiet unraveling of the familiar, leaving the community to grapple with a reality far more complex and unsettling than they had ever imagined. The certainty of the everyday had been replaced by a gnawing uncertainty, and the task of rebuilding their lives, their trust, and their sense of normalcy had only just begun.

The days that followed the revelation were a study in muted disruption. The rhythm of West Seneca, once as reliable as the sunrise, was now syncopated, out of step with itself. The marketplace, usually a cheerful cacophony of vendor calls and animated bartering, had settled into a subdued hum. Vendors found their usual pitches faltering, their minds often drifting to the implications of Elias Thorne's research. Farmer McGregor, known for his booming voice that could carry across the entire square, found himself struggling to engage potential customers, his usual spiel about the crispness of his apples interrupted by a recurring thought: had the artifact's influence made them sweeter, or had it subtly altered their very essence? He'd shake his head, a flicker of bewilderment crossing his weathered face, and offer a hesitant smile, his usual hearty demeanor replaced by a newfound introspection.

Even the simple act of sharing a meal became a more somber affair. Families gathered around their tables, the familiar comfort of shared food now tinged with a subtle unease. Conversations, which had once flowed easily, now often stalled as individuals found themselves searching for words, struggling to recall details of shared experiences. Young Lily Thorne, Joseph's younger sister, who had been blissfully unaware of her father's scientific pursuits until recently, would often ask, "Papa used to tell me stories about the stars. Do you remember, Mama? What did he say about that bright one, the one that looked like a diamond?" Her mother, Sarah, would try to recall, her brow furrowed in concentration, but the clarity was often elusive, the memories blurred at the edges. She'd offer a vague reassurance, a gentle touch, but the unspoken question hung between them: how much of their shared past had been tainted?

The village blacksmith, Elias's closest friend and confidant among the tradesmen, found his forge unusually silent. He'd spend hours staring into the glowing embers, not shaping metal, but piecing together fragmented memories of Elias's increasingly desperate visits. Elias had spoken of "subtle energies" and "vitalistic drain," terms that had seemed like the eccentric ramblings of a brilliant mind pushed to its limits. Now, those words echoed with a terrifying resonance. The blacksmith, a man whose hands were usually steady and sure, found them trembling as he contemplated the possibility that his friend's frantic warnings had been accurate, and that he, too, had been affected, his own focus dulled, his own vigor subtly sapped. He'd sometimes stop mid-swing, the hammer hanging suspended in the air, lost in a sudden, inexplicable forgetfulness.

The local tavern, 'The Weary Traveler,' typically the hub of social life and a place where the day's worries could be momentarily forgotten over a pint, now presented a different scene. Patrons sat in smaller, more isolated groups, their conversations hushed and serious. The usual boisterous laughter was absent, replaced by a low murmur of speculation and concern. Bartender Silas, while outwardly maintaining his usual stoic demeanor, found himself observing the subtle shifts in his patrons. He noticed the increased frequency with which they'd ask for another drink, not out of revelry, but out of a subconscious desire to rekindle a dulled spirit. He saw the way they'd sometimes stare blankly into their mugs, their thoughts seemingly miles away, lost in the labyrinth of their own altered perceptions.

The town council, which normally met weekly to discuss matters of infrastructure and local ordinances, found their agenda completely derailed. The revelation had rendered their usual concerns almost moot. Instead, their meetings became intense, often fractious sessions dedicated to understanding the extent of the damage and devising strategies for mitigation. Sheriff Brody, attempting to exert his authority, found his pronouncements met with a weary skepticism. He'd recall Elias's journals, attempting to explain the scientific principles at play, but the complexity of the information, coupled with the villagers' own lived experiences of subtle cognitive and physical decline, made it difficult to achieve a unified understanding. The very trust that Elias Thorne had sought to build, and that Brody had inadvertently eroded, was now a vital commodity that was desperately difficult to reacquire.

The children's games, too, had changed. The carefree abandon that characterized their play was now tempered by a nascent awareness of their own vulnerabilities. A game of tag might be abandoned mid-chase if a child suddenly felt inexplicably fatigued, their energy reserves seemingly depleted by an unseen force. The simple act of learning, too, was affected. The schoolmaster, a stern but fair man named Mr. Abernathy, noticed a marked decline in his students' ability to retain information. Lessons that had once been readily absorbed now required constant repetition. He found himself struggling to maintain their attention, his own patience tested by a phenomenon he couldn't quite comprehend, a creeping lassitude that seemed to affect not just his students, but his own ability to impart knowledge.

The relationships between villagers were put to a severe test. Husbands and wives, friends and neighbors, found themselves scrutinizing their interactions, searching for signs of manipulation or subtle influence. Had that argument been a genuine disagreement, or a manifestation of the artifact's divisive tendencies? Had that act of kindness been a true gesture of affection, or a calculated response to an alien prompting? The very foundations of trust, built over years of shared experience, began to feel precarious. A sense of isolation began to creep in, as individuals retreated into their own thoughts, uncertain of whom they could truly rely on.

Pastor Davies, while offering spiritual solace, found that his sermons had to adapt. He spoke not just of faith and redemption, but of vigilance and critical thinking. He acknowledged the limitations of human understanding, the ways in which even the most devout could be susceptible to forces beyond their comprehension. He organized prayer vigils not just for comfort, but for clarity, for the restoration of clear thought and purpose. He'd often quote from Elias Thorne's journals, allowing the scholar's meticulous observations to frame the spiritual struggle they faced, emphasizing that understanding the nature of the threat was as vital as faith in overcoming it.

The revelation had created a vacuum, a period where the old certainties had been stripped away, and the new realities were still taking shape. West Seneca found itself in a state of suspended animation, its routines disrupted, its relationships strained, and its future uncertain. The immediate impact was not a singular, cataclysmic event, but a pervasive, unsettling shift in the very atmosphere of the town. The normalcy they had known was gone, replaced by a shared understanding of a profound vulnerability, a secret that had permeated their lives, demanding a complete re-evaluation of everything they thought they knew about themselves and their world. This was the fragile dawn of their new existence, a dawn shrouded in the lingering shadows of revelation.

Joseph, however, was beginning to navigate this altered landscape with a different kind of purpose. The initial surge of exhilaration, the almost desperate need to understand the mysteries his father had left behind, had transformed. It was no longer a thrill-seeking chase for esoteric knowledge; it was a profound, almost sacred duty. The boundless curiosity that had once propelled him into the woods, eager to uncover every secret of nature, was now tempered by a sober understanding of the consequences that such unearthing could bring. He had seen firsthand the disruption that even a partially understood truth could unleash. His father's journals, once a source of intellectual fascination, now felt like heavy tomes of responsibility, each page a potential weapon or a shield depending on how its contents were wielded.

He found himself lingering over Elias's meticulously detailed observations of the artifact's effects, not with the eager anticipation of a budding scientist eager to replicate experiments, but with the cautious diligence of a historian piecing together fragmented accounts of a devastating plague. The scientific jargon, the complex diagrams, the speculative hypotheses – these were no longer mere intellectual puzzles to be solved, but critical pieces of a larger, dangerous puzzle that had ensnared his entire community. The thrill of discovery had been replaced by a gnawing awareness of the inherent risks. He recalled the exhilaration he'd felt when first deciphering a particularly obscure passage, a sense of intellectual triumph that now felt naive, almost shameful. He understood now that knowledge, particularly knowledge of this magnitude, was not a commodity to be hoarded or a prize to be won, but a burden to be carried with immense care.

His explorations, once driven by a youthful exuberance and a touch of recklessness, were now undertaken with a newfound deliberateness. He still ventured into the familiar woods surrounding West Seneca, but his steps were more measured, his senses more attuned not just to the rustle of leaves or the call of a bird, but to the subtler shifts in the environment, the almost imperceptible hum that Elias had described. He carried Elias's journals not as a treasure map, but as a guide, a warning system. He was no longer simply looking for *what* his father had discovered, but *how* to manage the repercussions of that discovery. He analyzed Elias's notes on the artifact's energy signatures, not to marvel at their complexity, but to understand how to shield himself and, by extension, the town, from its insidious influence.

This shift was most apparent in his interactions with Silas. Previously, Joseph might have chafed under Silas's pragmatic, often blunt, assessments, seeing them as an impediment to his own more ambitious explorations. Now, he actively sought Silas's counsel, valuing the blacksmith's grounded perspective. When Joseph would excitedly present a new interpretation of Elias's findings, Silas wouldn't just offer a gruff affirmation; he'd probe Joseph's reasoning, asking about the source of his certainty, the potential for misinterpretation, the practical applications of the knowledge. "And what good does knowing that do us, Joseph?" Silas might ask, his voice rough but his gaze sharp. "Can you build a fence with that knowledge? Can you keep the frost from the crops?" These questions, once a source of mild irritation for Joseph, now served as vital anchors, pulling him back from the precipice of abstract theory into the realm of tangible reality and immediate need.

Joseph found himself scrutinizing his own motivations. The boy who had once delighted in the daring nature of his clandestine investigations, the thrill of venturing into forbidden territory, was being replaced by a young man who understood the weight of responsibility. He began to see the potential for harm in his own eagerness. He realized that his initial curiosity, while genuine, had been intertwined with a desire for personal validation, a need to prove himself, perhaps even to outshine the memory of his father. Now, that element of self-aggrandizement had withered, replaced by a quiet, determined resolve to protect his community. He understood that revealing the truth was only the first step; the true challenge lay in managing its aftermath, in guiding West Seneca back towards stability, not through ignorance, but through informed vigilance.

He spent hours in Elias's study, meticulously cross-referencing different entries, searching for patterns, for contradictions, for anything that might provide a clearer path forward. He wasn't just absorbing information; he was dissecting it, questioning it, evaluating its potential impact. The boundless, almost naive, enthusiasm for knowledge had been replaced by a more discerning inquisitiveness. He was learning to ask not just "What is this?" but "What does this mean, and what should we do about it?" This transformation was subtle, an internal metamorphosis rather than an outward show. It was evident in the way he listened, the way he spoke, the way he approached every piece of Elias's legacy.

The weight of his father's sacrifice was no longer just a source of sorrow, but a constant reminder of the stakes involved. Elias Thorne had not merely been a scholar; he had been a sentinel, a man who had recognized a danger and dedicated his life, ultimately to its exposure. Joseph felt a profound connection to that dedication, a lineage of responsibility that transcended blood. He saw his father's research not as a collection of arcane facts, but as a testament to the courage required to confront uncomfortable truths. This realization instilled in him a quiet respect for the process, for the slow, painstaking work of understanding, and for the humility that must accompany the pursuit of knowledge. He understood that true wisdom lay not just in acquiring information, but in knowing how and when to share it, and how to mitigate the potential harm it could cause. The boy who had once charged headlong into the unknown had learned to tread carefully, his curiosity now a guiding force, not a reckless impulse, leading him towards a future where knowledge and responsibility walked hand in hand.

The raw, unvarnished truth of the artifact, and the terrifying fragility it had exposed within West Seneca, had irrevocably altered Joseph Thorne. The boy who had once chased the thrill of discovery with an almost reckless abandon now moved with a deliberation that belied his years. His youthful exuberance hadn't vanished entirely, but it had been tempered, refined by the crucible of his father's legacy and the near-catastrophe that had threatened to engulf their quiet town. He carried himself differently, his shoulders less prone to the nervous slouch of uncertainty, now set with a quiet, nascent confidence. It wasn't the swagger of arrogance, but the steady assurance of someone who had stared into the abyss and understood, with chilling clarity, the precipice upon which they all stood.

The hurried, often impulsive nature that had defined his explorations of the surrounding wilderness had given way to a more thoughtful, methodical approach. He still felt the pull of the woods, the undeniable allure of the unexplored, but his ventures were now guided by a profound sense of purpose and a hard-won prudence. Each step he took was considered, each observation meticulously cataloged not just in his mind, but in the ever-growing collection of his father's journals, which had become his constant companions. He understood, with a clarity that was both exhilarating and terrifying, that the knowledge contained within those pages was not a game to be played, but a formidable tool, capable of both immense good and unimaginable harm. The thrill of discovery was still present, a flicker in his eyes when he unearthed a particularly insightful passage from Elias's meticulous notes, but it was now underscored by a heavy awareness of the responsibility that accompanied such revelations.

This newfound maturity was most evident in his interactions with Silas. The gruff blacksmith, a man of action and grounded pragmatism, had always served as a foil to Joseph's more speculative inclinations. Before, Joseph might have bristled at Silas's pointed questions, viewing them as attempts to stifle his intellectual curiosity or, worse, to dismiss his father's work as the ramblings of an eccentric recluse. Now, however, Joseph actively sought out Silas's perspective, valuing the blacksmith's ability to cut through theoretical complexities and focus on the tangible, the practical. When Joseph would present a new hypothesis gleaned from Elias's journals, perhaps a subtle correlation between specific atmospheric conditions and the artifact's energetic fluctuations, Silas wouldn't offer a dismissive grunt. Instead, he'd lean back on his anvil, wiping sweat from his brow with a calloused hand, and ask, "And what does that mean for us, Joseph? Can we use that knowledge to mend a broken wagon wheel? Does it help us predict the coming frost?"

These seemingly simple questions, which once might have felt like an accusation of theoretical indulgence, now served as vital anchors for Joseph. They pulled him back from the ethereal heights of abstract scientific inquiry and grounded him in the immediate, pressing realities of West Seneca. He understood that his father's work, while groundbreaking, needed to be translated into actionable wisdom. He began to see his own role not merely as a successor to Elias's research, but as a bridge between his father's profound discoveries and the practical needs of his community. He realized that the true measure of their success would not be in the intellectual elegance of Elias's theories, but in their ability to implement that knowledge to safeguard their lives and livelihoods.

The clandestine expeditions into the woods, once fueled by a youthful desire to escape the mundane and uncover hidden wonders, had undergone a significant transformation. Joseph still sought the solace and intellectual stimulation that the wilderness provided, but his journeys were now imbued with a heightened sense of purpose. He was no longer simply exploring; he was observing, analyzing, and, most importantly, learning to anticipate. He meticulously studied Elias's notes on the artifact's unique energetic signature, its subtle fluctuations, and the environmental factors that seemed to influence its behavior. He learned to recognize the almost imperceptible hum that Elias had described, a resonance that could be felt more than heard, a prickling awareness of an unseen presence. His senses, once honed for the thrill of a hidden discovery, were now sharpened to detect the faintest anomaly, the subtlest shift in the natural order.

He recalled the day he had stumbled upon a patch of unusually vibrant moss, a shade of green so intense it seemed almost otherworldly, a detail his father had meticulously documented in his journals as a potential indicator of localized energetic saturation. Before, the discovery would have elicited a simple gasp of wonder. Now, Joseph approached it with a scientist's caution, carefully noting its precise location, the surrounding flora, the atmospheric conditions, and cross-referencing it with Elias's broader observations. He understood that such anomalies were not merely curiosities but potential warning signs, clues that could help predict and, hopefully, mitigate the artifact's influence. This meticulous attention to detail, this disciplined approach to observation, was a direct product of the harrowing experiences he had recently endured.

The boy who had once dreamed of grand adventures, of unearthing ancient secrets and becoming a renowned explorer, was beginning to embrace a more mature vision of his future. The recklessness that had often accompanied his youthful explorations had been replaced by a considered courage. He understood the inherent dangers, the potential for unintended consequences, and he was learning to navigate those risks with a newfound respect. His desire for validation, for recognition as a clever young man who could unravel his father's mysteries, had begun to recede, replaced by a deeper, more profound sense of duty. He felt a burgeoning responsibility to his community, a quiet determination to protect them from the unseen forces that had so nearly undone them.

This internal shift manifested in subtle ways, in the way he now approached the delicate task of sorting and organizing Elias's sprawling collection of research. Where once he might have eagerly devoured the most sensational findings, he now approached each document with a measured patience. He spent hours cross-referencing notes, seeking corroboration, questioning Elias's own interpretations with the critical eye of a seasoned scholar. He understood that his father, despite his brilliance, was still human, prone to moments of intense focus and, perhaps, occasional overstatement. Joseph learned to discern the objective observations from the speculative theories, the empirical data from the emotional responses. This discernment was not born of cynicism, but of a dawning understanding that knowledge, especially knowledge of such a potent and potentially dangerous nature, required rigorous examination and a constant awareness of its limitations.

He found himself drawn to the more pragmatic aspects of Elias's research – the detailed accounts of the artifact's physical properties, its material composition, the precise measurements of its emissions. These were the elements that Silas, and by extension, the rest of West Seneca, could readily grasp and, perhaps, even utilize. Joseph realized that to truly help his community, he needed to translate his father's complex scientific endeavors into a language they could all understand, a language that offered not just explanations, but solutions. He began to see himself as an interpreter, a conduit between the esoteric world of his father's research and the everyday reality of their lives.

The constant presence of his father's journals, once a source of intellectual stimulation, had also become a profound source of personal guidance. Joseph would often spend his evenings poring over the carefully penned pages, not just for information, but for solace, for the comfort of his father's voice in the familiar cadence of his writing. He would trace the lines of his father's diagrams, imagining the intense focus and quiet determination that had accompanied their creation. He felt a deep, enduring connection to Elias, a shared understanding of the world that transcended the years that now separated them. This connection fueled his resolve, reinforcing the immense weight of the responsibility he carried. He understood that Elias Thorne had not merely been a brilliant scientist; he had been a vigilant guardian, a man who had recognized a profound threat and dedicated his life to understanding and, ultimately, exposing it. Joseph now felt that same calling, a solemn obligation to carry forward his father's work, to ensure that Elias's sacrifices had not been in vain.

The boy who had always been eager for adventure, for the thrill of the unknown, was slowly but surely becoming a young man of quiet purpose. The harrowing events had acted as a powerful catalyst, accelerating a natural process of maturation. He was learning to temper his impulses with reason, to channel his considerable intellect into practical applications, and to approach the world with a newfound sense of self-reliance. The inherent dangers he had faced had stripped away the last vestiges of youthful naivete, replacing them with a clear-eyed understanding of the complexities and perils of the adult world. Joseph Thorne was no longer just a boy lost in the mysteries of his father's legacy; he was a young man stepping into his own, guided by wisdom born of hardship, ready to face whatever the future, and the artifact's lingering influence, might hold. His adventurous spirit remained, a vital ember within him, but it was now a flame carefully banked, its heat directed by the steady hand of experience and the unwavering compass of responsibility.

The weight of knowledge settled upon Joseph Thorne not like a comforting blanket, but like an ill-fitting, heavy cloak. It was a constant, perceptible presence, altering the very way he moved through the world. Before, West Seneca had been his uncomplicated home, a place of familiar faces, predictable rhythms, and the comforting certainty of the ordinary. Now, beneath that placid surface, he saw a far more complex, unsettling reality. The tranquil facade of his town, once a source of security, now seemed a carefully constructed artifice, a delicate veil drawn over secrets that had almost consumed them. He understood, with a gnawing certainty, that appearances were not just deceiving; they were actively misleading, designed to obscure a darkness that had very nearly plunged them all into oblivion.

This realization was a far more profound and personal burden than the physical dangers he had faced. The artifact, with its terrifying power, was a tangible threat, a force he could, in some ways, comprehend through his father's research. But the human element, the capacity for calculated deception, the willingness to harbor such a perilous secret for so long – that was a darkness that resided not in strange energies or otherworldly materials, but within the hearts of men. He found himself scrutinizing the casual conversations in the general store, the friendly nods from neighbors he had known his entire life, with a new, unnerving vigilance. Every smile, every offered pleasantry, seemed to carry a double meaning, a potential for hidden intent. He saw the quiet resignation in the eyes of some, the carefully maintained cheerfulness of others, and wondered what unspoken stories lay behind their facades.

The knowledge of what had transpired, of the near-catastrophe and the hidden machinations that had led to it, was a constant, internal hum, a resonance that echoed his father's descriptions of the artifact itself. It was a reminder that even in the most seemingly peaceful communities, shadows could lengthen, and hidden currents could run deep and treacherous. He remembered the initial days after the artifact's influence had been, by all appearances, neutralized. The relief in the town had been palpable, a collective exhaling of a breath held for too long. But Joseph couldn't fully share in that unburdened joy. He knew the truth, the fragility of their safety, the razor's edge upon which they had all teetered. This knowledge created a subtle, almost imperceptible distance between him and those around him. While they celebrated their return to normalcy, Joseph remained acutely aware of the abnormal forces that had so recently threatened their existence.

He found himself dwelling on the quiet admissions, the hushed confessions that had followed the revelation of the artifact's presence and its near-unleashing. These weren't grand pronouncements of guilt or remorse, but small, almost involuntary acknowledgments of complicity, of a shared silence that had allowed the danger to fester. He recalled the hushed conversations overheard between town elders, the nervous glances exchanged when certain topics were broached, the way conversations would abruptly cease whenever he entered a room. Each of these moments, once dismissed as the natural reticence of a small community, now seemed imbued with a deeper significance, pieces of a puzzle that revealed a tapestry of unease and complicity. He understood that for years, a select few had known, or at least suspected, the truth about the strange object buried beneath their town, and their silence, whether born of fear or a misguided sense of protection, had carried its own insidious weight.

The memories of the artifact's raw power, the chilling sensations he had experienced, and the sheer terror of witnessing its potential, were etched into his mind. These weren't fading images; they were vivid, intrusive replays that would surface at the most unexpected moments. A sudden drop in temperature, a peculiar shift in the light, even the distant rumble of thunder could trigger a visceral surge of adrenaline, a phantom echo of the energies he had felt. He learned to recognize these triggers, to mentally brace himself, but the underlying anxiety remained. It was the anxiety of a child who had seen something he shouldn't have, something that had irrevocably shattered his innocent perception of the world.

This newfound awareness of human fallibility and the potential for hidden darkness also affected his trust in Silas, though in a different way than one might expect. Silas, with his blunt honesty and unwavering loyalty, represented a bastion of integrity in Joseph's increasingly complex view of the world. Yet, even Silas, in his own way, had been a part of the town's collective silence. He hadn't been privy to the deepest secrets, but he had lived alongside those who were, and his understanding of the artifact had been, initially, limited to what Elias had confided in him. Joseph knew Silas's heart was in the right place, that his actions were always guided by a strong moral compass. But the experience had made Joseph question the very nature of trust. Could he truly rely on anyone's outward demeanor to reflect their inner truths? Could he ever be sure that everyone in West Seneca was truly on the same side, sharing the same desire for safety and transparency?

He began to understand that his father's dedication wasn't just about scientific curiosity; it was about an ethical imperative. Elias Thorne had recognized a potent force, and he had also recognized the moral obligation to understand and manage it responsibly. He had grappled with the implications of his discoveries, the potential for their misuse, and the burden of ensuring that such knowledge did not fall into the wrong hands or, worse, remain unchecked, its destructive potential unleashed upon an unsuspecting world. Joseph now felt that same burden, the crushing weight of responsibility that his father had carried for so long. It wasn't just about deciphering cryptic notes or conducting experiments; it was about safeguarding the very fabric of their reality.

The secret of the artifact had been a tightly guarded one, and its revelation had come at a cost. Joseph understood that the unveiling had been necessary, a desperate measure to combat the immediate threat. But he also knew that the truth, once exposed, could be a double-edged sword. It had saved them from one peril, but it had also introduced a new kind of vulnerability. The knowledge that such a power existed, and that it had been so close to being unleashed, would forever linger in the collective consciousness of West Seneca. It was a scar that would not easily fade, a constant reminder of their near-demise. He saw it in the hushed conversations, the lingering unease, the way people sometimes looked at the sky as if expecting something to descend from it.

He found himself re-reading his father's journals with a different perspective. No longer was he solely searching for scientific breakthroughs or solutions to immediate problems. He was now also looking for the emotional toll that Elias's research had taken. He saw the frustration, the isolation, the moments of profound doubt that Elias had so carefully documented. He understood that his father's brilliance was intertwined with a deep sense of personal sacrifice. Elias had carried the weight of this secret alone for so long, and in doing so, he had isolated himself, not just from the wider world, but from the very community he sought to protect. Joseph felt a pang of empathy for his father, a deeper understanding of the loneliness that must have accompanied such a solitary pursuit.

The transformation in Joseph was not just about gaining knowledge; it was about internalizing the profound implications of that knowledge. He understood that the world was not as simple or as safe as he had once believed. He had learned that true strength lay not in recklessness or bravado, but in a quiet, unyielding vigilance, a constant awareness of the unseen forces that could shape their lives. He was no longer the boy who chased adventure for its own sake. He was a young man who understood that some adventures carried an immense, almost unbearable weight, and that the greatest adventure of all might be the quiet, persistent effort to protect those he cared about from the shadows that lurked just beyond the edges of their everyday lives.

The weight of this knowledge wasn't just a mental burden; it was beginning to manifest physically. He found himself sleeping less, his mind constantly churning, dissecting the events, replaying conversations, searching for any detail he might have missed. The easygoing demeanor he had once possessed was often replaced by a furrowed brow, a pensive gaze that seemed to look beyond the immediate present. He would catch himself staring into the distance, his thoughts miles away, lost in the intricate web of his father's research and the precarious state of West Seneca's newfound knowledge. He understood that this vigilance was necessary, a crucial element in preventing future crises, but he also recognized the toll it was taking on his youthful exuberance. The spark of carefree joy was still there, but it was now often overshadowed by a solemn awareness of the responsibilities he bore.

He had to consciously remind himself to engage with his peers, to participate in the simple rituals of their shared lives. The temptation to withdraw, to retreat into the world of his father's journals and the solitary pursuit of understanding, was ever-present. But he knew that his father's work was not meant to be a solitary endeavor. It was meant to serve the community, to protect it. To do that effectively, he needed to remain connected, to understand the pulse of West Seneca, not just through Elias's notes, but through his own lived experiences and interactions. This internal struggle, between the pull of solitary study and the necessity of community engagement, was a testament to the multifaceted nature of the transformation he was undergoing.

He began to see the subtle ways in which the artifact's presence, even after its apparent neutralization, might still linger. Elias had theorized about residual energies, about subtle shifts in the natural world that could be attributed to the artifact's proximity. Joseph now found himself hyper-aware of such anomalies. A patch of unusually fertile ground, a flock of birds behaving erratically, a sudden, inexplicable silence in the woods – these were no longer dismissed as mere coincidences. They were potential indicators, whispers of an underlying truth that remained just out of reach. This constant scanning of his environment, this heightened sense of perception, was both a testament to his father's teachings and a source of his growing weariness. The world, once a place of comforting constants, had become a dynamic, ever-shifting landscape of potential threats and hidden meanings.

The revelation had also brought a strange sort of immunity, or perhaps it was merely a desensitization. The sheer magnitude of what they had faced had, in a way, recalibrated his sense of danger. Lesser threats seemed less daunting, the everyday anxieties of youth faded into insignificance when measured against the existential peril he had recently confronted. This was a curious side effect of his transformation, a paradoxical byproduct of intense exposure to the extraordinary. He found himself more resilient, less easily startled by the unexpected, but also, perhaps, more distant, less able to connect with the simple concerns that occupied the minds of his peers.

He knew that this was just the beginning. The artifact, and the knowledge it represented, was a Pandora's Box that had been opened, and there was no truly closing it. The secrets of West Seneca had been laid bare, and the consequences of that revelation would continue to unfold. Joseph Thorne, the boy who had once chased the thrill of discovery, was now a young man burdened by the weight of profound truths. He understood that his journey was far from over, and that the knowledge he now carried would continue to shape him, to guide him, and to challenge him in ways he was only beginning to comprehend. The innocence was gone, replaced by a hard-won wisdom, a solemn understanding of the delicate balance between the visible and the hidden, the known and the unknown, and the enduring responsibility that came with holding such knowledge in his hands. He carried the memory of the danger not as a ghost of the past, but as a constant, guiding principle for the future, a reminder that true preparedness lay not in forgetting, but in understanding, and in a vigilant, unwavering commitment to protecting the fragile peace they had so narrowly preserved.

The weight of his father's cryptic warnings, once dismissed as the anxieties of an overprotective parent, now settled upon Joseph with a clarity that was both humbling and profound. He replayed Elias Thorne's hushed admonishments, the stern pronouncements against delving too deeply into the unknown, the fervent pleas for caution that had seemed, to his younger, more impetuous self, like mere attempts to clip his wings. He had seen them then as barriers to discovery, as unnecessary constraints on his burgeoning curiosity. How misguided he had been. The very nature of the forces he had encountered, the chilling whispers of ancient power and the suffocating presence of malevolence, underscored the prescience of his father's fears. Elias hadn't been trying to suppress his spirit; he had been trying to shield him from a reality so dangerous, so fundamentally unsettling, that it threatened to unravel the very fabric of their existence.

He recalled specific instances, conversations etched into his memory with the stark detail of a nightmare. The time he'd stumbled upon his father poring over ancient texts in the attic, the air thick with the scent of aged paper and a palpable tension. Elias had slammed the books shut with a force that startled Joseph, his face a mask of grim determination, warning him away from "paths that lead only to ruin." Or the evening he'd been caught trying to decipher some of the more obscure symbols in his father's study, only to be met with a torrent of concerned words, laced with an urgency Joseph had never before witnessed in his usually measured father. "Some doors," Elias had said then, his voice low and resonant, "are meant to remain closed, Joseph. For your own safety. For everyone's safety." At the time, it had sounded like an unfair decree, a denial of his intellectual burgeoning. Now, it was the echo of a desperate plea from a man who had glimpsed the abyss and understood its terrifying pull.

Joseph also thought of his mother, Eleanor, and her own quiet anxieties. Her concerned glances, the way she would hover, her fingers often finding their way to his arm, a gentle pressure that conveyed a world of unspoken worry. He remembered her soft inquiries, her attempts to steer him toward more conventional pursuits, her subtle suggestions that perhaps a weekend spent fishing or helping with the town's historical society would be more beneficial than deciphering arcane texts in the dead of night. He had often interpreted these as attempts to keep him tethered to a mundane existence, to prevent him from straying too far from the comforting predictability of their lives in West Seneca. He hadn't understood that her motherly intuition had sensed the undercurrents of danger, the subtle dissonances that hinted at forces beyond their understanding. Her desire for his safety, for the preservation of their peaceful existence, was not a sign of weakness, but of profound, protective love.

He realized now that his parents' warnings were not born of a desire to control him, but from a deep-seated, hard-won knowledge of the true nature of the world they inhabited. They had seen, perhaps through his father's research or through some other, as yet unknown means, the shadow that loomed over West Seneca. They had understood the allure of forbidden knowledge, the seductive whisper of power, and the devastating consequences that often followed in its wake. Their caution was a testament to their love, a shield forged from experience and a fierce determination to protect their son from the very darkness he had unknowingly brushed against, and ultimately, had to confront.

The realization brought with it a pang of guilt, a sense of regret for his past dismissiveness. He had been so eager to prove his independence, to forge his own path, that he had failed to see the wisdom embedded in their guidance. He had mistaken their protective instincts for stifling control, their concern for a lack of faith in his capabilities. Now, standing on the precipice of a world irrevocably changed by his discoveries, he understood that their fears were not only justified but had been a vital, if unheeded, safeguard. They had been trying to prepare him, not to dissuade him, to equip him with caution where he only saw opportunity.

He felt a strong urge to bridge the distance that his youthful arrogance had created. He wanted to articulate this newfound understanding, to convey the depth of his appreciation for their foresight. He envisioned a conversation, not one filled with accusations or regrets, but with a quiet acknowledgement of their roles in his journey. He wanted to sit with them, perhaps in the familiar comfort of their living room, the scent of his mother's baking a gentle counterpoint to the gravity of his words. He would look them in the eye, the same eyes that had held concern and worry for so many years, and express how their warnings, once perceived as impediments, were now recognized as beacons of wisdom.

"I understand now," he would say, his voice softer than usual, stripped of the youthful bravado that had often characterized their previous interactions. "About what you always told me. About being careful. About the things we don't always see." He would pause, allowing the weight of those words to settle, watching their reactions, hoping to see a flicker of recognition, of understanding. He would explain how his recent experiences had stripped away his illusions, revealing a world far more complex and dangerous than he had ever imagined. He would tell them, without embellishment or exaggeration, about the artifact, about the power it held, and about the sheer, terrifying fragility of their peace.

He would acknowledge that he had not listened, that he had been too quick to dismiss their concerns, too eager to rush headlong into the unknown. "I thought you were just trying to keep me safe from everything," he would confess, a hint of vulnerability in his tone. "But I see now that you were trying to keep me safe from something truly terrible. Something you knew was real, even when I couldn't see it." He would articulate how his father's research, which he had once viewed as a solitary intellectual pursuit, was actually a lifelong battle, a silent vigil against forces that threatened to consume them all. He would speak of his mother's intuition, her quiet strength, and how her gentle nudges had been more than just parental concern; they had been a mother's innate understanding of the hidden dangers that lurked around their seemingly idyllic town.

He wanted to convey that their wisdom had been a guiding star, even when he had refused to look at it. He would explain how the knowledge he now possessed had amplified his respect for their foresight, not diminished it. He would share how the very act of facing the darkness had illuminated the brilliance of their cautionary words. It was a strange paradox: the more he had seen of the world's hidden dangers, the more he had come to appreciate the protective embrace of his parents' warnings. They had been preparing him for a fight he hadn't known he was in, and their guidance, however subtle, had been his first line of defense.

He imagined his father's reaction, perhaps a quiet nod, a softening of the stern lines around his eyes, a subtle acknowledgement of the son who had finally, truly, understood. He could picture his mother's gentle smile, a smile tinged with relief and a quiet pride. It wouldn't be about admitting fault or seeking forgiveness, but about forging a new understanding, a deeper connection built on shared experience and mutual respect. This conversation, he felt, was not just about reconciling with their past warnings, but about solidifying their bond for the future, a future that, while still uncertain, would be faced with a newfound unity.

He would express his gratitude, not just for their love, but for their wisdom. "Thank you," he would say, the words imbued with a sincerity that had been missing in his younger years. "Thank you for trying to protect me. Thank you for seeing what I couldn't. Your warnings... they were more important than I ever realized." This acknowledgment would be the bridge, spanning the gap between his adolescent rebellion and his newfound maturity. It would be a testament to the transformative power of facing genuine adversity, and to the enduring strength of parental love and foresight. He understood that the knowledge he now held was a heavy burden, but sharing the weight of that understanding with his parents, acknowledging their role in his preparedness, would make it immeasurably lighter. He was no longer the boy who ran from warnings; he was a young man who finally understood their true value, and the profound love that fueled them. This realization was not an end, but a beginning, the first step in a new chapter of his relationship with his parents, one built on the shared foundation of hard-won knowledge and a deepened appreciation for their unwavering guidance. It was a reconciliation not just of perspectives, but of hearts, a coming together in the face of a world that had proven to be far more mysterious and perilous than any of them had initially conceived. He felt a sense of peace, a quiet satisfaction in knowing that he could finally acknowledge the wisdom that had been there all along, waiting for him to have the eyes to see it.

The primal call of the woods, a symphony of rustling leaves and the distant murmur of unseen streams, had always resonated deeply within Joseph. It was a siren song that had lured him from childhood, a promise of secrets whispered on the breeze and mysteries waiting to be unearthed beneath a canopy of ancient oaks. In his younger years, this magnetic pull had been fueled by an unbridled curiosity, a desire to conquer the unknown with sheer enthusiasm and a boundless, often reckless, energy. He'd scrambled over fallen logs with the agility of a squirrel, his mind alight with imagined adventures, each foray into the dense foliage a testing ground for his burgeoning independence. The woods were his playground, his canvas, a place where the rules of the ordinary world seemed to loosen their grip, allowing his imagination to soar. He'd spent countless hours tracing the meandering paths, charting his own course, often returning with scratched knees and muddy boots, his heart brimming with the quiet triumph of exploration.

Yet, the events that had recently transpired had undeniably shifted the lens through which he viewed these familiar terrains. The ethereal glow of the artifact, the chilling resonance of ancient energies, and the suffocating aura of malevolence he had inadvertently touched, had irrevocably altered his perception of the world, and consequently, his own place within it. The woods were no longer merely a place of innocent discovery; they were a landscape imbued with a newfound, palpable significance. The rustling leaves now carried the echo of hushed warnings, the dappled sunlight a reminder of hidden shadows, and the very air seemed to hum with a latent power that was both exhilarating and deeply unsettling. His father's admonishments, once dismissed as the overprotective ramblings of a fearful man, now echoed with a profound and urgent wisdom. He understood, with a clarity that pierced through his former youthful arrogance, that the unknown was not always benign, and that curiosity, unchecked, could lead to paths fraught with peril.

This realization, however, had not extinguished the explorer within him. Instead, it had tempered it, refining the raw, untamed desire into a more focused, discerning intent. The woods still called to him, but the call was no longer a simple invitation to frolic. It was a summons to understand, to investigate with a keen intellect and a healthy respect for the forces that lay dormant beneath the surface. He found himself approaching his explorations with a newfound deliberateness. Before stepping into the emerald depths, he would pause, taking a deep breath, not just of the crisp, pine-scented air, but of the very atmosphere of the woods, attempting to discern its mood, its inherent energies. He'd learned to observe the subtle shifts in the environment – the way the birds fell silent in certain areas, the unusual stillness of the undergrowth, the peculiar patterns of light filtering through the dense canopy. These were no longer mere sensory details; they were indicators, subtle clues that hinted at a world beyond the ordinary, a world he was now compelled to understand.

His father's well-worn books, once subjects of secret fascination and defiance, now served as invaluable guides. He'd spent hours poring over the faded pages, deciphering the intricate symbols and cryptic texts, his father's marginalia offering glimpses into a lifetime of dedicated, albeit perilous, research. Elias Thorne's meticulous notes, his careful observations of ley lines, ancient rituals, and forgotten lore, provided a framework for his own burgeoning understanding. Joseph found himself connecting the dots, seeing how the seemingly disparate elements of his father's work interwove with the strange phenomena he had personally experienced. The woods, once a wild and untamed frontier, were slowly transforming in his mind into a complex tapestry, woven with threads of history, magic, and a power that demanded respect, not just awe.

He started carrying a small, leather-bound journal, not for idle sketches of wildflowers or whimsical observations, but for meticulously documenting his findings. He recorded the precise location of unusual rock formations, the unusual growth patterns of certain fungi, the faint, almost imperceptible hum that emanated from specific clearings. He noted the time of day, the atmospheric conditions, and any anomalies he detected, cross-referencing these observations with the texts he studied. His approach was no longer about haphazard discovery; it was about systematic investigation, a quest for knowledge driven by a profound sense of responsibility. He was no longer a boy playing in the woods; he was a nascent scholar, an investigator of the hidden, armed with a sharpened mind and a deepening understanding of the stakes involved.

The artifact, though its immediate presence was no longer a tangible threat, remained a powerful presence in his thoughts. He understood that its power, and the knowledge it represented, was not something to be trifled with. His father's warnings about certain doors remaining closed resonated with renewed force. He realized that not all knowledge was meant for immediate consumption, and that true wisdom lay not just in acquiring information, but in understanding its context and its potential consequences. He found himself more attuned to the ethical implications of his explorations, constantly questioning the purpose behind his curiosity. Was he seeking to understand for the sake of illumination, or was there a lurking desire for personal power, a temptation to wield the knowledge he was uncovering? This introspection, this self-awareness, was a crucial component of his transformation, a testament to the maturity he had gained through facing genuine danger.

He revisited the places where he had encountered the most potent energies, not with the reckless abandon of his youth, but with a quiet reverence. He would sit, meditate, and simply observe, allowing his senses to expand, to pick up on the subtle nuances of the environment. He noticed how the very character of the woods seemed to shift depending on the unseen forces at play. One grove might feel warm and inviting, radiating a gentle, nurturing energy, while another might exude a palpable sense of unease, a silent warning to tread with caution. He was learning to read the 'language' of the woods, a language spoken not in words, but in vibrations, in shifts of light and shadow, in the subtle interplay of life and unseen forces.

His mother's quiet worries, her intuitive understanding of the potential dangers lurking beneath the surface of their seemingly ordinary lives, also played a role in shaping his new approach. While his father's knowledge was rooted in esoteric texts and ancient lore, Eleanor's insight seemed to stem from a more primal, instinctual connection to the world around her. She had always possessed an uncanny ability to sense shifts in mood, to anticipate trouble before it materialized. Now, Joseph understood that her gentle inquiries and subtle attempts to steer him toward more conventional pursuits were not born of a desire to stifle his spirit, but from a deep-seated maternal instinct to protect him from unseen threats. He found himself sharing more with her, not in exhaustive detail, but in a way that acknowledged her concerns and her wisdom. He'd mention his walks, his observations, framing them in a way that reassured her without minimizing the seriousness of his burgeoning understanding.

He even found himself re-examining some of his mother's own interests, her fondness for gardening and the quiet rhythms of nature. He began to see a deeper connection between her gentle stewardship of their small garden and his own explorations of the larger, wilder landscape. Both involved understanding the needs of living things, the delicate balance of ecosystems, and the profound interconnectedness of all life. He realized that his mother's nurturing spirit was not so different from his father's pursuit of hidden knowledge; both were expressions of a deep engagement with the world, a desire to understand and connect.

The woods, then, became more than just a place of investigation; they became a sanctuary for introspection and a proving ground for his evolving philosophy. He still felt the exhilaration of discovery, the thrill of peeling back the layers of the unknown. But now, it was tempered by a profound sense of responsibility and a deep-seated respect for the forces he encountered. He no longer sought to simply conquer the unknown, but to understand it, to integrate its lessons into his own burgeoning worldview. The explorer within him had not been extinguished; he had been reborn, a more mature, more capable, and infinitely more mindful seeker of truth. His steps were no longer driven by youthful impetuosity, but by a steady, informed purpose, a quiet determination to navigate the shadowed paths with wisdom and a profound respect for the mysteries that lay ahead. He was ready, not just to explore, but to learn, to understand, and perhaps, to protect.

10

The Lasting Impact on West Seneca

The silence that had descended upon West Seneca after the revelation was more deafening than any outcry. It was a silence born of shock, of a dawning, bitter understanding that the familiar landscape of their lives had been built upon a foundation of secrets and, for some, outright deception. The very air seemed to thicken with unspoken accusations, with the weight of a trust that had been shattered like fragile glass. For Joseph, witnessing this pervasive quietude was a stark reminder of the invisible threads that bound their small community, threads that had now been strained to a breaking point. He saw it in the averted gazes at the general store, in the hushed conversations that ceased abruptly when he or his mother entered a room, in the subtle, yet palpable, distance that now existed between neighbors who had once shared meals and laughter. The shared history, the common experiences that had woven West Seneca into a cohesive whole, now seemed to mock them with their superficiality, for beneath the veneer of normalcy, a deep chasm had opened.

The immediate aftermath was a period of profound introspection for many. For those who had been complicit, either through active participation or passive silence, a gnawing guilt began to manifest.

They wrestled with the knowledge of their involvement, the realization that their actions, or inactions, had contributed to the pervasive atmosphere of deceit that had permeated the village. For the deceived, it was a raw, open wound. The betrayal was not just about hidden facts; it was a betrayal of the inherent belief in the good intentions of those around them, a belief that formed the bedrock of any healthy community. This was especially true for the younger generation, whose innocence had been shielded, perhaps too effectively, by the adults who had carried the burden of the secret. They were now confronted with a reality that was far more complex and disillusioning than they could have ever imagined.

The first steps toward mending were tentative, almost hesitant. They began not with grand pronouncements, but with small, almost imperceptible gestures. Mrs. Gable, whose husband had been one of the original custodians of the secret, started leaving small bouquets of wildflowers on the doorsteps of families who had been most directly affected by the deception. Mr. Henderson, the taciturn owner of the blacksmith shop, found himself offering unsolicited help with repairs to homes, his usual gruff demeanor softened by a quiet remorse. These acts, though small, were significant. They were silent apologies, acknowledgments of a shared burden, and the first tentative reaches across the divide that had formed.

It was at one of the impromptu gatherings at the town square, initially conceived as a simple 'Sunday social' to try and recapture some semblance of normalcy, that the real work of rebuilding began. The usual chatter was subdued, punctuated by long, awkward silences. Joseph watched as his mother, Eleanor, her presence a quiet anchor, began to engage with Mrs. Peterson, whose family had suffered a significant loss indirectly related to the secret. Eleanor didn't pry, didn't demand explanations, but simply listened, her gaze steady and compassionate. It was a masterclass in empathy, a quiet demonstration of how to acknowledge pain without exacerbating it.

Then, a bolder move was made. Old Man Hemlock, a man who had always been a pillar of the community, a repository of its oral history, stood on the makeshift stage – a collection of stacked crates. His voice, raspy with age, carried an unexpected gravitas. He didn't shy away from the truth. "We... we kept things from you," he began, his gaze sweeping across the assembled faces, a mixture of apprehension and weary resignation. "For what we thought were good reasons. To protect. To preserve. But protection can become a cage, and preservation can lead to stagnation. And in the end, keeping secrets only serves to isolate us from each other."

His words, so direct and unvarnished, hung in the air. There was no elaborate excuse, no attempt to justify the past, only a plain acknowledgment of a collective failing. This, Joseph realized, was crucial. The rebuilding couldn't happen if the past was glossed over or rationalized. It required an honest confronting of the truth, no matter how painful.

Following Hemlock's impromptu address, a more structured approach emerged. The town council, comprised of individuals who had been either directly involved in maintaining the secret or deeply impacted by its revelation, decided to organize a series of open community meetings. These were not designed to be accusatory, but rather to create a forum for dialogue, for shared understanding, and for the collective charting of a new course. The first meeting was held in the old community hall, a place usually reserved for harvest festivals and town debates, but which now felt heavy with a different kind of expectation.

The agenda was simple: 'Moving Forward, Together'. The initial moments were tense. People sat in uncomfortable silence, their eyes scanning the room, searching for familiar faces, for reassurance. Then, Sheriff Brody, a man whose gruff exterior masked a deep sense of responsibility, stepped forward. He had been one of the younger men tasked with subtly enforcing the secrecy, a role he now deeply regretted.

"I... I owe an apology," he began, his voice a little rough, but clear. "To many of you. For my part in keeping things hidden. For looking the other way. For not questioning. We believed we were doing what was best, but we were wrong. Our silence made us complicit in the deceit. And for that, I am truly sorry." He paused, letting his words sink in. "West Seneca is built on trust. And we broke that trust. Now, we have to earn it back. And that starts with honesty. With transparency. With each of us being accountable for our actions, and for our silence."

His words were a catalyst. One by one, others who had carried the weight of the secret, or who had simply been bystanders, began to speak. They shared their fears, their justifications, and, most importantly, their regrets. They spoke of the pressure to conform, the fear of ostracism, the genuine belief that they were protecting the village from something far worse. It wasn't about assigning blame anymore; it was about understanding the complex web of human emotions and motivations that had led to the current situation.

Joseph's mother, Eleanor, played a crucial role in these meetings, not by speaking at length, but by her quiet, observant presence. She had a remarkable ability to diffuse tension with a well-timed nod, a gentle smile, or a softly spoken word of encouragement. She had experienced betrayal firsthand, yet she embodied a spirit of forgiveness that was contagious. She understood that healing required acknowledging the pain, but also actively choosing to move beyond it. She would often share anecdotes about her own childhood, about how her mother had always taught her the importance of looking for the good in people, even when it was difficult.

One of the key themes that emerged from these discussions was the need for a more robust system of community governance, one that emphasized open communication and shared decision-making. The old ways, which had allowed a small group to wield significant influence and control information, were no longer tenable. Proposals were made for a more democratic council, with rotating members and greater public input. There was a tangible desire to ensure that such a widespread deception could never happen again.

Furthermore, the community recognized the need for proactive measures to foster transparency. This included establishing accessible public records, creating a regular newsletter that detailed town business, and holding frequent, well-publicized town hall meetings. The aim was to create an environment where questions could be asked freely, where concerns could be addressed openly, and where any attempt to conceal information would be immediately visible. It was a commitment to a new era of accountability, one where every resident felt empowered to participate and to hold their leaders responsible.

The healing process, however, was not a swift or linear one. There were setbacks, moments when old resentments resurfaced, or when trust faltered. Joseph witnessed a particularly difficult exchange at one of the meetings, where a long-held grievance between two families, exacerbated by the recent revelations, nearly erupted into a public confrontation. It was only through the patient intervention of Eleanor and Sheriff Brody, who managed to steer the conversation back towards common ground, that the situation was de-escalated. These moments served as stark reminders that rebuilding trust was not a one-time event, but an ongoing process, requiring constant effort and a genuine commitment from all involved.

Joseph himself found his role evolving. While he had been at the heart of the events that had brought the secret to light, he now found himself advocating for open communication. He shared his experiences, not to boast or to assign blame, but to illustrate the importance of understanding and dialogue. He spoke about how, in his own journey, he had learned the value of asking questions, of seeking out different perspectives, and of never assuming that he had all the answers. His youthful naivete had been replaced by a quiet wisdom, a testament to the profound lessons he had learned.

The artifact, the source of so much of West Seneca's hidden history, remained a sensitive topic. While its immediate danger had passed, its existence represented a fundamental shift in the community's understanding of its own past and its place in the world. The decision was made, after much deliberation, not to re-bury it, nor to display it publicly, but to establish a small, secure archive, accessible only to a designated committee tasked with its careful study and safekeeping. This ensured that the knowledge it contained would not be lost, but that it would be handled with the utmost responsibility and ethical consideration, preventing its misuse or its further exploitation. This approach symbolized a commitment to learning from the past without being defined or threatened by it.

Crucially, the community began to actively engage in shared projects that served to reinforce their collective identity and their renewed commitment to one another. They organized volunteer efforts to revitalize the town park, which had fallen into disrepair during the years of secrecy. They initiated a mentorship program, pairing older, more experienced residents with younger ones to share skills and knowledge, fostering intergenerational bonds. They even revived the annual Founder's Day celebration, not as a commemoration of a hidden history, but as a celebration of West Seneca's present and its hopeful future, a future built on honesty and shared purpose.

The rebuilding of trust was a slow, often arduous, journey. It required a willingness to be vulnerable, to admit mistakes, and to extend forgiveness. It demanded patience, empathy, and a steadfast belief in the inherent goodness of people, even after that goodness had been tested. Joseph watched as the fabric of West Seneca, though scarred, began to mend. The silences grew shorter, the averted gazes began to meet, and the hushed conversations started to include him and his family once more. It was a testament to the resilience of the human spirit, to the innate desire for connection, and to the profound truth that even in the face of deception, community can be rebuilt, stronger and more authentic than before, on the bedrock of shared honesty and mutual respect. The lasting impact of the revelation was not merely the trauma of the past, but the hard-won wisdom and the renewed commitment to a future where truth and transparency would be their guiding stars. The scars remained, a reminder of the fragility of trust, but they also served as a testament to their collective strength and their capacity for healing. The process of rebuilding was, in essence, the act of rewriting West Seneca's story, not as one of hidden secrets, but as one of courageous honesty and enduring community spirit.

The revelation of West Seneca's most guarded secret did not simply alter its present; it irrevocably reshaped its understanding of its past. What had once been a foundation of quiet contentment, built on what many believed to be unwavering communal integrity, was now recognized as a narrative deeply entwined with omission and carefully orchestrated silence. The truth, unearthed by the persistent courage of a young boy and the quiet strength of his mother, had peeled back layers of carefully constructed normalcy, exposing the complex machinery of communal memory and the often-unseen forces that shape it. This was not merely a story confined to the whispers of a few or the hushed anxieties of a generation; it was a chapter that demanded to be written, etched not just into the minds of its inhabitants, but into the very fabric of the town's historical consciousness.

The decision was not made lightly, nor was it a unanimous decree born of immediate consensus. For months, the community grappled with how to acknowledge such a profound disruption to their shared identity. Some advocated for a deliberate forgetting, a pragmatic approach that suggested dwelling on the past served only to reopen wounds. Others, however, felt a moral imperative to remember, to ensure that the sacrifices made and the deceptions endured would not be erased by the convenience of a tidy narrative. It was this latter sentiment, championed by those who had witnessed the slow, arduous process of rebuilding trust, that ultimately prevailed. They understood that true healing wasn't about erasing the past, but about integrating its lessons, transforming its pain into a source of enduring strength and vigilance.

The physical manifestation of this commitment took several forms, each carefully considered to reflect the town's journey. A modest, yet dignified, bronze plaque was eventually commissioned, its inscription a testament to the resilience of truth and the power of community. It was placed not in the bustling town square, nor within the hushed halls of the town council building, but at the edge of Willow Creek, near the very spot where the artifact had first been unearthed. The location was chosen deliberately, a quiet nod to the clandestine nature of the secret and the unassuming setting where its unravelling began. The plaque itself bore simple, unadorned lettering: "West Seneca: Acknowledging our past, building our future on truth. Remembered herein: the courage to uncover, the strength to rebuild." It was not an accusatory monument, but a solemn dedication to the ongoing process of transparency and accountability.

Beyond the physical marker, the story of West Seneca's secret became an integral part of its oral history. The elders, those who had witnessed firsthand the slow, painful unwinding of the deception, took on the mantle of storytellers. They shared their experiences not as sensationalized gossip, but as cautionary tales, woven into the fabric of local lore. At community gatherings, during the long, crisp evenings of autumn, or beside crackling fires on winter nights, the narrative would unfold. They spoke of the quiet fear that had once pervaded the town, of the subtle pressures to conform, and of the profound relief that came with the eventual exposure of the truth. They recounted the small acts of defiance, the hesitant questions, and the ultimate bravery that had illuminated the hidden corners of their history.

Joseph, now a young man, often found himself at the heart of these retellings. He didn't seek the spotlight, but his presence served as a living testament to the events that had transpired. He would speak not of his own heroism, but of the collective responsibility they all shared. He emphasized the importance of vigilance, of questioning when something felt amiss, and of understanding that silence, however well-intentioned, could be a potent accomplice to deception. His mother, Eleanor, would often be beside him, her quiet wisdom a gentle counterpoint to his earnest pronouncements. She would share her own perspective, focusing on the importance of empathy, of understanding the human frailty that could lead even good people to keep secrets, and the profound power of forgiveness in the arduous process of healing.

The younger generations, who had grown up in the shadow of this revelation, absorbed these stories with a mixture of awe and sober understanding. They learned that their history was not a pristine, unbroken line, but a complex tapestry of human choices, both flawed and noble. They were taught to appreciate the value of open dialogue, to understand that differing perspectives were not threats but opportunities for deeper understanding, and that the strength of their community lay not in uniformity of thought, but in its collective commitment to truth, however challenging that truth might be. This instilled in them a unique form of civic responsibility, a deep-seated awareness that the health of their community depended on their active participation and their unwavering commitment to transparency.

The artifact itself, the silent catalyst for so much change, was not merely stored away and forgotten. It was placed in a climate-controlled, secure archive within the newly established West Seneca Historical Society, a testament to the community's renewed commitment to preserving its past, both the celebrated and the difficult. Access to the artifact was strictly regulated, requiring a formal request and approval from a specially appointed committee comprised of historians, community leaders, and descendants of those directly involved in its original concealment. This ensured that its study would be conducted with the utmost care, sensitivity, and scholarly rigor, preventing its exploitation or misinterpretation. The archive became a place of quiet study, where the complexities of West Seneca's past could be examined, debated, and understood in a context of respect and intellectual honesty.

Furthermore, the lessons learned from the era of secrecy directly influenced the town's governance and its approach to public life. The town council implemented stricter protocols for transparency, establishing a publicly accessible digital archive of all council proceedings, including minutes, financial reports, and public comment submissions. A 'Civic Dialogue' initiative was launched, a series of regularly scheduled forums where residents could engage directly with their elected officials, ask questions, and voice concerns without fear of reprisal. The local newspaper, which had initially struggled to navigate the aftermath of the revelation, became a staunch advocate for investigative journalism and open reporting, recognizing its crucial role in holding power accountable.

The annual Founder's Day celebration underwent a significant transformation. No longer a simple commemoration of the town's origins, it evolved into a broader 'West Seneca Heritage Festival.' This festival embraced all facets of the town's history, acknowledging the periods of both struggle and triumph, of darkness and light. It featured historical reenactments that depicted not only the founding of the town but also key moments in its evolution, including the careful and often fraught process of confronting its hidden past. Joseph and Eleanor were often invited to participate, sharing their perspectives and reinforcing the festival's core message of remembrance and forward-looking commitment.

The impact of the secret, once a source of shame and division, became a unifying force, paradoxically. By openly acknowledging and integrating this difficult chapter, West Seneca forged a stronger, more authentic collective identity. The shared experience of confronting and moving beyond deception fostered a profound sense of solidarity. Residents learned to trust each other not because secrets were absent, but because they had demonstrated a collective capacity to address and overcome them. This resilience became the defining characteristic of their community, a quiet strength that radiated outwards, influencing their interactions with neighboring towns and their approach to broader societal issues.

The story of West Seneca served as a powerful example of how a community could confront its own buried truths. It demonstrated that while the uncovering of secrets could be painful, the subsequent act of integrating them into collective memory was essential for genuine growth and healing. The bronze plaque by Willow Creek, the hushed retellings by the elders, and the transparent governance of the town council were all manifestations of a community that had chosen courage over complacency, honesty over convenient illusion. The young boy's bravery had not just unearthed a secret; it had ignited a revolution of truth within West Seneca, a revolution whose lasting impact would continue to shape its destiny for generations to come, a perpetual reminder that the most enduring legacies are often built not on what is hidden, but on what is bravely brought to light. The past, once a burden, was now a teacher, its lessons etched into the very soul of the town, ensuring that West Seneca would forever remember the profound importance of vigilance, integrity, and the unwavering pursuit of truth in the ongoing construction of its shared history.

The aftermath of the revelation, while initially unsettling, catalyzed a profound shift in the collective consciousness of West Seneca. The shared experience of having a fundamental truth obscured had served as a stark, albeit painful, lesson in the fragility of communal trust and the insidious nature of unchecked silence. It became evident that the town's newfound commitment to transparency and historical honesty could not merely be a passive sentiment; it required the active cultivation of new structures and a renewed dedication to communal engagement. The question that lingered, not in fear but in earnest determination, was how to ensure that West Seneca would never again find itself vulnerable to the same kind of pervasive, deeply entrenched deception.

This imperative led to a deliberate re-evaluation of their existing governance and oversight mechanisms. The town council, now acutely aware of the potential for blind spots, began exploring initiatives designed to foster greater citizen involvement and immediate feedback. One of the most significant developments was the establishment of a 'Community Watch Liaison' program. This was not a revival of the more overt, almost accusatory neighborhood watch groups of the past, but a more nuanced approach. It involved training and empowering a network of volunteers to serve as conduits between residents and the town council. These liaisons, carefully selected for their discretion, empathy, and understanding of community dynamics, were tasked with attending town meetings, monitoring local discourse, and, most importantly, creating accessible channels for residents to voice concerns or report observations that might indicate a deviation from accepted norms or a potential brewing issue. They were not investigators, but facilitators, designed to ensure that no murmur of unease went unheard, no subtle shift in the town's equilibrium went unnoticed. The emphasis was on early detection, on addressing potential problems when they were still small enough to be managed with open dialogue rather than crisis management.

Furthermore, the town's budgeting and administrative processes underwent a significant overhaul. In the past, financial reports had been available, but often buried in dense municipal documents, accessible primarily to those with a keen interest or the time to sift through them. Post-revelation, the town council committed to a far more proactive and accessible form of fiscal transparency. A dedicated online portal was created, presenting the town's budget in an easily digestible format, complete with interactive charts and explanations of how public funds were allocated. Regular 'Budget Briefings' were instituted, open forums where residents could ask direct questions of the town treasurer and council members, delving into the specifics of expenditures and revenue. This initiative was born from the understanding that financial opacity can be as damaging as any other form of hidden truth, creating fertile ground for mismanagement or even malfeasance. By demystifying the town's finances, West Seneca aimed to build a stronger foundation of accountability and shared responsibility.

The role of the local newspaper, The West Seneca Chronicle, also evolved significantly. Previously, it had been a reliable source of community news, but perhaps too accustomed to a certain level of passive acceptance of the status quo. Following the uncovering of the secret, the Chronicle recognized its pivotal role in safeguarding the town's integrity. The paper's editorial board made a conscious decision to invest more resources in investigative journalism, dedicating staff to delving into local issues with a more critical and thorough approach. This meant more in-depth reporting on town council decisions, greater scrutiny of local development projects, and a commitment to publishing a wider range of community voices, including those that might offer dissenting or challenging perspectives. The aim was not to be adversarial, but to be truly vigilant, to act as an independent watchdog that held all institutions, including the council itself, to a higher standard of accountability. This shift was met with initial apprehension by some in authority, but the overwhelming support from the community, recognizing the vital function the Chronicle now served, solidified its new direction.

Education became another critical pillar in West Seneca's renewed commitment to vigilance. The historical society, invigorated by its newfound relevance, began developing educational programs for schools and community groups that focused not just on the history of West Seneca, but on the principles of critical thinking, media literacy, and civic responsibility. The story of the uncovered secret was used as a central case study, illustrating how assumptions could be challenged, how important it was to question information, and the power of collective action when faced with difficult truths. Workshops were held on identifying bias, understanding the importance of verifiable sources, and the ethical considerations involved in public discourse. These programs were designed to equip the next generation with the tools to be informed, engaged, and vigilant citizens, ensuring that the lessons learned from the past would be actively perpetuated.

Moreover, the town council itself adopted a more structured approach to risk assessment and internal oversight. Recognizing that even well-intentioned systems can develop blind spots, they implemented a mandatory biannual review of all town policies and procedures, with a specific focus on identifying any potential loopholes or areas that could inadvertently facilitate secrecy or a lack of accountability. This involved not just internal review, but also the solicitation of external expert opinions, ensuring an objective assessment of their systems. A formal 'Whistleblower Protection Policy' was also ratified, providing clear guidelines and robust protections for any town employee or resident who came forward with concerns about misconduct or impropriety, ensuring that speaking truth to power would not result in professional or personal repercussions.

The emphasis on collective vigilance also extended to social interactions. While the community celebrated its renewed openness, there was a subtle but perceptible shift in how residents interacted with one another. Conversations that might have once skirted around sensitive topics now often embraced them, albeit with a newfound maturity and respect. Neighbors were more inclined to engage in open discussions about local issues, and there was a greater willingness to share perspectives, even when they differed. This was not about fostering suspicion, but about cultivating a shared awareness, a collective understanding that the well-being of the community depended on its members looking out for one another, not in a prying or intrusive manner, but with a genuine concern for the shared integrity of their home. This created a more robust social fabric, one where transparency was not an obligation imposed from above, but a value lived and breathed by its residents.

The physical landscape of West Seneca also began to subtly reflect this shift. While the bronze plaque at Willow Creek remained a quiet testament, small, tangible reminders of the importance of openness began to appear in other public spaces. Signs encouraging civic engagement and open dialogue were posted in community centers and parks. Public forums were regularly held in well-lit, accessible locations, fostering an environment where anyone felt comfortable to participate. The town library expanded its collection to include more works on civic history, ethics, and investigative journalism, making these resources readily available to all. These were not grand gestures, but consistent, reinforcing signals that West Seneca was committed to a future built on a foundation of enduring vigilance and unwavering transparency. The subtle yet persistent integration of these principles into the everyday life of the town ensured that the lessons of the past were not confined to historical markers or commemorative speeches, but were woven into the very fabric of their shared existence, guarding against the resurgence of any hidden threats that might seek to undermine the hard-won integrity of their community. The town had learned that vigilance was not a solitary act but a collective endeavor, a constant, evolving practice that required the active participation of every single resident to safeguard the hard-won truths that now defined them. This commitment to an ongoing process, a perpetual tending of the garden of transparency, was perhaps the most profound and lasting impact of the secret that had once threatened to divide them, but ultimately served to unite them in a shared purpose.

The unsettling revelation had, in the most unexpected way, redrawn the lines of trust and respect within West Seneca. For too long, the quiet hum of the town had masked a deeper dissonance, a truth buried not by malicious intent, but by a collective, almost unconscious, agreement to overlook. The unearthing of this buried history, a task spearheaded by the almost incidental observations of the town's younger residents, had not only shocked the adults into a new awareness of their town's past but also, and perhaps more significantly, instilled in them a profound respect for the very individuals who had, through their innocent yet piercing curiosity, brought it to light.

Joseph, in particular, found himself the unwitting symbol of this paradigm shift. His relentless questions, his meticulous piecing together of fragmented clues that had been dismissed by many adults as childish fancy or overactive imagination, had proven to be the key that unlocked the town's hidden narrative. Before the revelation, Joseph was, to most adults, simply a bright but perhaps overly earnest boy, prone to getting lost in his own world of historical minutiae. Now, he was seen differently. His persistent inquiries, once a mild annoyance to some, were now viewed through the lens of prescient insight. The adults who had tutored him, who had patiently indulged his fascination with local lore, now felt a tremor of awe. They recalled instances where his seemingly off-topic questions had, in retrospect, pointed towards the very heart of the obscured truth. His detailed drawings of the old mill, his fascination with the seemingly innocuous differences in architectural styles, his insistence on understanding the 'why' behind certain local traditions that had long since lost their context – these were not the ramblings of a child, but the instincts of a nascent investigator.

This recalibration of perception extended beyond Joseph to encompass the younger generation as a whole. The narrative that had unfolded served as a potent, albeit unintentional, lesson in the power of unfettered observation and the inherent value of a fresh perspective. Children, unburdened by the ingrained assumptions and practiced complacency that often characterized adult thinking, possessed a unique ability to notice anomalies, to question the status quo, and to perceive the world with a clarity that had been dulled in their elders. The adults of West Seneca began to understand that a child's persistent 'why?' was not a challenge to authority, but an invitation to deeper understanding. They realized that their own eagerness to provide simple answers, to maintain an undisturbed peace, had sometimes led them to dismiss the very questions that might have prevented the long-held secret from festering.

This newfound appreciation manifested in tangible ways. Town meetings, which had previously been dominated by adult discourse, began to see a subtle, yet significant, shift. When younger residents offered observations, especially those related to community history or the seemingly minor deviations that Joseph and his cohort had noticed, their contributions were no longer met with polite but dismissive nods. Instead, there was a genuine eagerness to listen, to understand the perspective from which these observations arose. Parents, too, began to engage more actively with their children's inquiries. The casual 'that's just how it is' was replaced by a more thoughtful dialogue. If a child pointed out an inconsistency in a local legend or questioned a perceived tradition, adults were more inclined to explore that question with them, to research the answers together, or to admit when they themselves didn't know, fostering a shared journey of discovery.

The local historical society, revitalized by the events, took a leading role in nurturing this intergenerational dialogue. Recognizing the unique skill set displayed by the young investigators, they began to organize workshops and historical walks specifically designed to highlight the importance of observation and critical thinking for all ages. These events were not framed as lessons *for* children, but as collaborative explorations *with* them. Adults were encouraged to bring their own knowledge and experiences, while children were invited to share their fresh perspectives and their innate ability to spot patterns that might elude adult eyes. Joseph, along with several of his peers who had been involved in the uncovering of the truth, became unofficial mentors in these sessions, their youthful enthusiasm and sharp observational skills serving as living examples of what could be achieved when curiosity was both encouraged and respected.

The curriculum in West Seneca's schools also began to reflect this shift. Educators, working in collaboration with the historical society, started to integrate more project-based learning that encouraged students to become local historians in their own right. Assignments that involved interviewing long-time residents, researching family histories, or even documenting changes in the town's landscape were introduced. The emphasis was not solely on the factual accuracy of their findings, but on the *process* of investigation: how they approached their research, how they formulated their questions, and how they interpreted the information they gathered. The story of the town's hidden past became a central pedagogical tool, illustrating the real-world impact of diligent inquiry and the courage to question widely accepted narratives. Students were taught that their observations, no matter how small or seemingly insignificant, held potential value, and that their questions were not to be stifled but to be explored.

This focus on young investigators wasn't about turning children into adult detectives, but about recognizing and valuing the inherent strengths of their developmental stage. Children are naturally attuned to sensory details, to inconsistencies in narrative, and to the emotional undercurrents that adults might unconsciously filter out. Joseph's ability to recall the precise scent of the old, unused room in the historical society's basement, or the subtle discoloration of a particular patch of wallpaper that differed from the rest, these were the kinds of sensory observations that adult researchers, focused on archival documents and official records, might overlook. His seemingly inconsequential habit of tracing the patterns of water stains on the ceiling of the town hall, noting how they formed peculiar, almost animalistic shapes, had, in retrospect, provided a visual clue to a hidden structural element that was directly linked to the secret.

The adults of West Seneca were learning to see the world anew, through the unfiltered eyes of their children. They understood that fostering this childlike curiosity, rather than suppressing it in the name of order or propriety, was essential for the town's continued health and transparency. It meant creating an environment where children felt safe to ask 'difficult' questions, to point out inconsistencies, and to express doubts without fear of being dismissed or ridiculed. This was a significant departure from a time when children were often expected to be seen and not heard, or when their observations were relegated to the realm of fantasy. The revelation had proven that the fantastical, in West Seneca's recent past, had a very real and potent basis in the suppressed truth.

The 'Community Watch Liaison' program, initiated in the aftermath, also saw an unexpected benefit from this newfound respect for young investigators. While the liaisons were primarily adult volunteers, the program actively encouraged the inclusion of younger voices. Children and teenagers were invited to share their observations of the town's subtle changes, their perceptions of any unusual comings and goings, or even their feelings about the general atmosphere of different neighborhoods. These were not formal reports, but casual feedback sessions designed to capture the ambient awareness of the community. The liaisons learned that the younger residents often possessed an intuitive understanding of the town's social pulse, a sensitivity to shifts in mood or behavior that could signal emerging issues. They became valuable, albeit informal, sources of intelligence, their perspectives augmenting the more structured observations of the adult liaisons.

The local newspaper, The West Seneca Chronicle, embraced this intergenerational approach with enthusiasm. They began featuring a regular column titled "Young Eyes, New Insights," which highlighted observations and questions submitted by children and teenagers. This not only gave young people a platform but also educated the wider community on the valuable contributions they could make. The stories showcased children who had noticed changes in local flora and fauna, young artists who had captured overlooked details of historic buildings in their drawings, and budding historians who had unearthed fascinating tidbits from family archives. The column became a popular feature, demonstrating that keen observation and insightful questioning were not the sole province of adults. It reinforced the idea that vigilance was a collective responsibility, shared by every member of the community, regardless of age.

Furthermore, the very act of adults listening to and valuing children's perspectives fostered a sense of empowerment in the younger generation. They learned that their voices mattered, that their observations could have a real impact, and that they had a role to play in safeguarding the integrity and truthfulness of their community. This sense of agency was a critical component in ensuring that West Seneca's commitment to transparency and vigilance would be a sustainable one, passed down through generations. The adults weren't just teaching the children about the importance of truth; they were demonstrating it by valuing their children's contributions and by actively seeking out their unique ways of seeing the world.

The experience had also subtly reshaped the town's collective memory and its ongoing narrative. The story of how the truth was uncovered – a narrative increasingly centered on the sharp eyes and persistent questions of the town's youth – became a cherished part of West Seneca's identity. It was a story that spoke of the resilience of truth, the importance of curiosity, and the unexpected power that could be found in the most unlikely of sources. It was a story that reminded everyone that the future of the town was not solely in the hands of its leaders, but also in the open, observant minds of its youngest citizens. This shared narrative served to strengthen the bonds between generations, creating a more cohesive and vigilant community, one where the lessons of the past were not just remembered, but actively lived and perpetuated by the very people who would shape West Seneca's future. The town had truly learned that the most insightful detectives might just be found in its own playgrounds, their innocent questions holding the keys to enduring truths, and their innate curiosity a beacon for a more honest and accountable tomorrow.

The hushed tones that once characterized hushed conversations about the past had been replaced by a more open, if still somewhat somber, discourse. West Seneca was no longer a village content to slumber under a blanket of comfortable, curated history. The unveiling of its buried truth had acted like a powerful solvent, dissolving the complacency that had allowed the darkness to persist. The fabric of the community had been strained, stretched to its limits by the revelation, but it had not broken. Instead, it had been rewoven, stronger and more resilient, albeit with the visible mends of its ordeal. The innocence that had defined West Seneca for so long was gone, replaced by a more mature, a more grounded understanding of its own complexities. It was a transition that was not always easy, marked by moments of lingering unease and the quiet processing of a shared trauma, but it was a transition that was ultimately, and irrevocably, for the better. The town had looked into its own shadowed corners, acknowledged its imperfections, and in doing so, had found a new path forward, one illuminated by the stark, clear light of honesty.

The physical landscape of West Seneca, too, seemed to bear the imprint of its recent awakening. It wasn't a dramatic, overnight transformation, but a series of subtle shifts that collectively spoke of a community no longer willing to ignore the whispers of its history. The old mill, once a silent, brooding sentinel on the edge of town, had undergone a renaissance of sorts. It was no longer merely a relic, a backdrop for childhood games of make-believe. Now, its weathered timbers and stone facade were the subject of genuine historical interest. Guided tours, often led by the very young residents who had first stumbled upon its secrets, became a regular feature. These tours were not sanitized retellings; they acknowledged the full spectrum of the mill's past, the labor, the ingenuity, and the shadow of what had been hidden within its walls. The town council, galvanized by the renewed interest in local heritage, had allocated funds for its careful preservation, not as a monument to a forgotten era, but as a tangible reminder of the lessons learned. The very presence of the mill, now a site of open contemplation rather than hushed speculation, served as a constant, silent testament to the town's altered perspective.

Similarly, the route taken by the old abandoned railway line, once a forgotten scar across the landscape, was being re-imagined. The initial discovery of artifacts along this forgotten track had been the first, almost imperceptible tremor that signaled the deeper truths hidden beneath West Seneca's placid surface. Now, plans were afoot to transform portions of it into a heritage trail. This wasn't about romanticizing the past, but about reclaiming it, about walking the very paths that had once carried the burdens of the town's history. Local schoolchildren, armed with trowels and magnifying glasses, participated in carefully supervised archaeological digs, their findings contributing to a more nuanced understanding of the area's development. Each unearthed fragment, each carefully documented discovery, was a piece of the puzzle that had been painstakingly reassembled. The trail, when completed, would serve as a narrative path, inviting both residents and visitors to engage with West Seneca's story in a visceral, tangible way.

Even the town square, the heart of West Seneca, seemed to beat with a different rhythm. The old oak tree, which had always been the customary spot for casual gatherings and impromptu picnics, now held a more profound significance. It was under its sprawling branches that the community had first gathered in the immediate aftermath of the revelation, seeking solace and understanding. Now, the benches beneath it were often occupied by individuals, young and old, lost in thought, their magazines turned not towards idle gossip, but towards a quiet contemplation of the town's journey. The annual Founder's Day picnic, once a straightforward celebration of West Seneca's origins, had been subtly reimagined. It was now a more inclusive event, acknowledging the diverse strands of the town's history, not just the triumphal narrative. The stories shared were richer, more complex, embracing both the triumphs and the tribulations that had shaped West Seneca into the community it was today.

The schools, as previously noted, had become vibrant hubs of historical inquiry. The curriculum had been overhauled, shifting from rote memorization to active investigation. Joseph, whose keen observations had initiated the cascade of revelations, found himself a sought-after resource, not just for his knowledge, but for his approach. He, along with his peers, were invited into classrooms not as students, but as collaborators. They shared their methodologies, their techniques for noticing the overlooked, and their passion for uncovering the truth. This was more than just an academic exercise; it was a civic education in its purest form, teaching the next generation that vigilance and a commitment to truth were not abstract concepts, but lived experiences, essential for the health of any community. The library, too, experienced a surge in patronage, with children and adults alike poring over local archives, seeking to deepen their understanding of the narratives that had been so carefully constructed and then, so dramatically, dismantled. The quiet hum of turning pages was now a sound of active engagement, of a community actively seeking to understand its own complex tapestry.

The social fabric of West Seneca had also undergone a significant metamorphosis. The incident had, in a very real way, stripped away the polite pretenses and superficial pleasantries that often mask deeper divisions. The shared experience of confronting a difficult truth had, paradoxically, fostered a deeper sense of unity. Neighbors who had previously only exchanged fleeting pleasantries now found themselves in deeper conversations, sharing their anxieties, their hopes, and their newfound understanding of their shared responsibility. There was a palpable sense of mutual reliance, a quiet acknowledgment that they were all in this together, navigating the currents of a history that had, until recently, been deliberately obscured. This shared vulnerability, once a source of potential shame, had become a source of unexpected strength. The collective act of facing and rectifying the past had forged bonds that were far more enduring than any superficial cordiality.

The adults, in particular, had experienced a profound recalibration of their relationship with the younger generation. The once-firm line between childhood innocence and adult wisdom had blurred, replaced by a mutual respect built on shared discovery. Parents were no longer simply custodians of their children's futures; they were also students of their children's insights. The casual dismissal of childish notions had given way to a genuine curiosity, an eagerness to understand the world as seen through younger, unclouded eyes. This shift was not confined to families; it permeated the entire town. The town council meetings, previously dominated by the concerns of established adults, now actively solicited and valued the input of younger residents. Their observations, often focused on minute details that had been overlooked by their elders, were no longer dismissed as trivial. Instead, they were seen as vital clues, potential indicators of something larger at play, something that might otherwise remain hidden.

The concept of "community vigilance" took on a new, more profound meaning. It was no longer just about adult watchfulness; it was a collective endeavor, an intergenerational commitment to the truth. The children who had so effectively uncovered the past were now seen as integral guardians of the present and future. Their innate curiosity, their unvarnished perceptions, were recognized as invaluable assets, crucial for maintaining the town's newfound transparency. Programs were established to formalize this collaboration, creating avenues for young people to share their observations and concerns in a structured, yet accessible, manner. These initiatives were not about infantilizing the youth, but about empowering them, about recognizing that their perspectives were not merely peripheral, but central to the ongoing health and integrity of West Seneca.

The scars of the past, while undeniable, were not to be a source of shame, but a testament to resilience. West Seneca had grappled with its hidden history, a history that, in its own quiet way, had cast a long shadow. The courage of a young boy, armed with nothing but an insatiable curiosity and a keen eye for detail, had been the catalyst that brought this shadow into the light. He, along with his peers, had navigated a labyrinth of buried truths, their youthful innocence a stark contrast to the adult complicity that had allowed the secret to fester. This journey had irrevocably altered the town, stripping away its naive veneer and replacing it with a more robust, more authentic identity. It was a transformation born not of convenience or expediency, but of a difficult, yet ultimately cathartic, confrontation with its own past.

The legacy of this period was not just in the physical restoration of historic sites or the pedagogical shifts in education, but in the intangible, yet profound, transformation of the town's collective consciousness. West Seneca had learned that truth, however uncomfortable, was the bedrock of any healthy community. The experience had instilled a profound appreciation for the power of observation, the importance of questioning, and the inherent value of every voice, regardless of age or experience. The town was no longer defined by what it had tried to hide, but by how it had chosen to reveal itself, by its commitment to honesty and its willingness to learn from its mistakes. The future of West Seneca was no longer a matter of passive inheritance, but of active, vigilant stewardship, guided by the enduring lessons of its own extraordinary awakening. The young boy who had dared to ask "why" had, in doing so, illuminated a path for his entire community, a path towards a brighter, more truthful tomorrow. The narrative of West Seneca had shifted, from one of quiet conformity to one of courageous self-discovery, a testament to the enduring power of truth, unearthed by the most unexpected of heroes.

11

Echoes in the Wilderness

The crunch of fallen leaves underfoot was a familiar melody, one Joseph had not heard in what felt like an eternity, yet the instant his boots met the forest floor, the sound resonated deep within him, a forgotten chord struck anew. It had been years since he'd last walked these woods, years since the summer that had irrevocably etched itself into the very fabric of his being and, in turn, reshaped the quiet town of West Seneca. The dense canopy overhead, dappled with the late afternoon sun, cast long, dancing shadows, much as it had that fateful summer, but now, the shadows held no menace, only the gentle patina of memory. He was no longer a boy of ten, filled with the boundless energy of discovery and the naive courage of innocence. He was a young man, his face a little leaner, his eyes carrying the quiet weight of experience, but the pull of this place, this particular stretch of wilderness, remained as potent as ever.

West Seneca itself had changed, of course. The immediate aftermath of the revelations had been a whirlwind of activity, of hushed whispers giving way to open discussions, of old certainties dissolving and new understandings taking root. The town had weathered the storm, emerging not unscathed, but undeniably stronger, more honest. The physical landscape mirrored this internal shift. The old mill, once a forgotten relic shrouded in whispers, was now a hub of historical interest, its weathered timbers a testament to a past that was no longer denied but actively explored. The heritage trail along the abandoned railway line, conceived in the wake of his discovery, had become a beloved local amenity, a place where children now learned about their town's complex history by walking its very paths. The town square, the old oak tree standing sentinel, felt different too; less a stage for pleasantries, more a place for quiet contemplation, a silent witness to the town's journey from comfortable ignorance to hard-won truth.

But it was here, in the heart of the wilderness that had held the town's deepest secret, that Joseph felt the most profound connection to his own past. He found himself standing near the old creek, its babbling a constant, soothing murmur, a sound that had been the soundtrack to his childhood investigations. The very spot where he had first noticed the anomaly, the subtle disturbance in the earth that had led him down a path no one else had seen, felt hallowed. He knelt, his fingers tracing the rough bark of a familiar oak, the same oak that had offered him shade and a vantage point as he'd painstakingly pieced together the puzzle. The world had moved on, as it always did. His own life had taken its course; he had pursued his studies, nurtured his burgeoning intellectual curiosity, and found a calling that still involved uncovering hidden truths, albeit in different arenas now. Yet, the wilderness had a way of calling him back, of reminding him of the foundational experience that had shaped his worldview.

The intervening years had been a period of healing and growth for West Seneca. The initial shock had given way to a collective introspection. The adults, once the keepers of the narrative, had learned from the keen observations of the children. A new dialogue had been forged, one where age and experience were tempered by the fresh perspective of youth. The town council meetings, once predictable affairs, now often saw younger voices contributing, their insights valued, their questions embraced rather than dismissed. Joseph recalled the early days, the tentative discussions, the moments of disbelief and then, finally, the dawning realization that what he and his friends had uncovered was not a figment of their imagination but a tangible piece of their shared history, a history that had been deliberately buried.

He remembered the way the adults had initially reacted – a mixture of protectiveness, confusion, and a deep-seated reluctance to confront the implications of the truth. There had been those who wished to sweep it all back under the rug, to let the past remain buried. But the evidence, once unearthed, had been undeniable. And it was the unwavering persistence of the children, their refusal to let the matter rest, that had ultimately forced the town to confront its own buried truths. His own parents, initially hesitant, had become his staunchest allies, their pride in his tenacity slowly eclipsing their initial apprehension. He had seen the gradual shift in the community's perception, from viewing him as a child who had stumbled upon something unpleasant, to recognizing him as the catalyst for an essential reckoning.

The wilderness, once a playground filled with the promise of adventure, had become a classroom. The trees, once just trees, now held a deeper significance, their roots intertwined with the history he had unearthed. The quiet solitude he had once sought for escape now served a different purpose. It was a space for reflection, a place to reconnect with the boy he had been and to appreciate the man he was becoming, a man whose life had been fundamentally shaped by the revelations that had blossomed in this very spot. The summer of 1852, as it had come to be known, was no longer a dark secret, but a pivotal moment, a turning point that had forced a community to examine its foundations.

He stood by the creek, the water flowing over smooth stones, its relentless movement a metaphor for the passage of time. The immediate intensity of the discovery had softened, like a sharp edge worn smooth by years of water flow. The raw emotions, the fear and the excitement, had mellowed into a deeper understanding, a more nuanced appreciation for the complexities of history and human nature. He remembered the feeling of revelation, the spine-tingling certainty that he was on the cusp of something significant, a feeling that had propelled him forward despite the whispers of doubt and the subtle discouragement from some adults. That feeling, that unyielding pursuit of truth, had become a guiding principle in his life.

The town had embraced its history, not as a source of shame, but as a testament to its resilience. The lessons learned during that transformative summer had permeated every aspect of life in West Seneca. Education had been revolutionized, with a new emphasis on critical thinking and the courage to question. The library, once a quiet repository of dusty tomes, had become a vibrant center of historical inquiry, a place where young minds were encouraged to delve into the past, armed with the knowledge that truth was not always readily apparent and often required a diligent search.

He tossed a small pebble into the creek, watching the ripples spread and dissipate. It was a quiet act, a solitary gesture in the heart of the woods, but it felt significant. It was a moment of acknowledgment, a silent tribute to the forces that had converged in this place, shaping not only his own destiny but the future of his hometown. The innocence he had possessed as a child was gone, replaced by a mature understanding of the world's intricate layers. But in its place, he had gained something far more valuable: a profound respect for the power of observation, the importance of integrity, and the enduring strength that comes from confronting the truth, no matter how deeply it might be buried. The wilderness, this ancient, silent witness, still held its allure, but now it was a place of profound contemplation, a sanctuary of memory where the echoes of the past served not to haunt, but to guide. He knew, with a certainty that had been forged in this very place, that the lessons learned here would continue to shape his life, a constant reminder of the extraordinary journey that had begun with a simple, unanswered question in the quiet heart of the wilderness. He turned to leave, the setting sun casting a warm, golden light through the trees, a comforting farewell from a place that had given him so much. The path back to West Seneca felt familiar, yet different, the weight of years and experience settling comfortably upon his shoulders.

The years following the uncovering of West Seneca's hidden history had been, for Joseph, a period of quiet consolidation and profound redirection. The raw, unadulterated thrill of discovery, the heady rush of piecing together a narrative deliberately obscured, had settled into a more tempered, yet no less potent, drive. He hadn't, as some might have expected, retreated further into the solitary world of childhood investigation. Instead, the very skills he had honed in those sun-drenched woods, in the hushed corners of forgotten attics, and in the deciphering of cryptic clues, had found a broader application. He had been drawn, almost inexorably, to the pursuit of truth in its many guises, understanding with a clarity born of lived experience that truth, like the creek that wound through the wilderness, was often obscured by sediment and debris, requiring patient, dedicated excavation.

His formal education grew naturally from his innate curiosity. He pursued philosophy and history fields that let him explore both the sweeping forces and the finer details that shape human societies. While his peers might have focused on theoretical constructs, Joseph often found himself seeking the tangible, the verifiable, the bedrock of evidence upon which any credible understanding was built. He remembered the skepticism he had faced as a child, the polite dismissals and the veiled incredulity, and he carried that memory not as a wound, but as a reminder of the importance of tangible proof. He learned to articulate his findings with precision, to present his arguments with an unwavering logic, and to anticipate the counterarguments with a foresight developed from having anticipated the very skepticism that had initially met his own revelations. His professors often remarked on his maturity, his ability to engage with complex ideas not just academically, but with a visceral understanding of their real-world implications.

This led him, after graduation, to a path that felt both inevitable and deeply satisfying: investigative journalism. It wasn't the sensational, headline-grabbing kind of journalism that thrived on fleeting outrage. Rather, he gravitated towards in-depth reporting, the kind that delved into the systemic issues, the forgotten histories, and the quiet injustices that often went unnoticed by the wider world. His first major assignment, for a respected national publication, involved an exploration of historical land disputes in a rural county, a story that, on the surface, seemed far removed from the shaded trails of West Seneca. Yet, as he meticulously traced property records, interviewed descendants of original settlers, and navigated bureaucratic labyrinths, the parallels were unmistakable. He saw the same patterns of obfuscation, the same subtle manipulations of narrative, the same vested interests seeking to maintain a comfortable status quo by burying inconvenient truths.

He remembered the feeling of sitting in dusty courthouse basements, the air thick with the scent of aging paper and forgotten intentions, carefully cross-referencing deeds and wills. It was not unlike sifting through fragmented diaries and cryptic annotations back home. The tools were different – microfiche readers and online databases replaced hand-drawn maps and deciphered inscriptions – but the underlying process, the relentless pursuit of corroboration, the instinct to question discrepancies, remained the same. He learned to be patient, to build rapport with sources who were often reluctant to speak, to understand the complex motivations that drove people to both conceal and reveal information. The summer he had spent uncovering the truth about West Seneca had, in essence, been his apprenticeship in the art of the investigation, a rigorous, albeit unconventional, training ground for the life he now led.

His approach was characterized by a quiet determination, a refusal to accept superficial answers. When a story seemed too neat, too easily explained, Joseph's investigative instincts would sharpen. He would dig deeper, seek out dissenting voices, and meticulously examine the edges of the accepted narrative. This often meant facing resistance, encountering individuals who preferred the comfort of ignorance to the discomfort of truth. He learned to navigate these encounters with a measured calm, understanding that outright confrontation was rarely as effective as persistent, well-supported inquiry. He recalled the subtle pressures exerted by some of the older residents in West Seneca, their desire to protect the town's reputation, and he recognized that such dynamics played out in every community, in every facet of life, albeit often with higher stakes.

His work gained recognition not for its sensationalism, but for its depth and integrity. He published extensively on topics ranging from environmental negligence to corporate malfeasance, always with a focus on the human cost of hidden actions. He found particular satisfaction in bringing to light stories that had been marginalized, voices that had been silenced, and histories that had been deliberately erased. It was a conscious effort to counterbalance the forces that sought to bury or distort truth, a mission that resonated deeply with the formative experience of his childhood. He understood that the past was not a static entity, but a living, breathing force that continued to shape the present, and that understanding it accurately was essential for navigating the future.

Beyond his professional life, Joseph remained deeply connected to West Seneca. He returned often, not as an outsider looking in, but as someone who understood the town's complex tapestry of history and community. He saw how the lessons of that transformative summer had been integrated into the town's consciousness. The annual "West Seneca Heritage Days" often featured him as a guest speaker, not to recount his childhood exploits, but to discuss the broader principles of historical inquiry and civic responsibility. He found it heartening to see generations of children growing up with a more nuanced understanding of their town's past, a past that was acknowledged in its entirety, both the triumphs and the shadows. He had witnessed firsthand how confronting difficult truths, rather than fostering shame, could lead to collective growth and a stronger sense of identity.

He had also found personal fulfillment. His understanding of the interconnections of things, fostered by his early explorations, translated into a deep appreciation for human relationships. He learned that just as communities could obscure truths, individuals too could carry their own hidden burdens, their own private histories. This fostered in him a sense of empathy and a commitment to treating everyone with respect, recognizing that each person's story was likely more complex than it appeared on the surface. He maintained close relationships with his parents, who, having witnessed his unwavering pursuit of truth in the face of considerable pressure, had developed a profound respect for his character and conviction. They were his earliest champions, and their unwavering support had been a silent anchor throughout his journey.

There were moments, when walking through the familiar woods, when the younger Joseph would surface – the boy brimming with an almost reckless curiosity, eager to unravel the next puzzle. But now, that curiosity was tempered by wisdom, by the knowledge that some truths were not easily unearthed, and some discoveries carried a heavy responsibility. He understood that the world was a place of both light and shadow, and that the most meaningful work often lay in bridging the gap between them, in illuminating the obscured corners. His life had become a testament to the enduring impact of a childhood awakened, a journey where the echoes of the wilderness served not as a haunting reminder of past trauma, but as a constant, guiding force, urging him always towards the persistent, illuminating pursuit of truth. He had learned that the greatest mysteries weren't necessarily those hidden in the woods, but those woven into the fabric of everyday life, waiting for a keen eye and a determined spirit to bring them into the light. His path was a quiet affirmation of that principle, a life lived in service to the clarity that comes from seeing the world, and its history, with unvarnished honesty. He had found his voice, not in shouting from the rooftops, but in the persistent, patient act of uncovering and articulating the stories that deserved to be heard, a legacy forged in the quiet persistence of a boy who dared to look deeper.

West Seneca, a town that had once been a quiet sentinel on the edge of the wilderness, now pulsed with a different kind of energy. The unveiling of its carefully guarded past had not shattered its foundations, as some had feared, but had instead forged them anew, tempering the resilience of its inhabitants with the quiet strength of acknowledged truth. The shadows that had clung to the periphery of its existence, whispers of a history deliberately obscured, had receded, replaced by the clear light of understanding. The town had not simply recovered; it had been irrevocably changed, its identity deepened by the very secrets it had once struggled to contain. This transformation was not a singular event, but an ongoing evolution, a collective journey of remembrance and redefinition.

The narrative of the young boy, the catalyst for this profound shift, had naturally woven itself into the fabric of West Seneca's lore. He was no longer just Joseph, the persistent investigator, but a symbol, a living embodiment of the courage that could bloom in the most unexpected soil. His story, retold in hushed tones around hearths and shared with wide-eyed younger generations during town gatherings, served as a potent reminder of the power inherent in curiosity and the moral imperative of seeking out truth, no matter how deeply buried. It was a legend that underscored the notion that significance was not dictated by size or prominence, but by the willingness to look beyond the surface, to question the established narrative, and to champion the obscured realities. The woods that had once been the backdrop for a solitary quest now represented a space of potential discovery for all, a testament to the idea that history was not confined to textbooks, but lived and breathed in the very landscapes that surrounded them.

The legacy West Seneca embraced was not one of shame or regret, but of a hard-won clarity. The adversity had been real, the historical injustices undeniable, yet the town had chosen to face them, to integrate them into its collective consciousness. This act of confronting its past, rather than burying it further, had become its enduring strength. It fostered a unique form of civic pride, a quiet affirmation that they were a community capable of introspection and growth, unafraid to acknowledge the complexities of their heritage. The annual West Seneca Heritage Days, once a more conventional celebration of local history, now took on a deeper resonance. Joseph, often a featured speaker, spoke not of sensational discoveries, but of the ongoing responsibility that came with knowing, the importance of critical thinking, and the vital role of preserving historical integrity. His presence was a constant reminder that the pursuit of truth was not a singular triumph, but a continuous endeavor, a commitment to vigilance that ensured the past would not be so easily forgotten or manipulated again.

The children of West Seneca grew up with a different understanding of their town's narrative. They learned that history was not a static entity, but a dynamic tapestry woven with threads of both triumph and tribulation. They heard the story of Joseph not as a tale of a lone hero, but as an invitation to become investigators themselves, to question, to explore, and to understand the world around them with a critical yet compassionate eye. The woods bordering the town were no longer just trees and trails; they were repositories of untold stories, potential sites of unearthed truths, a constant prompt to consider what lay hidden just beyond the visible. This instilled in them a sense of agency, a belief that their voices and their observations mattered, and that they too could contribute to the ongoing, evolving narrative of their community.

This shift in perspective extended beyond the purely historical. The town's engagement with its past fostered a greater openness in its present interactions. The willingness to confront uncomfortable truths about their origins translated into a more nuanced approach to contemporary issues. Discussions on community development, local governance, and social challenges were often framed with an awareness of historical precedent, a recognition that present-day circumstances were frequently shaped by long-unacknowledged forces. The spirit of inquiry that Joseph had embodied became a communal trait, a subtle but persistent current that encouraged dialogue, challenged complacency, and fostered a more robust and engaged citizenry.

Furthermore, the shared experience of uncovering and accepting their history had strengthened the bonds of community. It provided a common ground, a shared narrative that transcended individual differences. While the specifics of the past might have been difficult, the collective act of coming to terms with them had forged a deeper sense of solidarity. Neighbors who might have previously existed in polite, distant coexistence found themselves united by a mutual understanding, a shared commitment to the town's evolving identity. This sense of shared purpose was palpable, an invisible current that ran through the town, imbuing its daily life with a quiet but profound sense of belonging.

The legacy of West Seneca was, therefore, multifaceted. It was a legacy of resilience in the face of historical deception, a testament to the enduring power of truth, and a vibrant example of how a community could transform adversity into an opportunity for profound growth. The story of the boy who dared to look deeper had inspired not just his own town, but had become a quiet beacon for others, a reminder that the most significant discoveries often lie not in grand pronouncements, but in the patient, persistent uncovering of what has been deliberately concealed. West Seneca, forever marked by its secret, had emerged not as a town defined by its hidden past, but by its courageous embrace of its complete history, a legacy etched not in stone, but in the collective memory and the unwavering pursuit of truth. The quiet corners of their world, once repositories of silence, now resonated with the echoes of a story that had the power to enlighten and to inspire, a narrative that would continue to shape generations to come, a testament to the enduring, vital legacy of truth. The children who now played in the town square, their laughter echoing against the familiar buildings, understood implicitly that their heritage was not just a collection of dates and events, but a living testament to the courage it took to unearth what was hidden, to confront what was difficult, and to build a future grounded in honesty. This was the enduring legacy of West Seneca, a legacy forged in the wilderness and refined by the light of truth.

The quietude of the wilderness, once a veil for obscured narratives, now served as a contemplative space for West Seneca, a place where the town could reconnect with its foundational truths. The transformation of the town's identity was not merely an intellectual exercise; it was deeply intertwined with the physical landscape that had borne witness to its hidden history. The woods, the very spaces where Joseph had meticulously pieced together fragments of forgotten lives, had become emblematic of the town's commitment to acknowledging all facets of its past. They were no longer perceived as merely a natural resource, but as a living archive, a reminder that the land itself held memories, and that understanding its history was intrinsically linked to understanding the town's present and future. This connection fostered a deeper environmental consciousness, a respect for the natural world that had, in a sense, preserved the very secrets that had once threatened to define the town's hidden narrative.

The integration of Joseph's story into the town's collective memory was a carefully nurtured process. It wasn't a story that was forced upon anyone, but one that had organically woven itself into the town's fabric through shared experiences and conversations. The annual West Seneca Heritage Days became a crucial platform for this, evolving into a vibrant forum where the past was not just commemorated, but actively discussed and interpreted. Joseph, with his characteristic humility, would often guide these discussions, encouraging attendees to consider the broader implications of historical truth-telling. He would speak about the importance of critical inquiry, the need to challenge easy narratives, and the ethical responsibility that came with knowledge. His presence was a constant reminder that the uncovering of truth was an ongoing endeavor, a commitment that required continuous vigilance and a willingness to engage with uncomfortable realities.

The younger generations in West Seneca were perhaps the most profoundly affected by this shift. They grew up in an environment where historical authenticity was valued, where the exploration of the past was encouraged, and where the stories of those who had been marginalized or silenced were given voice. This fostered in them a sense of empowerment, a belief that they, too, could uncover truths and make a meaningful impact. The woods surrounding West Seneca were no longer just a playground; they were a landscape ripe with potential discovery, a tangible connection to the historical narratives they were learning about. This hands-on engagement with their heritage instilled in them a deep appreciation for their town's journey, a recognition that resilience and truth were not abstract concepts, but lived realities.

The enduring legacy of West Seneca was thus a testament to its capacity for self-reflection and its commitment to authenticity. The secret it had once held, while difficult, had ultimately served as a catalyst for a more robust and honest community identity. The narrative of the young boy who had dared to question the established order became a cherished legend, a reminder that courage could be found in unexpected places, and that even the most deeply buried truths held the potential to illuminate and transform. West Seneca's story was a quiet affirmation of the idea that a community's strength lay not in its ability to erase its difficult past, but in its willingness to confront it, to learn from it, and to build a future grounded in the enduring power of truth. The echoes of the wilderness, once whispers of concealment, now resonated with the clarity of acknowledged history, a legacy that continued to shape and inspire, a testament to the profound impact of a single, determined pursuit of truth.

The unveiling of West Seneca's most significant secret, the one that had cast a long shadow for generations, had indeed brought a profound sense of catharsis and clarity to the town. Joseph, no longer the solitary boy chasing whispers, had become an integral part of the community's renewed identity. Yet, as is often the case with the unveiling of one truth, it sometimes merely serves to illuminate the vastness of what remains unknown. The wilderness, which had yielded its most guarded secret under Joseph's persistent gaze, was a landscape of immense scale and ancient history. It was a realm where time itself seemed to operate on a different plane, and where the echoes of the past were not always as clear or as easily deciphered as the grand narrative that had been brought to light.

Even with the central mystery resolved, a certain contemplative stillness settled over Joseph whenever he found himself drawn back to the woods. These were not the anxious, driven expeditions of his youth, but rather a return to a place that had profoundly shaped him. He would walk the familiar paths, the rustle of leaves underfoot a comforting, rhythmic sound. The towering pines and ancient oaks, which had once seemed like silent witnesses to a singular event, now felt like custodians of countless untold stories. There were moments, standing in a sun-dappled clearing, when he felt the almost palpable presence of other lives, other moments, that had unfolded within these very trees, lives and moments that had left fainter, more ephemeral traces.

On one such recent excursion, a crisp autumn afternoon, the air carrying the scent of damp earth and decaying foliage, Joseph found himself tracing the familiar route towards the gully where the most significant discoveries had been made. He wasn't searching for anything specific, merely allowing the familiar contours of the land to guide him. As he rounded a particularly dense thicket of ferns, his eye caught something unusual. It was a faint marking on the bark of a venerable oak, a tree that had stood sentinel over this part of the woods for centuries, long before any of the events that had so dramatically altered West Seneca's understanding of its past. The marking was small, barely discernible beneath the rough texture of the bark, and certainly not the deliberate, recognizable symbols that had led him to the heart of the central mystery. This was different. It was a series of curved lines, almost like a stylized wave or a crescent moon, etched with a delicacy that suggested either a tool of immense precision or a considerable amount of patience.

Joseph ran his fingers over the carving, feeling the slight indentation. It didn't immediately spark any recognition, nor did it seem to connect to the known symbols of the past. It was a small, almost insignificant detail in the grand scheme of things, yet it stirred a familiar sense of curiosity within him. He remembered the sheer multitude of trees in these woods, the endless variations in their bark, the natural patterns that the elements could etch. Could this be just another anomaly of nature, a trick of the light, or perhaps a random scratch from an animal? But the regularity of the curves, the deliberate nature of the incision, seemed to suggest otherwise.

He pulled out his small notebook, the pages filled with his meticulous observations from years past. He sketched the symbol, noting the tree's location with the same precision he had employed when mapping out the broader area of his initial investigation. He tried to recall any stories, any anecdotal accounts from the older residents of West Seneca, that might shed light on such a marking. Had there been other, less significant, historical events in these woods? Other groups who had sought refuge or passage here, leaving behind their own subtle signatures? The town's history, now more openly discussed, was still a layered thing, with many depths yet to be fully plumbed. The primary secret had been a monumental one, but it was entirely plausible that other, smaller enigmas lay scattered like fallen leaves, waiting for the right conditions to be noticed.

As he continued his walk, his gaze became more attuned to the subtle details of the environment. He found himself looking at other trees, scanning their bark with a new, albeit mild, sense of anticipation. He didn't expect to find another elaborate cipher, but perhaps another small, enigmatic mark that might hint at a forgotten presence or a lesser-known aspect of the wilderness's past. The woods, he realized, were not a static entity, their history not confined to a single, dramatic revelation. They were a living repository, constantly shaped by nature and by the ephemeral traces of human passage.

He recalled a conversation he'd had recently with Mrs. Gable, one of the oldest residents of West Seneca, a woman whose memory was a veritable library of local lore. She had been recounting, with a wistful tone, tales her own grandmother used to tell her. One particular fragment surfaced in Joseph's mind: a story about a "lost piper," a figure from very early settlement days, who was said to have wandered into the woods during a particularly harsh winter and was never seen again. The story was vague, bordering on folklore, with no concrete details of where he might have gone or what happened to him. The piper was said to have carried a distinctive, intricately carved wooden flute. Could the symbol he'd found have any connection to such a figure? A personal mark, perhaps, left on a tree as a signpost, or a brief, melancholic communication with the wilderness itself?

The idea was speculative, of course, a mere whisper in the wind. But it was the kind of whisper that Joseph had learned to listen to. The central mystery had taught him that even the most obscure clues could lead to profound revelations. The woods were a vast tapestry, and while the main thread had been pulled taut and revealed, there were undoubtedly countless smaller threads, weaving through the fabric, each with its own story to tell.

He found himself looking at the patterns of the trees themselves, the way they clustered in certain areas, the ancient game trails that snaked through the undergrowth. These were pathways, used by creatures and perhaps by people, for generations upon generations. Had there been more than one group seeking solace or anonymity in these expansive woods? Had different eras left their subtle imprints? The thought was both exciting and a little overwhelming. The wilderness was far larger than any single secret.

He continued his exploration, his steps now carrying a slightly different cadence. It wasn't the frantic energy of a young boy on a quest, but the steady, deliberate pace of someone who understood that the world still held wonders to be discovered, not always through grand pronouncements, but often through quiet observation and persistent curiosity. He knew that the true legacy of his past endeavors was not just the resolution of one central mystery, but the ongoing understanding that the pursuit of knowledge was a continuous journey. The woods, in their profound silence and enduring presence, were a constant reminder of this. They were a vast, open book, and while he had deciphered a crucial chapter, he knew that many more pages, filled with their own unique and perhaps equally compelling narratives, remained to be turned. The very vastness of the wilderness, which had once felt like an obstacle, now felt like an invitation – an invitation to keep looking, to keep wondering, and to never assume that the story had reached its final page. The faint symbol on the oak was a small, yet potent, testament to this enduring truth, a subtle nudge from the past, suggesting that the wilderness, and indeed the world, always held more to uncover. It was a mystery, perhaps, but one that promised the quiet thrill of potential discovery, a gentle echo in the vast expanse, beckoning him, and perhaps others, to listen more closely.

The late afternoon sun cast long, amber shadows across the well-worn floorboards of their living room. Dust motes danced in the golden shafts of light, remnants of a day that had been filled with the quiet hum of domesticity. For months, perhaps even years, the air in their small West Seneca home had been thick with unspoken tension, a shared anxiety that clung to every object, every conversation. Now, a different kind of stillness had settled, one born not of apprehension, but of a profound, almost sacred, peace. Joseph sat by the window, his gaze fixed on the familiar silhouette of the woods at the edge of town, a landscape that had once represented fear and mystery, but now held the quiet solace of understanding.

His mother entered the room, a soft smile gracing her lips as she observed him. She carried a tray with two steaming mugs of tea, the comforting aroma of chamomile filling the air. She sat beside him, her presence a warm, grounding force, and placed a mug gently into his hands. They didn't need to speak for a moment. The shared experience, the unraveling of the town's deeply buried secret, had forged a bond between them, a silent language of empathy and resilience that transcended words. The wilderness had demanded much, and in its own way, it had given back even more – a clarity, a catharsis, and a profound appreciation for the simple, enduring strength of family.

"It feels different now, doesn't it?" his mother said softly, her voice barely disturbing the quiet. She gestured vaguely towards the trees, her eyes reflecting a similar contemplation. "The woods. They don't seem to hold the same... menace."

Joseph nodded, his fingers tracing the rim of his mug. "They're still the same woods," he replied, his voice quiet. "But we're different. Or maybe, we understand them differently now." He remembered the breathless terror of his childhood wanderings, the fear of what lurked in the shadows, the gnawing sense that something vital was hidden just beyond his reach. Now, those shadows had receded, replaced by a deeper, more nuanced appreciation for the resilience of nature and the layers of history embedded within it. The grand secret had been a dark one, a heavy burden that had weighed on generations, but its revelation had lifted a collective sigh of relief.

"Your father and I," his mother continued, her gaze distant for a moment, "we were so caught up in protecting you, in keeping the past buried, that sometimes I think we forgot to simply *live* in the present. The weight of what we didn't say, of what we didn't understand ourselves... it was a heavy cloak." She looked at him then, her eyes filled with a mixture of pride and gentle remorse. "You carried so much of that weight, Joseph, even when you were so young. You sought the truth, and in doing so, you freed us all."

He felt a warmth spread through him, an emotion far more comforting than any external validation. It was the quiet acknowledgment of shared struggle and ultimate triumph. He thought of his father, who now moved with a lighter step, his silences no longer burdened by unspoken anxieties but filled with a newfound contentment. The shared journey had been arduous, marked by fear and uncertainty, but it had led them to this quiet harbor of understanding. The wilderness, the very place that had harbored the town's darkest secret, had also provided the sanctuary for its healing.

"It wasn't just about finding the truth, Mom," Joseph said, turning to face her fully. "It was about understanding why it was hidden, and what it meant. It taught me that some things, even the painful ones, need to be brought into the light. Like clearing away the dead leaves so the new growth can come through." He thought of the faint, enigmatic symbol he had recently discovered on the ancient oak. It was a reminder that even after uncovering a monumental truth, the wilderness still held its quiet mysteries, its own subtle language waiting to be deciphered.

His mother reached out and gently squeezed his hand. "You have a wisdom beyond your years, Joseph. You see the world with a clarity that many spend a lifetime searching for. The wilderness whispers its secrets to you, and you listen." Her voice was soft, imbued with a deep maternal love. "It's a gift, this understanding. And it's one you share with all of us now. We are all a part of this story, and you have shown us how to read it."

The conversation flowed easily then, a tapestry woven from shared memories and quiet reflections. They spoke of the palpable shift in the town, the way the averted glances had been replaced by open smiles, the hushed whispers by communal reminiscences. The narrative of West Seneca had been rewritten, and Joseph, the boy who had chased shadows, was now an integral part of its brightest chapter. The wilderness, once a place of fear, had become a symbol of resilience, of the enduring power of truth, and of the quiet strength found in shared understanding. The echoes of the past were not erased, but integrated, woven into the fabric of their lives, a testament to the enduring lessons learned and the peace that followed. Joseph knew that the journey was far from over; the wilderness still held its whispers, but now, he understood its language, and he was ready to listen.

Glossary

Catharsis: The process of releasing, and thereby providing relief from, strong or repressed emotions.

Enigmatic: Difficult to interpret or under-stand; mysterious.

Petroglyphs: Prehistoric or ancient art executed by removing part of a rock surface by incising, picking, carving, or rubbing.

Runes: Letters in a set of related alphabets known as runic alphabets, which were used to write various Germanic languages be- fore the adoption of the Latin alphabet.

About the Author

From his earliest days, P. Hartwell has been drawn to the mysteries and the potent enchant-ment of the wild. His background, abundant with crafting intricate stories and exploring lim-inal spaces where the ordinary dissolves into the extraordinary, has honed his keen eye for detail and instilled a deep respect for atmospheric res-onance. With the dramatic beauty of coastlines and the enduring echo of ancient lore fueling his creative engine, He strives to unveil the veiled histo-ries embedded within our world. His cre-ations powerfully captures this burning passion, immersing readers in a captivating riddle where human grief and elemental forces intertwine. He makes his home in New York, near the tran-quil expanse of Lake Erie.

www.ingramcontent.com/pod-product-compliance
Lightning Source LLC
Chambersburg PA
CBHW030622310726
48979CB00003B/835
* 9 7 8 1 9 6 9 9 2 9 0 4 5 *